With deep appreciation to all those who shared their Vietnam experience with me, especially Jim, counselor, friend, and healer to so many.

D1569137

"For he would never acquiesce to it. He could never acquiesce to his own feelings, to his own passion. He could never grant that it should be so, that it was well for him to feel this keen desire to have and to possess the bodies of such men, the passion to bathe in the very substance of such men, the substance of living, eternal light, like eternal snow, and the flux of heavy, rank-smelling darkness.

"He wanted to cast out these desires, he wanted not to know them. Yet a man can no more slay a living desire in him, than he can prevent his body from feeling heat and cold. He can put himself into bondage, to prevent the fulfillment of the desire, that is all. But the desire is there, as the traveling of the blood itself is there, until it is fulfilled or until the body is dead."

—D. H. Lawrence, from the canceled prologue to *Women in Love*

"Gerald moved uneasily.—'You know, I can't feel that,' said he. "Surely there can never be anything as strong between man and man as sex love is between man and woman. Nature doesn't provide the basis.'

"'Well, of course, I think she does. And I don't think we shall ever be happy till we establish ourselves on this basis. . .'" [said Birkin].

—D. H. Lawrence, from the key passage censored in many earlier printings of *Women in Love* (in Chapter 25, "Marriage or Not")

MEN TOUCHING

A portrait of two gay men bonding into a marriage before its time, *Men Touching* is Henry Alley's poignant new novel of the healing powers of intimacy.

In 1986, Robb, a Vietnam veteran now living in Seattle, tries to go off drugs and enters a nightmarish world, when he recalls his involvement in a hit-and-run accident in Saigon during the war. After he emerges from treatment for his addiction, he seeks help from his partner Bart, a high school drama teacher, who is in the process of coming out to his family, just as a friend is dying of AIDS. As the two stories unite, Bart and Robb reach a reconciliation both between and within themselves.

PRAISE FOR THE WRITINGS OF HENRY ALLEY

"Henry Alley is an excellent writer. His fiction is artfully artless, clear, concise, and real. Best of all, he regularly tells stories that nobody else is telling."
—Christopher Bram

"*The Dahlia Field* is an impressive introduction to Alley, whose work I wasn't familiar with beforehand but will now purposefully seek out."
— Christopher Verleger, *Edge*

"Henry Alley delineates an endearing picture of the Pacific Northwest as well as some points beyond. In his precise yet vivid prose he gets to the heart of both a physical setting and the emotions of its inhabitants. These inhabitants, more often than not, are gay men of a certain age who are still at the height of their sexuality and draw. The men he writes of are waking up to the possibilities of their sexuality and striving to break free of society's limitations. But the problems of those cities, especially the scourge of AIDS—the very fear of it—still touch their everyday lives."
—John Francis Leonard, *A&U*

Henry Alley is the author of four novels, *Through Glass*, *The Lattice*, *Umbrella of Glass*, and *Precincts of Light*, and a collection of stories, *The Dahlia Field*. His fiction has appeared in journals and anthologies over the past fifty years, including *Virginia Quarterly Review*, *Seattle Review*, *Best Gay Stories 2017*, and *Chelsea Station*. He was awarded a Mill House Residency by Writing by Writers. He lives in Eugene, Oregon, with his husband, the poet and teacher Austin Gray.

To Austin

MEN TOUCHING

A NOVEL

HENRY ALLEY

CHELSEA STATION EDITIONS
NEW YORK

Cover and book design by Peachboy Distillery and Designs

Published by Chelsea Station Editions
www.chelseastationeditions.com
info@chelseastationeditions.com

Print ISBN: 978-1-937627-35-5
Ebook ISBN: 978-1-937627-78-2
Library of Congress Control Number: 2018964617

The author graciously thanks the Oregon Humanities Center, University of Oregon, for its generous support in the writing of this book.

MEN
TOUCHING

Part One

Going Under

One

He drifted from downtown block to downtown block, in the fray of Monday afternoon Seattle. He felt he was in crisis. In the store windows and displays, men on books and magazines and video covers climbed out of greenery or jungles or bedrooms, with long stripes of muscle down their backs. It was the same magnetism, he knew, that pulled him, haunted him whenever he saw something heartbreakingly beautiful, the splendor of a touch he had once thought to be God's, the heart and soul of man fashioned within a form so handsome it bulldozed the sight: Adam, in slow rise, awakening from the dust, and supporting himself on two magnificent arms, the extended back indenting. In his mind, his hands went out and felt the contours tenderly. It had been exactly the same when, as a child, no more than four, he had found a purple tulip growing like a miracle beneath a laurel, and, overcome with happiness in that front yard of Olympic peninsula sun, had gone running for his mother, who, smiling at his delight, had retrieved it for him and put it in a crystal vase.

Another man passed in a purple polo shirt, the contours of his body so very clear. The pressure was in the soles of his feet, and Robb felt he could not outlast the next three hours. The physical therapist—and then the doctor—were down there at the end of the afternoon; they would help him, but not at this moment.

Remember, he told himself, this is the day of the Body, when you can't fight it any longer; you can only give yourself to those who know more than you do.

So he must find a way of waiting it out. He would go to the Y. For the pain was moving again, typically, rising to the base of his spine, an injury from the war, although he could never be absolutely sure—had he been in a war, really? A workout at the gym would ease things, though; there would be stretching and lifting and running and deep tubs of hot water to take the edge off—loosen him, hopefully, and still, maybe, the clanging of his heart.

That morning, he had not been in Seattle but in Port Townsend on the Peninsula to spend the day with his daughter. But when he had reached the bed and breakfast, now owned by his ex-wife, he had found it locked. There had been no daughter to meet him. Restive, humiliated, he had looked about for a someone, anybody, even a customer, who would have a key. But there was none. The 8:30 breakfast was over, and all who had needed to had checked out. It was the lull hour of 10:30. He looked through the window of the front door, and saw, on the ceiling, the four muraled Seasons, frescoed maidens of the nineteenth century, holding their garlands up, looking down. Together they seemed conspirators keeping his daughter from him.

Below, Robb rang and rang, and he knew that if he waited much longer, he might lash out and punch through the glass.

And so the afternoon found him back, by ferry again, in Seattle, roaming the streets first and now taking his clothes off at the Y.

Over by the steam room, there was a man sitting, looking lonely, a towel draped over his knees. He was distinguished, for the years seemed to have etched in his muscles rather than aged them, and the moment he had gotten up with Robb's glance, his back seemed roped with thick vines. The man was older. Older! Perhaps the seasoning of the years had brought kindness to his face; perhaps that man knew, too, what it was like to be cut off from all your resources.

But a moment later, the man was gone, and Robb found himself alone in the weight room. On the bench press, another man was yelling out, horsing two hundred pounds towards his partner. On a leg-lift table, a figure Robb imagined to be an executive tried to draw up fifty pounds with his boyish calves, and, looking as though he could draw five at best, sighed out in pain. Robb, doing his stretches before the mirror, looked at himself—a bearded sullen man with well-developed shoulders in a maroon tank top. Dark but Nordic-looking, morose, a part-time biologist and gardener, browned by the sun with copper highlights. He was a man who had enormous potential—that was for sure—which had been growing since the 1970s, when he and the rest of the country had emerged from the Vietnam War. Since then he had gotten good degrees, a Ph.D. in biology, with a promise of becoming a brilliant teacher. But every time he just about reached his goal, a little minefield would go off, tripped by a wire he had carefully strung himself. He never failed at that. He was a Vet. It was 1986—what was he going to do about it?

So that: just before his separation and divorce from a woman who had been married before, he had been commuting between two jobs, one in Port Townsend, his home town, and the other in Seattle, his second home—working, basically, as a gardener for his wife (with the grounds of the State Park thrown in) on the Peninsula, and as an adjunct professor at Jutland College in the city. For all its forty years, his life had never quite come together. Initially hired on by the place which had awarded him his degree, he had found the University of Washington to be a near Eden. But his untenured work had only resulted in what the committees determined "disappointing sidetracks"—a book on the anatomy of weightlifting and a handful of articles vaguely exploring the question of sexual orientation. Among seagulls. Obviously not enough to win tenure and promotion, and so Robb had been promptly jettisoned out of the city, back to his Port Townsend, where he had met and married Laura, who had then slowly but surely taken over his family home, Rose House, and made it into a bed and breakfast.

He had been reduced to routine work. Had felt privileged to find another side job as groundskeeper at the state park, while his wife's business was trying to find its wings. Not ten minutes from home, he drove the John Deere mower all over the bluffs of the Park, a shaggy, shaded, hatted spectacle no doubt, more formidable and embittered than the sound of the engine. People would ask him, "What do you do now?" and he would answer, acidly, "Work other people's gardens."

He had done the family grounds at Rose House, now presided over by his wife, and the business prospered and took off. She was written up in every tourist and bed and breakfast magazine in the country. A famous cereal offered three nights' lodging at her place as a box-top prize, and put a picture of it on the back. But feeling crowded out of his own life, he had fled Port Townsend one morning and pounded the pavement in Seattle—one day after another, until the job at Jutland College had surfaced. As compromise, he and Laura agreed three days a week would be his own—to work, sleep, and room in Seattle, away from his home—Rose House, where he had grown up.

He now stretched out and started working the bench press. The strange thing was, he thought, how good sex had always been at Rose. So fantastically good! That was the legend of the place. Ann Rose had had the mansion built by her husband because their marriage had been failing: the ornate, stick structure rising, under her hand, filled with rose-colored corridors, nave windows, and the dancing maidens at the top of the spiral staircase, had been meant to make love better.

In the weight room, now, Robb tried to get clear on that as he pushed off and lifted the bar—170 pounds, his own weight. How many delighted consummations had they had, with the light coming through the vined windows? Again and again he had made love to her; again and again she had mounted him, so many times he thought he would be too dizzy for safety coming down, when it was over, the banistered stairs of Honduras mahogany. The place worked so well in its mystery. Ann Rose had been absolutely right. Their historical marriage had healed, been a success—as had the ultimate marriage of his own mother and father, who had lived there—and if it hadn't been for this matter of a little room for himself, maybe they would still have been together, too.

He turned to the butterfly machine, adjusting the leather support belt he had fastened around his waist. There was this matter, he went on, of a little privacy. He could remember, on tour days, every tourist—on foot, in the car—going by the place, peeking in the windows, ringing the door when the schedule plainly said not to, even coming by and rapping the glass of the guest cottage, where he often fled (occupancy permitting) as a last resort. Nothing in that house was sacred, sacrosanct from their eyes and endless curiosity except what he and Laura did so beautifully behind closed doors. But it was not enough. He became surly and rude to the customers, started telling some of them to fuck off, and that became the end of it. Laura had had to side with them. Things changed and permutated in the divorce proceedings, so that she ended up with full possession of the mansion. Part of the reason was that Robb had not ended up speaking well for himself in court. The family name and monument had been taken from him. His sister, alien to him for many years anyway, would hardly speak to him now. The family name and monument were gone. And he—retreated permanently to the third floor he rented in Seattle, except when he visited Port Townsend to see his daughter.

Nearly half-way done with his routine now, he stood before the mirror again, doing the biceps curl and wondering, Is this really me? Do I exist in my own skin? And putting the free weight down for a moment, he felt of his own flesh—it was there all right, but it didn't quite connect to what he might call the bone, the hard tissue of his being. It was always attempting to secede from the union.

Racking the weight and still feeling a bit dizzy, he almost collided with the man who had been sitting, woebegone, beside the steam room. He didn't look woebegone now. He was suited up and ready to run.

"Going out?" Robb asked out of the blue, surprised.

The man smiled. "Yes, once I've done a little here." Then one eyebrow up. "And I swim, too—"

"I'll be out there running—" Robb, not knowing what to say next, watched the man take up work at the lat pull, bringing the long bar down, exposing long stretches of muscle—several inches with each rep—through the back and chest. On "up," the man looked thin and tightly wrapped in his veins; on "down," he looked burly—enough to pull the whole stack down, easily, if he wanted to.

For a moment, Robb lost all sense of the room, his blood so much on the rise. Through the window, the huge autumnal lake spread, with the summery, light-clad figures running beside it. That was it—he was done, ready to go out, be at one with the burnished leaves, his tan almost the same color, but he had hardly taken off his tank top, when the man had come up again and was touching his arm—"Have a good run. Maybe I'll see you out there."

Robb smiled and nodded too but—he had to turn, for he was stung with the touch. How long had it been?

A few minutes later, out in the September air, light with the salt from the sea, he was aware of his chest rising, the light bit of sweat beginning to form, as his back first froze with the temperature drop, then eased slowly as he moved into his usual rhythm. The sun threw splinters of light on the water, and they cropped up again, in the form of the other runners, beautiful men and women passing along at different speeds, with different expressions, some running with him, some running opposite. One man going past in compression tights looked like a god newly risen from the water, his chest and shoulders seemingly cast in bronze, and fashioned into a complex network of sinew. Another tanned runner (in white) breezed by saying hello, his blonde hair radiant as a sunflower in early bloom—and in fact, he seemed to turn like one, steering his chest toward the light as if he couldn't get enough.

From the city came sirens and screams, and sometimes Robb used to think that a city was like a child—you could tell when its screams were serious and when they were just for attention. Right now, he ignored them and let the city go on, for he was too caught up in this burnished square of hours, harvested from late September, so breathtaking he even forgot the pain he thought intolerable before coming here, and then—his heart leapt—there was the Man from the Weight Room, without his tank top, too, incredibly light on his feet, for all his brawn, not far from him now, seemingly intent on overtaking him. The fifty-year-old Olympian suddenly increased speed and tore by him with a wave—"Looking good," the man said, and was a half mile ahead before he knew it.

The flames in the lake dimmed some. He rounded a turn and the wind hit him head on, tightening his back. Pain, again. If he was to get out of this, he must swim and do the hot tub before leaving.

Resigned, he finished out the arc, and went back into the building. Showered long, put on a tight bikini and got into the pool, beneath the solar dome. The water received him; he opened his fingers the way he had just been taught, and pulled himself through, feeling all the magnificent strength from his weight workout. Other men had mentioned that. The great residual pull. Strength, Herculean sometimes, through the water. Like that god he had seen in the black lycra tights, his butt almost busting. Triton, coming up for air on land.

And within moments of completing his first lap, he was aware of someone in the lane beside him, adding strength to the water. The fleetness of the swimmer said it must be the friend, but Robb was afraid of finding it too good to be true. The free style went hand over hand, arm over arm, but he could not be sure—then up, for a breath of air, and, yes, Robb saw the distinguished gray hair, and now, as his friend did the breast stroke, powerful as a frog, he could see him smiling ear to ear. Robb waited at the end of the pool, seemingly to catch his breath, knowing he must leave in a few moments if he was to straighten out his back in the hot tub and still make his appointments. But this man, he knew, would be better than any doctor or physical therapist, if only he could only make contact! But, no, the man was intent on his laps. And what, after all, Robb wondered, had been his own intentions? A little assignation in the steam room, with the hope that no one would step in? Quick sex out in the bushes? No, Robb told the critic. Not that at all! Then what is it, the voice came back, what is it you want from this total stranger? You know as well as I you can't come here past nine on a Saturday night without taking your life in hands, there are so many men who want what you think you don't. What makes you different from half the lonely men in Seattle which are half the men anyway? And Robb, having no answer, pulled himself from the pool, and, defeated, got into the hot tub in the next room.

Nearly scalded, he could feel his minimus muscle begin to give for the first time that day. And, looking across into the practice pool, now that the pain had subsided once again, he saw the specially-abled people doing recreational therapy in the water, with one young girl (was she young?), her breasts ballooning to enormous size, being held on to by a child on either side. Up and down in the water they went, her face mute and ecstatic with the contact.

Robb turned to pull himself out of the water one more time, when he found the man standing directly above him. He was holding his hand out. "Seems like we enjoy the same things. My name's Buddy."

"Buddy?" Robb said, smiling. "I've always wanted to know a man named Buddy. My name's Robb."

They shook hands as the man leapt into the tub. Robb held on for a few extra moments. Or was it Buddy who did? I must act now, Robb thought, I have to leave in the next two minutes, and I simply cannot lose this man. He's all I've got.

But Buddy made it easy. "I've been noticing you for a while. The similar patterns we have. Maybe we could work out together sometime?"

"Yes, I'd like that."

"My hours are uneven," Buddy went on. "But you can call me. I live out in Harcourt Lake. My last name's Wilson, and I'm in the book."

"So am I. But I'm here in town. Last name's Jorgenson." Robb sat there in the water, not wanting to leave. Of all the times to have to. "I simply must go," he went on, feeling ridiculous holding out his hand again. "But I appreciate the suggestion. I'll look forward to it." And despite himself: "As a matter of fact, I've been pretty lonely lately. And I guess I've always wanted a 'buddy.'"

"I understand," the man said. "My wife's been gone a while, and this life of a bachelor is awful."

Was this the signal, the sign that there could be—more than just a workout ahead? In the past, Robb, because of his handsomeness, had been cruised, propositioned, sized up one side and down the other—come on to by every human being conceivable, men and women alike but mostly men. But never, never, had he met someone like this aged and muscular Hercules, lounging here under this solar dome, his powerful chest firm against the water, one curved arm resting along the top of the tub, as he smiled and offered him the overwhelming chance to get to know him.

"Well, then," Robb said, "I'll call you soon."

"I'll count on it," Buddy answered.

Two

But sitting in the clinic an hour later and waiting for the secretary to come back, Robb started to feel invisible. Surrounded by the chromium and steel of the brand new medical building, where you could still smell the glue of the carpeting, he could feel no connection with the other people around him, even though all of them, obviously, were in pain. Kept waiting for the second time that day, he sat and tried to keep his temper, because he knew, as in the case of so many, many professionals, this was going to be Game Day for the clinic—they were going to tease you with your appointed time; one minute would tick past another, and as the pain from the insufficient furniture would mount up, they would act dumb about this little matter of common courtesy, that any fool kept this long, now, would stand up for himself, but no, not you, we've got you, because everybody wants to see this man who's on the other side of the entrance, who's got what you want, and there's not enough to go around, because everybody's in pain these days, why do you think the city's screaming anyway? So just stay put and you'll get your turn, and by the time you do, you'll be properly reduced to this groveling, crawling sycophant, an insect gloriously thankful for this little sliver of time with a "professional" who may or may not touch you and make you human again.

And, still feeling a ghost, Robb got up and spoke to the receptionist, who had materialized at last. "Robb Jorgenson to see a therapist named Tyler."

The woman, whose name was Ardis, consulted her sheet. "Oh, yes, I tried to call you several times. We have no referral from your doctor. It was supposed to come in last week."

"My doctor's office is just upstairs," Robb said, illogically. "Why wouldn't it come?"

But suddenly he was struck from behind by the pain, as though on the fifty-yard line.

"I have no idea. They're responsible for getting the referrals to us."

"Could you call?" Robb asked.

"We need it in writing."

"I'll tell you what"—he paused and spoke consciously to his temper rather than to her. "I have an appointment upstairs with the doctor in an hour. If you'll call now and request the referral, I'll personally walk it down when I'm through."

Ardis still eyed him with skepticism as she lifted the phone. After all, her assigned task was to guard—ardently, if you will—this fort from all invaders who didn't rightly deserve touching. Isn't that what the chromium and steel said—right down to that water fountain, which, like all stainless steel water fountains in buildings such as these, newly installed, actually worked! And with full force!

But Ardis, now speaking to one of her own kind, was softening her expression. Robb, she was discovering, did, after all, possess the Doctor's Referral. The secret code, the password, the talisman, the decoding ring. He wasn't trying to slip past the gates and steal a touch after all. Already, while still on the line, Ardis was smiling toward him and pulling out "the few information sheets" that would let him past her.

"I'm so sorry," she said, putting down the phone. "They had a change of receptionists this week. The letter of referral was still in your file. They'll send it down in the morning, and I'll simply write 'forthcoming' on your chart."

So he was instructed about the papers. One requested the usual background, but the other was a basic diagram of the human body, one front, one back, and on it, he was asked to put an "x" in the areas of pain. Sitting down in the insufficient furniture again, and feeling totally invisible, he wanted to "x" through both bodies, adding the caption "I am here, I feel pain. Everywhere."

But instead—and delighted to find he was carrying a pencil—he took it out and shaded in the various muscles, transforming the sheet into an anatomical chart—outdoing Leonardo—and precisely drawing in his piriformis, his minimus, and then covering his whole lower back area with the cartoon-like static that always follows a "Biff!" or "Whomp!" or a "Sock!" in the funnies. He also figured in his soleuses in his calves and drew circles around them. He shaded in massive pectorals—come on, they don't look that good—and wrote "tight" in all caps. As an afterthought, he added the rhomboids and upper traps and circled two little coins of anguish just at his shoulder blades.

Now for the questions sheet. Rheumatism, no, heart attacks, no, headaches, yes. Medication? Well, he'd come back. Any major diseases? No. Exposure to AIDS—well, they had a nerve. But, no. What is your primary complaint. And Robb almost wrote in, "Lack of contact," but instead wrote, "probable overextension of S-1 on L-5, leading to chronic pain in minimus and surrounding areas."

As though rewarding this precise diagnosis, his name was called out down the hall: a glaring and incongruous informality on this brightly lit clinical set. He was shown into a discussion area where he was introduced to Tyler, a powerfully handsome man in a sail-white polo shirt and jeans. In fact, his completely bleached appearance made him look as if he might be launched at a regatta or as an angel into an angelic choir at any moment. Within seconds, Robb noticed the massiveness and acuity of his hands.

Tyler was glancing through the papers with merry eyes, "So you were having a little fun with this, I see." The charts were in view. "Either you're a great imposter or you know your muscles."

"I'm a professor of biology," Robb said, rather grandly. But then added, "But I'm in pain."

The power shift caused Tyler's eyes to change. "You're way ahead of me, then, but I'll see what I can do. You work somewhere close by?"

"At Jutland College. Just here in the district."

"I did night school there," Tyler said. "And how long have you had this pain, Robb?"

"Two years."

"And was there an injury involved?" he asked.

"No," Robb answered.

"No overstrain of lifting, no car accident?"

Robb shook his head. "Nothing that I can remember. Except going way back."

"When was that?"

"It's hard to say. There was a truck," Robb said. "I was in it. It stopped suddenly, and I was thrown against the dash."

"How long ago?" Tyler repeated.

"Many, many years—I can't really say."

Tyler could see Robb didn't want to go on. "Well, we'll have a look. Also, there's this part you didn't fill out about medication. Are you on any?"

Robb hedged again. "I'm getting off some as we speak."

"But you're actually on some now?"

"Yes."

"Which is—?"

"Ativan—for sleep. That's all," Robb said.

"Is your back keeping you awake?"

"No—it's not that."

"Then what?"

"Listen," Robb said, feeling the man had gone too far, "I'm not here for a psych eval. I came hopefully to have my pain alleviated." How hard it was saying this to such a handsome man. Alienating him before they even got started. Now Tyler would never give him what he wanted.

"We need to know these things, before we can help you," Tyler said. "The Ativan, as you probably know, relaxes large-scale skeletal muscles, and under normal conditions, you might be tighter than you actually think."

"I understand," Robb said, conciliatory, "it's just that the issues around my insomnia I want to save for my doctor—who I'll be seeing as soon as I'm out of here."

"Sounds fair enough," Tyler concluded, putting down his chart. "We'll just try to work within the limits of the information you've given us—and you have given us a whole lot about where the pain is—at least."

And after a few more routine questions about Robb's exercise schedule, Tyler told him to disrobe in one of the cubicles, divided by curtains. And in a few moments, Robb found himself lying there in just his shorts.

And on either side of him, he was aware of other people getting treatment, or waiting for it, murmuring voices—one set he recognized, lying there long enough, as probably a mother, grandmother, granddaughter. The grandmother was the patient, and the therapist, a woman, was working on her arm. "I haven't been able to lift it," the grandmother said, "since he threw me against the wall."

Just then, Tyler came in, touched his back to check for tightness, and Robb started to cry, silently and unobserved. The practiced and firm hands found the center of pain almost instantly—and in the next moment, Robb was asked to sit up and then stand, for a check on further asymmetries—Tyler working so fast and efficiently, Robb was able to wipe the tears still unseen. Robb was absolutely clear he felt naked and child-like, almost like a baby, and was surprised to find this was what he had been hoping for.

"All right, my friend," Tyler said. "We're just going to do one thing today. Then next week we're going to try something more intensive. How does that sound?"

With that, Robb found himself lain on his side, and his legs parted, as though in a dream-like race. He was then asked to push all he could against Tyler's resistance, and suddenly he found himself entering into Tyler's very bone and sinew, as though their bodies were fusing, the anguish seeming to be like a flower, opening like a bud, unfolding into ease, with his brain instantly shooting itself back into the backyard of a childhood friend; the friend and his sister were wading with him in a little pond, below a rockery of heather and carnations, a little pond in cement normally used for goldfish. The laurel was scented and in white flower, and the swing made an easy shadow on the lawn. Then from out of nowhere there was a commotion, and Robb, as a boy, was loping off, in hot pursuit by the brother and sister. He found himself hiding under a laurel—what was it he had? Something he had stolen. A call was going up through the neighborhood. Robb had taken something that belonged to Ellen—that was her name. The ease of pain in his back was allowing him to remember it. Robb came in for a closer look at the memory, and saw what it was. It was Ellen's doll. A boy doll, handmade by her mother, with a sweet sewn smile, in red. And blonde hair. The doll's name was Gordon.

Just then, Robb was, once again, asked to push all he could against Tyler's strong arm, and something snapped into place. Tyler's face became Gordon's. And because of the very configuration his body formed with Tyler's, it was impossible now for Robb not to grasp the man's wrist—his fingers just rested lightly over. "It's O.K.," he now heard Tyler saying—and there was even a soft pat on the back, for Robb discovered that he was sobbing bitterly without realizing it.

"It's O.K.," Tyler said with tenderness. "Some people groan, some people scream, some people cry. And I think we got lucky the first time. I think I heard something. Did you hear the crack? We've rung the bell."

"Yes," Robb said, covering his face, and feeling more naked than ever before. For he realized that the change had come when Tyler's face became Gordon's. "I've never had anything feel so good in my life."

"I'd like to see you again next week? O.K." Tyler patted him on the shoulder. "O.K.? Ardis will set you up. And take all the time you want getting dressed. Let me help you stand. Feel a little light-headed?"

Yes, he did. And it was partly because of Tyler's strong grasp. He hardly knew how he got from this office to his doctor's, but somehow he did in the next fifteen minutes. He felt blessed that the most taxing thing he had to do now was take the elevator.

In the second waiting room, he didn't have to wait long. Inadvertently his doctor (an internist) had taken the day off for fishing, and had completely forgotten that he had saved this late hour for Robb alone, and had only remembered at the last minute, dashing in just seconds, according to the nurse, ahead of him.

When Robb was shown into the examining room, Dr. Simpson was smiling and wiping sweat.

"Well, this is our exit interview, I see," the doctor said. "Tonight's the night, right? For the showdown with Ativan."

"That's right," Robb answered.

He was ready, now, to admit to himself that he actually had been on Ativan for a long time. How long, he wasn't sure, especially when he was angling doctors for more. Sometimes he thought it was three years, sometimes four—maybe, reaching way back, he'd say five.

But for whatever length of time it was, he knew it was time to get off. Folded in his breast pocket were sheets painstakingly recording his long project, sketched out with Dr. Simpson, of titrating off Ativan, half milligram by milligram, over a period of six months. Today was D Day, or, as Robb privately called it, B Day, Day of the Body.

"Well," Dr. Simpson went on, "I have to say I admire you. I don't know who put you on this originally, but the little research I've done says you should have been on it only for a matter of months. Of course back in the seventies, people were put on valium and medications in the valium family without blinking an eye. And you could have gone on asking me for refills but you're really acted like a man in saying no to yourself finally."

"Thanks."

"Now. There's just one thing I want to say."

As though he hadn't done all the talking anyway. He liked Dr. Simpson—but these doctors!

"Yes."

"If you start feeling strange tonight when you don't take a pill, or if you wake up in the middle of the night feeling bizarre, I'd like you to call me, no matter what time it is. Am I clear?"

Suddenly a sense of alarm spread through Robb.

"Do you expect it to?" he asked.

"No, no, no." Dr. Simpson touched him. "No need to panic. It's just that I'm imagining, given the drift of some of the things you've told me, that something might emerge, once you get unmedicated."

Robb couldn't help but ask, "What things, exactly?"

Dr. Simpson smiled. "Now you're forcing me to be a psychologist. O.K., Robb, my friend, you asked. I think you might have some gay tendencies. That's all. And they might frighten you a little."

Robb smiled to himself. So Dr. Simpson thinks he's found a closet case.

But Robb found it hard to keep back a smile, especially because he was relieved beyond measure that Simpson didn't say something really frightening.

He played along. "I appreciate your concern," he said, "and I'll keep that in mind. But I know where I can get help on that if I need to."

Dr. Simpson looked relieved, too. "Well, then, go for it. I think we've accomplished all the ground work we needed to these past six months." He shook hands. "Welcome to the drug-free life."

Robb smiled with the grasp, which was sinewy and firm, too. "Thanks. He feels good already"—and instantly corrected himself, laughing, "I mean, it feels good already."

Three

Robb actually had a male lover, a young one; they had been together for some time. Having met quite by accident up in Port Townsend, he and Bart saw each other routinely on weekends here in Seattle, where they both lived—eating out, drinking, and dancing, and then sleeping over at least one night (usually Saturday) at Bart's place.

Coming out of the medical building, Robb considered the irony of Dr. Simpson thinking he'd be surprised by gay hallucinations, when really his and Bart's relationship was taken for granted within the narrow circle of friends they were out to. He knew he had that tendency in himself—and it was a weakness. He allowed people to make certain assumptions about him, because he rarely spoke up, volunteered much information. For a long time, for example, he allowed Bart to think he was still married, until at last Bart had asked—yes, he had had to say, the divorce had become final in 1984. And Bart had been so surprised.

Now, in 1986, when he and Bart had been together almost a year, the majority of the world, including his own family, was allowed to think he was still struggling with his sexual identity. Well, go ahead, because he was, just not in the way they thought. It wasn't over choosing whether it was going to be a man or woman, but, instead, what kind of man. That was one reason why he wanted to get off drugs—he knew it was causing him to make certain wrong choices. He had picked out Bart because Bart made no demands of him. A precise routine had surfaced. Outside of it, they never touched. But the kicker was—if you struck that kind of bargain, you never touched at all, became nothing but briefly adjoining amusement parks on Saturday and Sunday. You danced your asses off on weekends, drank within reason, fucked before sleep, and called it a night. Mondays, you were back on the conveyer belt, having lost all sense you had a relationship at all.

Like today, Robb thought. Today I completely forgot I'm "in a relationship," as they say. And maybe it's because I'm not.

The big word, the enormous word, "intimacy," cropped up, like the skyline now rising in rows behind him. Enveloping. It was the one thing he was incapable of, according to Laura, and he was out to prove her wrong. First by getting off Ativan, and second by letting Bart go and starting off fresh. With someone who knew how to be his friend.

Like Buddy.

With the evening coming on, he walked across Jutland in the initial ecstasy of being what he thought was pain- and drug-free. The abbreviated campus he entered—Jutland College—not only sounded with some gloriously archaic bells, punctuated by a few wisps of sails visible from Golden Gardens beach; it also arose, beautifully, with the couching forms of male students, still leaning over their books, some with their shirts open, or completely off, in the remaining warm air.

Some of them were throwing Frisbees, some passing a nerfball, a blonde Discus made whole loops on a tiny bicycle, a man almost thin except for the powerful steamer's trunk of his chest. The reclining forms were also beautiful—obliviously attentive to their books. He loved the varieties of men on campus, O.K., Big Men on Campus. The broad-shouldered ones who wore spectacles. The baseball cap ones who wore tank tops and muscle shirts to class and had almost laureled hair. The ones—he was thinking of a particular man—who lumbered in, wearing tight white sweatshirts, with enormous backpacks strapped to their shoulders and clutching cups of coffee to their barrel chests that looked like snowdrifts. He liked the way they hung around his office in their striped shirts later in the day, sensitive men who were sensitive to themselves and him, asking questions about the formulas and not quite getting them. But as he spoke with them patiently, always patiently—drawing on five sheets of paper, if necessary—very slowly the "Aha!" came to their faces and he was pleased beyond belief.

All around campus word had gotten around that "Dr. Jorgenson cared" about students. Men and women alike said that and they also said the Administration ought to be strung up for not making him more than an adjunct faculty.

But be that as it may, Robb said to himself now—approaching the campus parking lot where he had left his car—the main gift right at this moment is the sight of all these happy brilliant men, shirtless, reading, soaking in the last of the sun and knowledge through their spectacles. It was as though Michelangelo's David had put on reading glasses—the ultimate turn on. Because it meant there was a light on upstairs.

But as he entered the lot, something went wrong. He was about to overtake a woman ahead of him, when she turned and gave him one of the most suspicious looks he'd ever seen. Don't follow me, Male, her glance said, or I'll get out my mace.

And then there was something else, far worse. On the other end of the lot, Chester, his brother-in-law, was standing beside his car, watching him until their eyes met. Robb felt for a moment that he could melt from the intimacy of that glance, its intensity—and Chester, obviously feeling the same and looking away, instantly got in and slammed the door. To be sized up by his psychiatrist's glance. It was too much to bear. And instantly Robb thought with grief on his sister, how he had let her down by handing over Rose House. And how he rarely saw any of the family out of shame.

But the Mercedes was turning on its heel and pulling up.

"I just wanted to tell you if you haven't heard," Chester said with kindness, "there won't be class tomorrow. The whole campus is closing down because of that sexual harassment suit. Some woman is saying a math professor touched her in class."

"I heard about it," Robb said, "but I didn't know it had gone that far."

It was overpowering—the beautiful bearded man with his dark arm resting out the window. For the second time that day, Robb found he was at a loss for words. In a second or two, this man would be rushing off to the sister he loved but who considered him lost.

"It's devastating," Chester went on, "the male faculty have to back the man because there's no substantiation. But the women, as usual, have so many past injuries, they can't take the case on its own terms. It's a lightning rod. Lightning rods, lightning rods. Everywhere we men are lightning rods. The protests are closing down the classes."

"And it's not as though the women don't have a point," Robb said, not knowing why.

"No," Chester fired back, instantly guarding himself, too. "Of course not." There was a pause, and the softness returned to his face. "We hardly see you anymore, Robb. We miss you. Olivia cries about it sometimes. You've seen Ethan only twice. You do have our new number?"

"Yes. I'll get in touch soon."

But Chester was sizing him up again. "Do." And the car withdrew as the window went back up, leaving only a small silver star on the hood in the distance.

Standing there, islanded, Robb felt simplified down to his most basic point of consciousness: I am lonely. Gradually and subtly and even cunningly the day had been whittling him down, so that, without daughter, sister, brother-in-law or even job to go to the next morning, he was left with only this single and alarming fact of having to get to sleep tonight without a pill. Everyone had exited by now out of his life—into his own, her own. Dr. Simpson would be sleeping with his wife. Chester would be sleeping with Olivia. Laura would be sleeping with her lover. Whoever that was. And with his looks, Tyler would no doubt be sleeping with possibly every woman in town.

He looked over at the campus and saw that the shirtless men were gone—perhaps to the young women who would enjoy their naked shoulders before they took them or were taken in their beds. Even at this hour of six, Robb could feel the whole city of Seattle making plans to bed itself down, boy-girl, boy-girl. And he realized seeing his brother-in-law leave (a man, everyone said, who looked so much like him), that his own sleeping mate since losing Laura had been his sleeping pill.

The panic began to settle in.

Let's be perfectly logical about this, Robb thought. You're standing here as though you're out of options, when there are hours and hours and hours before going to bed. Think of it. Think of all the shows on television, all the people you can call—

And suddenly Buddy came back to mind, and he knew he had the perfect plan—he would call him from his office, where no one would be at this hour, especially if the college was on strike tomorrow.

The burnished office—burnished now with the light off the lawn and amber trees—greeted him. And—none of his office mates was there.

He dialed Information, was given a number and got Buddy Wilson in Harold Lake.

"This is going to sound strange," he said when Buddy had answered, "but I'd like to see you tonight. Is there any chance you're free?"

There was a pause. "That is strange," the voice said at last.

"Why?"

"Because I was just thinking about you," Buddy answered.

"May I come now?"

"Yes, come right away."

And Buddy gave him directions, which Robb rushed to take down, hardly sensible as to whether he got them right or not.

But he arrived there. After turning off the heavily trafficked freeway going North, he was plummeted down a short country road to the lake. Beside the beachfront home, newly built, he saw Buddy, wonderfully built, and without his shirt, leading a burnished horse to the barn. The two creatures were matching colors. Robb, stopping the car and turning off the ignition, just sat there, thinking he might pass out from the sight. Its splendor, against the blue of the water.

Buddy was signaling him to come to the barn. Slowly following, Robb noticed the lake was covered with water lilies, freshly opened, like perfectly carved white bowls. Inside, the horse was nodding up and down, as though on a merry-go-round; Buddy had put on his Pendleton back on.

"Meet Elsa," he said.

The horse nuzzled his hand from over the gate. She was no wooden horse. Her face was sweet with scent, her nostrils warm. At last she let out a big flutter from her lips, and her breath covered him. She was obviously delighted with his touch. And Buddy was reaching over the fence, stroking her side with delicate fingers. "All right, Elsa, it's time for us to go," he said, "but we love you."

Robb was almost sorry to lose the smell as they came out again into the light. But not really. "I can remember this farm we used to visit up on the Peninsula," he said. "When I was a child. They only had cattle. And I can remember that the only thing I wanted to do was pet them. The man in charge tried his damnedest to let me get near one with a brush for grooming, but nothing doing. That heifer kept me scared off. Later I went back and threw an ice ball at it, just because I couldn't touch her."

"Well, what you need," Buddy said, putting his arm briefly around him, "is to come here more often."

They went in the house and sat down on the sofa, in front of the picture window facing the lake.

"What is it you do," Robb asked, "that means you can have a horse and barn? Are you a gentleman farmer?"

"Hardly. I only have a few acres for Elsa, with a little left over for gardening. I sell hot tubs. You may have seen the sign coming off the freeway. We have a small hot air blimp above that says, 'Buddy's Spas.'"

"Yes, I have seen it. Big business?"

Buddy's arm was resting along the top of the couch.

"My wife and I are transplants from L.A.," he said. "I had a thriving doctor's business down there, and then I had one of those life changes people are having these days. I'm much happier now."

"And you have children?"

"Yes. Two different sets. I was married before."

Suddenly Robb felt the presence of women in the room, was aware of snapshots on the refrigerator, portraits through open bedroom doors.

"And you said your wife is gone?"

"It may be over," Buddy said, much to Robb's relief. "I may have to be starting all over again from scratch."

"Is that why you understood when I called?"

"Maybe. Or maybe it just didn't sound strange."

"Why not?" Robb asked.

"I'm a doctor," Buddy said. "We're supposed to touch people, provided we do it right. I think that's why I got into the profession in the first place. Maybe it could have been just as well if I had become a faith healer. Or massage therapist. But that would have been considered eccentric, bizarre. So I got all the best degrees I could. Then shortly before I set up my thriving practice, I went into the military as a second lieutenant. I was called to work on the men. And I did. Even in Vietnam. I would sometimes see all of them assembled there in rows, and I would think, 'Can I heal you when you come in? Can I push and prod in the right way?' And suddenly I found that I could, and I started to be loved by the men, and thought successful. And there was nothing on the battlefield that I was afraid of. But."

"But what?" Robb asked. And as he asked it, Buddy's hand touched his shoulder, just for a second.

"But I would long for another kind of contact. Something totally inappropriate. It would come over me like wildfire—the desire to get naked with them. Not 'take' them, you understand—"

"No—I understand—"

"But be with them," they said together.

"Cuddle," Buddy went on, "get some contact. And then, in the middle of the night, the sky being lit up all around, I would think myself insane. Buddy, what are you thinking about, when you're on a mission to blow other men up. Because that's what I was doing. I was patching up our men so they could do a better job of blowing up the Enemy—who were men."

"I was in Vietnam, too," Robb said, making the admission for the first time in sixteen years. "And all you said, I've felt, too. I've been afraid of looking at or even thinking of the Moving Wall for fear these feelings might surface, and I'd beat my head against it."

"So," Buddy said, "have you ever gotten any relief?"

"Never."

"Me, either. That's why my wife left. She just couldn't understand. And what could I do. I didn't understand, either. Still don't."

There was a pause. For a moment Robb remembered again the panic of facing the night without a pill. Buddy sensed the fear. "So," he said, "would you hug me?"

"Yes."

And Robb held on, feeling the steel-like muscles beneath the Pendleton. Then he came down and nuzzled him on the throat, thinking now of Elsa, and then rubbed his wrists, thinking of Tyler. It was as though all the components of the day, so near to embrace and yet never quite it, were combined. Buddy's shirt loosened, and Robb was reminded of all the power he had seen at the gym and in the water. There was the extraordinary mystery of seeing muscle emerge from bright-colored cloth. It was as though they were swimming in the same current again, but they were combined in the water in a dance of contact. Somewhere in the dance they lost all their clothes, and Buddy caught him between his strong thighs, while his hands went up and gripped Robb's own chest. Robb was brought back to remember the story of Michelangelo, blind now with old-age—how he had gone every night to the quarry and laid his hands over the naked torso of the stone Hercules—that's how it was, except every contour, every fold, was living flesh, answering back, as they went to the bed, and Robb, having prepared himself, mounted Buddy, with Buddy answering back, "I've wanted to be fucked so much. The burden of always having to be the one to!" while Robb, having entered him, thrust back and forth in rhythm, as though he were a rider, as they were both brought to the crest, and every tendon in Buddy's neck now stood out with strain and relief, and they passed over the wave together, with Buddy relaxing down into his arms, and Robb thinking of the doll Gordon again, and the memory—for he felt, once more, that he had stolen something.

They lay there for a moment, without questioning.

Then there was the terrible awareness of each other. Impossible to bear.

"You must be starved," Buddy said quickly. "I'll go and shower up, and get something ready. I assume you haven't had dinner."

"No," Robb said—and the door closed before he could finish—"I haven't."

He went over to the corner and removed the latex, then sat down on the bed again, feeling wet and exposed and vulnerable. And guilty—for there was, after all, Bart, who didn't make demands but was still a person.

He stood before the mirror, wondering if this was what he was supposed to do, was this the direction he had been getting from his body. For the hunger was still there; it had not been met, not even by this exquisite and caring man. Something bad was going to happen. That was for sure. And once again that day, he stood before a full-length mirror, this time naked, wondering if he was ever going to get a clear sign for living. Living right.

But Buddy was re-emerging and quickly putting on fresh clothes. Sweetly scented again, he looked terrific. "Oh, thank you, my friend. Thank you. You have no idea what you've done for me," he said, brushing his hair. "And how about dancing after dinner? Do you like disco?"

"Do I?" Robb said, instantly forgetting his reverie and his questions.

Four

Well, dancing.

There was more than just the joy of it.

Which was saying a lot.

Somewhere in 1984, shortly after the divorce, he made this wonderful discovery. Before, he had always been too embarrassed to dance, Laura having found him awkward. But now there was masculine music—coming straight out of Castro.

He started buying records—searching in the back bins for twelve-inch extended plays. There was something the way the rhythm crossed back and forth, and the lyrics, well, they were enough to blow you out of the water.

And then, as though shy no longer, the male leads started appearing on the covers. Terrific hunks. Sometimes with their shirts open. Sometimes without them at all. One album caption read, "The ten thousandth chest shot of Paul Parker." The women soloed, too, wonderful women, usually black, with extraordinary ranges, who sang about men just the way he felt about them. And underneath that powerful rhythm was something else, underpinning the lyrics—the closet was at first edging open, then swinging wide, spinning, like a revolving door, flipping all the unsuspecting gays out, like cartoon shoppers in a department store, but in this case out on to the dance floor.

On the rise, now, on a fresh wave of excitement as he got into Buddy's sports car, he felt all of Seattle opening up before them, with fresh strings of lights, as they roared above the various sights of the brilliant boats and bridges, like cigarettes, lit, handed across, to be enjoyed, and the night traffic became the thrilled lyrics of Ken Laszlo's "Tonight," or even better, Sylvester's "Call Me."

Sylvester. That man had changed his life. He remembered seeing *The Life and Times of Harvey Milk* for the first time on the Jutland campus, a gay pride event, when suddenly the scene changed to Castro, Gay Pride too, 1978, and all the bare-chested men were standing on their balconies, as the other men paraded past, and Sylvester's "You Make Me Feel Mighty Real" (Robb heard it as—"You Make Me *Feel*, Harvey Milk!")—came on. Nothing, absolutely nothing, could duplicate the sight of all those wild men going past the camera, their tanned and sometimes nearly naked bodies swaying to Sylvester's beat. It was though it all had been intended to heal every insult, every slight, every humiliation he had felt as a gay man.

After the film was over, and Harvey had been laid to rest, Robb, devastated, but still feeling he must know this singer, waited through all the credits. There at last it was. Sylvester. The magic name. Next day, he scoured all the record shops in town. Suddenly, in an obscure place called D. J. Mary's ("The Hottest Twelve Inches in Town,") there the singles were. All of them.

One of them, "Take Me to Heaven," he seemed to have been waiting for all his life. At last a gay singer addressing another man, transcending the century—in fact, the millennium. Let the poor proverbial woman go. The princess in the tower. Finally all the thousands of closeted composers and poets and singers were released and vindicated in Sylvester at last singing to him, in one courageous song about dancing, dancing, dancing, nothing but dancing (of course!), with the mix being perfect, and the crowd, too, and you wanting to dance with me, with the synthesizer exploding into red and blue-colored stars and finally—he said, "yes, Sir!" Not a woman but a sir.

And yes, there heaven was, all right, because in heaven you could sing to men. The absolute right on, right on the nail-on-the-head of it! It reminded Robb of the way he had felt when an extraordinary passage had flown out at him from out of the dullest porno—

The men were standing naked together, one of them about to experience gay love for the first time.

"I love you," the older man said.

"And I feel the same way," the other said.

"That's not enough. Say more."

"I love you, Mick," the other answered. "With my very soul."

That was it. With your very soul! That was the only way that meant business. You had to say the word love. And with all your heart and soul.

Getting out of the car with Buddy, Robb felt all the power of Sylvester with him. All of his heart. It was as if that man, that famous black cross-dresser with the extraordinary beat and power, gave him the courage to walk down the street with another gay man. That was it. For Sylvester had been celebrated for having walked down Castro in the sixties in nothing less than six inch heels, paving the way for Harvey. And you never knew, from one album to the next, how he would appear next. A Sphinx, a bejeweled Diva (blue eyes), a Bobbysoxer, or an Aretha Franklin, staring into her own image on the other side of a mirror. That was himself—Robb—looking into himself, who was a woman.

The thrill of all the sounds engulfed him as he followed Buddy into the bar. The lights percolated, fell on the men, who checked them over—so frankly, the way he had been checking men out ever since he could remember. But always undercover. He noticed that the man who had been screaming on the bench press this afternoon was there, all decked out on a stool, lounging against the bar. This was what he had been screaming for—to look that good, casually propped up, his cleavage nicely magnificent and glowing in an aqua tank top. And you could look all you wanted. That was what they were all there for.

The two of them, Robb and Buddy, threw themselves into Sylvester's "Do You Wanna Funk," with Robb chasing Buddy all over the dance floor, the lights changing red, blue, green, and with Robb thinking, getting a glimpse of Buddy's hindquarters in a mirror—Yes, I have fucked you, I have pumped the power into you—with Buddy flying all over, careening, and Robb thinking, Sylvester is God! Music like that. Do I want to fuck with you? Yes.

And he careened and flew himself, and as he did, he made a secret pledge to talk with Buddy even more intimately when they got back to the house, tell him something far deeper about himself than just his being in Vietnam—he was going to tell him that he had only been there a few months and then sent home.

He allowed himself to admit that, under the thrill of dancing. Something had happened to him that second month in Vietnam, and he'd been sent to Hawaii and then discharged. And something they'd shared back at Buddy's made him willing to confess. But that wasn't quite there yet.

Try again, Robb, he told himself. Take two.

He'd tell Buddy about it. And, feeling as good as I do now, Robb told himself, I know I'll sleep tonight. No doubt about that. Maybe Buddy will be sleeping beside me. I may wake up in the morning not only pain- and drug-free, but with a new lover.

But time was getting away from him. Buddy surprised him in the moment with a gigantic hug and kiss, feeling him all the way up and down, and with no one in the bar looking like that was strange, either. Not any stranger than if they'd just lit cigarettes. Somehow, the bar seemed the very antithesis of Rose House, where all the bed and breakfast eyes had always seemed to pierce right through the veil, while here he and Buddy could kiss forever and still maintain their privacy in public.

"We really should go," Buddy said at last. "I have to get up early in the morning."

Once again, Robb's heart stood stock-still. Did that mean he was included?

The sports car lifted them back home. Robb blanked out for a moment, and then found himself sitting in Buddy's living room, watching him put on more Sylvester before bed. So they were going to have those moments together. But as the music went on, Robb was aware of two things, suddenly. The pain had returned to his back—with a vengeance—and he could hear another car coming down the lone road to the house.

Fear was in Buddy's face, and he mirrored it.

"Jesus Christ, that could be only one person at this hour," Buddy said. "My wife."

He instantly flew about the room, as if he had something terrible to hide. Sylvester was buried in the row of albums. And all the clues to their previous lovemaking were in an instant picked up and put in place—what had fallen from the coffee table, the throw pillows that had been on the couch..

The gravel sounded, then the pavement. A creak of the handbrake. The car door, with Buddy running to meet it.

Robb stood there in a stupor, finishing his soda, like a man ready to be shot.

A beautiful wife stepped into the room, trailed after by her apologetic husband.

Robb found himself introduced. The woman looked lovely and sensitive, really. As might be expected. And totally naive. Robb heard himself termed a business acquaintance. On cue, he stood up. "Well, Buddy, my friend, I've got to get."

Buddy became a regular man too and held out a stiff hand. "Yes, we'll get back to you soon as possible."

"Take your time," he answered.

Yes, take your time. Because now that she's back, it'll probably take your whole life.

"See you at the Y maybe?" Buddy asked.

Right, the Y, Robb thought.

But the wife—Janine—had had to excuse herself before the goodbye was over. Robb could hear the bathroom door shut.

Instantly, Buddy grabbed for his hand. "I'm so sorry. She just took it into her head that she wants to talk and drove all the way up from California, leaving the kids with her mother."

Robb looked at him, his temper materializing out of nowhere, along with the pain, now that he had stood up. "That's fine."

"I can't invite you to stay. I know it's disappointing?"

"Well—as a matter of fact, it is, that's what I was dying for—to be sleeping beside you tonight," Robb said.

"I wanted it, too, but it can't happen. Only thing I'm worried about is—can you drive? You've got to cool down."

"Me cool down? Let's not do any projecting—"

But before he could finish, he heard a cry from the bedroom. The cry was anguishing.

Buddy, looking heartbroken, still had his hand on Robb's shoulder, "Robb—"

"For Christ's sake," Robb said, pulling it off, "go to her." And got into the car and went down the road.

Five

But what the hell, he asked himself, gunning the car, and seeing, bridged ahead of him, the easy and widely spaced traffic of the late-night freeway, how could I have known she was coming back?

How could Buddy have known for that matter?

Well, she had come back, and that was that. So where was he supposed to go now?

Not home. That part he knew. Vietnam was waiting for him there, in bed. Now that the pills were gone. He had to find somebody else.

It was obvious who. Bart. Even at this hour—which was? Midnight. Not that late at all. Bart might still be up.

As he turned into Bart's street, he felt that he actually belonged here. There were pieces of Rose House in Bart's home and its environs. Bart kept a nice mimosa tree stretched out in front of the living room window, which fanned out like a dancer—parrot green—and in the spring and summer, it blew pink with blooms. Inside, a soft rose light filled the one short hallway, dappled with leaf prints, and during the many times Bart would make him dinner, Robb imagined that he was being served with plates of light.

It seemed fitting, since Bart was a high school drama teacher, a job which Robb thought was something on the higher order of necromancer. He had not only seen Bart's student productions; he had actually seen him at work putting them together. Bart outdid him for rapport and even patience. He was expert, gifted. With a few rags and tinsel, he had fashioned out *The Wizard of Oz* for two full weekends and then next season had created his own musical

Houdini, with his own original script and lyrics, and had found a spot for everybody, even the students who said they couldn't dance or sing. You didn't have to qualify to work with Bart, didn't have to win an audience, because he was never too busy to find out who you were and recognize what you could do. And he was never too busy, because his emotional resources ran infinitely deep.

But thinking about that now didn't help matters. It was no consolation, as Robb pulled into Bart's driveway at midnight, probably rousing the Neighborhood Watch. It was always worse when you imposed on people who were open and generous. For a moment, he hesitated under Bart's mimosa, and some of the leaves brushed his face. As they struck, the pain went straight into his back again and he felt his chest tighten where Buddy had stroked it. The night had taken on a chill, and his pores felt open to the hour that had gone past midnight, as though he had been unnaturally cast out into utter darkness.

He knew the pain had returned because he had danced foolishly, too high on the sex to know when he had jumped up and come down on both feet, reinjuring the good Tyler had done. Another misdemeanor for this impossible day of outraging the Body. The only thing he'd not done was drink.

Sheepishly, he rang Bart's doorbell several times, knowing he would never wake him up otherwise—the man slept so deeply.

At last Bart poked his head through the curtains, and looked at him as a stranger in the porch light. It took a second or two for recognition to hit.

"Robb, what's going on?" he asked, as he showed the way into the kitchen—as if Robb had to be shown!

For the second time that day, Robb felt he had to be absolutely shameless about his feelings—and what he wanted. The Body was driving him to it. "I have no other place to go," he said.

Instantly fear went into Bart's face. It dawned on Robb, very suddenly, that his lover, for all his love of romance and the idea of being in love, wanted to hold him at a distance, especially on weekdays. Monday through Thursday, when they rarely saw each other, he ran a very tight ship. "What do you mean?" he asked. "No other place to go? You've got your home at Mrs. Molyson's."

"I've gone off my sleeping pills, Bart," Robb said. "And I'm scared to death. I have to make it through the night without them."

"And you want to sleep with me?"

"Yes."

Bart backed off, looking even more fearful. "I've got to get up early in the morning—"

"—I don't mean," Robb said, "having sex. I mean just sleeping beside you—"

"It's not just class preparations," Bart went on, apparently not hearing. "I've got a 7:40 rehearsal before school. I don't think I told you, but we're bringing *The Wizard of Oz* back by popular demand."

"Please let me sleep with you," Robb said. "Or I mean just in the same bed. I'll keep way over to edge and you won't even know I'm there."

"Of course you can stay," Bart answered judiciously, but getting up to find blankets. "But how about the couch? It folds out. I really need the whole bed to myself tonight. As you know, I travel a lot when I'm sleeping and I'm dead tired."

"If you say so," Robb answered, sullen.

The sullenness seemed to give Bart an edge.

"I don't know what else to say." He took Robb's coat and went to a linen closet, and started snapping sheets and the pulling out the bed frame hidden in the sofa. "I really don't. You have been so strange lately. Frankly, it would be hard to have you in the same bed with me. Always like a volcano, ready to go off."

"I've been taking less and less of the medicine with each month," Robb said. "It's put me on the edge. It's been like a countdown."

"And how was I supposed to know that?" Bart asked, showing an extraordinary side to himself, now that he was completely riled and awake. "I don't read minds."

"I'm sorry," Robb said, sitting on the bed which still had blankets flying about it.

But by then Bart's edge had gone, and he kissed him, while tucking in the sheets. "Hey, O.K., no big deal."

But Robb felt it was, and his unworthiness hit again. And he felt that if he was to sleep tonight—what was left of it—he must be honest. "Before you go, I have something else I have to say," he told him. "I was with a man before I came here."

"I told you already," Bart said sternly. "I don't want to hear about it. It's none of my business."

But Robb tried to reach for him. "Please just hear me out. I was with him, because of something that happened to both of us a long time ago."

"I told you I don't want to hear about it"—and was about to turn on his heel for the bedroom.

"Vietnam."

Bart stopped. "What?"

"Vietnam."

But now that he had set up his drama, Robb didn't feel he was worthy of it, either. For as had been the case lately, in trying to tell several truths at once, he had ended up lying by connecting them.

"You?" Bart asked, his hair on end. "You in Vietnam?"

"For a few months, yes. I never told anybody."

"Seems like there's a lot you haven't told me." Protectively, Bart tightened his robe. "I'm going to bed. I need my sleep, especially after this. We'll talk tomorrow when I get back home."

But as Robb lay there at last, having put out the lamp, he knew Bart must be lying awake in there, too, stiff as a poker.

Six

He had met Bart in the midst of what they sometimes whimsically referred to as a bakery brawl. One morning, on one of the visitations to see his daughter in Port Townsend, he had arrived early, and stopped in for a cup of coffee at the Crescent. This, in fact, had gotten to be something of a routine.

As usual, one of the senior fishermen—obviously off season and holding court interminably in a corner, never buying anything but talking, talking, talking—was going on and on about the injustice of Gays having rights. It was the third or fourth time Robb had had to listen to this moron. The man had a very loud voice, and thus half of the busy bakery—a coffee shop, really—was cowed into silence, during what was becoming a sort of discourse. What drove Robb up the wall was—the other fishermen, trim whereas this man was fat—just sat there at his table and smiled and listened to him, obviously delighted as his captive audience.

Meanwhile, a handsome dark-haired man had come in, with steel-rimmed glasses—Italian and intellectual looking. He had a wide, smiling open face, which grinned like a jack o'lantern when he took in Robb. He obviously found the man's voice offensive, too, and sat down as far out of earshot as possible, taking out a sketchbook, already full of drawings, which he turned. Robb, intrigued—and this man was younger, by at least ten years—was trying to improvise an opener, when he heard, "And the thing about these gays is—give them an inch and they'll take a mile." Immediately Robb's gaze hit his new friend's, and they burst out laughing.

The Pontificator instantly stopped. "Maybe you two will tell us what's so damn funny."

Bart—for it was Bart—sort of shrunk into the corner and looked longingly at the patio tables through the French doors.

But Robb had been needled in just the right way. "We're laughing," he said, "because you're so full of shit, it's coming out your ears."

The bakery came to a standstill, like a bell which has just been clasped. Outside, there were lovely silver lines of sunlight, but not in here.

The fat man stood up. So did the fishermen, as though royal guardsmen. "Maybe you and I had better have a little talk outside." He came over and shoved Robb in the chest. Robb shoved back, so the man—who curiously looked now like Humpty Dumpty— almost rolled backwards into his ten pins, which were the fishermen.

At that moment two strange things happened. One was, another fat man, whose spoon Robb had picked up and handed back when he'd first come in, sauntered over and told the other three hundred pounder to back off. Confronted, the two looked like sumo wrestlers. Immediately chairs flew when they touched, leading to the second thing, which was, the sidekick fishermen went for Robb, but they were surprised from behind by two militant lesbians, who shouted they wouldn't put up with this shit any longer, either—and caught them with full-Nelsons.

A table turned over.

Two bakery maids screamed.

Three coffee urns went down. Like fallen idols.

And Bart joined the fight, in Robb's behalf.

That's how they met.

Before the more moderate citizens of Port Townsend could end the Saturday Morning Massacre, Robb and Bart left with a cut ear (Robb) and a bloody nose (Bart). Ironically, it was in the aftermath of St. Valentine's Day, and, as consolation, the bakery had given them each a bag of day-old heart-shaped cookies, with red sprinkles.

"Well," Bart said, as they hobbled out, "we can't go on meeting like this. These tough bakeries have got to go. How about a safer place next time—like the drugstore fountain?"

And he laughed. And Robb remembered it, now. Bart's laughter. The man was always up. And honest.

And Robb had said, "I was willing to do just about anything to meet you, but this is ridiculous."

"Was ridiculous," Bart said. "We don't have to do it again."

Within weeks, they were lovers.

As Robb now lay there in the strangeness of Bart's living room, Robb found that sleep-time without the drug was just as he had feared—it was an odd and foreign country itself, full of his own thoughts, which he had never fully looked at before. He remembered, with longing, how the pill, settling into his system every night, had caused him to take a nose-dive, and everything that had disturbed him that day had found its way, as it were, under a mushroom cloud, whose explosions had occurred long ago—maybe in the chemist's laboratory—one he had never been forced to witness or to hear. And was safe from.

Now there was no cloud but plenty of explosions. One right after the other. One was, Bart might toss him out on his butt the minute he'd had time to think about harboring a pill head who was also a Vietnam Vet, when all along Robb had been secretly planning to jettison Bart himself, but of course with greater style and finesse, once the right man came along.

But Buddy (this was another one of the explosions), in the cold gray light of back pain and failed dancing and lovemaking, was not so much of an angel after all. His act didn't add up. Not in the least. What had he been doing just sitting there beside the steam room anyway—and already naked, to boot? What if only to pick someone up who was happening along? Didn't anyone who was legit take his clothes off directly and then suit up immediately afterwards? Buddy had been parading around the shower room first, and then, most probably, had put on his running clothes to net a good catch once he'd turned someone on. Robb. It was not just a coincidence that he had popped up in the Weight Room, then the running trail, and then the pool and the hot tub. Their talk had been way too immediately revealing to be on the up and up. Telling him right away about his separation before they had known each other ten seconds. Right—Buddy didn't know his wife would be coming home. Sure. Was there any better way of dodging all the intimacy and closeness and touching that usually follows getting fucked? A surprise wife. A perfect out. A trick question. An instant ringing down of the curtain. But notice how Buddy had even gotten in a little dancing, before tossing him out on his ass. In the wake of his wife's grand and tragic "entrance."

And I was worried—Robb started tossing and turning—I might have jeopardized their marriage, when I really just walked right into a trap which has probably destroyed what I had with Bart.

What a pushover.

Robb lay there, praying for sleep, so that he wouldn't have to face the next round. Which could only get worse and worse as he neared dawn.

A light veil of a doze did fall on him for just a moment, and under it, the anatomical charts of Tyler's office arrived once more, although it was better to say he felt the anatomical charts this time, rather than actually saw them. He felt every muscle, scientifically identified, as a shape of pain located in its precise location in his body.

And under the veil, his mind recovered an old, sly habit of shooting down, with heavy artillery and anti-aircraft probably borrowed from World War II Hollywood, all the worries and people who were keeping him awake. And the explosions went off in huge flashes, and in them, there were some ugly bits from R-rated films he'd glimpsed on video in dance bars, thinking at the time, they aren't bothering him at all, they'll never come round again and jump me. But here they were after all, coming round the bend, ugly, ugly things, viewed or gawked out, laughed over or tuned out by the inured barroom crowd but saved for this terrible moment of reckoning when he, of all people, lay flat on his back.

Robb almost screamed at one of them. Saw, suddenly, a turning bicycle wheel. Turning silver spokes, and he knew he was back in an odd place somewhere, just as he had feared. It wasn't the movies now. And there was no one's hand to hold this time. Not Bart's, not Buddy's. And no pills to get him safely through this territory and into the comfortable bed of sleep which rested in the safety zone at the back of his mind; for he found himself ship-tossed, plane-tossed (he had been flown to Vietnam in one infinitely long plane ride), for he was guilty, and now after fifteen years of getting away with it, he was going to have to face this music of hearing and seeing these bicycle spokes tick past and a man named Mason.

And as they ticked, he was arriving in Cam Ranh Bay for a day of processing. And that was how I met Mason, he thought, who drove us to MACV headquarters. That was how I lost Mason— it was because of that jeep. Mason had his shirt off, and I could see his back muscles change every time he shifted gears. (And Robb, lying in bed, could feel those muscles, a replay from Buddy, with his very hands.) Saigon, which they passed through, was a delight, with those back muscles. And the helmet and the khaki fatigues. He didn't pull rank on us, and laughed when they said he was going to catch hell for being without the shirt. He went on watching that tan, that back, those pectorals glimpsed in the windshield, bright with sun; he saw him sweat and laugh, and his dog tags swaying like a rosary on a god.

But in the middle of Saigon, Robb noticed that something was wrong—Mason's affability dissolved with impatience over the streetlights and the pedestrians. With all the acuteness of lack of sleep back then, he began to smell danger, like ripe apples. Mason's very body seemed to ferment there, with impatience and fury. It was the presence of the Vietnamese. Mason obviously loathed them. And a long barking set of words popped up now, and Robb felt the bed move and rumble toward the inevitable intersection where he knew the bicycle wheel waited turning.

The men in the jeep had begun to quiet and slowly cower, like the greenhorns they were—they knew the party was over until they got to Headquarters just a few miles off. Their faces withdrew and hung, and they looked suspiciously and sympathetically about, fearful for the people whose land they were now entering—for the people whose city they were now trying to leave.

But I can remember it, Robb told himself, I can remember it exactly. There was nothing traumatic at all. The sun was just above the main bar we went to later; it flooded the street and the jeep, so that Mason could not see. He meant no harm. And then all at once, there she was out of the blue—I swear even now she was aiming for us, for she struck us broadside. The woman on the bicycle. I saw a flash of red—it was one of those beautiful *ao dais* the women wear—it was so beautiful, like a bird, a cardinal, against the glass of a greenhouse, which was what the jeep had become, everything, everything seemed to come at us—and we were all so scared and shocked, and before we could even see her, Mason was pulling away, hightailing it out, and laughing and telling us about the Saigon rules of the road, but I was the one who looked back—I shouldn't have looked back! Everyone else somehow knew not to, that way they didn't have to hold themselves responsible—but I looked back and saw her lying there crying beside the broken wheel of her bicycle with the Vietnamese people staring at us in a circle as we retreated into the distance, staring at us like they weren't surprised at all.

Hit and run.

Was she hurt? In need of the hospital? Did she die?

Hit and run.

The phrase slammed up against Robb. "Hit" hit every muscle and caused his heart to race like a hooked salmon running thirty feet ahead of the boat.

Robb tried to forget about it, the way the others did, the way he was trying to forget about it now, but it didn't quite pass. He had the job, 6 AM to 6 PM, working as an ordinary clerk in the huge MACV headquarters—Pentagon East, they called it—a routine job much like what you'd put in at some high rise in Seattle, one that was so routine and American-like it was supposed to make you forget the artillery that lit up the sky like the aurora borealis after dark. But he did not forget, because the bicycle wheel was there every night, and one night he even dreamed a childhood memory of next-door neighbor Ellen falling from her bike in the alley in back of the schoolyard, and holding her knee and sobbing, with Robb on the other side of the cyclone fence laughing for a moment, before realizing she was hurt. How bad he had felt then! "Brew, brew," Ellen seemed to say, as she held her knee and sobbed. It might have been his first real understanding that someone else besides himself could feel pain and not deserve it.

He mentally reached out in the darkness for her, for Ellen, and for the Vietnamese woman he called Lily. He thought of the hundreds and thousands and even millions of women like her, in this rustling, crying, screaming, outraged country, a veritable anguished Body which America had picked out for a target to vent all its fury upon.

Mornings, he would go in to see the Colonel for his orders, and each morning he would nearly make a clean breast of it, willing to serve time in prison or the guardhouse. But "I didn't do it" would always stop him, and then the compunctions would follow, along with the terrible fear that he would be hunted down and even destroyed if at last he told. Suddenly Mason's body, so beautiful and godlike, became a terror to him, all that slick and eeling muscle could very easily make short work of him while he was sleeping—if he ever slept!—if he found out who squealed. Sometimes, in the huge two-story unit, they would pass in the hall, and exchange significant glances, and Mason's look would always be the same—at first guarded and inquisitive, then a forced smile would appear from out of the muscular jaw line. "You're not telling," his face said. "You're my buddy." Because maybe he had heard she was dead.

Sometimes his look was so significant, Robb expected notes or even a letter to appear in his locker, but day after day, there was nothing. I must settle this, he told himself, it must be resolved.

For I had stopped eating, Robb remembered, the bicycles at night had gotten so bad, I couldn't sleep and therefore eat. The bicycles I would see in my mind's eye. The woman in the Mess started to look exactly like Lily on the bike. The name I gave her.

Lily after all was Lily. You couldn't change the Vietnamese people. Never, never, never. And Lily in the Kitchen was kind to me, teased me for not eating enough, for trying to throw things out on the sly, so no one would notice. And the nicer she was, the more the spokes turned at night, and the more I saw the flash of the *ao dai*, like a cardinal now in a tree, flying from branch to branch. Then one night, everything stopped at once.

Robb remembered it, now. It was a hand. Mason's. He'd gotten into the bunk with him. Naked. Had found him out. Somehow. And he was blowing his breath upon him and rubbing him all up and down, and while Robb was overcome, all of him was giving way to those gigantic hands moving up and down, slipping off his shorts, while he planted a kiss on his mouth strong enough to take his breath away.

While he lay there, feeling the sharp ecstasy of what he had wanted all his life but never had, while Mason had his way with him—with him at twenty-four and still a virgin with men—while he lay there he could only imagine how many years in prison both of them would spend for what they had done and were now doing. Someone stop him, he wanted to yell, but the other part of him was yielding, was dissolving, beautifully and finally, into that flesh— Mason was being gentle now, kissing his chest and whispering how beautiful he was, for no one else was in the bunkhouse, he remembered; all the others were gone out on a Saturday pass.

But then there was another voice at the back of his mind, borrowed from boot camp, Are you good fine sissy girls? the D. I. had screamed. Yes we are good fine sissy girls, *sir*! Are you good fine sissy faggots? Yes we good fine sissy faggots, *sir*! Louder, I didn't hear you! Yes we are good fine sissy faggots, *sir*!

And suddenly I remember taking my hands back at last, pushing Mason aside at last, and throwing off the covers—"You son of a bitch. You hit that woman on her bicycle."

And all Robb could say now was—Mason seemed to go all cold like ashes, and break, in the light from the window, into a mask of anguish. He was gone, out of the bunkhouse.

Out.

Next morning, Robb received a letter from his father. "I know why you enlisted," it said. "I gave you the wrong advice. I was drunk. Have been drunk for many, many years. Please forgive me. I'll make it up to you. I'm sober now. My dear Robb, find a way of getting out of that hellhole and come home. If only I could hug you and have you forgive me it would alleviate everything I have ever suffered."

Robb wrote back, "I don't know when I can come home, Father. But I'll do it as soon as I can. In the meantime, don't blame yourself. I got myself into this, I have to get myself out."

He did not say anything to anyone about Mason. Later he'd heard that the man had died of an overdose. He'd been on heroin all this time. Even through the short memorial they held, he didn't say anything. Only cried when the others weren't looking. Cried on the side.

But afterwards, the bicycle wheels got worse again; they spun up in flames. And by day, he was sure that Lily in the mess hall must have been the woman on the bike, and if he spoke to her, made a clean breast of it, he could finally sleep.

He caught her one day in a corner, just as she was picking up the plates from lunch. She was happy to see him and smiled. Pretending in his gestures to be speaking about the meal, so no one would suspect, he said, "You're the woman, aren't you, whose bicycle broke? It hit the car?"

She continued to smile. "Broke? Yes." And she moved her head up and down, in laughter.

Feeling, for the moment, totally exonerated and relieved, Robb smiled and laughed, too. "That's what I thought. I want to tell you that I was in that jeep, and that I should have said something, and I am so sorry it happened. And I want you to have this—"

He drew out an envelope with folding money in it.

He could never be sure if it was just then that her look changed to suspicion and fear, or while he'd been telling of the accident. It became very important later at what point she'd started to change. But why had he gone on at all? Why hadn't he stopped while he was ahead? He had lost his reprieve. Thrown it away! Because, as usual, he'd sabotaged himself. Fucked himself over.

For her eyes had focused on the envelope by now and had seen the money, in shadow, inside. Funny money, they called it.

And just then—"Jorgenson, what's your business with this woman?"

The Mess Officer was standing there, right beside him.

Lily looked terrified.

"I—understand her family is in difficult circumstances, Sir."

"You know the rules about giving money."

"Yes, Sir."

The officer took back the envelope and placed it in Robb's hands.

"I don't want to see this again."

"Yes, Sir."

Next day and every day after, Lily did not appear in the mess hall, and Robb was sure she had lost her job on account of him.

That's when the panic attacks started. Set in.

He would get into the office at 6 AM, and his hand would start to shake while filling out the forms. He would try to complete the simple act of walking the papers down the hall, and everything would go slantwise on him. He would wait out, agonize over, the minutes that would finally take him to the Mess, so he could see if she was there, back at her station, but the moment when he would arrive and find her still missing, he'd find it impossible to lift a spoon.

One morning, while working, he thought he saw her from the window, and sprang from his chair and ran out into the parking lot. Fell face forward on the pavement.

When he came back, he almost collided with the Colonel, who commanded him to account for himself on the spot. But he could not. And the Colonel, giving him the once-over and obviously aware of his behavior for days, took out a form himself and ordered him to the hospital, which, in turn, forwarded him on with a prescription of Ativan to Hawaii, where he was discharged. Medically. The diagnosis: panic disorder.

And that had been the end of it. His military "career."
And so he was no veteran.

Seven

In the bed, Robb turned on his side, tried to envision the darkness of sleep, but he could still see the bicycle wheel in flames. It shot them out, like the straw-turned-to-gold of Rumpelstiltskin's magic spindle, accentuated by the light and rumbling from the sky he had known just above MACV headquarters. You left your post early, the voice said, you're not a Vet, don't flatter yourself with that. A two-month "tour" in Vietnam! Two months. Who ever heard of it? Don't expect your life to work out, don't expect to sleep, because you can't finish anything, you'll always sabotage it. And don't fool yourself for one minute that the men bought "panic disorder" when you got out. A wastebasket for all hysterical pansies. Like "nervous breakdown." A wastebasket. You'll never sleep again, you titless Wac.

Robb fell asleep just then, thinking about the "no questions asked" box, which he had passed just before leaving Vietnam and how he should have put that large vial of Ativan in that vile box, too, and how it was like the check point on the Oregon-California border, where they skin-frisked your car for fruit and the maggot-causing flies that could cut down all the orchards of California just the way drugs wiped out whole droves of people—and how he had often thought that while he had been busy invading Vietnam, everyone back home had been busy invading their own arms and stomachs and noses with dope and alcohol, and that when he passed that no-questions-asked box without putting anything in, he'd joined the rest of the damned. And in sleep, he sailed into flames, was sent screaming down a slide, where he was yelling at Lily to get out of the way.

With the scream, Bart came running into the room. "Robb, what is it?"

And Robb, rubbing his face and finding it wet again, said, "It's just this vile drug I'm withdrawing from."

Bart looked terrified. "Well, then, maybe it isn't such a good idea you go off. Least right now."

Robb shook his head violently, "No it is, it is. I need to stay off. Just hold me a minute."

And he felt his terrible fatigue as Bart caught him. "You are a very kind and good man, Bart," he said at last. "You remind me of a dog I once had named Teddy."

"Teddy?"

Robb was feeling his shoulders beneath the pajamas. "You're absolutely solid. Like my dog. And loving. But you don't do well taking up with the likes of me."

"Don't say that," Bart said. "It's just that you haven't slept a wink, it looks like."

"I'll do all right. But you don't do well taking up with the likes of me."

He was held in Bart's arms, and when he awoke again, his lover was gone, having left the breakfast table set for him.

The day was veiled and gray, and he found it impossible to hop in the shower the way he always did. It was all he could do just to sit down to the empty coffee cup in front of him—his back was screaming so much. And it was very right that it was screaming; he knew now where it had come from. Lily. The impact of the jeep had thrown his whole body into a skew. It was surfacing now, at last. Sixteen years later. He had heard and read of such cases. And he felt at this moment that he should never be alleviated until he got things right with her. And that was impossible.

He did not know what to do, with all his joints feeling as though they had sand in them. He simply stared into the newspaper Bart had left folded neatly on his plate, as though in a rotogravure of what one gay partner might do for another when he's sick and ailing. One thing was for sure, though, all plans to get rid of Bart were out. Robb felt panicked even thinking how close he'd come—

to losing what was fast becoming his last foothold. With one sip of coffee, his heart was pounding all over the place, up, down, and around.

He dressed and got into the car. He was going to try to see his daughter again. The first thing would be to give himself six hours to get there instead of two. The second thing would be to have only pleasant memories while he was driving, instead of nursing his anger. That had been his mistake yesterday. He called ahead, and left a message at Rose House, saying he was coming, and where Valerie should meet him. Chetzemoka Park. The stone bench.

And for a while, he managed the drive north out of the city just fine. He steadied himself. He kept clear of the freeway for the time being. He thought of the photograph of the three of them—Laura, Valerie, and himself—under the rose trellis behind Rose House. He thought of how much love there had been, constant kisses and hugs—and beautiful flowers rising high out of their Victorian garden, like airborne sparklers. He thought about their sitting out by the stone urn one evening when the guests had been taken care of, and singing, the three of them, with Laura on guitar. He had wondered, then, how any three people could be so happy and so well taken care of—Laura with her pliant but unshakable common sense, he with his dauntless energy, Valerie with her child's sense of wonder, rescued from the shadow of her first father, and the three of them together with their Rose House, a working unit, renovated from the ground up by Robb's preciously dead father.

But Robb also remembered how that lilac on the east side of the house would bloom purple every spring, and how that would put him into what he called his pornographic mood and he'd have to take a trip to Seattle. Laura knew exactly what it was for, and had to let him go. And go, he did. Further and further down First Avenue in Seattle he would hurry, like a tiger let out of his cage, looking for the safest and most unlikely place. Sometimes it would be a loose rack at the back of what appeared to be a smoke shop; sometimes it would be an unabashed "arcade" with twinkling globes and Master's Card signs, where the gay porno was stacked in hundreds behind the desk, and you ordered by giving the clerks a number from tags stapled to demo copies left out front.

But it was just at that moment—in that memory—when the car started giving him trouble.

He must keep it straight in the lane, if he ever was to get to Port Townsend. He was nearing a major shopping center—maybe that was his cue to stop. Giving himself calming messages, the way a former counselor had once told him, he said, of course, that's it, I got scared because I wanted to remind myself that I need to get Valerie something. And turned into the huge parking lot.

Walking through the aisles of the mammoth "all-purpose mart," which even downtown people flocked to, the prices were so low, he paused in the magazine section and picked up a copy of *Vietnam Pictorial* (September, 1986), and was immediately jolted by another memory he'd thought he'd left behind.

The men were pictured with rifles, trudging through swamps, or shown feeding each other when downed in battle, or talking amiably on cots. They were exactly the pictures he remembered seeing in a porno store—that had been the magazine he had found there!—except the men had been completely naked (well, except for an occasional helmet or pair of camouflage underpants), and instead of shooting or bayoneting one another, they had been embracing or hugging or fucking in the barracks. At the back of the magazine, there had been photographs of real-live "Hot Numbers," whose p.o. boxes promised you the time of your life if you tried them—the exact replacement for the knives and plaques and bullets which now gleamed in the classifieds between his thumbs.

He stood there and started to sweat. Why? What harm was there in looking at a magazine at Mammoth Mart? So what if his shopping cart was empty? Was there any crime in browsing? And no one, no one could tell what he was actually seeing into. Hot Vets (which he had bought and smuggled back to Port Townsend—why smuggled?—Laura knew) had long since been burned in the Rose House fireplace.

Nevertheless he was sweating. And not in the way he normally sweated. Big, globe-like drops hung along his forehead and nowhere else.

"Excuse me, sir," a clerk asked. "Can I help you with something?"

"No," Robb answered, wiping his forehead. And added, for this own comfort—"Do I look like I do?"

The girl could hardly have been much older than Valerie—seventeen, eighteen maybe? "Well, it's just that you've been standing here for such a long time."

Robb smiled her away, but felt himself go cold as she retreated, and he became aware of his watch. He would give himself a few seconds before he actually looked. Several seconds to calm himself. Cautiously, he turned his wrist and glanced. One o'clock. It couldn't be—for that meant he'd been standing there half an hour.

But he had to go on standing, because, in the fluorescent lighting, he knew he didn't know where he was. Actually. Which way was the prescription desk or even the checkout counter. Or the toy department, his original goal. Even though people might have noticed him—maybe even the whole store had noticed—he must go on standing there like a shipwrecked seaman, until he could figure out his next move.

He looked over and realized why he had been frozen. He was within an aisle of "Bikes and Accessories"—something that sent him off like a shot—off and running, until he almost collided with the teddy bears.

And then the Ken dolls. And remembered how badly Valerie had wanted to buy one when she'd been younger—how after months of saving up coins in a Mason jar, she had gone with him to the dime store, and they had bought Ken together.

He wheeled the shopping cart around, put in two teddy bears and found a check-out corner as fast as he could. And was glad when the clerk put the bears into a huge sack, so no one could see.

He put them in the car. On the back seat.

Eight

So he got to Port Townsend O.K. Somehow he held steady. The ferry was a great breather for him. Although there was another moment of panic when he thought, on deck, he wouldn't be able to find his car, and that he might hold up the whole ferry, he did fine.

He got across with flying colors, and in the veiled day above the two-laner, little searchlights of sun broke through above Hood Canal and beside the farmlands afterward. There were glimmering isolated horses in a field, and for an entire half hour with not another car in sight, he felt his shoulders relax, the pain in his back subside. He had made a tear in the paper sack, so that the heads of the teddies were out and smiling, and formed a kind of cheering section at the back.

In town, he still saw that he had a few minutes, for all his worrying, and so he drove up to the seaside park and sat waiting upon a stone bench. The place was blissfully deserted. A refuge from the sight of Rose House, which, although not three blocks away, was basically out of sight, the hill was so high, if he didn't look for the turret above. And so he was safe.

Valerie was coming now, running down the hill towards him in a cheerleader's outfit. So young to be wearing it, he thought. Barely sixteen. And still running to him the way she did as a child. Above her, he allowed himself to see Rose House's crest. He allowed himself to see it. He thought about the maidens on the circular ceiling again and how, not long from now, really, the winter solstice would be lighting up one of them. For that was the way the sun behaved within the house; it was guided by a mysterious feat of engineering, lost over a century ago, which zodiaced the seasons.

"Hi, Dad," she said, hugging him. "Have you been waiting long?"

"You're right on time, honey," he said. "How was school?"

"We had tryouts," she answered. "I want to show you my routine before I go."

He smiled. But he didn't like to hear about her having to go. Not when she'd just gotten here. He sat down again, and started to suspect that she could tell he wasn't himself. His face must have given it away.

"You look wonderful," he said. "I'm sure you'll get it. It's just that—"

"What?"

"It's so hard to believe you're this grown up. And that we've come this far."

And he meant it—that was the case. But he had also meant something else. He could hardly believe that he was here. Not just that he had managed the car—which was a miracle—but that he was actually sitting here, seeing his daughter in a public place, as though one of them was on leave from prison. That just three years ago, they had been living happily, apparently, beneath that turret that was just barely visible, and that now all was lost. That not thirty-six hours ago, he was up here, pounding at Rose House, trying to get in. That not twelve hours ago, he'd been involved in the delirium of dancing with another man as though there were no tomorrow, and at this moment, he was sitting here, trying to be Valerie's father. Instantly he realized what Buddy must have been feeling when his wife returned—the man had found himself between planets—and was falling.

Valerie was taking a sidelong glance at the car. "Dad, what are those teddy bears doing there? They aren't for me, are they?"

"Why, yes," he said.

"Dad, you know I'm too old for that. What would my friends think?"

"O.K.," he answered, embarrassed, ashamed, while thinking of the Ken Doll. He tried to smile. "I guess I should try to remember you're old enough to drive. You are getting older."

Obviously aware he was disappointed, she took some pom-poms from her tote bag. "Look, let me show you my routine."

There was a little light left from the autumnal day— magnified a bit by the very glimpses of beach and waves beyond the trees. October seemed to sketch her in as she got up, checking first, of course, to see that no one else had come into the park. Her cordova-colored uniform seemed at one with the leaves, with the euonymus, already going gold. Suddenly she danced and shouted, lifted her pom-poms—such a surprise from such a shy girl. Robb couldn't help but smile.

When she was done, he applauded. "Thanks, Dad," she said. "This will bring me luck."

Nevertheless, there was a sense, as with the sun, as with the afternoon, as with the season, that it was all very soon coming to an end; he knew she would be leaving, and she said so.

"Leaving?" he asked. "But why? You've only been here a few minutes."

"I didn't know you would be coming today," she answered. "I thought you would be teaching."

"Yes." And he was astounded that he'd actually be expected to teach tomorrow. Which was impossible.

"I thought you would be teaching," she repeated, "and I have to get back to the house. I need to call and see if they want me for call-backs at five."

"Couldn't I come with you and watch if they do?"

"With my father? Are you kidding?"

"I guess I should be."

There was an awkward silence. Usually, in the past, Robb always thought of something to say. He'd seen to it that he'd become a master. Since coming out to her on the eve of the divorce three years ago, he'd followed her lead in never referring to it again—she knew nothing, for example, of Bart—and so he had learned quickly how to fill in. But nothing, absolutely nothing, came to him now. At last, he said, "Well, at least let me drive you home."

She looked frightened. "All right."

She got in and they drove up the hill. The sight of Rose House, coming into view, rolled over him like a sweat. An awful flash came upon him of the day he had moved out. Before going, the three of them had formed a huddle in the dining room and cried. "I will always love you," he had said. Fortunately or unfortunately, it was still true.

He drew up to the front. As a miracle, the guests had left a parking space.

"Mom says you can't come in," she said.

"I know—but can you just go in and phone? And see if—just by some slip of judgment—you didn't make the finals, and we could still have dinner?"

"I have to stay here," she said firmly. "Mom said I could only see you a few minutes."

Some guests were going up the stairs, looking at them quizzically over their shoulders. Crouching they let themselves in with their room keys. Robb remembered when his father had fitted that glass—etched with a wreath of roses—into that door. Then he looked up and saw a man on the second landing, obviously vacuuming.

"Who is that?" Robb asked, pointing.

"Please let me leave, Dad," Valerie said. "I have to go and call."

"But who is it?"

"My father."

Robb set his jaw like stone. "What?"

"He's back. Mom's seeing him again," Valerie said.

"How long has this been going on?" Robb asked.

"Since spring. I didn't want to tell you, because I knew you'd be upset."

"That man in my house." And Robb felt a flame go straight through the top of his head. Valerie saw it and grabbed for the door handle.

"Please, Dad, that's all I can say. You will always be my father, so don't worry. But I have to go. If I miss the call-backs, I won't get another chance."

"Go, then." And they hugged.

Watching her run up the stairs and then wave before opening the door with her own key, he saw the maidens, too, in the third story window, in a grand dance, still, while the sound of the vacuum cleaner continued. She disappeared and he felt all the loss—of the spiral staircase, the faceted glass, the rose rooms. His heart settled at the bottom of a sorrow such as he had never known, and when the rage came again, and he got back into the car and turned to pull out without looking, he almost collided with a cyclist, who gave him a helmeted look of disgust and superiority.

"Dirty motherfucking cocksucker," Robb said.

So now I'm down to calling people names, too, he thought.

Nine

He had a pick-up dinner at the Ben Franklin dime store fountain, and started up out of town before the dark set in.

But just on the outskirts before the speed change, he saw the sun go down and began to worry that in the dark, his foot would not be able to find either the brake or the gas pedal. It made a lot of sense, that worry, and so he turned around, and found—the hardware store would be closed by now—a pencil flashlight with a suction cup, in the accessories section of the giant Port Townsend Safeway..

He looked at the clerk and suspected he knew what this strange device was for—this customer was bonkers, needing to drive with a flashlight on his feet, so he could find the pedal. The clerk, an older man, eyed him up and down, and Robb eyed him up and down, too, unable to tell who had been first.

But, pocketing his cash, he went back out to the car and surreptitiously planted the light in just the right spot anyway, and pulled off before anyone could notice. The light was going to help him not think about Valerie's father vacuuming up the stairs of Rose House. It really was going to help him. If he could just see his feet, he could drive. And if he could drive, he could get back home—two homes, really, one at Mrs. Molyson's (she must be ready to call the police by now, wondering where he was) and one at Bart's (who was probably ready to do the same). All these people were waiting there in the city, ready to care about his whereabouts, if he could just get back. And he would.

As the darkness descended, with the farm fields (the horses were gone) not looking so friendly this time, Robb did have to admit he saw the passing cyclist take flame somewhere out there. He knew it was just a mirage, or "false fire," known to be seen in some places like Mississippi on June nights—it was just there, an hallucination, and he shouldn't be too worried. He could hold steady with it there, off in a corner of his vision. He just wished that that cyclist had not come round the bend just when he had— that had been bad timing—then he wouldn't have to deal with this after-image now.

But his mind was not going to accommodate him completely. As he got on to the floating Hood Canal bridge and was very aware that he could not pull over, if panic should strike, he found that he was starting to think about Valerie's father anyway, the man who had abandoned Valerie when she was a baby, and who had not sent checks or cards or money orders or letters but only left his wife and his daughter with a lot of memories of neglect and drunken outrage—after finally disappearing. It was unfathomable, when Laura had carried on for years about her foolishness in having taken up with such a man in the first place and how far she had grown in learning to look after herself and her daughter, and first and foremost by choosing such a caring person as Robb. He had gotten countless points for not being Scott, and he realized now how much he had depended, through the years, in not being like him.

But now as soon as things had gotten tough for Laura, she had simply gone back to the familiar. After twelve years. It was safe to say that as soon as she had discovered these lavender periods in Robb, she had simply kicked him out and brought in whatever stand-in was handy. One she conveniently shared a history with. Judging by a few stray photographs, Robb could well imagine tourists coming back from a few years ago and thinking the family was exactly the same one they had seen before. Scott was, after all, doing the vacuuming on the second landing the way he, Robb, had done the vacuuming on the second landing for years.

It was totally dark in the car. Robb leant down and switched on the light. The apparition was gone. He had only twenty more minutes to the ferry. He would get back after all. And even if he never saw Valerie again, at least he could say he had been there for her cheerleading routine. Because he wasn't altogether sure he would live much longer. And if he did live, he might be locked up. Because if he went on running on to himself like this, about Laura and Scott, he would want to be locked up. And it was better to be dead than locked up.

It would be better to be dead than thinking as he did about Rose House and who was in it. Thinking as he did about Basic Training. Thinking as he did about Mason. Lily, Bart, Buddy.

And this whole country.

And he wanted to be in right relationships with everyone. And he was in right relationships with no one.

He got to the ferry landing. Haul out the regal robes, he got to the ferry landing, he said to himself without irony. It was a major achievement. But the man in the toll booth saw the half-sacked teddy bears, and those alone must have been enough to make him think he was nuts, and then one glance down, and Robb realized the suction flashlight was still shining between his knees. For a moment, he wondered if the man would let him on—and if not, the only way back would be the four hour route via Olympia, demanding a full hour and a half on the freeway, which was beyond his capacities.

But Robb was now getting change, and in relief, he was breaking into a sweat again and gripping the blessed ticket in his palm. The ferry, the Rhododendron, was just landing, and would take him on, if he could just get his ass into the right lane. Hurrying, but so afraid he'd drive into the wrong one, he actually took up two for a moment, and had to be honked back on track by the car behind.

Get in line. Get up on that bar, over those sandbags, one false move and you're hamburger. Robb reached down and very carefully turned off the pencil flashlight. With this much of a glow from the dock, he was sure his feet could find the pedals. In just a few more minutes, he would be on, and then he'd be home free. Driving off would be a piece of cake.

The man with the red flashlight was signaling. The seagulls were sounding, flying up like scattered paper. He started the car again, felt the ramp thud between land and sea. A second attendant, burly and also looking like G.I. Joe, pointed with a certain number of fingers to indicate the lane he should go into, just ahead, on the ferry. But Robb, flustered, and thinking of all the people he was in wrong relationships with, could not see how many fingers there were. Two fingers, second lane—a guess, but clearly the wrong one, because the man started yelling at him immediately from behind. "Lane Three." Robb pulled over sharply, to compensate, and was almost struck from behind by another honking motorist. For a few seconds, the quick and intense procedure of filling a ferry came to a complete standstill. Everyone seemed awakened from a sleep they had been in for years. A near decade of commuting and then this schmuck comes along.

At last it was over. For shame, Robb could not get out of the car right away but huddled there until he heard the sound of the ropes and chains, and the boat started forward over the water.

Someone was at the window. A man in uniform.

"Excuse me, sir, are you all right?"

He shone a flashlight into the car, hitting him in the face. A security officer.

"I'm fine."

"Have you been drinking?" the man asked.

"No, I haven't."

But suddenly Robb wondered if Ativan—or withdrawal from it—could change the size of your pupils. For the man—G.I. Joe—seemed to be checking.

"It's just that I saw you hunched here—and you had some difficulty getting on"—the man almost seemed attentive—"I wondered how you were doing."

"I'm all right. If you want to test for alcohol, go ahead" Robb told him.

"That won't be necessary. Just be careful getting off."

The man made a gesture vaguely resembling a salute and left.

But Robb, stranded again, felt he had no choice but to get out of the car and prove that he could walk a straight line. For he was sure the man would still be watching. He went up on deck—three full flights—and stood in the dark with the stars and the smell of seaweed, which used to take his breath away, but not now. He was scared out of his wits. He thought, if I ever get out of this one alive, I'll go home and throw the covers over my head and never come out again.

But then the voice came back—if you do that, Vietnam will be there waiting for you. Right there in bed. No sleep for you, not without Ativan, because you know that under the covers, there's Lily and the man on the flaming bicycle and Laura and Scott, who you'd like to throw through a plate glass window. You'll never survive, because by going one night without your drugs, you've kicked something into gear that just won't stop.

Robb, looking down at the rushing water, thought it might be an excellent idea to throw himself off. His heart was beginning to swell again with the thought of Valerie going back into that house.

But the ferry was approaching the bright city, which told him to hang in there, if just for a few more minutes, hang in there.

But I have to get this car off the boat, Robb said. G. I. Joe will be watching me especially. How can I do that? It means I'll have to go exactly between the white lines. You know I can't do that.

But he turned and followed everybody else back down to the cars. No way out, no way out—he slammed the car door, and felt himself coffined. Wherever he turned, there Lily and the cyclist were, under the covers.

Waiting for the signal to turn on his motor, he stared between his knees again. The pencil flashlight. Thank you, pencil flashlight, he thought, for getting me this far.

The ferry actually thudded against the dock. A trapdoor sprung. He was out. Free. He remembered he had stashed away, in the bottom of his chest of drawers, a lovely little bottle of green pills. He couldn't remember exactly what they were. But it was a lovely little thing. *If*—and he only meant if—he couldn't get to sleep tonight, he'd just take a pill or two from it. He was sure he could guess what the appropriate corollary doses were.

He was saved in the nick of time. All the flames and the apparitions came to rest, as the horn sounded, the seagulls flew, the ropes were thrown, and, once again, the platform was fitted into place. He found he actually was able to start the car and pull off glibly and smoothly, thinking of that bottle waiting for him back home, instead of Vietnam. It was so simple! Why hadn't he thought of it? And only thirty more minutes to go before he hit the Seattle Center exit. What a nightmare he had been through. It felt like ten years, when really it had only been a mere twenty-four to thirty-six hours. He had been in hell since Monday afternoon and now it was only Tuesday, and he was getting out.

Well—he smiled—I'll make a few apologies tomorrow. Explain the circumstances, and all of us will be as good as new. It will be as if nothing had happened.

Comfortably, he saw the green signs cropping up, showing the way to Interstate Five and Seattle, and he gave them each a friendly thumbs-up. Yes, absolutely. No problem, no problem there at all. What a spook ride it had been, though. The main thing was, he had not divulged any of these terrible secrets—which had just passed—to anyone. Not anyone.

For a moment, a doubt flickered over him, as he got into the right lane, which would put him on the ramp which would put him on the freeway. Had he shared any of these terrible thoughts with anybody? Laura, no, Valerie, no, Bart—.

And then he remembered he'd told him about Vietnam.

But he'd just say, he'd just say that the whole episode had suddenly surfaced because of the one-nighter with Buddy, but now he just wanted to bury the whole thing.

Which Bart would be more than happy to do, because he didn't like dramatic incidents. Let's just let the past stay buried, O.K.?

O.K., Robb heard Bart answer, as clearly as if he had sitting in the backseat, beside the teddy bears.

Smiling (he was just a little afraid, now that he was actually entering the freeway, where he would have to stay for twenty minutes), Robb reached down, and, just for good measure, turned on the pencil flashlight again, noticing also that the flaming apparition was coming up and pacing the car once more, just above the night shrubbery and the speeding random motels. It was a little closer this time, he had to admit, but no sweat, really. In fact, if he blinked his eyes at appropriate intervals, he could actually drive without seeing it at all. It was just fine! The apparition was no brighter than the freeway lights, which were, in fact, sometimes blinding, but he also discovered that if he put on a pair of sunglasses and kept on with the timed blinking, he actually had a normal road in front of him. He also considered that once home, he could take this blessed jewel of a pencil flashlight into the house and attach it to the wall just above some consoling picture he'd tack up—one just like the old painting above his mother's couch. One which she had kept years ago. A green pill from that lovely green bottle, and a nice companion of a picture, and Vietnam didn't have a chance. Not a chance. He'd be asleep in two minutes. And if he woke up in the middle of the night, there that companion would still be. No need to make a fool of himself again, begging Bart to sleep with him—or Buddy—he was done with all that crawling and fawning. Was relieved he had only spent one night doing it. No, this time, his own bedroom would supply him with everything he needed. In fact, it had been there all along. Why hadn't he thought of it in the first place?

Now, what picture would he put up? It was a wonderful thing just to sit there and think about choosing, as he finished out these twenty miles on the freeway, which, after all that worry, were not that hard at all—not in the least—now that the goal was in sight.

The goal was the picture. Perhaps something erotic. Or something spiritual. A protector of some sort. Like his father. A snapshot of his father? No, that might bring back the wrong thoughts. Bad idea, Robb. Something with green in it—let's go back to the original inspiration. Or maybe a picture of a saint.

As a matter of fact, Robb actually did remember there was a carved wooden icon buried somewhere in the house. Not of St. Paul. But Joseph. Joseph the Carpenter. He'd always liked the rugged masculinity of him, and the beautiful ebb and flow of the gown, the veins wrapping around his ankles. Yes, now where was it?

Robb took off his sunglasses, and tested his sight. Normal, again! Just come up with a master plan like this one, and the apparition makes a B-line for the door. There Joseph would be, placed on the nightstand beside the bed with the good old pencil flashlight above him. He'd seek him out.

The relief to be out of this nightmare. At last his exit was coming up. On safe city streets now, just past the dinner hour, with no whizzing lanes. Just this one last hill in the neighborhood.

But as he climbed, some aggressive cyclists were coming down at the same time, on the wrong side of the road, for Christssake, and without helmets. The after-image jumped the windshield, as Robb pulled up in front of Mrs. Molyson's, and got out his key, climbing, once inside, to the third landing. If those cyclists hadn't appeared, maybe he could have even gotten to sleep tonight without a pill, but now he would have to make sure. (He found the bottle. Right there, just where he had remembered, once he got into the house, under the socks he never used.)

But he had hardly shut the door when there was a knock. Mrs. Molyson.

"I was beginning to worry," she said in the doorway, in a tone extremely attentive for her. "You were gone all night, and I didn't know what to do with Tara, who was whimpering to get out."

The dog. Valerie's dog. He'd forgotten all about her.

"Where is she now?" Robb asked, flushed with embarrassment. And trying not to see any cyclists over her shoulder.

"Downstairs. I fed her. Do you want me to bring her up?"

"Not just yet, if you don't mind." For some reason, he wanted to set Joseph up and take the green pills without Tara there. "I'll be down in just a minute. And thank you so much."

He was aware of cutting her off before they could exchange their usual wry remarks. She smiled, puzzling over his face. "I'd appreciate it, if you'd come down as soon as you can. It's late."

"Yes. Right away. And thanks."

Blissfully, she disappeared. He had only to go back to his sock drawer, withdraw the bottle, and take the pill. Which he did. He felt the green float through his system. Yes.

Now it was easy to look his answering machine straight in the eye, alight with so many calls. Running through, he found they were all from Bart—desperate by the fourth one.

While he was easily and steadily erasing them, the phone rang. "Robb?"

"Yes"—very easy.

"Where on earth have you been?" Bart asked.

"I went up to see Valerie."

He could hear the relief.

"Are you O.K.? I was so scared after last night—"

"Please let's not mention it again," Robb said, rather hastily, considering his new mood.

"All right. But aren't you coming over? We were going to talk."

Robb could tell, even as he was sinking into his new ease, that Bart had come round to the idea of sleeping together. He could hear it—Bart had come round, was even a little desperate for it, but now he, Robb, was beyond all that.

"I told you I don't need to talk now," Robb said. "Anyway, it's rather late."

"But I'm upset. You really seemed sort of frantic." A pause. "There's no two ways around it. We need to talk and—"

"What?"

"I just need to be with you, now. Hold you," Bart said.

"No," Robb heard himself saying, "no holding. No touching. I just need to be left alone." The thought of how he'd once begged for it made his skin crawl.

But he could also hear Bart start to cry. "Robb, I've just been so worried about you today. And I just wanted to hold you close and let you know everything is O.K. I had no idea you'd been through something like Vietnam."

"Please stop it, Bart," Robb said. "I'm trying to wind down before going to sleep—or will soon. This doesn't do wonders for that."

Bart was still breaking. "I'm sorry. It won't be the same without you tonight, but I'll try to understand."

"Good," Robb replied. "Now I have to get off. Thanks for all the calls. I'll talk to you sometime soon."

But by the time he had stood up, he knew that Vietnam had gotten into the room anyway. Bart had spoken the word. So it was there. He dashed out and got Tara from Mrs. Molyson's living room—and when he came back in, it had gotten even bigger. He knew he was in for trouble.

He stripped and got into bed. Tara got into her basket, exhausted from her delight in seeing him, which he had not even thought about until now. But with the lights out, he remembered he'd forgotten his altar to Joseph. He closed his eyes, but was aware of some fire off in a corner. No, Joseph it would have to be.

Getting up, he found the icon over in a box in an instant. And it took no time to fasten the pencil flashlight and have it switched on above the nightstand. Settled once more, he at last felt the relaxation and comfort ease through his body a second time, all the way to the base of his back, which had been screaming and which he had forgotten again to notice. All the pain floated under. He thought of green parrots flying about—and green parrot tulips, flicked with color like peacocks; there were small little eyes of purple. He sunk further and further, until another ghost of a flaming apparition swam through, and he knew he ought to kneel by his bed and pray it away. Just for good measure.

With the pencil light on.

And so he tried, with Tara staring at him with raised head.

God, save me from dying. Because I think this pill is going to kill me.

There's no hope for you, the voice came back. You pushed God out of your life years ago. What makes you think He's going to pull you out now, just because you're in a mess.

He remembered a devoted Catholic friend of his who, suddenly turned atheist, had said, "Well, if I find out I'm wrong when I die, certainly God will forgive me for making an intellectual error."

How much laughter that had brought him then. But it wasn't funny now.

He lifted his head and tried to concentrate on the icon of Joseph once more—the wooden folds, the beautiful back, the carefully carved beard. But there was something in Joseph's hand—something round. Against himself, Robb felt his forehead bead with sweat. It's just a loaf of bread. Round and circular like they had in those days, Robb! But he couldn't stop himself, it still looked like a bicycle wheel.

Robb snapped off the light, and in desperation, tried to sleep again. But now the flaming bikers and their spokes and wheels were everywhere in the dark of his head, everywhere, with clear, luminous crackling faces. He started to hear the snap of wood burning. Could smell the smell. Of shit burning, Vietnam. Even so, like a firefighter fighting flames with memories, he tried to call back the earlier green moments, and for a second, Rose House loomed before him, at just the touch of April, with its lilac wafting through, and its lattice just budding, and Laura and Valerie signaling him to join them. Bart's house was somewhere there, too, with its mimosa in full leaf, flushed with the pink of blooms, and the man's soft face smiling in the window between parted curtains. They were all there; people who had loved him.

My great love for them will pull me through.

And as he thought of his love easing through every vein, he also saw his father, now on the camping spree, where he had rowed himself out to the center of the lake. Robb saw the boat capsize, and the life preserver, circular, float up, like a marker.

And the water turned green.

The cyclists were at him to do that, too. At last everyone was in agreement. And for every fiery apparition he now saw, he remembered he got up and took another pill. Each time he turned out the light, he could see the flames lessen and lessen on the borders of his bedspread. One last one and he was out.

Ten

The next time he could fix on as a date, it was November 28. November 28.

He went to the mirror and looked at his face. He recalled he had been in a fight. Actually two. There was a shadow of a bruise under the left eye, and he knew it had to do with a note lying open on the top of his dresser from Valerie, saying she didn't want to see him again.

He tried washing the bruise the way you would try to wash away a stain, but of course it didn't leave. It was clear to him that he would be able to conduct class much better if he didn't look beat up, but that there was basically nothing he could do but fix his panic-free breakfast, and stay clear of all circular objects. As he turned back to the bedroom, he felt, now, with some degree of satisfaction, that he had completely stripped his place of everything circular—even the clock dial was covered—and how, combined with the pills he had finagled from a whole slew of doctors, this safeguard had gotten him to sleep at night. He could not think of a single dream in the past month where Lily had gotten in. He had made himself safe from her and the other cyclists, and that had been a miracle.

His panic-free breakfast consisted of dry toast and eggs and one small white pill specifically designed to keep off the attacks, which of course might come up at any given moment during the work day, especially in the classroom. No sugar, either—that was clear, because the least little granule would send his heart into a flutter.

Now—he pulled on his clothes, while the eggs were boiling. Thought of Valerie's note.

That's right, he had punched Scott into and almost through a window of Rose House. The window of the door. For calling him a faggot.

The way it had happened was—Valerie had phoned and said, "Dad, my birthday's coming up, and I want you to go with me to get my learner's permit. You were the one who did all the teaching anyway."

Robb's heart had been alive enough then to leap, and so it had leapt, and he had said, "I'll be up tonight, if you want."

"Not tonight, Dad. They're not open, then. Tomorrow. Tomorrow afternoon."

"And what about your birthday? Couldn't Mom give us just a little corner to celebrate your birthday in? It's never the same in a restaurant."

"I'll see. I'll tell you when you pick me up."

And then Valerie had gone on to ask him about one of her geometry problems, and Robb, struggling to visualize three dimensions over the phone, knew that his mind wasn't working right, and that what was coming out of his mouth about angles and bisections wasn't making any sense at all, although Valerie, infinitely polite, was saying it was. And he knew, sitting now at the kitchen table, that his mind would not let him continue to think about the fight, and that it somehow had to do with the garden he could see three floors below, the part which was his responsibility, the part which Mrs. Molyson had been delighted to give him at one time and which he had turned, once, into a veritable bouquet of lilacs and dahlias and roses, accented by gold, and blooming in the spring with rhododendron. But now his garden plot caused his landlady embarrassment, because it had not been cleared or pruned since he had taken out the green bottle that night apparently so long ago, and so the ugly frozen blooms and weeds and fallen frozen leaves just simply stacked up there, and Robb, every time he looked, saw the rhododendron die just a little more, and then he would kick himself a little more, and make himself just a little less capable of doing anything about it, either, the next time around.

It was just like the Geometry over the phone. Besides, there had been a wheel in it somewhere. A circle, with pie-like spokes. He just couldn't think when things figured in like that.

He had been in another fight—this one at the Y, before the fight with Scott.

He had gone to the Y with the best of intentions. That was one thing that was for sure. Working out, since the Night of the Green Bottle, had been one of the few things he could still do. He found that if he put certain blessings on certain circular objects, they caused him no harm, and so he had blessed all the round weights in the gym. He was doing so well, actually. His body looked even better, and although all his excitement in glorying over the Human Body in general had dropped behind a thick curtain, he could still admire certain men individually. And there were several at the Y he still found especially nice to look at.

He'd been minding his own business, when this man he'd had come to identify as the Marauder (obviously an i.v. drug user, he had decided) started making wisecracks about gays. They were supposed to be *sotto voce*, but they were clearly meant for Robb's sensitive ear.

The surprise was, the man the Marauder was talking to, was the man with the magnificent cleavage Robb had seen in the bar where he'd gone dancing with Buddy. For some reason, this crawl back into the closet seemed overwhelming now, as he, Robb, stood, all tank-topped, surveying the gloomed-over weight room. He even took a look out the window for a breather and found the lake to be a regular bone yard of post-autumn. The leaves that lay stacked along the water looked like saturated Wheaties. There wasn't going to be any breather in this room today.

Unless it was the basketball court. That might offer something. He'd have a nice look at the guys playing ball, before picking up where he left off. There was one man in particular, a sultry young Italian, built like a brick shithouse, who worked out with weights, too, and was always especially friendly at the lift stations; in fact, he had the build Robb wished Bart had. Both this man (Larry) and Bart had the same handsome face and beautiful, long-lashed eyes, but Larry's back was like a god's compared to Bart's. And it had taken all this time for Robb to get the chance to see him with his shirt off. What a gift to find him playing Skins that morning, late. Every time Larry turned to throw a pass, it was like getting a free ticket through a gallery of Grecian statues.

And so Robb took his breather, but when he went back to his workout, the Marauder was still carrying on. This time more loudly.

Robb, lying on the bench press, felt himself stiffen with hatred every time, not so much for the man who was talking, as that Closet Queen, who stood there listening and laughing.

"Oh, so what you're saying is—he's a man's man"—and started to guffaw.

"Do you mind?" Robb called over. "I'm gay and I take it as offensive. Besides, I'm trying to concentrate."

"Oh, excuse me," the Marauder said. "Looks like this dude's doing some pretty serious stuff."

"I don't know if I am or not," Robb said, still supine. "I just want you two to be quiet." A rather long pause came in between, and Robb felt some clicking inside. It seemed to him the Marauder was like the monster in *Forbidden Planet*—a huge gorilla-like shape, visible only under artillery fire. And he was more than happy to supply the blast.

"So this man is a 'man's man' too."

Robb said the "click"—what the click told him to—and the two men didn't hear.

"What did you say?" the Closet Queen asked.

"I just said I want you to shut the fuck up with your homophobic shit."

The two of them were so surprised, they did stay shut up for a minute, and Robb was allowed to finish his twelve reps in peace. But while he was finishing them, Larry had come in, so that when he got up, there the god was, glistening as though newly risen from the sea. Now this veritable statue started in joking with the

Marauder, and Robb, pushed, at this moment, even beyond the "click," felt an altogether new force within him which said, "You looked spectacularly beautiful out there." And found he was actually saying it.

Larry, blushing all the way to his navel, quickly put his tank top on, while the man-at-the-bar said, "Better watch it, Man, he'll start asking for your phone number next."

And Robb, still beyond "click," yelled back, "So what if I do? What business is it of yours?"

In that instant, Robb saw immediately how much this barfly looked like him—same coloring, same build, same height—and just as he was thinking these things, he saw also that this man was just now realizing Robb knew him as the barfly.

It was an awful moment, then, when this enemy, who shouldn't have been his enemy, got up and gave him a shove, because it was totally fortuitous: unmeant, ashamed, self-loathing.

"Why don't you just leave," the Closet Queen said, shrinking after the push and looking either like Charles Laughton's Hunchback, or Margaret Hamilton's Wicked Witch of the West, after the douse from the bucket. ("Oh, I'm melting! What a world! What a world!")

Right, what a world, Robb thought, skulking off, too, but not leaving the weight room until his routine was done.

So that when he got to Rose House later that afternoon, things were not right in his head. He remembered something else that had been said at the gym—or somewhere—that "that guy over there is always pissed about something. Ever seen his face?" "Pissed?" another said, "That man is enraged. He needs professional help." And now he knew they meant him.

He'd have to say that he even felt some grief, too, over losing that closeted man—for losing him as a passing friend or acquaintance. There had been a time, before that disastrous day, when they had joked, the two of them, about what physical twins they were—so much so, people had sometimes mixed them up, had given them credit for being there seven days a week as the same man—and both Robb and his friend had felt gratified by the connection. It was like saying, now, that part of yourself was gone. As it was gone now, too, in Scott, although that part Robb did not really understand.

Nevertheless, Valerie getting the learner's permit had gone fine. And Robb had felt an extraordinary sense of pride, not only in signing in as her custodial parent, but also in having been the one to teach her how to drive. He had spent hour after hour, that summer, driving up to Port Townsend just for a few minutes, sometimes, of demonstration and practice in the car.

Maybe, then, it had been this—this feeling of pride, which had brought on the sudden change as they had gone back to Rose House, to celebrate her birthday in the back kitchen.

They were at the doorstep at the time—Robb remembered that—and there was something to do with the silver-wrapped birthday presents he'd bought for her and which she stood holding (not everything was quite behind a veil yet); she stood holding them and she said, "Could you open the door for me?" and he opened the rose-etched glass, and just when he had, there Scott stood, holding a pipe of the vacuum cleaner and telling him to get the hell off his porch.

"Dad," she said, "Robb's got Mom's O.K. We're just going back to the kitchen."

It took Robb several seconds to grasp which of them she was calling Dad.

"It's not O.K. with me," Scott said, and put his magnificent (most likely trucker's) bulk between them.

"Get out of my way, bum," Robb said, not even waiting for "a click" and still holding the key. "I don't answer to kept men. Just go on with your housecleaning."

Robb then couldn't remember which he felt next, the vacuum cleaner pipe to his stomach or the word "faggot." They both felt the same.

But what he did remember exactly was the delirium of the fight that followed. It was a perfect dance of the two of them in the lobby, just beneath the Victorian torchbearer—over and over they went, like wrestlers on the carpet; it was a delirium of contact

84

for Robb, suddenly, when he had not been touched by anyone since the night with Bart, over and over they went like wrestlers, their blood pounding together, the only possible way of uniting—a steel ball colliding with a cathedral. Robb, in temporary and mad embrace, felt the full wonderful solidness of Scott's body, and, flashing suddenly again on "like a brick shithouse," knew why men only used it when admiring each other; it was their way of showing attraction and then flushing it down the toilet.

In another flash, they were up and standing, Valerie yelling the whole time, and Robb was punching her father straight against the glass roses, and Valerie—and Laura, now, too, who had come running—were screaming for him to leave, with all four of them standing still somewhere in those moments watching the rose glass vibrate and thud, almost certainly exploding but ultimately vibrating to silence nonetheless.

That had been a while back, Robb thought, standing, now, miraculously dressed before the mirror in his rooms.

But glancing still at the bruise.

That had been a long while back, because back then he had been capable of passion for men's bodies, one way or the other, and now, maybe as a result of that fight, and in particular, the drugs, he felt nothing but revulsion—and in particular, towards himself. Scott's pipe still lay across his stomach. For it had been because of the fight, Valerie's note lay open on his dresser, and he could no longer see her. And he had hardly been able to touch food since.

He got into his car and drove to work. He had blessed the tires and steering wheel enough so he could manage them as circles. However, he was very careful to stay clear of streets with bike shops and in particular those with bike lanes. A glance at one circular red reflector could ruin his whole day. He had to admit, sometimes, that his life was becoming more and more like his car when it got fogged in—he could scarcely see out sometimes, and because of that, he had to reduce his speed to a crawl to avoid collisions—and yet he still moved in his car. That was the miracle.

Likewise teaching this morning would be hard but manageable. He only had one class, The History of Science. It was a basic seminar for bright non-majors, with discussion in the round, which Robb always loved. There had been some problem with getting the sentences right, but he had worked out a solution in a pill case which he kept on himself at all times, and which he took out now like a compact. Choosing among the six divisions, he decided he might have a panic attack this morning, so he swallowed the little white dot, with some special herbal tea derived from Valerian root. With it, he could maintain lucidity for at least the ninety minutes required. Of course, he could always give them a break if things got too weird even so—and he'd actually done it once, when an hallucination had popped up right over in the corner of the classroom, and wouldn't go away until he had given the surprised students a ten minute break.

Today the topic was—"Are Human Beings the Inevitable Apex of Evolution?"

And as Robb spoke, a minotaur-like shape did materialize over in the corner. He wasn't two minutes into his lecture—had just switched on the overhead projector—and there the little fucker was, gray, a little bit of refuse from his dreams.

Nevertheless, he felt the tea and pill hold him steady on, and he managed to take in all the loving, intelligent faces of his some twenty students. For they really did love him—many, many of them had had him before. Were devoted to his classes. It was obvious, he supposed, that lately they had noticed a few changes here and there, and yet in the past few weeks, all of them had kept their individual conferences with him, and had all seemed pleased when they had left.

He did have, in the top drawer of the desk in his office, a developed plan for a substitute teacher, who could finish out the term for him, should anything happen. But that was only a precaution. And although he could decide he didn't want to continue with that minotaur over there, he was, in fact, going to.

"Give me some reasons," he said to the class, "why you think human beings might be the apex of all life."

The hands went up. And as he stared at the faces, many of them masculine, he was almost reduced to tears thinking of how once he had sensed their beauty, illuminating the autumnal campus, even though he had thought nothing of the feeling back then. What he would give to feel that now! He could feel nothing but the nostalgia for feeling itself. The student who was speaking now—Howard—was a brilliant pole-vaulter who still came in his tank top, even in November, possibly to give his gay-rumored professor a thrill, but Robb was all cold to that now. The windows of his mind were all fogged in. Maybe that was why the minotaur was there.

"There are several things," Howard said, "the operable thumb, the large brain, conscious thought, bipedalism, and stereoscopic vision."

Robb, writing the words on the film of the overhead projector, nevertheless allowed himself to digress, as a way of feeling better. He posited the idea, once the words were down, that once human beings reach consciousness, they begin to resist mutation; they become protective of who they are; they hound out freaks. He then allowed himself to say that if a "diversified man or woman" should ever arise, whatever that might be, then conscious civilization as we know it would hunt it down and kill it, and in considering this, he realized just what he had said, and with the realization, the whole class exploded into a sea of interest and hands, all trying to suggest who or what the diversified man or woman was.

"The diversified man," Alice said, "would be capable of love, not programmed for war."

And with the Minotaur watching—with small bicycle wheels of fire like earrings hanging from the thing's ears—it became clear to Robb that the discussion was going to work.

For the class, delighted, was still expending itself on "diversified"—so much so Robb had to cut things off so he could get back to the topic. Hastily, he finished out the list of characteristics on the overhead, and then disqualified each one, with the exceptions, of course, of the *opposable* thumb and the large brain. And as for self-consciousness and such things—well, even porpoises had been proven to recognize themselves in a mirror, and a gorilla had been shown to teach her baby sign language—tidbits which, as usual, delighted everybody.

He made it to the bell.

Robb, gathering up the sheets of film, just checked to see if the students registered anything odd as they were gathering their things. Nothing at all. They were talking and laughing as usual.

And the Minotaur?

He was still there.

Robb left him behind. He was due for another pill in his office, and had to run to get to the running group at the gym.

But when he was out on the trail with his friends, things went weird again. He hadn't been running two minutes when every one of them started in with questions about what was going on. He had been keeping himself so scarce lately. And in answering, Robb didn't feel he at all accounted for himself. The Minotaur was gone, and there were no full-fledged wheels about, and the running path they chose promised to be free of bicycles—thank God he didn't have to ask for that—but the new man who showed up on the gym steps, just before they took off, proved to be Chester again, that brother-in-law, and now Robb felt his cover at last was blown. Of course Chester, being a psychiatrist, could see what was wrong with his eyes—the pupils were probably gone by now. And what could Robb say about not calling even on Thanksgiving? And what about the bruise?

So he ran from Chester as soon as he appeared. He tried to make it look like a frisky burst of speed (how was it possible to look energetic on a day like this—which was like a sepulcher?), and he did get hoots and laughs from the men close behind to go for it, but even just a few minutes into the run, he could feel his hamstring begin to snag like a bear trap, while all the drugs and herbs inside his stomach rallied to sicken him and work themselves into a witch's brew, causing his heart to flutter and spin.

Nevertheless, he left Chester in the dust.

He left Chester in the dust, and managed to get into the shower, before his brother-in-law could get back. With the water raining down over him, very hot, Robb almost thought he was

O.K., but then both hamstrings pulled at once, with just the least turn, and he knew he had to get home, before anyone could see. He also had a vision, still, of the temple-like structure they always passed on this run, one on a deserted corner of the campus, edging on to one of the oldest parts of the city. There had been trees with banana-colored leaves guarding it, and an image above the doorway—a wolf-faced god or goddess. Was it a sign of healing or a destruction? No one had ever been able to say.

Suddenly, he was aware of someone in the shower next to him, and, turning, he got a rear view of Chester's handsome body. How long had he been standing there anyway? With those psychiatric blue eyes upon him, he knew he must answer truthfully to any question that might be asked, but fortunately all he was hearing Chester ask was something completely beyond him. After their talking a while, Chester said something which, sounded out, basically was, "Olivia wants to know why you've shut her out of your life. And Ethan doesn't even know he has an uncle."

And as if the question and statement were the only reason he'd shown up, Chester vanished just as suddenly as he had appeared, taking his lithe, powerful body elsewhere. Soon the dark man was lathering himself very, very far away, down at the end of the long corridor of showers, and Robb remembered, with love, his sister, and that she was the last being on earth who could save him—if, in fact, he could be saved at all.

But then, of course, there was the other alternative—another prescription from another, easily hit up doctor. And if he had too much trouble managing the car to go out and hit the doctors up, he could always get Bart to drive, the way he had so many times before in the past few months. He could get him to do most anything now.

Whatever his decision, something had to be done, and soon. For the Minotaur was standing there now also, just about opposite Chester. Getting a shower. The bull-man matching the apex of creation.

Which one am I more like? Robb wondered, still under the water.

But he couldn't answer, because the fact was, he really didn't feel he existed at all.

Eleven

Olivia lit the candles for Christmas. The important thing to remember was, the house was perfectly trimmed, all arranged in neat rows; Ethan would be up from his nap just in time for Christmas Eve dinner, and they could all go off to the evening service. Out of all these extremities of light, for Christmas, sometimes star-shaped, sometimes waxen, with angels hovering over there in the corner, was the long scale of music—from Handel on the stereo—rising in rows, like candles in ruby glass—lifting her in multi-tiers of memory. Then, in memory, Rose House itself, hovering above this house, which hovered above her mother's, which hovered somewhere above Robb's, wherever that happened to be.

She lit the candles, and thought of him. He was there, along with the other tapers—lit—she kept for her father. Smell of paraffin.

Once she had been at the Easter Sunrise service at Washington Cathedral on Capitol Hill, sitting in the benign pew with Chester. First light came through the rose window, and with that, the fragmented light combined and fell like a curtain upon all the flowers which, in the sanctuary, had been lost in shadow. And as the curtain slowly fell (like a cloud seen in aerial passing over a mountain landscape) the flowers—crocuses, daffodils, and tulips, maroon, coaxed out early—began to rise, as though from darkened spring soil.

She lit the last of the candles, below the brass rubbings, lit the fire in the hearth, tinted for Christmas.

She turned the security system off, so the guests could get in, and get in they did. Their voices sounded through the house like a bell, and with them, the sound of Nathan's, as he got up from his nap at last. The relief they all felt when he came into the room! Something to talk about.

But Seymour, Chester's brother—the physical therapist in a wheelchair—could still put a damper on things. As the Christmas circle continued to close in on the child, and every member of the party talked at the top of that voice which was Christmas, Seymour said to her privately, "I don't feel comfortable here, Olivia."

And she laughed. "Why not?"

"All these lights going off and on. This fucking security system." She didn't answer.

"Is there any time he doesn't show off?" Seymour asked.

"I don't know," she answered.

"Does it bother you?" he asked.

"I don't know," she repeated..

And his huge body seemed to close over her.

Seymour's—and Chester's—father had misheard. "You're right about this security system. It is something else."

And the-odd-friend-they-have-every-year said, "You bet. It's the only way you can live in Magnolia these days, and keep your things from being run off with. Why, I know someone whose Cadillac was lopped off piece by piece right on the street, night by night until all that was left by the end of the week was the little 'v' of the grill."

"Well, I wonder," Chester's mother said, dryly. "All these systems run their gamut. And run to extremes. At the hospital, everything is so tight, I wonder if sometimes any of the patients can get in, not to mention out."

"Can you just see some poor schmuck expiring on the street waiting to clear Capitol General's security?" Seymour asked.

"Well I don't know about you"—Seymour's father ("Howard the Mechanic") had put his arms behind his head—"but if I had a system like this, I'd just lie back on the couch after dinner and watch the lights blink. Better than TV."

"Howard is so easy to amuse," his wife put in, and the whole group burst into laughter.

However, Chester arrived at that moment and put an end to that. Instantly, Howard's arms were folded in front of him again, his face filled with the rapture of the admiring and almost star-struck father. With that, she could sense the hostility flaring out of Seymour and finding its target right in Chester's back, which stiffened. Joyce, their mother, noticed and took no notice.

"It's a shame," she said, looking at Olivia, "that none of your family could come."

And there it was—the note was struck, at one with Handel—that that was what she had been feeling all along, her enormous homelessness through all of this, mixed in with her constant blame and criticism of Chester for it—her perennial resentment that her poor, dear decimated family could not get itself together once again, and so she had to look to them, Chester's people, once more, to fill in the space.

"My cousin should be here any minute," she said defiantly.

"You mean she'll be going with us to the cathedral?" Seymour asked.

"Yes, I think . . ."

"It'll be interesting for her to go with us to the service, since she's the one who usually provides the entertainment."

"I thought she was on tour," someone else said.

"Not for Christmas, evidently," Olivia answered. "Anyway, we won't be holding dinner for her. In just a minute"—getting up—"I'll be wanting all of you to come through the kitchen. Tonight it's buffet style."

The mahogany of the dining room table flashed her image back as she passed through. She dimmed the kitchen light first, before getting the potluck ready, for it was to be not just a potluck, but a feast, she decided, and she could hear now the special record of St. John's Choir sing out the mysterious minor chords of "Coventry Carol," and she felt herself nearing that nether world which contains all of one's Christmases at once on the Eve, as though someone like Keats had grabbed the pen of your life and started writing everything in Spenserian verse. The hobgoblins of the season did such fairy tricks as make "lime" rhyme with "thyme" as she prepared the turkey one last "time," and thought of those moments when she and Chester had watched *The Bishop's Wife* late one Christmas Eve, when all the windows had been wreathed with frost, and she had thought back even then to that moment when, as a child, her crazy father had shown her Jack Frost outlined in one of the panes. The image had been so perfect—he must have, imp himself, snuck in and etched it out just a little, here and there, just to fool and delight her later on. Make it exactly a troll. It was just like those old-fashioned pictures for children, where you were supposed to find the buried face in the branches of the trees, the shape of the kangaroo in the campfire. There are seven things hiding in this illustration. Find them. He'd do something like that. That was him all right. Buried pictures.

With that, Nathan came bursting in—he had just tied his shoe—for the first time, just himself, alone for a moment in his bedroom. "How wonderful," she said, overcome, somehow, with him, and with this dinner, and with the holly on the table, the berries as red and glossy as the candle glass, with the music coming in and changing to "Angels We Have Heard on High," and thus creating mountaintops, gold-painted clouds, and foil shepherds bowing, Christmas-pageant style (for a shepherd was what Nathan would be in the pageant).

And so they all filed in, her "family," bringing with them her cousin Cindy at last, the rock star, who was no angel, certainly, but who had been, once, a school teacher back in Ozarks country, along with her husband, that gorgeous man who played bass in back of her (his wild-haired wife), the man who, in contrast to her outrageous get-ups, always wore a plain white t-shirt very tight and smoked in more ways than one in the back corner of the photos on the album covers.

"You didn't bring Rick?" Chester asked.

"No, he's sleeping somewhere in Cincinnati under an eyeshade," Cindy answered.

And before Olivia could answer, everything was whisked away from her, out of the kitchen, into the dining room, with everyone laughing or sighing over Cindy or Nathan, depending on who got the floor first, with Olivia knowing why, suddenly; for just at the moment she tried to say grace, no one would hold hands.

There it was. Cindy and Nathan did that for everyone. Touching. They were the substitutes.

"I wonder when Nathan will begin collecting your albums," she said, trying to bring her cousin into the circle and smiling.

"I'll give him just one more year," Cindy answered.

"Tell me," Seymour asked, "when do kids these days make the quantum leap from 'Row, Row, Row Your Boat' to Megadeath?"

"I wouldn't know," Cindy answered, "because I'm not Megadeath."

"Then what are you?" Seymour asked.

"Straight-on rock and roll, honey," she answered, looking him direct in the eye without a flicker. "And I'll tell you something else. There's not much difference between what I was as that one-room schoolhouse teacher back in the Bible Belt and who I am now fronting at the Kingdome. No matter what it is, teaching or singing, it's show biz for the kids from first to last."

Oh, my God. And although Olivia resisted, she felt a slow fade of herself at the head of her own feast, with the Cathedral Mass so close at hand, there seemed to be a rose window overhead curtained in glass, contained in the choir music, still audible above the voices of her beloved second family.

But there was a pounding at the door—so loud it set the security system off—and she suddenly saw, like the Ghost of Christmas Past himself, her brother Robb standing there, in answer to her prayers.

"Please don't turn me out," he said.

And she ran to him in tears.

So he staggered in, with her and Chester just in time for the catch, for he collapsed in between. "Please hold me," she could hear him say, as they walked him instinctively to the couch.

Joyce, good Nursing Supervisor, instantly went and checked him over, saying—"This man could probably stand Detox," right next to Chester, who said, "You'll be O.K., Buddy. We're glad you're here," caressing his cheek in that alarming way he hadn't used since the day Nathan was born.

"Do you mind, everybody?" she heard herself saying. "This is my brother."

And they cleared off.

"Olivia," Robb said, "I'm sure Tara died because of me—what am I going to do? I'm out of pills. I can't take anymore or I'll die."

"Then you've come to the right place," she said, "because there aren't any here."

"Tara," Robb said, "Valerie's dog. She got out. I'm sure she got hit. I had forgotten about her again, and left the door open."

"All right," she said. "All right."

"I just want to die," he went on. "I just want to die thinking of Valerie."

"Of course you do," she said, in a way which shocked everybody. They went away to the Cathedral, with Chester at the head.

The door was shut. They were alone.

"You have to listen to me," she said, "and listen very carefully. It's not you that's talking. It's the drugs."

"But drugs can't create fires, can't create demons on bicycles, can't cause these horrors," he almost screamed.

"Oh yes they can," she said. "And if you want to live in that you can. But there is a way out."

But in the next moment, which she knew was also rather extraordinary, too, she realized he would not listen.

Twelve

Well, he ran.

He had to.

Straight out of Olivia's Christmas house.

Years later, he would think about some flowering quince he had cut and put in an old tin teapot on the dining room table by the window in Mrs. Molyson's flat. For weeks it would be there. A final standoff against death. Apparently.

But for now he ran. Ran through spring.

He recollected going to doctors, traveling across the state line to Oregon, and going to doctors again. He told them that he was sick, that he couldn't sleep, that he was working on it with a counselor, but for now, he simply had to get his rest. And—strange, though he pleaded with them, desperately sometimes, he never mentioned that he was either gay or a vet. Not once. He told them it was family matters.

He started getting the idea that it was good to start mixing drugs. Why not? A doctor had not yet given him strict orders not to. It was around Valentine's Day when he began doing that. Everything seemed to be behind the bars of a doily of a card he sent his mother. A delicate white latticework. But jail bars just the same. He couldn't remember exactly where she was, but he had her address. Yes, she was off on one of her regattas—sailing off—but he thought he might send her one last card before he died.

Because that was what he was going to do. No doubt. He knew that when this arc of doctors was finished, so was he. It was very clear now—easy to understand—what was going on. His life at last had become uncomplicated.

His mind started to give him a very pleasant logic. Or, if it wasn't pleasant, at least it was comprehensible. Whereas everything since that one night of not taking that one pill had become one terrible and horrifying tunnel, now it was easy to understand that whatever doctor gave him pills at the present time, that man was his master. That man presided over his sleep, whatever that was, and saw to it that he was safe, at least for a few hours. For several weeks—while the flowering quince and wild plum got ready and even opened here and there on the twigs in the tin pot—he was able to subsist, and somehow teach his classes. Valerie and the news he had to tell her about Tara hovered somewhere there in the background, but his job went on and his failure with Valerie dominated his sleep.

Then the pills ran out, and a Wednesday morning saw him in the office of a doctor who asked him how long he had been taking Ativan.

"About three years." (What a lie, but it just slipped out. Usually he said three months.)

"You know, your brain," the doctor said, "is like a pressure cooker under those pills. They seal everything in. Nothing can get out, and the steam's still rising. So what we're going to have to do is set up you up on a taper program until you're off. You need ventilation."

He wrote out a prescription.

The man was known for being a black belt in Karate.

"You are to alternate all of this with a protein called tryptophan."

Robb thanked him, carrying a bundle of samples out of the office with the taper schedule, but he knew he would have to hurry and find another Master, if he was to sleep on just his regular drug tonight. No telling what the tryptophan might do—if it ventilated his brain, Lily was sure to emerge again. But he must follow these orders unless he got another Master.

Nevertheless, the next—and final—doctor on the list proved to be out until Easter, and Robb saw himself suddenly going through another night exactly like the one at Bart's. There had been no

Lily since the Minotaur, and that was a gift, and he wanted to stay more with the monster than with her.

But when Bart picked him up in the car, Bart laid down the law that there were to be no more rides—Bart would drive him to his sister's, if and when Robb ever got the nerve to try to get clean once more. But that was it—he had given up otherwise. Bart had. On love, especially.

So out of spite, Robb had him drop him off at a bar which opened at noon, where the spring trees beat against the walls, even though he couldn't see them, and he stared into a glass of gin, wondering what he could do next, now that he was driven into a corner. It was either expire from seeing Lily again, under the Master's orders, or collapse in a different way from having nothing at all—for the withdrawal would surely kill him—he'd read about such cases. But as he stared into the glass, which was green again, he saw the solution clearly. Suicide. The perfect out. It slid blissfully between the horns of the dilemma, like an Alka Seltzer dropping fizzing into a glass. And he had nearly gotten it right the first time, after returning from seeing Valerie.

He would get his house in order. He would write letters to his near and dear and then sign himself out. He knew now that he had actually written one already—couched in that lesson plan addressed to his boss, should he ever get sick and not show up for work.

Finishing his drink, he went out into the waning afternoon and knew he had the rest of it to die in. Actually some of the trees were starting to flower. The March he would never live to see was closing in. He would stop in at a nursery and buy some hollyhocks and leave them newly planted as a token for Mrs. Molyson to remember him by.

Somehow, all at once, the Nursery materialized and vanished.

He had the little cartons in his hands.

But here Dr. Simpson's office was coming up, too. He'd just leave the cartons outside for a minute, and stop in to thank him. A clandestine goodbye. To the original Dr. Simpson. And Dr. Simpson did just happen to be walking through when Robb came in. His glance—or did he say it?—told him he was an "Addict!" (it came to him in a shout), and Robb could just remember picking up the cartons again—as delicately as though they held eggs—and rushing out, amazed that Dr. Simpson, whom he had known for so many years, could speak to him like that.

Now he would have to write him a letter, too.

He went home and, even though there was lovely daylight coming in, turned on the light above Joseph. He would lie down just for a minute and then he would write his letters. Afterwards, he would make a call to Bart's answering machine so he would find the body. ("I'll never forgive you if you do," Bart had said not long ago.)

But as the rose image of Joseph filled the room, he could hear his answering machine switch on, with the voice of Tyler, the physical therapist of long ago, asking where he had been all these months. He just wanted to know how he was doing.

The machine switched off.

But as he lay there, an image far different than Lily or the Minotaur or Joseph or even the picture in his mother's living room arose.

Arose.

It was Rose House. And with all the people he had loved drawing near to again, it occurred to him that the perfect way to commit suicide was not by downing all the pills, but rather, by grasping one of the horns of the dilemma—he would not take any at all, and die of withdrawal. He was sure to have a seizure—he was thinking of what he had read—and that would be fine.

So he got up and dumped vial after vial into the toilet—pills, red, white, green, blue. Oblong, square, flat. All of them went with several flushes. A little plumber's jingle kept running through his head while he was doing it. But he couldn't remember everything.

And when he was free again, he lay back down on the bed, under the shadow of Rose House, which seemed to brighten his room, although it was a shadow. He felt delighted with himself and in his haze of abstention, switched on the TV using the remote control.

He got all thirty-six channels, even though he had forgotten to pay for months, so there was a lot to watch all at once.

There were two wrestlers jumping on each other.

A special on inner-city violence, where black men were being hauled off on stretchers.

There was William Bendix in a navy cap saying his men were the best damn men in the world. (He didn't say "damn" in the 1950s exactly but you knew what he meant.)

There was an H-bomb going off on Bikini island, and then an announcer's voice saying, as the footage suddenly shifted to a shimmer of tide pools of today—"But despite man's devastation, there's something we can see now—life beginning to stir, almost forty years later."

There was a gay male couple being interviewed, who had a thousand different piercings of their ears and noses.

Toward these scenes, Robb nodded with familiarity.

A male chorus was singing "From the Halls of Montezuma." Richard Widmark.

Three suitors were elbowing each other on "The Dating Game."

William Bendix's ship was going down, and in a gesture so motherly it set your teeth on edge, he offered his commanding officer a life jacket, saying between tight lips, "We wouldn't want to lose you, Sir."

An elaborate detective story was coming on, with runaway scenes, the upshot being (old hat), that the male leads offered barrel chests to the ladies and barrel shotguns to the men.

But then there was hope. Because in *The Creature Walks Among Us*, burly Rex Reason, in just his pajama bottoms, was trying to save the poor thing from drowning, after it had been given a respiratory system like the rest of us. And the underwater rescue was so spectacular and erotic, the two male forms going end over end, Robb recalled his dreams as a child, where he had been saved by firemen, one hunk in the perfume of yellow oilcloth after another.

But then there were more blow-ups and gunfire.

The two detectives killed six men apiece before they took their clothes off for the ladies.

And then the news came on and said another man had gone berserk at a McDonald's.

And with that, he looked down into the garden, and saw that he had planted the hollyhocks anyway, even without remembering he had, and with that, he realized he would not be dying now—that in a moment, a memory of his daughter would be walking through that door, and, sure enough, there it was, there she was, dressed for her fifth birthday party, saying, in pink, holding a big globe in red, "Hey Daddy, want to play some basketball?"

"That's a beach ball, Dear, not a basketball, but I'll play."

And he reasoned that if he could face this memory, he could face anything, even the memory of Lily—maybe not now, but at some point in his life.

So the logic, suddenly, took another turn, and he found himself turning toward the phone.

Thirteen

"Expect," the Director of the Treatment Center said to him, "to see things."

They were high atop a building. They took up a whole floor of the hospital.

"You will," the Director said, "see things like bugs on the wall. And other things. But just ride them on through."

Robb did not feel very lucid, but he was sure this man sounded very much like a man who ran a spook ride at a carnival near Golden Gate. Years ago. In the fifties. Robb had been very small at the time, and the name of the ride had been "Dark Mystery." "What happens?" he had asked the man. "Do you see things? Feel things?"

"Yes, that's right. See things. Feel things."

And then Robb realized the Director was responding to a question he had just asked. But he couldn't remember the question. He was shown to his room and told to get into pajamas. They were standard greens. And paper slippers. The contents of his pockets were checked in with a nurse. He had nothing on him now except two vitamins.

Then he was shown into a large dormer where he was to sleep for a while, maybe for a few days, depending on how he did. He was given something as a slow taper—so he was to have a taper after all—and he went off to sleep, dreaming of "Dark Mystery," which had the surreal faces, in the shapes of shadowy trees on the front, with orange and red highlights to the eyes. He was passing through a forest of spooks, with a forest fire going on.

He had often thought at times that when his body was completely exhausted, he was like a log burning in its hearth, rolling over and over in sleep as though in the flames, which purged away the fatigue. He felt that was happening now and that he had completely given up—that his grasp upon life in the past few months had been a strangulation hold, and ironically it had been killing him, his own hold. He vaguely remembered a quick trip through a toiletries section of a drug store somewhere, and that Olivia had been with him—was it toothpaste he had needed?—but that everything had been like a kindergarten watercolor, like the ones which he had done with too much water, and that it had all run together. Olivia had then left him off at Treatment, like a child at an extended daycare, and there had been the inevitable "goodbye." He wished, now, turning in the flames, that he could remember the look of departure on her face.

He thought that would be just the beginning of it—the nightmare, downward—but in the next days, things became remarkably stable. The dreams continued, but life smoothed out. Quite suddenly. It was easy getting clean and sober! If only he had known, he would have done it right from the start. He found himself becoming quite charming. He'd sit in room after room, and listen attentively. So this was Treatment with a capital "t."

"Robb, your central nervous system is healing beautifully," his counselor would tell him.

And Robb, answering, would say, "Eight thousand dollars. Eight thousand dollars for a whole new central nervous system. Hey, that's not bad. Not bad at all, really."

And the whole group would laugh.

He found that he was getting into his street clothes in record time. He was permitted to go out bowling, on the next field trip—remarkably early again. Olivia came to visit. And even though she didn't seem as pleased as he was, he felt an affection for her like never before.

But.

But. It was as though the walls were breathing funny. Inhale, exhale. There seemed a red outline to things sometimes, as in one of those old color TV sets, badly tuned. A halo. Which instead of disappearing got more and more pronounced.

Then it happened. It was at a St. Patrick's Day party—an exchange with the next ward below—when he walked in and felt that everyone standing there had been carefully rehearsed to humiliate him. The fruit punch had been dyed green, and they were all there to see if he noticed. Would he say anything? That was the plan. The room began to turn on him (probably some rotary device), and he started to wonder how in the world, only days prior, he had actually been able to throw a bowling ball down an alley. Another field trip. An impossible feat.

Now everyone's voice was speaking to him at once. He opened his mouth to show that he meant to scream, to howl at least—to let all the people know that he wasn't putting up with this shit; he knew that things had been made crazy on purpose. But just then, or perhaps on cue, the Director, grown to colossal size, ushered in a sweet-looking Asian woman. Dressed as Lily, just before she had fallen from her bicycle. That Director had found his way into his head after all by reading his chart, and was giving him the ultimate test. Yes, yes, Robb thought, I will let everybody know I'm on to them. I'll let out the biggest yell I can make up.

And so, with the room still turning, he yelled, and slid slowly into a corner, bracing himself between two walls.

"Post-symptomatic withdrawal," the counselor said, as people rushed about, trying to help, but Robb knew that had been written into the script, too.

He was helped back to his room. He was allowed to call his sister. "Everyone," he told her, "is acting crazy here to see if I'm sane. I need to ask you," he said. "Do I sound crazy now?"

"No," she answered.

"Then will you try to get me out if they try to start making a conspiracy out of it?"

"A conspiracy?" she asked. "What kind of conspiracy?"

"They're trying to trap me into a confession—about being gay"—this was the first time he had said it sober (and never before to her)—"and about something else. And if I don't fess up, they're going to commit me."

"You're telling them you're gay? Robb, how wonderful."

"No, I haven't told them," he shot back. "I haven't let them trick me into it. That's just my point."

"They're not trapping you. They're only trying to help."

So that was it. Proof. She'd been scripted, too. The last one. As in *Invasion of the Body Snatchers.*

"And there's something else," he went on, "but now I can't tell you." And hung up.

A creepiness came over him as he went into the bathroom, under the close eye of the one attendant who was left on duty. A sudden sense of shame about his own body, which had all gone to slack, since he had been confined. As if—as he sat there on the toilet, as if he made one wrong move, he'd give everybody a disease. AIDS, probably. That was it, they were all wanting a confession out of him, so they could make sure they wouldn't get a disease. Maybe they'd even checked up with Buddy or Bart to see how safe he'd been, and they had found he'd been slack. They wanted him out of here—off the face of the planet. So everybody was safe, free of him, and his stains.

And with this terrible, ugly feeling about himself came such an urge to confess—to the Director—such as he had never felt before. It was overpowering, inexorable, like defecating, which he was just finishing now. If he made that one false move with the toilet paper, he must confess to the Director. Or at least his counselor.

It was terrible, it was horrible, because he knew these people were conspiring against him, but it seemed the only way out. How many days was it he waited? He couldn't be sure, but he kept on thinking he must tell.

And then the false move with the toilet paper came, and he called his counselor into his room.

"We stopped the valium taper," the counselor explained. "And now all the withdrawal is happening at once. That's what you've been experiencing."

"But what do I do?" Robb asked. "I'm afraid of destroying the whole hospital. Maybe even the world."

"Destroying?"

"It just feels like I could do that. So how can I keep myself and everybody safe?"

"Tell us what's going on with you," the counselor said, taking out a tablet of paper. "That's what you can do. Tell us what happened. What did you see at the St. Patrick's Day party?"

"Well, there was no monster," Robb answered.

"No monster," the counselor said. "Good."

The sheet of paper she worked on seemed to have one box for "Monster Yes" and one for "Monster No." She checked one.

"Have you been seeing monsters lately, Robb?"

"Yes."

"How many?"

"One."

"What did it look like?"

"A minotaur."

So this must be it. What he was supposed to confess. Nevertheless, there was still a clutch at his throat.

"That would be half man, half bull, Robb?" the counselor asked.

"That's right."

"Anything else?"

Robb tried to reach back to that night when he had first gone without the pill. He actually remembered there had been such a night. But beyond that there was nothing—only this conspiracy to prove that he was crazy. And gay. Overhead, came an enormous thudding and crash. It rained in heavily. The sound. Why were they doing this to him? He had confessed about the minotaur.

"And did you see anything else at the party?"

Robb broke out into a sweat. "Well, I saw this Asian woman."

"Yes. Cheryl Ann. She's Vietnamese. And how did you feel about her, Robb?"

"Like I wanted to help."

"She's a patient here like everybody else. The staff helps her, and she helps herself. Your job here is to take care of you. Do you understand that?"

"Yes."

He wiped the sweat. Well, he actually got out of that one. Cheryl Ann did exist, after all.

"Can you tell me, Robb," the counselor went on, putting down her tablet, "what day it is?"

Robb saw that she looked exactly like a grandmother. But severe. She had put down on her tablet and was listening very closely and gravely to how he would answer.

"No, I can't. I think it's Saturday, but I'm not sure."

"And the date?"

"Can't help you."

"And the year?"

"1987."

"Good."

"And the President of the United States?"

"Ronald Reagan."

A terrible despair came over him. He must tell. But what was it they had in mind? Something to do with Cheryl Ann. And the bicycles—whose wheels he'd stopped seeing since the Minotaur. The staff would stop this conspiracy if he divulged his secret about the bicycles and the flaming spokes.

"Well, that's enough for now, Robb," she—Irene—said. "If you have anything more to tell me, you let me know. And let me say this—much of this is happening to you, because at the St. Patrick's Day party, you were at the end of your valium taper."

He realized when she left, however, that he had failed to mention his real reason for asking her to come in the first place—the toilet danger. He was sure that if he mentioned that, they would leave him alone, and he would start to heal. And then maybe his sister would come back out of the conspiracy, too.

He fell asleep, dreaming of an enormous forest of stripped trees—Dark Mystery—but when he looked closely at the trunks, he saw that each was a man, buried inside. The symbolism was obvious and friendly, for the branches reached toward one another but could not touch, even though each man buried inside the sinewy wood was an overpoweringly beautiful specimen, and he came alongside one which was particularly dark and teary and waved to himself inside, but all that the buried Robb could do was grimace and cry very gross-looking tears. Even when his body in that wood was even more developed and more muscular than the one he had known in his best days. What a hunk. Of wood.

His dream passed into another, where he got the chance to exercise—something his body longed for miserably. He stood before the mirror in the Y once more, but this time totally naked, while flexing the barbell, and with Buddy, also naked, coming up behind, and kissing him on the shoulder, the way straight men do their partners on the covers of romances.

He woke up again, and realized people were having family week, and that for some reason and for some time, he'd been taken off the regular schedule. Many of the patients looked new, and some of his friends there, people he'd known for a while and distantly loved, seemed to have already graduated. He wondered when they'd be giving him a roommate.

He was sitting there wondering just that, when a new man came in, followed by Olivia. He could tell, just by looking at her, that there was a fresh conspiracy afoot. Far from advocating, she now seemed to lead the pack which wanted to humiliate him. Wring out the truth. Nevertheless, as he mustered up all his strength to resist, he could feel welling up inside the overpowering need again to confess.

The doctor's—the psychiatrist's—name was Wells. "I've talked with your counselor," the man said, "and we think it best to consider giving you some medication."

"Medication! But that's just—"

His sister had taken his hand.

"This is not the addictive kind," the psychiatrist answered. "Also we need to find ways of getting you talking."

"Why?"

"Because you're seeing things," the psychiatrist answered.

"So she told you?"—a furious glance towards Olivia.

"Yes."

"Traitors!" Robb yelled. "Traitors all!"

The psychiatrist and Olivia exchanged looks.

But Robb, spent, had slackened in his chair, and felt now the sense of full confession about to emerge. He would tell them all about his slip at the toilet, and how a global plague might result because of him.

"I want to tell you about—but instead of his fear of germs, he said, "Lily."

"And who's Lily, Robb?" Olivia asked, with compassion. Her hands were almost on his face.

"Lily is the one our jeep hit in Vietnam," Robb said with ease at last but bursting into tears. "Mason hit her and then tore off. He and I made love together soon after. Since going off the pills, I've seen the spokes of her bicycle, along with people dying. Burning up. I couldn't look at a wheel for months. And Mason killed himself afterwards. And then Dad."

"An overly developed superego," the psychiatrist said, making a note.

"Vietnam!" Olivia said. "Robb, I never knew that happened there."

But although her hands were stroking his face, and Robb felt, her skin on his, tissue on tissue, part of him was quite sure now these two people would pounce—they would persuade him to take the medicine, so they could watch how he behaved. He could tell that they were still not satisfied, even though they had wrung his secret out of him.

Fourteen

In the days the psychiatrist followed up with his evaluation, Robb was told that no visitors, save his sister, would be allowed in. But once he stabilized, others would be O.K. Yes, he thought, they really want me in this medical experiment.

To his surprise, one of the first people was Mrs. Molyson. She looked dark and anguished.

"I had no idea you were going through all this," she said. "I became so concerned way back in the fall, when your garden started going to wrack and ruin. That wasn't at all like you."

"Thank you for taking care of Tara," Robb said, fighting back to the memory. "I know that you took care of her. And then I couldn't find her."

He was aware he couldn't cry right now. He would have cried right now.

"There is something else," she said. For a moment the lines in her face aligned themselves. "I need to tell you, Dear, that your daughter called me."

His daughter. He remembered himself, way back, pounding on the door of Rose House. And now he had forgotten her—for how long?

But then he remembered she had been refusing to see him all along. Yes, there had been a fight. A very cruel one. Of his own making.

"She called saying, 'Where is my father? What's happened to him?' And I really couldn't say, except that there had been this note you had left, saying you were gone to get help."

"I wrote that?"

"Yes."

"And then when your sister came to get some of the things you had forgotten, she told me where you were—said you had given your permission to see you."

"That's right."

And then he didn't know what else to say. There was a great wall in his mind. And he couldn't surmount it. Somewhere—perhaps the room was bugged—people were noting that he couldn't speak any further.

A nurse came in to bring him his medication.

"I won't take it," he said, very suddenly. "Take it back."

It was only then that he realized that he had snapped at her, and had spoken in a very cruel and mean fashion. Mrs. Molyson had disappeared.

"You stop by the Nurses' Station and take it in a few minutes then," the nurse said on her way out.

"I will not."

He sat there, pleased with himself that he had caused such an upset in the Experiment. Now all their scripts were off; they'd have to meet in secret to decide what to do next.

What happened next was that the Nursing Supervisor appeared with glass and pills. "You must take this. If you don't, we'll have to give it to you by injection."

Robb smiled again. He had her on this one too. "It says right there in your pamphlet that you won't do anything against the patient's will."

She—her name was Alice—looked as though she was about to cry. "You won't believe any of us here, will you? That we have your best interest at heart?"

"Stop the Experiment, and I will," Robb insisted.

"Experiment?" she asked. "What experiment?"

Then he became exhausted, and had to sink back on the bed. He could hardly hold his head up.

His sister came in. "Please, Robb, do as they say. I've thought about it. I've prayed about it. I understand how you feel about drugs. I feel the same way. But it's not the same. These are only temporary and they're to get you better."

"You know my brain will never be the same once the medication has been in there," Robb said. "It's just like the way it was before. Ativan has fucked me up forever, and so will this."

"No, I've asked about it," Olivia said. "I know. And if you'll just let yourself get stable, we'll get you to somebody you can talk to about being gay, about being in Vietnam. Maybe even Valerie will come."

Robb made a slow groan, cradling his head. "Oh, Valerie—I still haven't told her about her little dog."

"One thing at a time," Olivia answered. "Take the fucking medicine!"

"No, no." And then the phrase occurred to him which he wanted to say. "This nightmare is over."

And then the Director appeared.

"You stick with us," the Director said, "trust us, and we'll see about getting you some counseling about Vietnam and other things."

Robb, however, felt so closed down now, he was hardly aware that the Director's hands were on his shoulders. Not shaking him, but holding fast. "Believe me, Robb, we're trying our best to keep you out of the booby hatch, but that depends on cooperation from you. We know you're suffering the life of the damned, but trust us that there's something on the other side."

But as Robb lay back, spent and exhausted on his bed, too tired again to go to any of the meetings or lectures, too tired to eat—too stony, even, to lift his head—the reasoning went on that the Director was going back and cooking up the next part of the Scheme. Humiliation, once he was under the total influence of this medication and everyone else wasn't. Why, else, when he peeked down into the hall, did he see everyone at the telephones all at the same time, with each other speaking in a blatant mimic of his old way with Valerie, "Goodbye, I love you very much"—with a fourth man, appearing very suddenly and breathing very heavily into the pay receiver.

No it was starting up again. He passed down the hall, and he saw a replica of himself walking crying into a room, followed by a replica of his grandmother counselor, who carried her steno pad. He was even aware of being at a "social," again, and he was somehow the appointed host, and he was missing every mark of his duties. Yes, he was even forgetting to introduce a new patient around, and everyone was making faces again over the board games, and neglecting special party food that had been set out. Someone handed him a note right above the candy dish which said, "No nuts!"

Well, that was it.

He went back to his room and started talking furiously with himself. Somehow talking furiously gave him back his identity. Yes, I am me! He shouted. And when a male nurse (night) appeared at the door with another pill tray, he said, very cagily, "Would you just set it there. I'll bring it right back to the Nurses' Station."

"No, I'm supposed to watch you take it."

"Then no, then," Robb said again, handing cup and pill back. "This nightmare is over."

The nurse was gone, furious also, and Robb, taking advantage of the exit, threw on his heavy coat over his pajamas, headed straight for the ward door, and banged it open, allowing it to slam locked behind him. He had the sense that something inevitable and irrevocable had happened.

Going down stairway after stairway, he finally reached a side door where there was another pay phone. He tried calling Valerie but there was no answer. But there was always an answer. Then he tried Olivia and Bart—the same thing.

And so there was nothing to do but to go out into the night air, which received him, in a sudden rush—yes, it was frightening but so rejuvenating after all! It was right that Valerie and Olivia and Bart weren't there. This was where he was supposed to be.

He walked on to the avenue, growling with some of his fury still, but happy, too. He found himself in a little park, which allowed him to turn in circles—so convenient—with his fury. A couple passed by and pointed him out, as if he were just another transient. And crazy. They pointed him out and laughed. "He's nuts." Little did they know.

He turned again down the avenue and headed toward the bridge. That was the next step. He knew exactly where he must go.

The Jutland Bridge. It was just ahead, an arc of lights, just the way he'd seen it from the freeway, and it had one of the most beautiful drops imaginable—straight into the Bay. It was so perfect the way all of this was working out. Just a short walk in his pajamas and it would all be over.

Because, really, now that he was free, this was the only corner left to him. He stopped for a moment beside a bus shelter. Struck by the absolute pathos of his situation. There was no one left to call. No place to go. If he stayed out on the street too much longer, the withdrawal would catch up. Already a strange tingling was taking over his legs. Already it was getting difficult to see. And not long after this, there would be Lily.

He must have stood there frozen for a while. Because when he turned, a young man appeared, and asked him, Sir, for the time. Well, he knew what that was all about. So Robb just told him he didn't have his watch, and then there was nothing.

Nothing, but the turning water coming up ahead, for he had indeed started moving again. There it was, with little reflected lights dotted through. All the way down. He stood against the bridge railing and leaned. Then, taking off his jacket, he looked down again, and thought it was over. But then immediately for some reason, the word "golliwog" came into his head.

It flashed through.

Years ago, he had yelled at Valerie for something, and she had run to her room.

And with him following in secret, he had seen her leaning against her bed, squeezing the daylights out of something, and when he looked more closely, he made out she had chosen her gingerbread man with the minstrel face, smiling from ear to ear. And Valerie was smiling through her tears in secret to herself, too, getting comfort from holding the little minstrel. As if she had already found the answer, at four, to feeling hurt.

And Robb, unable to cry for years, found himself begin to flood.

Interlude

The cut-glass light from the sun fell upon the page; all the flowers in their vases seemed to carry sounds, chime-like, through the house, as though tolling the hour, and the Persian carpet formed a ruby diamond that was a luminous shadow. What was it Rose House wanted? The figures stood mid-meridian in their dance. The bellicose copper maiden held a clear globe as a torch, almost fully lit with sun.

Therefore, now: the diamonds of light, spread throughout the house from the refracted glass, hung down as clear, as rowed, as in a chandelier. All the diamonds, a diadem of light, gathered themselves together into a crown of two o'clock sun, radiating every tier. It moved itself, shimmered its way up the spiral staircase until into the deep crystal well of a gold-framed mirror, it vanished into a single spot once more, ruby, upon the Persian carpet.

Outside, the cherry trees held their buds tightly, resisting the southern sky. Early-spring autumn for a moment imbued every tree, every bush along the avenue: that moment when all buds, only fragments of gold, are caught in the sun and look as though they might become brazen with fall; when a few actual October leaves, still left clinging to the branches, shake in the chill of the March wind straight in from the sea, and the scene, if only for a moment, is taken back into fallowness. Then, when the corner is turned, the tulips, like paint brushes, newly dipped, arise sharply, and daffodils open in their yellows silently and proudly in their mansion beds, meticulously kept, now, with the approach of Easter.

And the rest of the grounds? The rest of the seascape? A single stone urn, with no pansies yet appearing, yet with arm-in-arm maidens dancing round the circumference—imitating their larger sisters on the fresco above and within the house—seemed to organize every cloud hovering above the profoundly uninhabited bluffs, set apart from the world by a continental drift, set adrift yet again upon the sojourning planet.

What is the equipoise between that still ruby hour of the house and the seasons themselves—of progress, emergence, change—such as the moon thinning itself to a fragment and then filling again in the wide blue triumphal arch of the sky? What is that truce? the house seemed to ask.

And as though in answer, she came, the artist, to scrape down the decayed places in the maidens' fresco, to lavish paint all over again—to mount up, new, a preservation of the year 1875, when the original painter from Seattle had come and completed her masterwork of the Seasons, her analogue, in paint, to the heroic couplets her mother had read aloud to her out of the eighteenth century, at night, by the fire (no doubt crackling), when she was a child; a masterwork, yes, in parade around the dome; and because of that fresh paint now, the pigments, new with all their latex and chemicals discovered recently on "the cutting edge," all the nineteenth century came closer and closer to the twentieth, before the very present itself could slip and eel itself away into the second millennium.

The ruby equipoise, the house answered itself, was almost struck in those dancing maidens, but not yet, not quite. For no artist had yet come again to paint a second garland, complementary to the first, of young men dancing together this time in harmony and balance, where limb might answer limb, muscle might answer muscle, free of fear of itself.

So the maidens danced on, waiting not for partners—as have appeared before—but another circle, as yet unsung, this time of men dancing hand-in-hand, so that a gyre of double garlands could unite both house and season, stillness and motion, progress and continuity.

And as the house waited, an interim came, not a complete answer, but a mainstay against the passionate wait of time and the appalling stasis of Wars; a figure, opening the door—masculine—who shouted in one long peal—"Father, I forgive you!"—and slammed the door after him, gone.

Part Two

Contact

Fifteen

Bart's Men's Group had done a good job of talking him into joining them up in Port Townsend. An outing, a getaway from the city. Just for the weekend. A rented beach house on the water.

They knew he simply couldn't go on, waiting breathlessly for Robb's next move in the hospital. And, really, they said, Robb's gone off the deep end this time. Better off without him. Now he's got religion and he's "no longer gay." Robb is someone to be avoided. And besides, Port Townsend was your former home.

Bart did not have the nerve (nor the disloyalty) to tell them also that Robb had gone AWOL from Treatment even before his private conversion to Jesus. Which had happened in Treatment, after they had taken him back.

"What are you going to do?" his friend Marcus asked him. "Wait for him to change? Back into what he was? It's not going to be a pretty sight when he does come out again. It never is."

"No, but I need to be there for him."

In general, Bart's friends did not at all like this solicitude, newly arrived, in Bart's nature. Really, they missed the spark, the total balance, of the Old Bart. He was the one always to get the party going, who always had an idea for getting out and about, even when he was busy with his ten balls in the air, as they liked to put it. Marcus said Bart was just like sunlight on an equator jungle: brown and agile and active. But lately he had turned almost morbid on account of that total jerk, a man no one had ever liked anyway, whose role at parties had been to sulk in a corner, "Like Captain Ahab's bear," Marcus had said, "sucking his honeyed paws of hibernation."

At thirty-three, Bart was one of those gay men who have always known they were gay, and have never made much fuss about it. He could remember that as early as childhood, he had admitted (just to himself) to being more attracted to James Bond than Ursula Andress, could remember almost swooning when Batman Adam West had gotten up off a massage table, loosely wrapped in a sheet. "Hey Mr. Wayne" the masseuse had said, "you're in pretty good shape for your age." Pretty good shape!

So it was, and Bart just didn't put on being attracted to girls. He simply hibernated through the whole dating scene in junior high and high school, not as one who didn't know what was going on but as one who thought the whole thing ridiculous, so far as he was concerned. The night of the Port Townsend High prom, he stayed home and wrote the middle scene of one of his "Rose Period" plays, in which a troubled youth is caught reading a porno paperback called *Naked Picnic*. He actually had the cover described (pantingly) by one of his own characters: a lovely teen queen is bending over a football type, who has his chest bare in the sun, his head resting on his letterman's sweater as a pillow. Back then, that was as far as his written imagination could take him. But to hell with the lovely teen queen. Let's just keep bare Mr. Touchdown for ourselves.

His parents kept a little Mom-and-Pops grocery store and souvenir shop right by the Marina on the water up here in Port Townsend. They worked long hours, and they had little time for him. Especially his father. His older brother had been blind since birth, and so what attention had been left over had gone to him. Bart, in fact, had grown up not expecting much attention from anybody, and since Port Townsend had been a safe place at night, even in the sixties, he had been given pretty much free rein of the whole town, and had been allowed to come and go from the basement door of their bluff-side house, just as he pleased.

The beautiful mansions of what the pioneers had termed "uptown" had become his friends after sundown. And although extremely well-liked at school, especially once he had come into the high-school drama scene, he had begun to see the big clock face of the Court House as his true best buddy, especially when he was making his way home after midnight, for there the face would be, lit up with its slender steeple and arch Roman numerals, like Maybelline eyes. He began to see that 1890s spire in fact as rather swishy, especially as he got to be so himself.

Of course Bart had considered himself a drama Queen from the very start, and his father had always been too busy and sometimes too drunk to notice. Bart had been Hannibal in *The Curious Savage*, Lion in *The Wizard of Oz*, and finally The King in *The King and I*. Always with whip and chain, his mother would corral his father into the back row of the auditorium just a few minutes before curtain, followed by his brother Daniel, who took his white cane but who didn't need any guiding at all. Bart would always watch for his family from the wings, and to him it became a grand symbol, an icon almost, of his connection to them. Sometimes, standing there, he would mentally set his timer, seeing how long it would take for his father to fall asleep. Once, as Hamlet, he had actually seen him zone out during "To Be or Not to Be." Another family symbol, Bart said to himself, if you really wanted to get nasty about it. Which Bart rarely did.

Although, suspiciously, Bart didn't date, he was never lumped among the "faggy" theater types (and "faggy" was used in high school), because he was too oblivious of the cliques to stay in them. He tried out for the swim team and made it. And although never a stellar swimmer, he had a naturally strong body, and never got in the way of his school's superb record. In the middle of his junior year, he contracted a strange chronic inner ear infection, and his doctor allowed him to stay on the team only on the condition he wear ear and nose plugs. These, combined with of course goggles, made him look, in some of his friends' estimation, like the Creature from the Black Lagoon when he got out of the water. A name which lovingly stuck to him ("The Creature" for short) and ended up tagged to his photo in the Yearbook.

In fact, throughout his sojourn in high school (and that's what it was, ambling, easy, friendly, but steady), he frequently saw himself as this amphibious man, turned amiable, of course, and with his claws removed. A domesticated Creature. He had had the privilege of traveling to Seattle once and seeing the old fifties film in the original 3-D, and throughout he had felt the most passionate sympathy for him, particularly when the hunky thing was seen swimming silently and secretly beneath the beautiful Julie Adams, in white bathing suit, in the Amazon, filled with large global bubbles, which the audience could almost pop. The poor "creature" was not wanted anywhere, but could operate on both land and sea—had the most pathetic way of breathing through his gills when his feelings were hurt—and was condemned to admire everything (how many thousands of years had he been around anyway?) and yet touch nothing. When Richard Carlson appeared in just his trunks, or even better, Richard Denning was shown sinewy and shirtless and cranky, sweating over an archeological dig, Bart felt sure he knew just how the Creature felt. When, later, he read a nasty retrospective on the film, Bart had taken it personally.

Bart was sure that all of this—this matter of being a displaced person—would have gone on indefinitely, had it not been for something which had happened his senior year. He could well imagine himself becoming a permanent fixture in Port Townsend, maybe, for example, taking up behind the counter of his father's grocery store (lovingly termed the "6-10" as one step up on either side from the "7-11"—and those were its actual hours!). But when a friend of his got accepted to Harvard, he called upon Bart, with his facility for all academic subjects, to tutor him in Calculus for the summer. With pay, of course, Brian's mother said.

Bart agreed, not thinking much about it, but when, in July, they actually sat down on the beach, both bowed over the book, Bart had a sudden moment, a vocational epiphany of sorts, of feeling instant and inexplicable delight in seeing somebody else learning. It was entirely a disinterested process—Bart could remember that, just as sure as he could remember the St. John's wart blooming, and the lilac turning white in the impossible wind not far from shore. It was entirely disinterested, because Bart knew that he was only being a medium to something that Brian wanted desperately to learn, and Bart knew not so much Calculus as he knew, instinctively, the avenues which could reach Brian's mind. With his extraordinary gift of patience and easy way of talking, Bart found Brian grasping the concepts which their regular math teacher had scared off the runway. It all came together, now. There was a place for the Creature. When the summer was over, Brian's mother made a special point of driving all the way down to the 6-10, and telling Bart's parents how gifted as a teacher she really thought their son was. And by then Bart knew it, too—so much so that he didn't even mind, when he saw that the compliment made no impression, except, "Thank you. That's nice of you to say," from both of his parents.

He didn't mind, because he had a direction. And therefore a ticket to get the fuck out of Port Townsend. The Vietnam War was in full bloom now, but with this insight and his low lottery number, he was provided with a key to the University of Washington School of Education. He didn't have to flounder, and by 1973, when he was a college junior, the War was over, and the chaos on campuses began to die nationwide. As in high school, he had ignored all the student movements—in this case, The Student Movement—all the turmoil and all the rebellious circles and groups. He proved as innocent of drugs as he did of sexual experience. Then, just when he thought he would spend the rest of his life with an easy monkish life teaching school and moonlighting in theater, a Director there at the University (hotly closeted?) decided to stage a panting production of *Measure for Measure*, and Bart, having made the audition, found himself becoming completely unglued. His hormones had hit at last.

In the part of Escalus, he did not get his own private dressing room, and one night, alone at the mirror, Angelo came in, stripped to the waist, because he was to literally flagellate himself (now Bart knew the Director must be queer) in his second soliloquy. Angelo looked a glorious anatomy chart, in hot black tights, and with abs and pecs accentuated by body make-up. Mercy. In fact, there was an extraordinary muscularity to his whole form, including his face, which was irresistibly craggy.

And now this anatomy chart was in Bart's dressing room. Talking about what trouble he'd been having remembering his lines. He knew Bart would understand, as he, Angelo, sat there, prone and vulnerable, all decked out in his make-up stripes, all over his torso, glowing red. Bart, taking them in, saw them as veins, turned inside out from the flesh. And was given another key. He was a goner for the massive man, because men like Angelo were God's most eloquent reminder that we are situated in the body. Made of flesh. And veins. Must never forget, Dears. Don't leave home without it. The body. He guessed that was the Director's point, too. And Shakespeare's—although the Director, while getting the anatomy, totally missed the humaneness and subtlety of the play.

Because when Angelo was done with his dressing-room confession, it was as though he became aware of Bart for the first time, and, drawing near—so close Bart could almost touch (and he wanted to—wanted to) this pictograph of the Body (in iambs)—said, "I love the way you play Escalus. Such quiet strength." And, putting a hand on his shoulder, squeezed in. Bart had seen medieval depictions of nearly this scene before. Of Death (Mr. Skeleton) taking a naked man (Man) by the dimples and giving them a little squeeze the way you would a baby. You little Dickens. God must have squeezed your cheeks before you were born. But there was this difference. This man seemed Life itself, especially when Bart took the stripes as veins.

After that, something was dislodged in him that never settled. He wished there could have been a Bessie Smith torch song about "The Massive Man." No matter where I go I'm just a goner for the massive man. Spelled, "massive," with many, many "s"es.

Well.

Well, there weren't any songs like that. Even the black culture couldn't dislodge that one, even though it had dislodged just about everything else, including how you felt about your own dog. Yes, Bart, adrift on the University of Washington campus, felt he was a man without song or metaphor for what was wrestling his heart to the ground. Whereas any other normal straight everyday Romeo could walk straight into a Hallmark Shop and find thousands of reasonable facsimiles for his feelings, he, Bart, and his Incredible Shadowing Hulk still had to hang out in the shadows.

And now there was this matter, this very day, of going up to Port Townsend, with his Hulk, his Body, still in the hospital. Bart felt guilty about leaving even if Robb had renounced his orientation.

Nevertheless, everybody needs a few days off. What was it that Richard Hooker said, "but then at last all of us must come to some pause"? Since that odd night in October, when Robb had barged in screaming Vietnam-and-an-affair-Ativan, Bart had been yelled at, stood up, pushed around, given silent treatments, and enlisted into every sort of drama, the final one being visits, now, to the Treatment center to talk things out with counselors, interveners, arbiters, psychiatrists, and finally the Director himself. A pause, that made sense. For when he got back on Monday, there'd not only be Robb, but an AIDS test, too. And then after that, auditions he was holding for his students for *Jesus Christ Superstar*. The whole high school—as well as the community theater—was excited about them. But that could be a pause, as well. Going into rehearsal was like going down a hallway—long, lamp-lit—a gallery of candle-flamed portraits which you painted and hung yourself. You became Leonardo. And if you wanted Mary Magdalene to look like the Mona Lisa, or vice versa, that was the way it was to be, with the daylight world of carpenter ants and insurance adjusters and ear infections and wrecking balls ever receding until you were in the world of Night Town, the Renaissance night club (always open) of L'Allegro, where Ben Jonson and Will Shakespeare stopped in, bringing their sheets of verse, and became rowdies just before midnight.

So he threw an athletic bag into the car (all he needed was a change of underwear and a few toiletries), and was there in no time. There had been a glimpse of Jutland Hospital (it was unavoidable), when he had driven round a particular turn in the freeway, and for a moment he had felt a certain gravitational pull towards one particular window (was Robb sitting there like a sentinel, or dutifully reading his Bible?), but then, in seemingly a matter of seconds, he was there in no time.

The men at The Place on the Point were out on the deck, most of them, sunning themselves. One warm hour on a Saturday afternoon in April was snatched up like a golden cloverleaf in a forest meadow. Eureka—and off with the clothes, men. Bart felt relieved he had the excuse of taking time to unpack. In the bunk room, he thought, Now what shirt can I change into? For he had an unwritten rule never to go without one, even as much as he had done other actors up to show off shoulders, chests, back. And yet he didn't want to come off as a wet blanket, either. So he compromised on just his A-frame t-shirt ("grandpa shirt," some of his friends called it), with a button-down pin stripe open over it, and went on out.

"Hey, Bart," one of them said. "Where's your body?"

Back in Jutland General, Bart wanted to say. Fifth floor. Most likely looking out the window.

The circle was a very eloquent bouquet of living, supple human beings, almost all in their prime, physically and professionally. In their twenties and thirties, they had grown up, most of them, as gay and accepted; some of them coupled, even, as childhood sweethearts. Also, there was an unwritten law in this group about being "out." If you were hung up on it, then leave until you got your act together. This was the post DSM-II generation—they were outside the shadow of "aberration"—so don't be hauling your baggage into our circle.

So they were watching *The Wizard of Oz* on video, of course. A sort of baby's bonnet had been put around the screen, so the sun wouldn't sun out the picture.

Dorothy had just hit Oz, and Technicolor. She had the munchkins were skipping around before finding the road.

Bart, literally decking himself out, said, "Tell me what's happened so far," and they all burst out laughing.

"It's all about Kansas," Marcus—the most massive, and eldest, of them—said. "It's the awful truth. About things like . . . the Midwest."

Everyone hooted in mock fright. "Don't even mention the Midwest," Andrew said. "That's worse than Idaho."

Bart had moments, during gay hilarity, when he wanted to crawl beneath the floorboards. This was one of them. His skin, duly covered with Number 30 sunscreen, felt porous and on the edge. He would have said horny, if it had been a rawer deal. Marcus, with his muscles and white mane, could have been the reason, but Bart was sure it was more than that. In the distance, he could see his beloved Rose House, Robb's former home, of course. Along with the house, the sea breeze was stirring up a hunger to be touched. And in looking around the circle—at men either carefully distanced or smack on top of each other, if they were couples—he knew touching was out of the question.

"I had a two-D-subscript-5 date the other night," Lance said.

"Oh, no, not another one."

"Excuse me," Bart said, taking the bait with mock innocence, "but what's a two-D-subscript-5 date?"

"Oh no," everyone said together. "You don't know what a two-D-subscript-5 date is?"

"You've been coupled too long," Andrew answered. (Andrew had always been shameless about his attraction to Bart, but the moment Bart had come anywhere near, he always fled like a mirage.)

"A two-D-subscript-5 date," Lance said, "starts at the bar with this absolutely gorgeous man who won't stop cruising you."

"Usually during 'Do You Want to Funk?'"

"Or some of the new stuff," someone else said.

(By now, Dorothy was witnessing the arrival of the Bubble.)

"He gives you a lot of encouragement, and you decide, in a really neat way, not to go home together."

"Because you want this one to last," Marcus said.

Uproarious laughter.

"So Mr. Two-D—"

" . . . SO4," Marcus put in.

"So Mr. Two-DS04 gives you his phone number, which you've wangled out of him, and you eventually call him—"

"—but only after a discreet number of days!" someone put in.

"Or at least two hours, anyway."

"And so you call him—"

"But he's not in—"

"No, but you do get his answering machine—"

"Which has the cutest message."

"'Hi, you've reached Dominic's house. I'm not home but my dog Toto is—'"

"—'whose voice you are now listening to.'"

"And so you leave your number, and he doesn't call for a while."

"Just two months," Marcus said.

"When his other long-term relationship is over."

"He calls you when things suddenly end on their two-month anniversary, when the wrong hunk jumped out of the cake."

"Because, you see, he's met other people at the bar, besides you."

"And so he calls you just to tell you that he's been sitting around hoping he meets the right man some day, but he doesn't know who that could be, given the way gay world is these days, but somehow, somewhere, sometime—"

"And so you maneuver him into a date—"

"Out to dinner, in *his* maroon sports car."

"And you have the most spectacular dinner, and speak of deep things, but just when he walks you to your door, and you invite him in—"

"He tells you he has to get home early—"

"—to finish packing for the movers who are coming the next morning."

Marcus had finished with that one, and so got the applause.

"And so at nine p. m. you're watching television."

"But thinking, definitely thinking about maybe going down to the bar, just to see who's there."

"You haven't been there in just ages."

"Ten minutes."

"But you need someone to tell your troubles to."

"Definitely that—because never again will you be caught believing Mr. Right will come walking through that door."

"Not right now, anyway," Bart said, his pun passing everyone by, almost himself included, and stopping the whole story.

Now in the pause, as usual, his own apparent cynicism left him melancholy and even more vulnerable. In a way, he almost hoped his hurt over Robb would be obvious, so that everyone would know that at least he was feeling something.

"How's your man doing?" Bill, another massive one, asked, looking over at last.

"All right," Bart answered. "But they're keeping him there another two weeks."

There was a little ripple in the group, as though Bill had said the wrong thing. Bill, propped up on his elbows, obviously sensed the change, and fell silent.

The group held the tension, while Judy Garland met Ray Bolger. Bart had time to notice that Marcus had left the group and was down walking along the beach by himself. The smell of the sea was overpowering, and the sight of that vulnerable man, as shaggy as father time himself—combined with Bill's discomfort (reflected in a muscular ripple, as he stretched)—caused Bart to rise and stretch his back.

"One thing we can say," diplomatic Andrew said, "is that Bart's a real trooper."

"Let's reserve judgment," Bart answered, getting ready to head down the embankment, "until Robb is back home and we're in our relationship again. For one thing, let's see if he stays off drugs and alcohol."

"He will."

"If he knows what's good for him."

"Where's his family through all of this?"

Aren't I his family? Bart wondered. Maybe not. Maybe I'm just his trainer. And in looking around, he saw that this combination—Body and Trainer—held true for many of the couples who were there.

"His family," Bart said, "has been pretty secretive. Or I should say, Robb's been pretty secretive about them. There's been some sister who's been coming and going through all of this. But our paths have never crossed, and we've never been introduced before."

His exit was one in character, for the emotion that had come had been so strong as to send him straight out of the circle and down along the beach, toward Marcus. The strange, curious and erudite man, who guarded himself with large bouquets of polysyllabic words and phrases from most of the Romance languages, was somehow a comfort to him. He was like the colossal head of The Wizard himself, at the end of a long rainbow of irony. He shimmered as he spoke.

"Lovely barnacles," he said, "of the order cirripedia. Their feathery fans remind me of fan dancers, if you have ever seen them underwater."

"Never," Bart said, "except in photographs."

"It's sort of an inspiration," Marcus laughed, "thinking of those little fish nets each of them have, scanning the water like screens for food."

The beautiful shoulders of the older man were hunched above the rock in the tidal pool. "Everything in the sea," Bart said, "hightails it off, the moment I get anywhere close. Same with fish. Same with clams."

"Like Proteus," Marcus said sadly, "the moment we touch him, he's gone."

Bart felt sad, too. A few years back, way before Robb, he and Marcus had shared a night together, they had done presumably the most intimate thing two human beings on the planet could do—making love and sleeping together—and here they were, as distant friends discussing Proteus and barnacles. He wondered if Marcus even remembered what had happened between them. There were other men in the circle Bart had been intimate with—just once—as well. And the years had sewn the seams tight again. They'd been sophisticated enough to go on being friends once they had passed through those intimately important Portals, these days, of "letting go." But I'm not going to be sophisticated right now, Bart insisted to himself, I'm going to be sad.

And there was something else about Marcus, who'd written a perfectly beautiful novel back in the 1950s—cadenced, imagistic, sensitive, compelling. It had been continental in texture, and hung with great draperies of moss. The film rights had been bought, and it had been made into a movie starring Jean Seberg, who had been nominated for an Oscar for her role. But Marcus disowned the book now, perhaps because Jean Seberg was considered faded these days. Bart could remember during their night of love together, his and Marcus', trying to get him to share his success story, seeing the book on the shelf, but those years had been dismissed; they belonged to that sensitive part of him which could have made their One Nighter into something with a promise. But that was equally lost.

Nevertheless, with the wind and sun on both of them now, Bart could not resist the urge to embrace Marcus now.

Marcus responded, being a good gay man, but immediately and gently pushed him away. "To what do I owe this honor?" he asked. "No one ever hugs me anymore."

Bart wanted to say, "Because I like you," but that would have been too much, so he had to go for an excuse which, nonetheless, was true. "I just have all this love to give, and Robb's been away."

"Yes, a month's a long time."

"It's been more than a month," Bart said, "way, way more. He's been distant from me since he first tried to get off drugs himself."

"When was that?" Marcus asked.

"At least a year ago."

"So you're sex-starved. You want to do the beast with two-backs. Well, listen, I'm available. The bunkroom awaits."

Marcus was smiling kindly when he said this; nevertheless, Bart felt stung. "You're joking about us?"

"Us?" Marcus asked, looking puzzled. "Us?"

Of course this man's going to look puzzled, Bart thought. With so many plant-identification hikes that he's put between us, so many polysyllabic parodic poems, so many perfect glasses of wine, sipped for age and bouquet, so many other men, chosen for their youth, how could he possibly remember the one night which had been important to *me*, for sentimental reasons.

Nevertheless, Marcus could sense, at least, that Bart had shut down.

"I have reason to feel close to you," Bart said. "Don't I?"

"Of course," Marcus said. "Pray forgive me."

They walked by the tide pools, in silence for some time. At last Bart said, "It isn't doing the beast with two backs I'm talking about. It's intimacy. It's accidentally saying something really hurtful and being willing to apologize."

"And what does this have to do with your physical needs?" Marcus asked.

"I don't know," Bart said, feeling as though they were both drowning in the sea smell. "But it does! It's intimately connected."

"So to speak."

"Yes, so to speak."

They had come to a log, covered with dried kelp. "Ah, the mysteries of nature," Marcus said, sitting down. "If only we could read them the way we read tea leaves." Suddenly he took Bart's hand, turning it palm out. "If only I could read the mystery there in your palm, why you need contact so much right now. Intimate contact. Whereas I"—turning out his own—"want it so little. My dear friend," he said, pausing again, "I'm dying. Of AIDS. I look into that sunlight right there and wonder how it could be the same light which sunned me into existence—and all the minuscule and rising life here—could have also countenanced those same viruses which invaded my body through some act of 'love.'"

An attack of fear overtook Bart's body as he said this, and all his openness contracted in on him, like a barnacle drawing in its fan. His memory winged back immediately to the bedroom scene which he had kept in loving shadow all this time, and immediately turned the lights on: huge, fluorescent, clinical. In an instant all the anatomical parts were named, what had gone where with Marcus. The semen was seen flying. Masturbation only. No exchange of bodily fluids. Bart settled down into relief again, but this time from behind a fortress of defensiveness. Gently, he removed his compared hand, and worried for Marcus.

"Marcus, I'm so sorry," he said.

"The wages of a libertine life," Marcus said, "much of it lived before Stonewall. We shared each other back then. It was a peak experience, as they say, exchanging bodily fluids, like these lovely little crustaceans in these tide pools here. But now one has to pay for the gift exchange. The White Elephants we gave everybody."

"When did you find out?" Bart asked.

"Six months ago."

"And you never told me?"

"I've told very few," Marcus answered. "And, please, don't tell anyone else."

"Of course not."

Another pause, in the heavy wind, which blew the sand against Marcus' beautiful, aged flesh.

"May I touch you? May I hug you?" Bart asked.

"No," Marcus said, getting up. "Because you wouldn't mean it."

This cloud followed Bart through the evening, where he watched Marcus over wine over dinner, and the next morning it followed him when Marcus teased Andrew and Steven for making love openly and narcissistically on the fold-out bed facing the 180 degree living room windows facing the beach. Sex seemed everywhere but contact non-existent.

Sixteen

A Sunday morning, dawning bright and early, fading to overcast and silences, along the beach. Men packing up early, some of them, leaving a few stranded at the breakfast table with only gossip and then a few dishes to wash. There was something cozy about it for Bart. As though he could take all day getting back to Seattle if he wanted to. If you wait as late as eleven in the morning, you may as well as wait until eight at night, the ferry lines are so long. Thousands of people, having stolen some time on the peninsula, were now anxious to get back so they could mow the lawn, put the garbage out and get ready for Monday morning.

He called his parents and told them he'd stop in before he drove out of town, and in turning into a corner of the hall of the communal house for more privacy as he spoke, he was struck, suddenly, by the sight of Marcus again, snapping a suitcase closed, and starting the round of hugs goodbye. The surprising moment on the beach and the closeness of the AIDS test tomorrow, all caused Bart some fright while talking to his father. He was not out to his family. And his pink triangle pin, which he had taken from one of his shirts this morning, was now like a weight in his pocket.

Putting down the receiver, and embracing Marcus last, he held on. Marcus was merry with the special tenderness, and sported it off, in words that were exactly Bart's father's, "Oh stop or I'll get all choked up."

Bart was quietly furious with this.

He packed and pushed off, deciding to give himself the whole late morning and early afternoon off. In Port Townsend, he would simply drift through town. He'd drift like a leaf. Maybe even take a guided tour, in off-tourist season. Pretend he didn't know any of the places he'd grown up with. Luxuriate in being a stranger until, inevitably, he got caught.

So, he parked the car at Chetzemoka Park, and walked uptown, unable to resist the gravitational pull of Rose House. It wasn't his planning which caused him to walk straight into a guided tour of the place. It just happened—he paid his two dollars and joined the camera buffs who were being led from landing to landing, by an attractive, dark-haired woman who Bart knew must have been Laura. An angel, also, hovered about, who must have been Robb's stepdaughter, for instantly he recognized Laura's features in her face.

And so they rose upon the stairs, with the light sidling itself down and the beatiful fresco of maidens coming ever closer. With each step, with each inevitable peek into each inevitable bedroom, Bart saw, with heartbreaking clarity, Laura and Robb making love together, the greater massive back covering her entirely, as he loved her, kissing her neck, and especially her breasts, as he bore down, again and again, but as Bart looked in and noted all details, and the photoflashes went off, and the stained glass deepened, he also saw that the body beneath Robb's was his own, which shared so many of the same outlines as Laura's. They came, in fact, to double mirrors in the master bedroom, and for an instant, the two of them were side-by-side.

"Ann Rose," Laura said, "did most of her sewing and poetry reading by this window."

That's me, Bart thought, when attending to parents at a dress rehearsal. I'm whispering in the shadows at the back, just the way she is. Observe. Admire.

And in that double moment, suddenly he felt attracted to Laura.

And yet the caressing voice continued on, caressing him, and the furniture, and the beautiful gilt lines embossing the freshly painted walls. And still they were circling toward the dome, moving along the staircase, which mirrored everyone's face back. And it occurred to him, as they ascended, that this was just like his gallery, inwardly lit, the private one of special phantoms, which he created every time he went into Rehearsal.

And as in Rehearsal, the rose light off the walls hushed her voice, or so it seemed. Ann Rose was spoken of as going to the Port Townsend library every week (so had he). And they even knew what books she read, for a careful record (note scrolled handwriting) had been kept on her card. And with Ann Rose, the maidens were arriving within his field of vision. The fresco of them on the ceiling, represented as the seasons. Instead of the troop ascending; the dancing ladies seemed to wing down toward them. "Look," Laura said, "right above each one is a piece of fitted glass, which lights up at each solstice. And the winter woman, once she was unveiled, was known for the scandalous brevity of her attire. For ten years she had to remain covered. And the irony is, of the entire four, she is the most scantily dressed—and yet she is Winter." And, in fact, Bart thought, the maiden did seem to shiver within a white mist of snow. And her face looked so surprised— like his own, when, one time, he and Robb had made love under a mirror—the vast body closing over him like a blanket and with him looking up all of a sudden.

But now they were at the top, and they had a grand view of the town to look out on. And also a dizzying look straight down: three stories of gloriously polished mahogany.

And the painter, someone was asking. What about the painter?

Nothing was known, except that she took an extended trip from Seattle and then returned. There is a coordinate mural in the Women's University Club. In a room that is never used.

A coordinate mural, Bart wondered. Of what? Men?

"I heard it said," another voice was insisting, "that all of this came to the painter, from poetry her mother had read to her. How do they know that?"

"There's a signed book somewhere," Laura replied. "From the mother."

The consoling hearth image of, somewhere, in the nineteenth century, a mother reading to a daughter.

"And the whole house," another asked, "who or what built it?"

"Seth Rose," Laura said. "The lumber baron. Who built half of this whole district. A millionaire, a traveler in Europe, seeking patterns and then copying them out to scale throughout these streets. He built this place to please his wife, who designed the rooms, she said, to reawaken his feelings of passion for her."

Bart wished she had not said that. In fact, he had been praying that she wouldn't. And only realized that now. For at this moment, all the mirrors were opening into full views of Laura-Robb, Robb-Bart, Bart-Laura; the joined bodies turned, on the rose-patterned sheets, as daylight cracked the windows open, and an unpleasant memory arose and then beat a hasty exit.

And at the topmost one, Bart still stood, euphoric and looking out.

"Sir?" Laura was calling from below, and now already one flight down with the rest. "We're going back to the foyer." And gave him a winsome smile.

That wasn't fair, either, Bart thought, smiling too and hurrying himself into the descending line. And I should never have come here, spying on Robb's life like this. Above, the maidens seemed to take him in, severely. Never, never should I have come.

They were, politely, shown to the door. For a bed-and-breakfast is the real property of its paying guests. However, he was allowed to buy a postcard of the mural and staircase for fifty cents. I must have this, he thought, despite his shame. Going down the painted stairs, and out into the carefully mown landscape, Bart felt he might disappear at any moment. So caught up in thoughts of Laura and Robb. He rubbed his eyes beside the roses, and thought of how Robb had talked with bitterness of being groundskeeper while holding down the teaching job in Seattle. This woman has got life down to a science, he thought, also bitterly. Who ends up with the spellbinding bed-and-breakfast and a beautiful child to match, while I end up with the booted-out, pain-in-the-ass, pillhead ex-husband?

The sense—consonant with what had happened with his men's group this weekend—of being nothing but a P.S. to other people's lives arose once more, and Bart was sure that if he stood there one second longer, the shadow from the huge place would snuff him out completely.

So he walked down to the Crescent, pushing himself to think wonderful thoughts of when he and Robb had fought in the St. Valentine's Day Bakery Massacre. And as he sat there, smiling, he reached into his pocket to pay for the refill, and came up with his pink triangle pin, which now came up as a good luck piece. His eyes misted, looking at it, and so, before he stood the chance of fading out, he simply put it on.

Next step, the Family.

And so he entered the Six-Ten, feeling armed almost, and centered, suddenly, in his own body. He smiled and kissed his mother, who was behind the counter, and shook hands rigorously with his father, who was running stock.

The pin was small—no bigger than a dime. They did not notice at first.

"So what brings you up here?" his mother asked.

"I was up with friends." A definite signal not to ask what "friends" meant.

"Oh, old friends?" she asked, not getting it. "The ones from high school?"

"No, new friends—we all came up from Seattle together."

"I'm hearing the ferry lines are getting longer and longer these past Sundays," his father said, getting it, that was for sure. And more than happy to change the subject. "I hope you brought a book."

"If he didn't," his mother said, "he can have one of those from the rack. Help yourself, Dear."

Bart looked at the rack of paperbacks—new since he'd been here last. Finally they were out of danger. Relief. It was as if each of them had popped a beer.

"And they're not all Harlequin romances," his mother said. "There's something there I'm sure would suit you."

"I've got plenty of things to read in the ferry line," he answered. "I'm up to my ears in school work."

"Maybe you're hungry, then?"

"No."

"Do you know if your kids will go to the Nationals again this year?" his mother asked, apparently trying to think of something else.

"I don't know," Bart asked. "If it happens, it happens. There's so much I can't control as far as their performance is concerned."

"I don't know," she said. "It's my opinion you always ought to be a winner. That *The Wizard of Oz* was one of the best things I've ever seen." And she turned to his father. "You should have seen it—so entirely professional."

"Well, I must be going," he began to say, "I—," but before he could turn toward the door and ask where his brother was, he was stopped by Jesse, who owned the marina close by and who always came in for a cup of coffee.

Jesse had always been such a hunk, was so gloriously put together, he always made Bart forget who he was. Presently, after getting his coffee, he was pumping Bart's hand, "Good to see you, Man, good to see you—and what's this pink triangle you've got on?"

"It means," Bart said, "I'm gay."

"Oh," Jesse said, "well . . ."

Never before had Bart been so aware of the sailboats bobbing silently up and down in the window. It was just becoming clear to Jesse that this was also news to his parents.

"Well," Jesse went on, "I can't say I've got anything against you guys, so long as you keep it to yourselves." Silence. "I always say, two things in life I'll never try—that and parallel parking."

Bart was charitable enough to feel sorry for Jesse when this totally failed, but for the most part, Bart had to suffer over the shocked look of his parents.

"Well, I best be going," Jesse said, still trying. "Guess I really put my foot in it. Hoof-in-mouth disease they call it. Had it all my life."

"You didn't say anything wrong," Bart said. "That's what the pink triangle is for. So people will ask."

"Well, you're a true gentleman and a scholar for putting it that way," Jesse answered, and exited at last with the coffee, very tenuously balanced indeed.

Bart looked at his parents. "Is there anything you want to say or ask?"

"Just give us time," his mother said. "We weren't planning on getting this information today."

"It's quite a snoot full," his father added. "One son blind and now the other homosexual."

"Jack, what a thing to say."

"I won't linger then," Bart answered. "Tell Daniel I'm sorry I missed him, and I'll see him next time."

"We'll let him know."

As Bart left, he felt this would be the last of the free paperback and lunch offers.

Seventeen

Just after the St. Valentine's Bakery Massacre, he and Robb had started going out to coffee at the Five and Dime, when Bart suddenly found himself with lots of reasons to come up for the weekend. They hadn't made love right at first, even though both of them had been used to first-date sex. It was quite strange, but Bart had known almost from the beginning that the attraction was not equal, that Robb felt nothing of the lust that he did. Nevertheless, they walked the bluffs together, thrilled by the spring madronas and wild lilac—and, when they were assured no one was looking, they walked hand in hand and kissed.

They had a favorite hike. It followed a magical path, unknown to many, which wound past a wild apple tree, in full bloom. Bart, aware of Robb's strong hand over his, felt that even with the disparity between them, that he had arrived, that this was the most he could hope for—the natural fulfillment of the longing which had struck him broadside, the moment Shakespeare's Angelo had walked into his dressing room, covered with his fake whip marks.

For some reason their conversations, the early ones, had always come to rest on Rose House. When, for example, they had tried figuring out how they could have completely missed each other in their growing up years, they had used Rose House as a chronometer. And the strange thing was, as they had talked of Rose, whom they had begun to call "she," they had created two separate histories, one belonging to each of them, but which, although braided apart, finally joined in her. As they had talked, she seemed, in some ways, a greater personality than either of them. Where were you in the sixties? That was when she was closed down for repairs. Dad was spending a mint on her. I was away at the University.

"Oh, yes, I remember," Bart said. "I can remember biking past one time. All of Port Townsend seemed shut down then."

"Yes, and then I went away a few years later."

"Where?" Bart asked.

"It's a long story," Robb answered, his grip tightening. "I'll tell you sometime. Not now, but sometime. But just the sight of Rose used to pain me then."

And then Bart could remember their pathway, still through the edge of the Olympic National Forest, suddenly falling away, opening out into cleared farmland dotted with horses, backed by a horizon of the Strait itself, limitless, ponderous under shapes of cumulus whose tones matched the apple tree's, in an unearthly pink.

"What was it like?" Bart asked. "Being married all that time and having your wife slowly take over the family estate?"

"Like a slow sleep," Robb answered. "Like waking up every morning with just a little more of yourself gone. It was like I lost the sense of being alive. Like every day going out for a walk and it taking just a little longer to get back. That was especially true after I started commuting. It was like having someone take over my life for me. And my daughter's. One day I came back after a week of teaching, and couldn't find either Laura or Valerie at home, so I just got into my dirty overalls and started working on the garden the way I always did. It occurred to me then I could have just as well been a hired man, hired on for gardening, and that was exactly it—that's what I was."

A tenderness spread through Bart as he listened to this story. He wanted to assure him that that would never happen again. As they turned to walk along the beach, a heavy wind hit them sideways, and instantly Robb hugged him from behind, and said, "Hey, that's enough talk now, warm me up."

They were looking at the sea-sprayed roses coming out of the fog, and Bart felt Robb would not rest until they had made love.

And so they had dinner back in town, and the fog, so typical of spring, came in, rolled over the waterfront street, so much Bart could not even see the steeple of his beloved court house—his compass, his north star, in that place—and it seemed that along Waterfront street, Robb ducked into every bar he could find, and Bart joined in enough, so that it did not at all seem so strange when he proposed they go up and pay their last respects to Rose, before they caught the late ferry back to Seattle. The fact that he had already been there that morning to see his daughter—why should he want to go back?—did not occur to Bart; rather, his mind began to follow Robb's, as they approached its curtained lights on every tier, always left on in case the guests needed to use the facilities in the middle of the night.

And out of nowhere, Robb produced a key, and, swaggering a little, said it's to the basement, which has been abandoned for years. "Do you want to just see if the key's still good? Just see what's still down there?"

"Are you kidding? Laura will catch us for breaking and entering, sure as the world."

"Not if we're quiet about it," Robb said, giving him a kiss.

And all of a sudden, as Robb was unlocking the place in the shadows, Bart's mind kind of went off rail, and started to flash scenes of *Basement Tinkerers*, his favorite porno number, where two hunky guys get it on down in the cellar, when they're both supposed to be fixing the water heater.

Because as they crept inside, switching on one silent light, a mattress appeared over in a corner, right below a full-length mirror. Just like in the magazine.

In no time, Robb had Bart's shirt off, and Bart was thinking this is insane! Insane! We'll get caught. But the effect of the house—something in that basement, perhaps the musty smell—was overwhelming, and Bart was trying to keep his head on straight, to get clear on this, but it was completely fogged by now, by wine, but even more by the pressuring sense that Robb wanted him—he'd better take this opportunity and run with it, it (or he) may never come again.

They were in just their jeans now, and Robb was starting to lick his neck. He saw the massiveness of his chest—and suddenly it was as though Bart had that chest, was that chest—it was like when he used to dream when he was a swimmer for the High School— he used to dream that he was plunging in, with a perfectly built body and tearing through the water, outdoing everyone with his butterfly. Or was it that he was a butterfly now, emerging as Robb's new body, out of the chrysalis, as it took over his?

He kept kissing his chest, over and over, and he was starting to feel prone already. His hands reached up, and although he'd been with men with his perfection before, he felt for the first time that it's O.K. to be Gay! It's O.K. to feel this chest, magnificently furred, as much as he wanted to! But while he was feeling it's O.K., it's O.K., Robb was opening his pants, unsheathing him like an ear of corn, as the desire to be him by having him inside him was taking over, like a madness.

Where the hell am I? Bart asked himself, as his hands rippled down his back, as they discovered his jeans were gone, too, and there was nothing there but taut hamstrings.

Where the hell am I? And feeling ludicrous, he turned his eyes heavenward, like a Victorian woman on her bridal night. And in that moment, he thought of the ultimate ceiling of this house—of the frescoed maidens, in their seasons, and in just that second, he thought, You're not going to throw yourself away, you're not going to kill yourself tonight. This is no hara-kiri mission. This sex is about to get dangerous, lethal, who the hell knows where this man has been? A closeted ex-husband. Are you kidding? You may feel like a bride, but you don't need to die in childbirth. Stop, think. AIDS. And as Bart thought this, he could imagine the maidens turn overhead, smiling in his mind's eye for the first time.

"Robb," Bart said, "this is far enough."

"Please."

"Robb," Bart went on, "we have nothing to protect ourselves. I don't want to be fucked tonight."

"I've brought something," he said. And got up, as long and erect as the Empire State Building, and produced just what they needed from his shirt. "Besides," he said. "I want you to fuck me."

The maidens were gone. Bart was no longer present. You want me to fuck you?

As if kerosene has been thrown on the dampened fire. You want me to fuck you? It would be better than having his body in a dream; it would be becoming the muscular lion tamer in tiger tights, with whip and chains. Or Jack Armstrong suddenly producing Kong from behind the curtain. In massive, billowing manacles.

Bart was so erect now, he could poke out the door, and he was back to *Basement Tinkerers*, and the two studs doing it down in the darkness, and he remembered one of the few lines, "the place is getting hotter than a firecracker," and he wondered if Robb, even Robb, would be big enough to receive him.

But Robb was lying there, a giant with his legs open, and they both were prepared now.

"You really want me to fuck you?" Bart asked, overcome with his new power. "Do you really want me to?"

"Yes, fuck me here in the dark," he said, "like Mason did. Fuck me silly."

Mason?

And he was inside him all at once, long-dicking him until he was smooth. With every thrust, he felt was getting bigger and bigger, until he was no longer there; it was just himself and his penis in a gigantic cavern.

A stroke up, and there were tears in Bart's eyes.

A stroke down, and he felt was about to give birth.

A stroke up, and he knew he was about to blow.

And then he let fly inside, and something was crossing his body like an earthquake, and Robb was letting go, too, in a fine shower of love.

Breathless and covered with sweat and semen, they folded down into each other, and became sheathed again. Overhead, they could hear a commotion upstairs.

And then Robb's face—he'd never seen it so ugly—tightened into fear. He separated himself from Bart like as though he had just crashed a car. Grabbed a towel that was placed there as though he'd planned breaking and entering, and Bart was aware, hideously aware, that he'd been a part of some terrible rite of revenge, and shamefaced, he pulled on his clothes, still wet.

This was unpardonable, Bart told himself. This was disgusting. It will never happen again. Never, never would he show anything but total respect for a house which had always turned such a tender face towards him when he was alone and teenaged and wandering through the town, afraid beyond belief and not knowing it. In his mind, he apologized to Rose, not for being gay, but for doing something he knew wasn't right.

Eighteen

The next day, at four o'clock, he drove into downtown Seattle, and went into Newberry's at Fourth and Pike. His friend Mariam had offered to meet him there, and see him through the test. "Oh you want to hold my hand?" Bart had almost mimicked at the time, but when he had thought better of it, he had actually said, very humbly, "Yes, I think I'm going to need it."

Mariam was a massage therapist and power-lifter, with huge shoulders and strong, knowing fingers. She was prone to being quiet, and Bart had always thought that if his psyche could have been turned inside out, his and Mariam's would have made a perfect match. It was a consonance he often felt with sensitive women jocks who were also lesbian. Mariam's living room also served as her massage studio, and it was hung with the intricate macramé which she had done herself. But Bart had always seen the flowers and leaves as the furnishings of her soul.

Now he sat with her at Newberry's and, over an old-fashioned coke glass, which people bought by the thousands these days, made himself nervous about his first HIV test.

Mariam was too tactful to ask whether he had anything to worry about. So he answered her anyway. "Robb and I have always been safe, even from the very start. But there's always that nagging little bit that maybe here, maybe there one of those dirty little viruses got through."

"Has Robb been safe with others?" Mariam asked. "That you've got to ask, too."

"I don't know," Bart answered. "I always considered it none of my business. Our unwritten agreement has always been—be safe, so there's no questions asked."

They had a little rain and a rainbow in the street. Sheer gold at the intersection of Fourth and Pine.

Mariam, always seeing the healing side of things, said, "Well, maybe that will change—I mean things won't seem so secretive— now that Robb is recovering."

"Thank you for saying that," Bart said. "That's the first time someone's come right out and said it that way. 'Robb's recovering.'"

"Haven't you seen it that way?"

"No. I mean, everybody's been so mobile around him— doctors, nurses, counselors. He's a moving target. But he's been like a stone wall."

"Sometime you have to slam into one in order to change yourself."

Bart sighed and looked up. "That's good to hear, too."

"And it's good to see you crying," she said.

"Am I?"

In the instant, he realized he was. He was centered in his own body again—had re-entered it just the way he had yesterday. And so, also, in tears, he put on his pink triangle once more. Mariam smiled. "It's just," he said, "that I realize I have so much going on. I came out to my family yesterday, just after an old friend shared with me that he has AIDS."

"All in the same day?" Mariam asked.

"I think," Bart said, "I did one because of the other."

Mariam looked uncomfortable. "It sounds painful."

"It is," Bart answered, leaning forward while knowing they must leave. "The only lovemaking I'll ever regret is the lovemaking where I hoped no one would ever find out or ever remember."

"Strange," Mariam said, as they got up to leave, "I never thought lovemaking could be lovemaking unless it was entirely private. Secret, almost."

Bart felt challenged, almost as though he were in class, but there was no time for that now. They were out on the street now, and a large stone white building was coming up before them, which was the best that could be done with the fact of AIDS in some places in 1986. He had had to give the nurse a pseudonym over the phone, since even anonymity could not be guaranteed unless you lied, so here he was, fake name and all, telling the receptionist he was here ("Henry James") to get the test, and he was given a number and a questionnaire to fill out while he waited.

All along, he had still felt slightly wimpish having Mariam there—who beside him, was simply doing her macramé with her massive hands. She looked like his bodyguard. He had thought having support made sense when he got the results. But why do I have to have somebody when all they're going to do is stick a needle in? But it did matter, because the first question on the sheet was, "How many sexual contacts have you had in the past twelve months?" And Bart, lifting the veil on many, many months in the calendar in his head (smiling moons, half suns, tides, fishes), could see only one. He counted again. Absolutely faithful. And only three times with him at that. Robb. And not very good times, either. In each one, he had been aware Robb had been sizing him up, at a distance, wishing, as he knew so well now, his body were otherwise.

A counselor—a sixty-year-old woman—showed him into a cubicle. "Right in here, Dear."

She withdrew a sheet, surrounded by posters of celebrities in semi-undress, smiling and telling everybody to be safe.

"And what causes you to think you might be high risk?" she asked.

"I'm a sexually active gay man," Bart answered rather proudly, but a moment later, he also wanted to smile at himself.

The woman—Ida—raised her brows. "Well, that certainly cleared the air, didn't it? No beating around that bush."

She made a check mark. "And this is your first test."

"That's right."

"Do you have reason to believe you have had contact with anyone exposed to the virus?" she asked.

"Yes. I was just told yesterday. Although if you mean by exposure—"

But the checkmark had already gone in. "Well, then, we're certainly glad you decided to come and see us. You do understand, Mr. James, that there is a two-week wait on results?"

"Yes."

"And you have a support system available to you during that time?"

"Well, yes, I think so," he answered. Even so, this was the first question, really, to take him off guard.

"Good. And do you understand, to the best of your ability, all the ins and outs of safe sex?"

Bart felt it would be almost indecent to say no. Otherwise this grandmother would start talking to him about penises and ejaculation. She'd almost done that with "ins and outs." "Well"—he hesitated—

"Please, Henry, we're here to answer questions. The only stupid question is the one that doesn't get asked." And then Bart suddenly realized, seeing her bravado, that she had been schooled in street language—she, who probably read *Jane Eyre* as a part of her nightly repertoire—and that she would use it on him, if necessary.

"Well, I'm just not sure what you mean by 'contact,'" he said. "I've done mutual masturbation—"

"Go ahead, you can say it, 'beating off—'" she said.

"Well, really, Ida, that isn't the way I'd put it."

"—Beating off is entirely safe, and we would not consider that contact—of an unsafe sort. However, there have been some cases, as yet to be verified, where cuts in the hand could leave one vulnerable. The one, though, to be really be careful about is when a guy fucks you in the butt—"

Bart was so appalled by this, that he had to grasp the little school chair he was allowed to sit in.

"Or if you fuck some guy in the butt, you also have to be careful, wear that rubber."

"I know about that," Bart said, to steady himself.

"Do you know also that you should wear rubbers—unlubricated ones—when somebody comes down on you, or you come down on somebody else. We now have"—pointing to a candy bowl—"a lovely assortment of flavored rubbers now, absolutely wonderful, and I especially recommend the 'kiss of mint'—"

"Oh dear," Bart said aloud. "Yes, Ida, I know all about those, too." He realized now that she reminded him, exactly, of his kindergarten teacher. He expected her, any moment now, to be handing out snacks ("You can have two graham crackers or four saltines"), or call for nap time and the unrolling of mats.

"We just want you to be as safe as possible. And now let's book you a date when you can come back and get your results."

He was prepared for this at least, and took out his calendar. While filing through the hours and finally coming up with one, while being led down the hall afterwards to the lab for the drawing of blood, he visualized himself naked in a perennial raincoat, like the hunk in the poster ("Don't forget your rubbers"), whenever he wanted to take off his clothes and have "contact" with another man. For the raincoat always stayed on, no matter how hard he tried, and he guessed these days, this was the way it was supposed to be. First there was the shield of your manhood as a man, and then there was the shield of safe sex.

He came out of the labyrinth of rooms, something like a diver who's got the bends.

"How did it go?" Mariam asked.

"Mostly the way you would expect," Bart answered.

Nineteen

Mariam asked if there was anything more she could do, and at first Bart said, "no." Just drop him off back at Newberry's, where he could have another Coke, and sit and stare off at all the alien faces, coming and going. Alone. He just felt a little off the wall right now, and he wanted to steady himself in an alien environment.

So Mariam did drop him off, but hung around, apparently looking at inexpensive perfume, but really, she was, at a distance, checking him out to see if he was O.K. It reminded Bart of the time he had taken a low-rent one-bedroom cottage in Lake City, and had immediately gone up on the roof to sweep off the needles— and all that time, his solicitous next-door landlady had clipped her already-clipped roses, just to keep an eye on him. She was quite sure he would tumble.

As was Mariam, who finally drifted back to the little booth and said, "You don't look like you're coming back down to earth at all. Come back to my place for a massage."

"Please, Mariam, I hate imposing, but just fifteen minutes or so." Bart said.

"You keep sounding like I don't want to. I suggested it in the first place," Mariam told him, somewhat nonplussed.

She guided him out, with her massive strength.

They didn't have very far to go—to her studio in her small house in Greenwood. There he stripped, while she stayed decorously in the kitchen as always, and lay himself on the table, with a sheet draped over. Also as usual, when he came for his regular appointment.

He called to her to come in, and as usual, told her the spots that hurt. The interplanetary orange of the living room, with the sun through, had taken over by then, so he also told her, in New Age language, what his dominant feelings were, as he watched almost as though he were an infant, a miniature mobile of an emotional solar system turn languorously above him. Except instead of screaming his emotions, he spoke them. Or it. "Mariam," he asked, "are there muscles you can touch which let go of grief?"

"Yes, of course," she said, pouring on the oil.

She began, as usual, by leaning into a particular spot on his back. His key spot, she called it. Not hard, really. Almost just a touch. Then she began to work things out intricately, almost as if his back (he was face down, with his face in the face-cradle) were a piece of tapestry, lit by the candles in the room. But she was also Penelope, because whatever she wove, she unwove. He was tight at first, became tighter, then slowly began to loosen, and as he did so, he began to think of the photo album he had kept as a child—a precocious one, because most of the pictures he had taken himself, even at six years old, with a 126 instamatic. Sometimes when the camera was handed across to his mother and she took the shots of the family, the pictures in there became the only instances when his father ever touched him. A hand on his shoulder. And it looked good. The strong, tall, and apparently sober grocer, with his young, good-looking Italianate son, Bartholomew Visconti. A distinguished name. An Italian sufficiently far from his native roots that he had lost all demonstrativeness. And the prim but firm Irish Catholic mother as photographer, a woman who, with her strong mind, later liked to stylize herself as something of a Port Townsend feminist.

As Bart's tension began to dissolve more and more as he lay there, conversely, he started to feel again that flame of being that clear, finite self, as it drifted amongst the recollected photos he had taken—totally fortuitous and whimsical ones, of plants, of birds, missed on a wire, once the shutter had come down, of a deer almost out of lens shot. The pictures you'd take as a child. And as his mind rested there, his father came back to him, falling asleep during his "To Be or Not to be" again, and Mariam must have found the grief button by then, because the crying came non-stop, along with the assurance that his father would never speak to him again, now that he knew he was gay, and what about his mother, and his brother, Daniel? The beautiful imaginary island known to him as Port Townsend rolled out of sight, as though washed away in a celestial wave, leaving him stranded with a possibly positive HIV test, in two weeks.

But I have to be strong, he told himself, despite the loosening. For the children, my children, and especially Robb, who is not yet well.

And the rhythms in his blood seemed to be articulated for him in iambs; they spilled and splashed, and he was swept back into a memory of his final senior theater project, where he directed the middle scene of *Pericles*, with Thasia rising from the coffin, with the smell of musk, and the sound of lutes—the doctor-god bending close, invoking the name of Aescalepius, the magic-sounding word, like a sprinkling of water over hallowed ground, a grave perhaps, from which he, Bart, was rising.

Tis known I ever
Have studied physic, through which secret art,
By turning o'er authorities, I have,
Together with my practice, made familiar
To me and to my aid the blest infusions
That dwells in vegetives, in metals, stones;
And I can speak of the disturbances
That Nature works, and of her cures: which doth give me
A more content in course of true delight
Than to be thirsty after tottering honor,
Or tie my treasure up in silken bags,
To please the fool and Death.

And in mentally rising, he became that doctor-god himself, was aware of all the virtues embedded in plants and herbs, could name their colors and Latin identifiers, the right combination of which held the secret to life itself: Thasia, who was also rising, out of his own body itself.

The crystalline scene, very delicately portrayed, had won startling applause, even from his supervising professor, who had harbored serious reservations about his talent, even though he had never said so.

And Bart, drifting, now, around the final curves of the massage, saw the scene of Cerimon and the resurrected Thasia as the same as the tapestries hung in this very living room, letting through the orange light:

This queen will live: nature awakes; a warmth
Breathes out of her . . . . See how she 'gins to blow
Into life's flower again!

And like Thasia, he must wait for someone to open his sea chest, wait for his own illumination. Or perhaps it was happening at this moment; perhaps his own stage directions were she moves, and he, in rising, was saying, "O dear Diana, Where am I? Where's my lord? What world is this?"—as Mariam continued with her extraordinary pressure, and he felt himself reintroduced to this stranger, whose midst he had been born into—his body, with whom he had been trying to shake hands, become friends with, since birth. His lord was his body—and his world was the same, the world of the flesh, whose demands were so great, so hard to decipher, especially when the shadows of AIDS and alcoholism were looming over, freezing, ever-present, imminent.

Well, enough. The thoughts had been ongoing since morning. He must finish out the natural course of the day—which was, to check Robb's phone calls and messages, so he would have information to give him tomorrow, during visiting hours.

He was taken around the final bend of the massage—Mariam disappeared again—and he got dressed. She had taken much longer than fifteen minutes. Scenes from that primary level photograph album flipped in front of him, as he put on his clothes. His crazy little neighbor Richard holding up Bart's own dog in front of him, as though the poor thing were a dead fish. Richard's sister Deborah looking sunward (also at seven) in a sundress. The log on the beach where all three of them used to search for agates, and where the kids on their bicycles used to shout, "Rockhounds,

rockhounds!" whenever they would pedal past, as though they were shouting obscenities.

But he had to move on—and he hugged Mariam goodbye, and thanked her, and she promised she'd show up in two weeks for the test results, if he wanted her, and he said, yes, yes, he wanted her; he knew that now! And she said, "Good luck with your family—and with Robb," and he answered, automatically, "And good luck with yours," when really he knew nothing about her family, except from surmise: that it was a source of deep pain, too.

But he also knew that the porno store was not far from here, and he might just stop in and have a look—after all, he had already given up his night at the Sultan Theater—and this time, he could ask for what he wanted. He would not stand there and peruse for hours what didn't have even the least appeal. No—their system there had become completely computerized, and they could now meet your exact needs by typing in all your fantasy categories (outdoor, workmen, leather, and so on) and finding just the right intersection.

So he went inside, under the frosted lights and the MasterCard sign, and went straight up to the man, and asked him to access the database. It felt odd, standing there, among all the sex-toy paraphernalia, and among all the little Halloween-like creatures that frequent such places, standing there as though he were at the bank, trying to work out a loan, or as though he were in the official building again, waiting for the AIDS test application.

Now a fantastic torso was filling the computer screen, of a man stretching every muscle, and "Male Base" appeared below. "All right," the clerk said, "what's your pleasure?"

"I want a video that's monogamous."

The clerk raised his brows but typed that in.

"And outdoor."

Typed.

"Violence free."

The man made a special note.

"That's explicit."

The man smiled. "They're all that."

"And very loving."

The man made a very special note, one that took an enormous amount of time; it was so odd.

Then all the commands were executed, and the computer, whirring away at first, started making sounds of extreme discontent. It sounded almost on the verge of explosion. At first frowning faces and then zeroes started filling the screen, replacing the torso, and finally a message appeared. "Bad commands." Obviously a total shock to its system.

"Well," the man said, "you sure blew its mind on that one. And I don't blame it. I've never had such a line of requests before in my life."

"Is it so weird?" Bart asked.

"Yes!" The man looked at him. "You're talking violence-free and loving and hot sex all at the same time? And with men? I never even get a request like that with the straight stuff. I guess you need to go to Hollywood."

"I do know it exists. I had a porno magazine once called *Men Touching*," Bart told him.

"Well," the man answered, "I'm afraid I can't help you. I think I've seen that magazine, too, but you'll never find it again. But I do have some great new prison stuff that's just in."

"Please," Bart said, "I don't even want to hear about it."

He turned to pick up his backpack.

"Hey, friend," he could hear behind him. "I couldn't help but overhear."

Bart turned.

"If you want what you're looking for," the stranger said, "try this." And handed him a card.

Bart, pocketing the card, said, "Thanks," and quickly moved on.

The man held out a hand, but Bart dodged it. The man was hooded, and seemed sinister. Young.

Out on the street, he felt crestfallen again, despite what Mariam had given him during the massage. The needles of desire were back with a vengeance, and all because he had blown it by going into that hole in the wall.

But when he looked at the card, it said, "Starlight Theater. Eleventh and Spring."

How odd. Because if the man had wanted a quick one in the back row, he would have put down the time. So what was the point? And what was the Starlight Theater? Never heard of it.

He got into his car, and went on over to Robb's.

But at Robb's, there was another strange message, this on the answering machine. From a man named Buddy. "Please call me, friend. I need to spend some more time with you. I know it's been a long time. And I'm sorry."

The message had been there several days. Bart, trying to sort out the puzzle of the day, was just in the midst of writing it down, when the door burst open, and there was Olivia, the woman he knew from "treatment family day" to be Robb's sister.

She was startled as well, and stared at him with the slightly exasperated eyes Bart had so disliked in the family session. Really, until now, they had been in each other's company only a matter of minutes, all sessions considered.

"What can I do for you?" they said together.

"I'm just getting his messages," Bart answered, feeling silly. "For when I see Robb tomorrow."

"Strange," she answered. "How long have you been doing this?"

"Ever since he went in."

She smiled. "He's been having me do the same thing. Guess it must be short-term memory loss."

Well, he knew who this woman was. A counselor. He could tell by her words already.

"Well here," she went on, handing him the mail he'd failed to collect downstairs, "you'll be seeing him before me. You may as well give him these."

"When did you last see him?" Bart asked.

"Just this afternoon."

"How is he?"

"Still seeing his chaplain" was the answer.

Bart felt stiff, and she seemed to feel it.

"I try not to judge it," she went on, as though having an inside track on his thoughts. "It's part of his process right now."

Process. Bart wondered if "gay" was in anyway included in this "process."

"I try not to judge it, either," Bart answered defensively. "It's just that a God on Mount Sinai has nothing to do with the Robb I knew."

She nodded. "I understand. Me, either."

They stood waiting. Bart folded up the slip of paper with Buddy's phone number and put it in his breast pocket.

"You know," she said. "I'm grateful to have met you. One of the good things to have come out of this is that a piece of Robb's life has come into mine. And you're part of that piece."

Piece! Bart smiled through it, just the same—knowing, although perhaps only faintly, that she meant no harm. But it was with some heat—maybe it was the heady spring air in the unopened room, too—that he answered, "I know what you mean— although, if you don't mind my asking, where have the rest of the 'pieces' of your family been through all of this? I was expecting to meet more than just you."

"Our mother," she answered also defensively, "lives down in California, and has not been allowed to fly up, because she's recovering from something herself. She had an accident while sailing. And our father's been dead for years. Robb's stepdaughter has not been allowed to visit, because of something he did just before he went under."

"What was that?" Bart asked.

"He evidently had a fist fight right on the steps of Rose House. With Laura's first husband."

Bart took a step back. For some reason—and because of the very nature of the day—the idea turned him on. Nevertheless, he felt flattened also by all the inside information she had over on him.

"Well"—Olivia looked uncomfortable, as though she had said too much—"I best get busy. Robb sent me on another errand." She took out a list. "He wants me to strip the house of all the alcohol and prescription bottles he's hidden over the years." She smiled. "He's given me a kind of treasure map, telling me where everything is. This is to make the place safe for when he comes home."

"Want me to help?"

"If you think you might know where some of these places are."

"I think I might know where all of them are," Bart told her.

He went to a special kitchen drawer and removed two flattened shopping bags, one for him (rainbow) and one for her (brown).

They made short work of the house, turning up every sort of conceivable hiding place. In one junk drawer, Bart found some pill bottles resting like decorations at the bottom of an old fishbowl. Robb had told him about those. Olivia found some pills in an old pair of socks, and the sock drawer itself was a veritable pharmacy. Plenty in envelopes under the mattress, which they turned over. Somewhere along the line, they started laughing. The treasure map also led to the cooler, and to the toilet tank, which held a cold beer, floating.

But when Olivia held it up as a trophy, instead of laughing, she turned quite pale.

"What's the matter?" Bart asked, his smile gone as well.

She had to sit down.

He came over.

She looked up at him. "I've been getting triggered and I haven't known it," she said.

"You?"

"Yes," she answered. "I didn't realize it, but I've gotten turned on while we were doing all this."

Bart was quite shocked; he had always taken her for a Grace Kelly. "Are you—?"

"Yes," she said, "a recovering addict and alcoholic." She wiped her sweat. Sweat? From Grace Kelly. Or Loretta Young? "You know what," she went on. "I'm going to have to turn all of this over to you." She handed him the shopping bag. Now Bart felt terrible for having given her the drab one. "Provided you feel safe with it yourself."

"Me?" he asked. "Sure. What do you want me to do?"

"I was going to take it over to the Treatment Center, and they were going to dispose of it themselves. But since you're going tomorrow, perhaps you could."

"Absolutely no problem," Bart answered, cautiously patting her shoulder. "I'll just keep it in the trunk of my car."

"Bless you," she said, briefly putting her hand over his. "And I'm sorry."

She stood up abruptly. Beautiful and slight, with points of gold to her hair. "And I must be going. All of a sudden, this place feels like a trap. Please give my love to Robb."

"I will," Bart answered, shopping bag in hand. And wanted to add, "If he'll take it."

"Oh"—she turned back at the door. "And don't forget this—this was his biggest request." Somewhere along the line, she had picked up Robb's statue of Joseph. "He was adamant about me bringing this over."

Bart sighed.

When he got home at last himself—having packed actually three grocery sacks into the trunk; everything clanking—he emptied his own pockets and found the note with Buddy's name and phone number on it. Thinking no harm, he decided he would call him and tell him Robb's situation, just before turning in.

Twenty

Robb was told Bart would be coming any minute. Still, he made no move to get up. He was fast in prayer. And prayer, lately, had been changing for him. At first God had appeared to him as a great shape of Jesus, hanging from the cross, and promising him salvation from his lusts, especially for men like Bart and Buddy and Mason, and all the guys down at the Y gym, but then the light changed, that irradiation, and there was something aglow first outside and then inside, widening the walls, brightening so intently he thought they would burst.

What was it he was being told? But he had no answer, because while his heart was full, his brain was sluggish, dull. His veins and his bones and his modes of thought felt positively blue with medication. Still.

But underneath that medication, there was a vibrancy, a life, a dormancy, which promised to flower somewhere down the line, and which would not exile him from men like Bart, or Buddy—or even the ghost of Mason. He was Frankenstein's Creature, still on the slab, but with his fingers rising—just so. You have value, a voice said. Not the voice of the past—the one which had given him to drugs and alcohol. You have value, you have a right to be here. Stay put. Don't run. Wait and see.

One time while his back had been turned in the room, a bird had crashed against the window, blue, hard. And Robb, terrified of what he might see below, had only edged to the glass, and waited before allowing himself only a glance down. But immediately he had seen that the bird had flown off—was O.K. And therefore had seen that she—the pigeon—was only a blue omen. Like

Lily. Who did not visit him with horror at night any longer. Her visits now were reminders. Only. That he must stay put, and let the memories hit him, until they stopped. He must let them keep coming, the voice said, until they were finished. One bird against the windowpane after another. A strike, and then a flying off. Given wings.

And the worst memory was Tara, Valerie's dog. He could remember her dropping into her bed night after night and morning after morning and afternoon after afternoon when all he had done was sink further into sleep and daylight dreaming. She'd take one look at him and drop, for she was taking on his living death, too. And then when Mrs. Molyson had told him she had been struck by a car, he had felt, at the time, almost nothing. A blank. And then the realization had hit him in dreams, and he had been driven, screaming, one more time from his bed. Straight to Olivia's house.

Well, the crack of that was upon him now. It rent him to pieces, but the difference was, he knew he must sit there now and not run.

Already he felt differently because he had sat through memories like these. These birds at the window. One thud and then it was gone, with the glass vibrating after. (He must think, for example, of the fight he had had with Scott, right in front of Valerie.) He knew, too, that just as he had torn Bart's feelings apart, this memory was now rending him. And so he spoke differently when Bart came into the room. He found it impossible to say anything mean, even though it was also impossible right now to say anything with real feeling even though he really felt it. The man had not quite become a person to him again, but Robb knew he soon would—and that this was a part of the new pulse of life. And in the meantime, he would not say anything mean.

One time Robb had called him at his house and had asked what he was doing.

"I've been outside," Bart had answered. "Working in the yard."

Were there still yards? People working in them?

He was fascinated by thinking of the underground life of the soil, which would be just giving way to flowers now—he'd been faintly aware of it there in the hospital. Bart was standing and digging in an oasis of spring, with the plume of the trees (cherry, apple) chalked in above him, like a mist, like a fog—the one which had hovered above them when they had first walked on the peninsula, holding hands.

The touch.

Bart belonged to that. Uncovering the moss, clearing away the leaves, and finding the hyacinth and crocuses like green stars below.

But as for himself, the world of touch was only a promise, a potential; right now, he must stay fixed here and hold himself accountable for everything he had done.

Everything inside of him made that demand. He would stop being a moving target. And face every bird at the window. In fact, he sometimes saw himself as the rock which the birds visited, his body slowly ossifying but slackening, too, and providing a perch. Although his mind was stony, his body was becoming limp, overweight, and flabby, whereas before his body had been hard as nails and his heart sometimes the same. Things had changed. One time, after a shower, he had caught a glimpse of himself in the hospital mirror. He could see that fat gathering at his hips, hanging down. He remembered himself as he had been at the Y— could this have been him, aged by twenty years?

And feeling the separation from his own body take over again, he started to pray once more. And in doing so, he felt the spring again, the life in the flower beds—they had done plant therapy on the roof last week—and he heard someone knock and come in. The Director.

"Well, you been through a war, man, and I don't mean Vietnam. I mean you've been through the war of drugs, and you're doing so well, we're thinking about letting you out in a week."

"Me?" was the most Robb could say.

The Director was sometimes given to jive talk when he wanted to make a point. "I do mean that. Can't you see what's changed in your head, man? I mean, really changed."

Sometimes, counselors passing him in the hall would say that, but he'd always been sure they'd been putting him on.

"I've changed in that I'll never go for men again." And Robb, even though he was staring at his portrait of Christ when he said this, even though he was emphatic, knew he was beyond this already.

"If I was you, seeing what you've been through," the Director said, "what we've all been through with you on this very, very bumpy ride—I'd stay gay. It's been one Zulu ride, man. I'd stay gay. I wouldn't fuck with that shit again."

Exactly! That's right! But Robb said, "I've been freed of the desire to sin. And I will sin no more. Perhaps my wife and stepdaughter will have me back again."

"Your wife is remarried, man. Or about to get herself that way. You got to get back into reality, if you're going to get yourself out on those streets. You hear what I am saying?" And he grabbed him by the shoulders once more. "You as queer as a three-dollar bill, and there ain't nothing to be ashamed of in that."

"I love my wife and my stepdaughter," Robb said—and it was true—that was true.

"Hey, man, I know that. You got plenty of feelings. Enough to go round for everybody. But you can't sit here thinking you're going to waltz yourself straight back to Port Townsend, and settle in carving turkey at the head of the table and slapping hands for taking rolls too early. There's ongoing life out there, man. It can change and leave you out. Or leave you with something new."

Robb stared straight ahead, still feeling like the rock.

"You've got feelings all right," the Director went on, "but that's different from the facts of the situation. You really looked at those feelings? You ever do your counselor's homework assignment on writing about them?"

"Not yet," Robb said. "I was waiting until you took me off all this medication."

"You going to be on it for a while," the Director answered, "so you may as well get used to it, understand? You stay really clear on the difference between drugs and medication, and you'll do just fine." Now he was writing some things on a chart. "You get to doing that homework assignment, and we'll maybe get a Viet vet in to talk to you, if that goes all right, and then we'll get you the hell out of here. Meanwhile you have a nice talk with your friend who's coming in here. Believe me, man, that's reality. Life again with your wife ain't no reality at all. And the minute you start writing about your feelings about her, you'll get clear on the difference."

Incongruously, the Director continued to write orders, presumably medical and in formal English, into the chart. "You hear me? You get on that."

And, honestly, the moment Robb did get alone again, he tried to grasp the spirit of what the Director had been saying. There was a scrivener's desk at the back of his head, rarely used, but still there, with the top up, and so he pulled it down, hung a mental icon above, and tried to think, as was per usual with him, how the icon was directing him to get back into his marriage. But the harder and harder he tried this time, the Director's three-dollar bill seemed to take him over, and he began to think, instead, about all the funny times there had been in his marriage. He was seeing it, all queered up. Laura had been so, so young when they had gotten together—so young no one would have believed she had been around the block with a first husband already. And with a child in tow. She had been ironing. That he remembered. The curtains. For this Rose House that wouldn't come together. And she had gotten so angry, with a seam going off, she'd kicked toward the window, her shoe had cut loose, and she'd screamed at her mistake, with the shoe sailing straight under the lifted sash and hitting the screen and bouncing back and knocking over a fortunately cheap vase. He remembered when he had fallen face forward in a cake once while carrying it, on just the day one of those bed-and-breakfast customers had been celebrating a huge birthday, with everything done up and perfectly lit by Laura's quick and somewhat architectonic imagination. And then for their first anniversary, he'd pinned on her corsage upside down. And then later, far gone on drugs and alcohol, he'd lost their car in a huge parking lot in Seattle, and he'd had to call someone up to help him find it.

Just like when they had been moving into a home above a ravine, and he'd tried rolling the truck's huge spare tire back up the ramp, because he'd taken it out to get more room, and the tire had gotten away from him, and started rolling down the cliff, rolling and rolling still, hitting a neighbor's wall, bouncing ten feet straight up into the air, and continuing to sail downward, crashing through trees and brush, and then dropping down hundreds and hundreds of feet, until landing splash in the lake below. Robb, following its trail, had finally had to flag two fishermen down and have them float it out to the other side. When he'd gotten to a pay phone at a little grocery store at last and was able to call home, Laura said, "You're where? With what?"

He couldn't keep it off his mind, either, the way they'd taken such ridiculous pictures at their wedding. And in December, too. The bridesmaids had been beautiful in their evergreen satin, with pine and holly bouquets, but the photographer had contorted all of the wedding party into all the postures of standard early sixties shots: Robb trying to sneak out the church door and the groomsmen pulling him back, feet forward; Laura showing the ladies her garter; Robb shaking his fist at Chester (the best man), to remind him not to lose the ring. The pictures were in a shoe box somewhere in Mrs. Molyson's flat—yes, and there was a picture of the marvelous ceremony in the cathedral sanctuary; it was somewhere there, too, that the dome had resonated with the organ. And then later on, during their wedding night, he and Laura had failed to connect in bed, and she, trying to roll over and sleep, had rolled straight on to what Robb had passed, saying, "Oh, there's something wet in here!" And Robb had roared with laughter, despite himself, and later that had been the family joke between them. "Oh there's something wet in here!"

The psychiatrist—who had been assigned to Robb—came in. Harangued him. Put him through the motions of testing for stiffness. Talked chemicals and milligrams, but Robb did not listen. Even under the layers and layers of what of what he'd been through in the past six months—under what he'd been through in his own life—he was getting better.

The door to his room became an open door into spring, and through it Bart came—hesitant, fearful, but still very loving. The icon at the back of Robb's mind told him to back off into a corner, and keep away from this man, for he brought danger, but the other side, which belonged to the landscape outdoors and to the inevitable motion of the day, said, "Just stand there."

"Well, your place is pill and bottle free," Bart said. "At last. I had to have a little help from your sister. Who showed up suddenly."

"You and Olivia were together?"

"For a short time."

The stiffness between them was overpowering.

"I never realized," Bart went on, "how much you had stashed away."

"It really was very bad," he answered.

More silence. It was as if he hadn't seen Bart since that last night when he had slept over at his house. He didn't know what else to say. "Did you bring my statue of Joseph?"

"Yes"—Bart pulled it from a backpack. "All intact and in tissue paper."

Robb, unwrapping it, caressed the wooden folds when it was handed across. He touched the circular loaf of bread, still amazed that he was no longer afraid of circles, of anything suggesting their shape. He sat there, as though meditating.

"Robb," Bart said, "do you remember the last sensible conversation we ever had together—back in October? When you came over to stay the night?"

"Yes."

"You mentioned Vietnam—that you'd been in it."

"Yes."

"You've never mentioned it since."

"No."

"Is it true?" Bart asked. "That's what I need to know. Were you actually there? Or was that your drug talking?"

"It is true," Robb said, "I was there."

And for a moment, it occurred to him that Bart might walk straight out the door because of this.

"For how long?" Bart asked.

"Two months."

"And are you getting help for it?"

"I am always getting help."

"No, I mean from other Vietnam vets, support groups."

"No," Robb answered. "Not yet."

Well, was this man going to run or not?

"They say you may get out in a week," Bart said at last.

"Yes."

"Do you want me to contact Dr. Oppenheimer, and let him know you may want to come back teaching?" Bart asked.

"Teaching?"

"Yes.

"Teaching?"

"Your job."

"I don't know. I haven't thought about it."

The fact was, he was having a hard time seeing Bart. In his mind, the bird came back to the window, and the bird was Bart, dressed in blue, like the pigeon, trying to get through the glass. How good this man looked—and smelling of cologne. Yes, yes, smells now were reaching him. Brut—exactly the wrong word for this man. And hair combed back, neat, pin-striped shirt, with tie, fresh from school. A man fully capable of standing in front of a classroom!

"It's just a matter," Bart said, "of getting some support, and then just suiting up, and getting back into the saddle."

At last Robb saw him completely. He approached him, a little nearer. "I haven't been good to you," he said suddenly. "I know I haven't. And I don't remember things too well. Just have faith, though, that I will, and that I will make things square between us."

The tears rushed to Bart's eyes. "Robb, there isn't anything you have to make up for." And took his icy hand.

Robb allowed it to be held, and somewhere, further along his mental corridors, he saw Laura and how Bart was like her in the early days. "The first thing I remember," he said, "was how I forced you . . . in Rose House. I'm sorry."

Bart, apparently startled, drew back—just so. "We don't need to mention that."

"Yes."

There was a void, there was a blankness now.

"Should I leave?" Bart asked, once again through the silence, and still holding his hand. "Do you like me here like this?"

Yes, yes, of course he did. The spring said so—his deepest tissue—like the emerging points of a rose, coming through the bark. "No," Robb said, just the same. "You've got to understand that right now I don't feel anything."

"I see"—and took back his hand.

Robb, however, felt the loss and said, "But you need to know that I don't mind either, if it helps you."

"Yes," Bart said ruefully, "I guess it does help. Robb—"

Robb took him in.

"I also have a confession to make."

"Go ahead."

Bart started to say something, but seemed to be stopped by the blankness of Robb's look. Robb knew the muscles of his face were as stiff as a poker. That wasn't him. It was just the wall inside coming out in his eyes, lips, cheeks—his countenance.

Bart looked down. "Maybe it's too much to confess right now. Maybe I don't want to give it up."

"All I can say," Robb answered, "Categorically, everything is forgiven. It has to be, in light of what I've done."

Categorically. That was a good word.

"Yes," he went on, "categorically I forgive you. You don't even have to tell me."

"Somehow," Bart said, laughing, despite himself, "that doesn't make me feel any better."

"How about if I took your hand again?" Robb asked.

"Take it."

Robb did so, and together they endured contact a few moments longer in the still room.

Twenty-one

To be honest, Bart had gone and seen Buddy the night before, and although they had not gotten very far, it still seemed to him like a complete act of cheating—and for the first time, too.

How he had justified it reminded him of how Robb must have talked himself into drugs and alcohol—he'd end up in the bar, sooner or later, no matter what the problem.

Only this time, it was himself, Bart.

Well, he'd gotten home, after the moments with Olivia, and had turned, over and over, in his mind, the prospect of following that hint from the stranger and going over and checking out the Starlight Theater. But what cold comfort that would be of a few naked wet bodies on the screen. That would simply never do.

But if he stayed home that wouldn't work, either. There'd been nothing on the answering machine from his family, and he simply couldn't call them right now. It would be forcing the issue, and screaming for comfort. And he was above that, at least for now.

And this March living room, going on April, with the mimosa tree mimicking living shapes on the wall with its new leaves, made him restless. There was a scent in the air like magnolia, and nights now did not die down early but seemed to be lit almost by the countless flowering trees outside. God I'm horny, he thought, feeling sorry for himself. And I've got to be up for rehearsal in the morning and up for Robb in the afternoon. Where can I go for a little R and R?

And then he remembered the second slip of paper, also in his breast pocket, from Buddy. A sense of obligation came over him to let the man know that Robb was indisposed—and a guess that this was his best "friend" calling—but underneath, in the garden of his head, tubers were starting to shoot out strange, carnivorous and bewitching purple flowers—so that if this Buddy was the lover of last October, this man would be as easy and horny as himself.

He was a little shaky when he lifted the receiver. He was also more than a little angry, too, as he remembered the moment when Robb had two-timed him that fall—when he'd come running back for succor and attention and guardianship (constant) the second the bottom had dropped out.

As he dialed the number and heard it go through, he realized, very uncomfortably and yet with some excitement, that he was more than capable of revenge. And he'd never thought so. He'd never thought he'd had it in him. Surprise.

"Is this a man named Buddy?"

The man said it was.

"Hi, my name is Bart Visconti. I'm a friend of Robb Jorgenson—"

The whole idea of Bart saying that he was just a friend made him cringe.

"Oh, yes, I'm glad you called."

"Robb has been sick and in the hospital, and he's not expected to be out for a while."

There was a pause of terror, Bart imagined, on the other end— so long, Bart knew this must be the man.

"May I ask," the man began, his voice tight, "may I ask what he has?"

"He was misprescribed some medication some time ago. It caught up with him, and he's having to have it taken care of."

"Was the medication for anything serious?" Buddy asked.

"Just a sleeping problem."

Huge relief on the other end. "Oh, I'm so happy it wasn't anything too serious."

"Yes, I'm relieved, too."

Now came the moment when the conversation absolutely refused to end itself. Bart felt a tug on the other end of the line as strong as a tuna's. Those nasty flowers had indeed arisen like purple cobras from their tubers and were now throwing off toxic pollen back and forth, in silence.

"Well, Bart, tell me what do you for a living?"

"I'm a teacher."

"Good, honorable profession," Buddy said. "You know some of my heroes have been teachers."

"Really."

"Yes, I'm a doctor by training, but you know, I could never have made my life's transition into my new calling—hot tubs—without a certain liberalness of mind, and that came from my teachers."

Great routine. One Bart was very familiar with. All he had to do was stay on the line. Pretty soon he was having his voice complimented, his vocation eulogized, along with, of course, his striking considerateness in calling in behalf of their mutual good friend, Robb.

I can't believe I'm doing this.

"This is going to sound awfully strange," Buddy finally led himself to say, "but lately I've been embarking on a new experiment."

"Oh yes?" Bart asked.

"My wife's out of my life again, and I've been calling upon my male friends to be my hug buddies. Do you know what they are?"

"Well, frankly, I know what fuck buddies are. But not this other thing."

"Well," Buddy went on, "I have what I have been able to identify as male touch starvation. I realize that I've been dying on the vine without it—"

So that was what you were doing with Robb. What a way to go!

"Anyway, lately, I've been asking men to come over and hold me for half a hour. That's it. And then I hold them, if they want it back. And I was wondering if you'd like to do that for me tonight. Especially because we have this mutual friend."

"Yes, as a matter of fact I would." And for a moment, the very sting of his skin, the very rawness of his nerves felt soothed. For the first time since October. "Only thing is," he concluded, "I want you to come here."

And so Buddy had agreed, had come.

But now, now that it was over, Bart, fresh from seeing Robb in the hospital, felt as though he had done incalculable wrong.

Well, they hadn't done much, really, he and Buddy, except stand facing each other at first in the living room, and look shy, at a loss for small talk. It was if they had a job to get done, and one of them was the handyman. Bart's skin felt raw again by now—as in those times when he had gone without Mariam for a while, or he had just been stung by some chance sarcasm from one of his friends.

"Tell me what I'm supposed to do," Bart had said. And he had been surprised by the sincerity of his tone—so different from when he had been called. "I'm totally foreign to this."

Buddy's beautiful shirted back was accentuated by the mimosa. "It's very simple," he said. "We just sit on your sofa, and take it from there."

Bart compiled, and Buddy settled into his lap. For such a big, muscular man, he actually folded up quite neatly. Like a piece of luggage. Bart, with his arms around him, recognized the perfect, chiseled shape of his body, beneath his shirt and pants, and then, almost at the instant of perception, found himself shrinking into shame. This was the body which Robb had been comparing to his!

Bart, sitting there, felt he was being paid back double, triple, quadruple for his sins. This was his wages for venturing outside the commitment.

Still, the man's body was an extraordinary gift. It was an extremely subtle one, beautifully fibered; once the warmth of the man had settled in long enough, Bart felt free to allow himself to wander with his hands. Every time Buddy would shift, his shoulders and chest would form new mountains and rivulets and crags—and yet they were so minute, it was as though Bart were pressing selected jewels on felt in a jeweler's shop, brought from the casement. Going over the edge of his trapezius was like rounding the cut face of a diamond, while sliding off, facet by facet, into the clavicle, the breastbone, and the rising ground of his pectorals.

Seated in this warmth, Bart found it impossible not to bend down and kiss Buddy's head, the way you would a baby's. It was just exactly the same. Holding a baby, you can't help but do that: a simple reflex. And the result was the same. Softness, and the most wonderful smell of hair. He seemed poised on a teeter-totter, right between fulfillment and desire. He did not slip into either, but was on the very pivot. Or was it that the fulfillment exactly met his desire, and this was the first time he had experienced such a thing? When he had been with Robb, lust had frequently carried one of them off like a football, leaving the other stranded on the sidelines. But here he was allowed to settle into the magnetism, and allow his own to rise, slowly, so that together they formed a continuous field.

Never, never had this happened before—that he had begun with something so completely foul, like those purple tubers, and have it turn into something beautiful. So often it had been the reverse. Bliss, then disaster. What was he to do with it?

Buddy's hand was now gripping his, and he could see the blue veins rising, in the wrist and fingers. "You're giving me such comfort," Buddy said, as his hand pressed. "My energy supplies were all but gone. The other night I tried calling a male prostitute, and when he came over, he thought I was nuts, when I told him all I wanted to buy was a hug. But this is all I want, all I want. The life is coming back."

And Bart for the first time believed him. What started out as plan for a quick one, turned out to be this. And the strange thing was, he couldn't tell if he was being unfaithful or not. What did this count as? And why did it seem to heal all the sores inside him, too?

"I think my half hour's up," he thought he heard Buddy say. "Can I oblige you the way you did me?"

"Yes, yes, please," he heard himself answer. "Only—let's take off our shirts first."

And so they did, and he felt Buddy's massive arms—they were massive, because he saw they were massive—over him, enclosing, warming—with the heat taking him back to Mariam's massage, and his body responding like a tapestry, or like a pattern of iambs, but only this time, there was skin and muscle against his, answering back, fiber for fiber, and the edges of Buddy's very sensitive fingers were finding the diamond shapes of his bones, his sinew, with Buddy saying, "Beautiful back, beautiful arms," and Bart saying, "No, no, not like yours, not like Robb's—I wish there were more for you, but this is all, this is it—I don't work out," and feeling wrapped in tears, he went on speaking, as though speaking to the body he wished he had, in a dream.

"There's something"—Buddy's hands were moving all over him—"there's something I heard from the leader of my Vet group—"

"Squeeze me harder," Bart said. "Squeeze me until I crack."

"Do you want to hear what he said?"

"Yes."

"He said"—squeezing—"'tissue needs tissue.' And that's all that matters."

And with that came the thought, overwhelming to Bart, that he was made of just this—tissue—and that his very skin had been crying out for its counterpart ever since Robb had closed him off. And there came also, in the aftermath, the recollection of when he had, as a child, an adolescent, stared straight into a mirror, naked, trying to understand the longing which none of his friends seemed to share—of wanting, like Alice, to step straight through, and meet the stranger, and enfold him in a caress, contact answering contact, just as was happening now.

The time was up—Buddy was up—but before Bart could even get completely off the sofa, his partner was coming up from behind and, burying his head in his back, was saying, "You're so obliging and tender. I've been dumped, dropped, and forgotten by almost every hug buddy I've tried, and you were here. Right here. Can we do this again?"

And Bart could only answer, "Of course."

Twenty-two

Bart wasn't sure what he should do now. Buddy, obviously thinking they had done the most harmless and natural thing in the world, had wanted to know where Robb was, so that he might go and visit, and Bart had not wished to tell him—since this man would be visiting his lover with some dread secret between them.

But dread—and a secret—only to him.

"I guess I have to tell you," Bart said, "that Robb and I are sort of partners. Or at least we were."

"I figured as much." And Buddy smiled. "That's O.K."

But it isn't with me, Bart wanted to tell him.

But Buddy had clearly seen what they had done as something on a par with a handshake. So why shouldn't he go see Robb? And with that plan in mind—and the address of the hospital in his hand—he had at last—after several fierce hugs—disappeared behind the mimosa.

Staring out the window, now, with both school and the visit to the hospital over, Bart felt alone as he never had before. He had yet another night ahead of him. Alone and with the spring, which was growing now, like ferns in a hothouse, like those purple tubers.

But someone was knocking at the door. Whoever it is, Bart thought hopefully, he's my answer.

But instantly he heard a car pull away and saw his brother standing there alone, big as life.

"Dad had to come into town," Daniel said, his white cane beside him. "So I told him to drop me off. We saw the light in the window."

Bart was so hurt seeing the car disappear, he hardly knew how to answer. And besides, he felt raw from Buddy. "Couldn't Dad stay?" Bart asked.

"He had to go out down to the district and talk delivery with some guy."

"Please come in." And automatically, he took Daniel's arm.

"I like the way you've got things arranged," Daniel said, smiling in his blind, inimitable way. Like a lion, yawning with his head turned.

"How would you know?" Bart asked.

That smile again. "I can tell. Every time I come."

Instinctively, he grasped his favorite chair.

"Can I get you something?"

"No," Daniel answered quickly. "Dad will be back too soon for that."

Bart, sitting across, just stared into the blind face, and felt the full force of his mother's absence, too.

"Mom and Dad tell me you just came out to them on the weekend."

"That's right," Bart answered.

The lion again—and a slap on the table (how he knew the table was there, Bart couldn't figure. It was a recent change.) "Damn! The one time I'm gone and you visit, you come out, and Jesse's there and I'm not."

"Nothing could have been more undramatic," Bart said, with some self-pity again. "You didn't miss much."

Daniel smiled, and with just a touch of malice. "And with you in drama, too."

"Daniel, I'm not at the stage where it's funny yet. Mom and Dad view it as about as much a catastrophe as your blindness."

"Tell me about it. I've been hearing a lot from them on that score lately," Daniel told him.

"So why are you here?" Bart asked, piqued and nettled because of the day.

Daniel waited. Obviously, he did not want to have this question put to him. He rocked a little, and tried to contain himself. "I was so moved by your courage," he said. "For as long as I knew, I never thought you'd have the fortitude to say so."

"How long have you known?" Bart asked.

"Since we were kids."

Bart had always felt that Daniel, being blind, had been gifted with a second sight into all things—except one, his, Bart's, being gay. In this, Bart (and he only realized this now) had been sure he'd been given special cover, and he could wave this "obvious" right under Daniel's nose, and have it go unnoticed. Maybe he had given himself that false assurance not just with Daniel but with many others. Somewhere, he felt a huge wall dropping—and not just in the "now," but in the past, too. He wondered, his fear rising, that if Daniel had known all along, maybe everyone else did, too—for example, the people at school, his students. The sense of vulnerability was coming in and taking over, like a sneak thief.

Meanwhile Daniel's face had changed.

"But I have to say, too," he went on, "that I've felt damned hurt that you never told me, that I've been waiting all this time, and then when the moment comes, I get it second, even third hand. It was Jesse who told me."

"I couldn't tell you," Bart answered, "when I never thought you'd understand."

"Understand what?" Daniel asked.

"What it's like to be different."

With that, Daniel held out both his hands. "Sure, sure—I'd have no understanding of that. Only years and years of being in blind school, years and years of being led about like a pet dog. And now I've got this overgrown white wand like the Fairy Godmother in Cinderella. Who were you waiting for to tell, Harvey Milk?"

"I don't know," Bart answered. "I kept coming to you with questions. Do you remember?" And suddenly it flashed on him that he had told Daniel once. "Do you remember when I was ten, and I was looking at those Life Magazine Books on Prehistory, and I came to you, and said I was afraid I was gay, because I was so attracted to the cavemen. Do you remember?"

Neither of them was smiling.

"Do you remember? I thought that the Neanderthals were hunky? And you just said, 'Well, Bart, you probably *are* homosexual,' and went on talking about something else."

Daniel just sat there. "Oh no, did I really say that?"

"Yes."

"Some compassion, right?"

"I'm not criticizing you for it," Bart told him. "You were only fifteen yourself," Bart said. But he did criticize him for it. For sure he judged him for it. "I'm only saying that I tried to tell you, and now that I think about it, there were other times, too."

Daniel was dropping tears. "I don't know how we got off on this—the past." He paused. "Yes, I do, I got us off. But now I'm ending it. The only point is—the only reason I came to see you—is to tell you I love you unconditionally. It doesn't matter to me who you are. You're my brother."

It wasn't the kind of "unconditional" Bart had been waiting for, but he was going to take what he could get. No doubt about that. In fact, he came over, and took Daniel's hands. As he did, he recognized the enormous gulf which had been between them, not because of sex but because of the huge favoritism in the family— for Daniel. Now Daniel's hands went up to Bart's face, and traced out a recognition, and Bart knew it was only possible for him to bear this because of Buddy. "I love you, too, Daniel," he said. "I always have."

"Do you really?" Daniel asked. "How interesting—because I feel so little of that for myself."

"Maybe we'll just have to be stand-ins for each other for a while," Bart answered.

"Yes." Daniel's tears had stopped. He opened his watch and felt the Braille. "Dad should be here any minute."

The same intolerable silence—of Robb's hospital room.

"It'd be nice," Daniel said, standing up, "if you came up and saw me sometime." He had even put a little of Mae West in his voice.

"You still working at the library?" Bart asked.

It was a family myth, shared by all, that Daniel actually had a job. "Yes. But my hours are flexible."

"I will, Daniel, you know that."

Their father's car did, at last, pull up. Bart, standing there, felt he might pass out from hurt, seeing his father stare straight into the windshield and not move a muscle until it was obvious that Daniel had approached the car. He felt the urge to run down and demand that his father say something, but, again, he realized he had been doing this all of his life, and that nothing had come of it, so why try it now? As the car pulled away, he turned again into the overpowering scent of the room and of spring, and as he did—as though in answer to his prayers—he heard the car turnaround in middle of the street and come back.

Feeling grateful—relieved—he waited for his father to come running up and hug him—he had changed his mind—but instead, he saw that it was only Daniel, crawling out again and tapping his way back. "Here, Buddy," he said, "I forgot to give you this. A letter from Mom."

The door closed once more, and Bart, feeling that the return had spoiled their almost perfect parting, sat down in the living room.

Twenty-three

"Dear Bart,

"I've decided to write to you because your father finds it impossible to speak to you right now. You know what loyalty means to him, and so I've worked it out that it would be all right to write you a letter. Daniel feels otherwise, and that meeting with you is the only right thing to do. We talked about that. So I'm giving him this.

"I love you, but I can't condone what you're doing. Your father strongly feels that you are putting yourself at risk in a whole lot of ways, not only professionally but also physically and emotionally. People get hurt when they turn gay. I've seen a lot more of life than you probably think I have, and I have seen it time and time again. When I was going to school, there was a whole nest of lesbians close to where I lived, and I saw them crying and hurting all the time. One of them was my best friend. Eventually she committed suicide. I never got over that, and her parents never did either, and I knew I had learned an important lesson from afar, should I be ever visited by those feelings, or anyone in my family.

"When you were growing up, we tried to let you go your own way. Especially with your friends and your theater. I tried to support you in every aspect I knew. And there was always Daniel to look after. And the store. We simply couldn't do everything for everyone. I suppose that there were times we suspected, and there were times when we were bitterly disappointed that you didn't bring any girls home, whose company we might have enjoyed. By then, most other parents our age were starting to look forward to the prospect of their kids getting engaged or at least going steady—to show them that their children had at last learned from their example what a good marriage is. Even some of my friends had grandbabies to brag about.

"But I knew that you and Daniel were different. I just didn't know how different in your case. Bart, with the store and your father and Daniel's special needs, there are times when I could use a little lift in my life. Something to look forward to. And things have gotten especially tight and difficult recently. Especially financially. I have been praying for a way out. And then when this news came, it was sort of the last straw. I worry so much—about your health and AIDS, about you losing your job, and I simply find it overwhelming at times, even to think about.

"Please, Dear, reconsider. You're still young, with your whole life ahead of you. Think about whether this is really what you are. Your father and I will support you. And I think this letter should give us all time to think. Nothing has to be decided that we can't change. And no harsh words have been spoken! Not one! I know that a lot of this has to do with being true to yourself, and I admire you for it, but try to consider also the question of stability. And if you do, we will never have to speak any harsh words.

"Let me know. You can write or call. But if Dad answers, don't expect him to speak to you. He's taking it harder than you'll ever know, and that's something which exhausts me so much. I fear he'll go back to his heavy drinking. So if he answers, just ask for me very quickly, and *don't* try to engage him in an argument. If you can't do it for his sake, do it at least for mine. Or don't call at all until you can do it calmly.

"Thank you. And take care.

"Love, Mom."

Bart just sat there.

Then, without another thought, he went straight to the bedroom for the address of the Starlight Theatre, and within minutes was out and driving at top speed.

The theater arrived very quickly, pumping light through the darkness. "XXXXX" was in its windows, and for a moment Bart didn't care whether it was straight porno or not—he was so far gone—but when he made it inside, he knew this was an altogether different place. There was an actual concession stand in the lobby, with no sleaze mags or sex toys, and the actual seating area was clean and well-lit. Also the men sitting waiting for the movie to begin were not only well dressed (not at all unusual), but were actually sitting together in twos, threes, and fours, and talking in a non-covert friendly way.

The place darkened, and Bart, feeling himself coming to rest like an exhausted, grateful top (grateful because of the darkness), saw "Men Touching Series" on the screen, and would have thought he had turned into the wrong theater, if the title hadn't immediately followed, "Episode One, Footballers."

It was a locker room story—almost a silent movie, with just a few lines of dialogue—and Bart had seen many of these before, but this one was strange, very strange. It took at least an hour for the characters to be developed before even one piece of clothing came off, and even then it was upstairs behind closed doors of their apartment that it happened. One of the players had just taken his shirt off, when, finding he was attracted, he had gone over to his friend, who was dressed in a Kelly green sweater. They engaged in a kiss. Kelly (for that was his name) was caught completely off guard at first, but then the camera did an extraordinary close-up on his fingers as they went up and down Martin's naked rib cage.

And then. Cut to the gridiron, and football practice. And massive Kelly lifting Martin high into the air and about to throw him, when suddenly the recollection of the fingers returns to him, and he, to the coach's fury, quietly and gently puts Martin back down on the ground. Looks of puzzlement from the few fans watching the practice.

Back to the apartment. This time both of the men have their shirts off. Close-up (extreme) of hands on Martin's neck, and the slow removal of his pants, and the eagerness of Kelly's mouth on his buttocks. A sense of surrender comes into Martin's face, and the massive legs part, as Martin unzips his zipper, and a huge tool, nicely condomed and lubed, enters the man with the same ease and tenderness as at the football practice. As Kelly begins to sway into him, the camera backs up, and shows the two naked men as though in a Grecian frieze, although living and mobile, too, and as Martin begins to peak, the film suddenly shifts to a close-up of his face, now with the stadium as backdrop—his face above the shoulder pads as he is about to catch the ball. With every return to his rising, surrendering naked body, caressed by the nearness of cuming, his face becomes like the one back at practice—and the pictures are interchanged—back and forth, with Kelly's face also caught in the same interwoven ballet, as though the film were a garment itself.

Bart, overwhelmed by the film, was also overwhelmed remembering the stranger back in the porno store—realizing that he'd been absolutely right. This was exactly what he was looking for. Had seen before in that magazine. As the film ended, and the two young men were seen walking off hand-in-hand into the campus sunset, Bart couldn't wait to see what was next.

"Episode Two. Red Hot Vets."

It was a pretty complex frame, with an opening, a closing, and a flashback. Two hunky older men were seen skiing down an icy slope; with every "whosh," a spray of snow would hit the camera. The time was evening, and the camera embraced their faces— rough, muscular, craggy. Suddenly there was a cut to a cabin, and the men were sitting by the fire, in their Pendletons, holding hands. "Remember the time?" "The way that lamp swings reminds me—"

And then they were back in Vietnam. A wonderfully studio Vietnam. Innocuous bombs were going off, and the two men, Ken and Jeff, marching through manufactured mud, suddenly stop, and survey the ravaged, violated, and outraged land.

Ken, the usual blonde and romantic, turns to his friend and says, "Let's get the fuck out of here."

Jeff, the dark and bearded one, nods, and points to a several hills in the distance, clearly borrowed from Hawaii. As the camera follows them, mists part, sounds of guns die, and a hut appears in a meadow. It is a Vietnamese family. Before knocking, Jeff throws his gun into a ditch, and Ken frees himself of all his lethal gear, as well.

Then the door opens, and the family, as though notified by telephone that their favorite nephews were coming, greets them heartily, pumping their hands, and giving bows of blessing. They sit down on their heels to plates of rice and fish, while the camera embraces each Vietnamese face, as well as Ken and Jeff's arms and necks, now accentuated by A-frame undershirts.

The meal over, the family shows them a room at the back of the hut, with an open window facing the meadow. With the twilight coming through, the men, stripped to their dog tags, embrace each other in the darkness—but with the lighting as such that every outline is visible on their bodies.

"That was the first time we ever made it."

And the voice from the present suddenly puts them back to the ski shack, with the two men, their age much more apparent now, in bed. Blonde Ken, his shoulders much more massive, is reading his poetry. Jeff, propped on his side, is poring over his manual on power tools.

"Yes," he says above his reading. "That's when we decided to desert."

And suddenly, the film was right back in Vietnam, where the love scene left off. The two men were joined, and Jeff was pumping into him. Every muscle was visible now on his back, as Ken yielded again and again. There were close-ups of Jeff's beard as it searched the crevices of Ken's smooth back—down on him until he returned to his pumping, like a horse at steady gallop.

Soon the couple was out-of-doors in the evening meadow, hand-in-hand, Adam and Adam, with the audience watching from an abandoned window in the house. They returned to their intercourse, Ken this time being the one to do the mounting and imprinting a subtler, more poetic rhythm upon his friend's body.

Dissolve back to the present and the snow. The kerosene lamp swings. Ken is now resting his head comfortably upon his friends' aged but still muscular chest. "How wonderful we knew that that was time to give up the War," Ken says, his face covered by the flickering.

"That family gave us our bridal night," Jeff says. "They must have known."

And the scene sways again, as Jeff mounts the older Ken—with the covers falling off, and with the snow peaks framed in the window, the tanned body gently lifts the slightly more slender one, adds a pillow, before slowly entering again and again, in time with the swinging kerosene lamp. "And Jeff," Ken says, "it's just as good now as it was then . . ."—with the screen splitting in half, the younger joined bodies on one side (in memory—a Vietnam sunset), the older on the other (American snowscape twilight).

There was a general sigh as the houselights came back on. Bart found he couldn't move. He thought, for a moment, that he had completely lost the pain of his mother's letter—like an injury that suddenly and miraculously goes away—but with the rising light of the theater, he found all the pleasure gone, and instead, and with some malice, there was a memory. Of a Father's Day card he had carefully India-inked years ago, which said (front): "Amid the myriad water lilies on the lake," and (inside), "I stood watching with Dad." It had been his fifteen-year-old attempt to recall a time when, even removed from another Father's Day years before, they had stood together and enjoyed something. Also to use the word he'd just discovered. "Oh nice," his father had said (as he had probably said when they had seen the water lilies), not remembering. "Very nice." But a few hours later, his mother had come to him and announced, "Your father was very moved by your card. He just couldn't say so. He's in the bedroom now reading his card."

Why did he have to remember this now? All from his mother. And as his anger arose, the letter flooded back upon him.

If he didn't get up and going right now, he would do something he'd regret later. He'd try to make the first man here who was handy—and they were everywhere—milling in the aisles and in the lobby, which he was now freeing himself from.

But out on the sidewalk, a hand thudded on his shoulder, and there was Andrew, from his Men's Group, the one who'd been after him for years.

"So caught you with your pants down, so to speak."

"I don't know," Bart said, after a familiar, rubber-stamp embrace. Cold, Collisional. "I found the films to be very—"

"Sweet," Andrew said. "That'll be the last of them, I bet. Not enough clientele."

For some reason, Bart felt his sense of abandonment increase. "Not going to be showing any more? The Director was absolutely brilliant."

"Brilliant? How?"

Andrew's persistent skepticism was not charming now. Unable to digest the hurt of his mother's letter, and feeling exposed and vulnerable out on this street (the people in their automobiles always slowed down to see who had the nerve to emerge from that theater), Bart could hardly think of an answer. But it was pretty good anyway. "It made the men into real people."

And, smiling, Andrew merely cuffed him on the shoulder, and sailed off into the distance.

But the evaporation put him back into Father's Day again and out on the lily pond—and back in his own fifteen-year's old bedroom, penning out the card ("myriad," "myriad," "myriad"), hoping for something, anything in the way of a response. But with his mother as oracular priestess (now he was turning away from the lights of the marquee, towards his car), moving in and out, the priestess, and in between, what chance was there of any communication? It was interesting—it was crazy, the family's favoritism for Daniel included himself, that is, he favored Daniel over himself, too. And what surprise was that? There had been nothing in the family, absolutely nothing, to indicate he had value, other than what he could help Daniel with, or what he could put together, could ink and eke out on that little bedroom desk. And this time for Dad.

To step, bodily, towards his father, was to create the mirage that Andrew always created. One motion toward him meant one more particle would be gone. Invasion of the Body Snatchers. The Corporal form known as Father, known as Andrew, was gone by the time you got there.

Bart smiled over it now, even though he didn't think it was so damn funny, really. Approaching his father and trying to date Andrew. You got your courage up, maybe started thinking of a little gift, like a card, or some flowers, and you started nearing this man who seemed to have spent his whole life getting ready to be "asked." Yes. Andrew worked out, bought beautiful clothes, kept his hair perfect, and hung out with the smoothest men, so that he was just begging to be asked. But just ask him—just try! Would go crazy if you did. Become all a-twitter, shower you with a thousand busy excuses, and then tell all his friends just what you've done, just to be sure you were known as needy.

And his father? Gone in a puff if you approached. "Nice. Very nice." And now enter Mother coming around the corner with her oracular news that he really was touched. Well, if he was so fucking touched, why did it take her to say it?

Twenty-four

Robb was told his daughter had been asking about him. And he was relieved to know someone had told her about Tara. He had thought, perhaps, she would never want to see him again after hearing that.

However, she did. And she finally got clearance from her mother to visit. It would be the day after tomorrow, she told him. During visiting hours. And only three days away from his being discharged.

Now, it was getting very clear to him that the staff was worried about how would do once he was on the outside. Very worried. Because he simply did not talk at the A.A. meetings they were taken to. Everybody else seemed to be healing so beautifully when they got there. But Robb had stayed shut up like a clam.

But now that Valerie was within two days of visiting, he got scared and started sharing. All of a sudden. Out of nowhere, he opened his mouth. It was slow, frightening, and laborious but he started talking. "I lived in a house," he said, breathless, terrified. "And that house was mine. And I had a wife and a stepdaughter, in that beautiful house, and I lost everything. And now my stepdaughter is coming to see me. It was because of me that her dog got killed."

And just after one A.A. meeting, they had gone and sat on the lawn in front of Jutland General. The little fishing village, turned Seattle district a century ago, now came to him in waving lines— the meandering, unfocused sidewalk, the masts of the boats in the distance, above the uncertain restaurant roofs, bobbing like restless needles. One time, on a field trip, they had walked the nearby docks on Shilshole Bay, and Robb had been scarcely able to keep his balance. And now, even though they were back on solid ground, things still felt as though they were on a float, out in the water.

Nevertheless, he was determined to face Valerie the way he had every bird at the window. Yes. He would still stay put, no matter what, and when he heard his name called, he simply thought, "Well, she's come early, and I simply must tough it out, too."

But it wasn't Valerie. It was a man introduced to him as Cliff. They sat in the lounge, with the TV off.

"I went through Treatment here, too," the man said. "And I also was in Vietnam."

"Oh," Robb said. And looked at his own dumbfounded expression in the glass plate over a poster. Shaded out somewhat by the picture itself. "Get a hit of endorphins," the poster said. And two men were shown running in silhouette. He used to do that.

"So," Cliff said. "What's your time here been like?"

"Rough," Robb said, and almost smiled; it was such an understatement.

Cliff lit a cigarette, and the way the smoke sketched up the air was reminiscent of a forties restaurant, in the movies. A rendezvous.

"It seems to me you're doing just fine," Cliff said. "But you probably don't know it."

"That's right. I don't," Robb said.

"Feeling kind of rocky?"

"Yes. Like I am still walking on quicksand."

"It passes. Don't worry. It passes. Before I was through here, I went up one hall and down the other, apologizing to everybody."

"I've already done that," Robb said, smiling at last. "Twice."

"Feels weird, doesn't it?" Cliff said.

"Yes—like I can't help myself. And then the medication they've put me on—"

"Makes you feel stiff and—"

"Blue," Robb said.

Cliff smiled, pleased with recognition. "Exactly. Good old Mr. Eskimo Iceberg, walking around like he's got a steel rod down his back. Like that's what Vietnam gave him."

"That's it all right," Robb said.

Now they were both stiff. Robb struggled to think of the next thing to say. Suddenly—and of course—he was very aware of Cliff, who was quite lean, very precisely veined. And behind Ichabod Crane spectacles.

"I'm here to say," Cliff said at last, "that if you want me to take you to an A.A. meeting when you get out, I'd be happy to. And then there's this other thing I go to at the Vietnam Vet Center, which is just getting started."

"I think that's a little beyond me right now."

"The Center or the A.A. meetings?"

"The Center. I'll try the Meetings outside."

"Then here's my number"—and the precisely veined hand handed it across.

For a moment, Robb felt like weeping, and he couldn't say why.

He stood up, as they shook hands. "Take care, and don't forget to call me," and then the room was silent again, and Robb was left with only the smoke.

After that, he didn't know where the time went. A nurse came in and quizzed him about what day it was, and he flunked again. He wondered if that meant he would have to stay longer. And with that thought, he wondered if this might be a good time to call the minister he had been seeing, and ask him to come and bless his exit from this place, but then he reconsidered.

But then she was at the door, arriving. All at once. She was in an outfit that was pink and white. She was all stripes. And she put out her hand, and hugged him. A candy striper. Valerie.

His eyes filled, and he remembered again, as during that moment on the bridge—looking down—that he was still capable of crying. Despite the medication. Despite the way he had disgraced himself these many months and years.

And she seemed to bring autumn with her. That day in the park. What was its name? Holding her, and thinking he'd crack, he thought it would be a good idea—a good sign of his recovery—if he could remember the precise and difficult name. Chetzemoka. There it was.

"They wouldn't let me see you for a long time," Valerie said. "In fact, Mom is waiting in the Gift Shop downstairs. I don't have long."

"It doesn't matter," he said. "I've seen you. It's enough to make me feel you've forgiven me."

"Forgiven you? Of course. But for what?"

"For Tara. I forgot about her. And I'm sorry."

"She came back," she said. "Mother called the pound the night Mrs. Molyson called. She was there. I have her."

How was that possible? He must have dreamed he heard Tara was hit.

But it was clear Valerie didn't want to talk about it.

Instead, she was about to say something else. She looked older—much, much older. And very frightened, too, apparently, that he looked so different. How red her lipstick looked!

"All this," she said quickly—as though she had been allowed only one minute—"put it behind you. It's over."

"Will you let me say one other thing?" he asked. "I must mention the past one more time."

"What is it?" she asked.

"Please forgive me for fighting in front of you. For the bad fight I had with your Dad."

"He's gone now, anyway."

How could that be? But he must stay on the point. "I was wrong. And it feels good to say so."

She looked frightened. She wasn't used to hearing him admit he was wrong. And he saw himself in the poster glass again. Darkened but intent. And he knew this wasn't the answer. Or least—this wasn't the way to do it.

"I forgive you," she said. "And Dad, I have to leave. I've got to get to my own volunteering back up in Port Townsend. At the hospital up there."

"I love you," he said, as she got up, parting from his hands.

"I do, too," she said haltingly.

And he felt almost complete, almost square with the world, when a nasty voice said, "But she doesn't know you're a Vet. Wait until she finds out. Or that you're gay."

But he couldn't drop any more on her. Not now. This was enough. He knew he'd been selfish with his amends already.

And with that, the corrosive voice went away, and he knew he had spoken to himself in a manner that was altogether new. For just one split second, he accepted her presence there with him, loving him, as a gift. They hugged.

"I will write to you," she said, parting. "I will send you a card. Easter is coming up."

"Thank you," he said. "I'll wait for it, and I'll cherish it. God bless you."

And left alone again, he felt the presence of light again. He saw that past autumn once more, with her in her cordovan-striped uniform, and the trees lifting gold over the entire park—there it was, right in front of him, his own precinct, individuated, sole—now that the hideous clouds of drugs and alcohol had been removed. And that uniform, that smile—which had just been with him—her touch was beyond almost anything he could bear or acknowledge.

Like the bird at the window.

Twenty-five

The day Robb was to get out, Bart was not at all in a good mood.

There had been complications. No doubt about that, he thought. And complications was a nice word. Robb's sister had been adamant (that seemed to be her style) about Robb not going back to the rooms at Mrs. Molyson's. Robb was not capable of taking care of himself, and she was going to see to it that he moved in with them—meaning her and her psychiatrist husband. Who was a total pain in the ass. But Robb would not hear of going and staying in Magnolia (who would?—just think of being psychoanalyzed in stereo, a counselor on one side, a psychiatrist, no less, on the other), and Bart had heard that house was like being under lock and key, it was so burglar-proof.

Nevertheless, Bart had become resigned to letting them have their way—what he was now calling the Dynamic Duo—when all of a sudden things went completely weird. Bart had actually convinced Robb to "play along"—to try humoring Olivia and Chester by staying with them a couple of days, and then going back to his rooms. But he no sooner had done that, when Olivia called him yet again, and, apologizing profusely, said that it was impossible now that Robb stay with them, and that she would have to appeal to *him*, and his enormous patience and understanding, to have Robb stay at his place until further notice.

Immediately Bart felt panicked; he had never even considered that. And although throughout all their days of seeing each other on weekends way back, Bart had longed, almost like the old-time "kept woman," for the day when his man would move in, he realized that'd be the last thing he'd want now.

"You must understand," Olivia had gone on, "that Robb is likely to drink or use at the drop of a hat. He must have companionship, and constant stimulation. And someone needs to see that he gets to the Meetings."

"Somebody else is doing that already," Bart said. "And I don't see why it's my responsibility to babysit. Robb is a big boy. He's taken care of himself for forty years."

"But not sober, not clean. We're talking about a seventeen-year addiction here."

"Olivia, I've got a play to direct—we open next week—I've got family issues of my own—and"—he was about to say the AIDS lady is just around the corner again but stopped himself—"and I've got my ongoing gay life, to be frank with you. I'm not sure Robb even considers himself gay now, and so it's not as though we're really partners anymore."

"But that's him at this moment. Who knows what he'll be next week."

"Exactly. But you came into this movie late—I've had to deal with his antics, from the start—where he started experimenting with going off those pills over a year ago. I've been jerked all over the fucking map—excuse me, but it's true—and I'm not about to lose my privacy now over him."

"Let's just give it a week. Just a week, Bart, and then we'll re-evaluate, and assess what's going on. Would you just agree to that?"

And aware that guilt was motivating her—as it certainly was him, he capitulated.

So now, on the day Robb was getting out of Treatment, Bart was pissed as hell.

So why, Bart asked himself, am I on my way to the florist before picking this asshole up? Because he was—he was actually stopping in, and buying some long-stemmed roses after work, and then of course there was the Hallmark Card Shop, which was always a slippery place for him, because he could easily enter with just an idea of "kind thoughts," and end up with a whole goddamn package of cards which neon-flashed "everlasting love."

Nevertheless, he was riding the elevator up to the Unit with flowers and card and even a little Hallmark love teddy bear in hand. It scared him to think of how much he was feeling at this moment, and all marked by a lot of sentimental fluff. Robb was waiting in his room, with his luggage all packed, and when they met in the presence of the nurse, Bart felt that she was smiling to herself over the obviousness of this courtly and fawning flake.

In fact, he was almost rude to her, as she signed Robb out downstairs, and Robb paid the last of his $8,000 tab.

"I'm busted," Robb said at last. "Flat broke. But I made it. And I didn't think I would."

"I've got dinner all made for when we get home. And Olivia's coming later on, once she gets done with some counseling work she's doing at the University."

"It will be nice to see her."

Without warning—and with nastiness—the slow envy and fury started taking over. What the hell had Robb said, anyway? Nothing. Except something nice about his sister. But why was Robb thinking it would be especially good to have Olivia come waltzing in his, Bart's, house? He, after all, had been the one to pick up the emotional check on every one of Robb's attempted re-entries back into the world. And he didn't even have the assurance he had any tangible relation to Robb anymore, anyway. If Robb was still planning to be a non-gay monk (as if that was possible) for the rest of his life, no wonder he looked forward to seeing just his sister.

With these sulky thoughts in mind—and after a basically silent ride home—Bart rather meanly took up his share of the luggage, and put it in the den, which had been altered back, overnight, into a second bedroom. A foldout bed from Abbey Rents rounded out the picture.

Carefully—and as instructed by one of the nurses—he took out Robb's "mediset" along with the three bottles of pills, and checked to be sure his mate had done his "Monday, Tuesday, Wednesday, Thursday, Friday, Saturday, Sunday" properly. The nurse had assured him that this overseeing need only be for a week or so, once Robb got his head screwed on right —provided he went to the Meetings and Aftercare (he must go to the Meetings and Aftercare). Bart still wanted to say, That isn't my responsibility!, but still held his tongue, and now, of course, and once again, that steam was leaking straight out his ears, as he slammed the last of the bottles on the dresser.

But here was dinner. Bart put the flowers in a vase (the flowers which Robb had not even mentioned), and lit the candles. Robb ate very slowly and deliberately, Robot #44357, and Bart was so caught up in the strangeness of it—he had not seen Robb eat since October—that he was hardly aware of what he was eating himself.

About six-thirty there was a bang at the door—and it was so much earlier than the time Olivia had named, he thought it might be Daniel again—or, possibly, just possibly, their father. He had heard nothing since his mother's letter, and he'd been so caught up in the present drama, he had not found himself collected enough to answer.

But when he went to the door, he found, to his extreme disappointment, that it was Olivia, and that she was at her worst.

"Well, I'm so glad to see that everything is under control," she said.

Nevertheless, she carried with her a sack of groceries and other sundry items. "But I just thought I'd bring along a few things which helped me when I got out of Treatment."

Almost as a Mexican standoff, Bart stayed where he was, and refused to take them from her hands.

But that didn't faze her. She just went to the kitchen, and started putting the stuff in the cupboards herself.

"That's very thoughtful of you," Robb said.

"Thanks," she went on. "And I've also made out a list of where the Meetings are, and how you can get to Aftercare while you're not in them. And"—she held up a second slip of paper—"I've designed a schedule with the nurse about when you're supposed to take your three kinds of pills. This should take care of you for the first week, until you're ready to go back and teach. By the way"—she held up a third thing—"I've talked with Dr. Oppenheimer at the college, and there's a note here from him encouraging you to come back next Monday when you're ready."

"Thank you," Robb said.

Olivia smiled, and then just stood there, waiting to be invited to dinner.

Robb did so, and Bart, flaming, ladled out the stew that was very, very deliberately wine-free, as per Olivia's instructions.

"I so appreciate this, Bart," she said.

Bart did not answer—and at last she got the message.

Dead silence.

Robb looked at both of them in dismay.

"I'm going to leave the two of you alone," Bart said, eating his food as quickly as he could. "I'm going to leave the two of you alone in just a few minutes. I'm busting my butt on these rehearsals—we go into full-dress in just a few days—and I need to hit the sack early. I've got another 7:40 in the morning. And I have some last-minute paperwork to do."

Olivia's eyes moistened in the reflected candle flames. "I feel as though I must be interfering."

"You're not," Robb said.

Bart stayed significantly silent.

"Am I, Bart?" Olivia asked.

"Of course you are!" Bart shouted. "This was supposed to be our first time together in five months."

Olivia looked like a wounded deer, and Bart felt terrible. "I'm sorry," she said, "I knew I should have found a way to bring Robb home with me. But I'm here to make an apology to both of you. Chester wouldn't hear of it—or better, he just wouldn't cooperate in making the house safe. And I felt so bad about it."

"Don't you see, Olivia," Bart said, not listening to her apology—and she cowered at the sound of her name—"Don't you see that it doesn't matter whose house he stays at? What matters is that he's allowed to do these things for himself."

"Yes, yes"—she shut her eyes. "Yes."

She sighed. Untied the apron she had stolen from the kitchen. "I don't know what I've been thinking of."

"It's all right," Bart said, catching himself up at last. "We've all been on edge lately. Pushed to the limit." He considered the backyard now. Its beautiful green March mist. That he had worked in just recently. "Things should settle out in about a week. Depend on it."

Then he became aware of Robb, as though they had been talking about him in his absence. "I'm sure," Bart said, deliberately looking at him, "that that will be true for all of us."

Robb nodded and then said, "It wasn't right—what I've put the two of you through for the past year. I need to say that. It doesn't make up for the past, but it at least tries to rectify it."

Olivia was crying. She went over to her brother, kissed him, and then got ready to leave. At the door she said, "I'll check in again later, but not this time to look over your shoulder."

"You meant well," Bart said, not very magnanimously, and relieved she was going. He found himself, curiously, believing that he and Robb might make love. "And call anytime."

"Thanks."

And all of a sudden, she hugged him, and Bart found himself almost overcome by the contact—a female version of Robb, who was so much more present in her own body than either of them were in their own.

He turned back to the kitchen table, and remembered that was where he had left that breakfast place setting, all laid out for Robb, before he had gone on his four-month rampage. An eternity ago.

Curiously he came up to Robb from behind and embraced him as the man still sat at the table, in front of this new place setting; he embraced him, and buried his face in his neck. It instantly flashed on him that he was no angel either—remember Buddy? what about Buddy?—that he had been sitting there like a queen getting apologies from brother and sister alike, and he'd been the one to do the cheating on the side.

Robb lifted his cold, stiff hand in partial acknowledgment. And then it was back down again, on the table. I wonder, Bart thought, if either of us has got what it takes to get through.

Twenty-six

For some time, Olivia had known she had been escaping into Robb's life. But she couldn't say exactly how or why until now.

Chester's total lack of faith in Robb—or at least the sort of recovery Robb had chosen—meant a total lack of faith in her own. She felt so stupid, now, for she could have figured this out without this interlude with Robb. She had tried—she could remember this distinctly—opening up her diary and sharing her Easter experience with Chester one time, and at first the small crocuses had come up and bloomed right before their very eyes, as they talked, and then a dark frown had come to his face, and she had shut the book, hid it away ever since.

What did she expect? she had asked herself then.

They were at a party. And there had been some talk about an AIDS patient—for the throng was a medical circle—and the word "dementia" had come up. It had arisen and floated above them. As if it were some large flower, growing in water. As though it were all outside of them. There had been some talk of what the AIDS patient had dreamed—had even seen from his bed. Stingrays. They had surrounded him while he had been swimming. And they had eaten from his hands. (It was said that this was even possible in the Cayman Islands. Had the patient been there, they wondered?) Great open mouths, with great gristle for teeth. And they had come at him in a circle, again and again, and the only way he could keep them at bay was to feed them from a diminishing supply of bait.

And the pause in the room that had come with this dream had not been respectful.

"The zanies," the host (an internist) had said.

"There was a man with AIDS at my Men's Retreat," Buddy said.

This man, she didn't know. Although Chester said he had been a doctor once. In Vietnam.

"Oh, you've been to one of those," Chester's mother said. "What was it like?"

"The Theme was 'I Sing the Body Electric,'" Buddy answered. "I felt completely rejuvenated. We did a lot of drumming."

"I went to one of those in the Seventies," someone in the party said—and with sympathy, too. "We had to do trust exercises. Pull each other off cliffs, in order to show team effort."

"You're confusing that with Basic Training," Chester said. And the group all laughed.

The unnamed man smiled but went on, "And then one man stripped to the waist, and we had to go up and touch his back, and talk about how repulsive that felt."

"That's something I wouldn't have any problem with," Buddy answered, smiling.

"But to come back to the point," the host said. "Those AIDS patients, with all their dementia, are a full-time job. If all we had assigned was one person, we'd be fine. But we have other people to think about."

"It'd take you all day," another one of the doctors said, "just to figure that sting-ray out."

The conversation was losing some of its center, and to one side, Olivia could see side talk forming. They eddied and repeated. She heard things in parallel tracks. And on one of them, she saw Chester pull a fellow psychiatrist aside, and put a hand on his shoulder. He was doing that thing again, with men. Whenever he was out of her magnetic field, he became tender—and with his own kind, especially. Why? Why? He was being kinder to this man—Branton—than he would be with her tonight. Why?

She closed her eyes, feeling pained, but still saw the circle of guests, at this distinguished home. It was, in fact, a home she had known in childhood when other people had owned it. Her memory was working in her favor, now, intent on springing her from this tightening circle (Chester putting a hand on Branton's shoulder, talking confidentially), carrying her away from this living room to the basement ("rec room"), where the eccentric owners of the original 1950s house had painted a mural of two paisley fish on the wall, bright red, bright blue. ("We saw *Lili* last night," they had said, way back then. "We liked it so much we stayed and saw it again.") And Olivia saw her, that tender young girl, Leslie Caron, like a flower in a vase, wooed by the lame man, at a time when they used words like "lame." And the fish put great blue bubbles on the wall back in those 1950s days, too.

She stood there, with the party in front of her, and saw doctor, physical therapist, psychiatrist, head nurse, psychologist, clinician, clinician supervisor, nursing supervisor, respiratory therapist, nurse practitioner, and as the names were repeated over and over in her mind, a clinician's blank wall, a despair arose. With the settled pain of seeing Chester in closing conversation with Branton—for then she would soon have to go home with him and they would be alone again, and incapable of talking—it was the slow, settled despair of knowing that these were the people who would ultimately "get" her when she got old. These people were the attendants of the stainless steel tables and stainless steel-framed loveseats of distant clinical places and waiting rooms. And that maybe Chester wouldn't be there to hold her hand upon her leaving this life, after all; or if he was, it might very well be in a locked house, under "close security" and with the palm very icy indeed. And then she wondered why she thought it would only happen when she got old, this medical ambush; for Chester had her now, locked tight in Seattle's Magnolia, under the guard of the most elaborate spook security system whose owl's eyes blinked and roved like Felix-the-Cat clocks in novelty stores, all in synch and in rows.

And yet it felt good to her—it saved her knowing that she had been in this house once—this house with the party—, when it had been innocent of these creatures. It had been whimsical and robust once; the owners, the Kaufmans, having etched "Kaufmanor" above the barbeque outside. She, Olivia, had thought the place the most beautiful in the world, as she had run through as a child, glimpsing the pipe organ upstairs, the Asian figures in the yard, and the blue fish at ground level, which blinked, looking out over a yard of their very own. And now that aquamarine wall had been painted over, but somehow remembering that it had been there— perhaps the fish were still there, would arrive in pentimento centuries later, when the house was razed—saved her. And who could prove that the eyes of those fish, even under a whole coat of paint, had no consciousness?

That was it. In memory, she ran through the house with Robb in tow, and looked at the fish wall as though it had been an under seas garden. Robb was there beside her, and as she stood alone in the present in that alienated and frightening party, she could suddenly feel—like a star, whose worth's unknown although his height be taken (perhaps the most beautiful line ever written)—the shadow of Rose House arise, and loom there over her and Robb, like an umbrella over the conversation, mysterious, protecting, reassuring. As it rose, turning all hues in the room slightly rose, she knew she was going to be all right somehow. That there would be a way out for her, given time. She and Robb would be saved, and in some mutual way.

But for now, the fear left and she found the right words. She asked her host about his stamp collection—and immediately she was whisked out of the circle—and given another parade of memories, unbeknownst to him. She was shown into his study which had once been the family room, and she was shown a book taken from a closet which she had once hidden in.

Tidy Graf Zeppelins were laid before her. His air mail collection. A commemorative sheet taken from an exhibition on the other side of the country. Then lovely triangles from South Africa, like old gold, just at the turn of the century.

These sights somehow served as her ticket out of the party; because she had pleased him, she and Chester were allowed to leave early, as though it were the most natural thing in the world.

The shadow of Rose followed her in the car; she even felt tender toward Chester now, and was even going to hold off pleading with him to let Robb stay with them. She could almost smell the sea air of Port Townsend, and feel the imminence of the Peninsula's Rain Shadow.

They were in bed soon enough, and, he said, loosening her gown, that it had been a long time since they had made love at night, and so she even put her arms around his bare shoulders in answer. She'd let him. There was a long slow sail of a kiss, and she felt everything go slack inside her, including her will. And with the slack, came the rise of her breasts against him, and she seemed to surround every part that was Chester. She arched her back, as he kissed her again and again, on her neck, on her breasts; and with the point of her nipples, she felt herself become a knife blade, honing him down to softness. For just a moment she felt she had the power to change him.

But then he was all muscle upon her. His body kept searching hers for something he could not find, or she did not have. His entry into her was not timely, only considerate. And as he spent himself inside her, she knew he was going to ask if she had had the magic experience—as though that was what he had been looking for. And Rose House, kindly and gently, spread its wing over them, and she became generous and loving in the instant, and so she did pass over the crest, like a wave at the foot of that strange and mysteriously healing place, overseen by her family.

He was pleased with himself.

They waited a few moments, and she could see that he was pleased with himself. He said, "It was so, so good to touch base with Branton tonight. You think that you're going to play phone tag with another doctor forever, and things just get settled by crossing a room at a party, and having a few moments of chit-chat."

She still felt easy, at home, but for some reason, she knew she must wrap herself up—just a little. He was going to say something that was going to be quite—.

With the sheet covering him at the waist, he was propped up against the bedstead. As though waiting for another lover—or for her to speak.

Still she said nothing.

"I don't know Branton," she answered at last.

"Strange man, in some ways—as we psychiatrists have a way of being." He patted her leg. "As you well know. But I thought he'd be the perfect man for Robb."

Then everything went rigid. Suddenly. He had said it. "You didn't say Robb, did you?" she said.

"I did. I've been worried about him. And Lord knows you are. I think he needs to see somebody. Be under somebody's care. Obviously. And it can't be me."

There it was again: perfectly and symmetrically formed: the formula, if Chester doesn't believe in Robb's spiritual recovery, then he doesn't believe in mine.

"Robb hasn't asked us for a psychiatrist."

"Do you think he'd be capable of asking? Somebody's got to show him where he's missing his insights. There's your father's suicide, and then—I told Branton tonight—that whole incident with hitting the Saigon woman. I hadn't realized—God, why didn't I think of this?—Robb must have been the one driving the jeep. That's what Branton pointed out. That other man who was supposedly driving, and that encounter Robb was supposed to have had afterwards, was just a figment. Or a 'pigment,' as that old client of mine used to say."

He sat there smiling, arms folded across his chest. But at last he saw her face.

"Who told you that?" she almost shouted.

"Told me what?"

"About that incident with the woman in Saigon."

"You did."

She sat still, in panic. "That's impossible. I never tell my brother's secrets. Haven't since we were children."

"Well, you did this time. I remember it distinctly because it was right here in this bed. Also right after being together. And in fact it was the last time we made love at night. Until now. That's why I remember."

And then she remembered. In the aftermath of intimacy.

The wing of Rose House was gone.

Chester went on. "I've already spoken to Robb. Actually. He's not hostile to the idea. Just stopping in once a week."

"Robb already has a re-entry plan of his own. Worked out with the Director and his drug addiction counselor. It's spiritually centered. And it's wrong of you to interfere."

"And how long is that going to last—this spiritual center. as you put it, before he hits bedrock and has to really look at that Vietnam experience—and everything else?"

"It's not for us to decide when and where that happens," she answered.

"It's strange hearing you say that when you've been trying to engineer Robb's every move ever since he stepped outside the hospital."

"And if I have, it's because I care," she said.

"And the same is true of me," Chester retorted. "I love the man. You can't expect me to sit idly by when I recognize all the symptoms, and just play like he's any other man in the street. Or that AIDS patient they were talking about."

"We need to keep clear," she repeated. "It's what we must do— what we must both do. Not tamper. That was obvious when I was with them at Bart's house." And very suddenly she recognized that she was pleading—that she had already given away her power. "He's in hands greater than ours," she said nevertheless.

Chester shut his eyes. "Please don't start that again. Not now. When we've had such a lovely time together. You know"—edging toward her—"I could make love to you forever."

She got up and put on her robe. To keep herself from growing faint with rage. He was actually getting excited again, as if nothing important had taken place.

She took a moment to scrub and wash in the bathroom. She was trapped, but there was a way out. Chester's slow invasion was nearly complete. First it had been her life, now it was her brother's. When this henchman Branton was through, next it would her father's and then her mother's. Or at least their memories. Rose House herself. The brain police. Then the plan would be complete—to make her and Robb totally invisible, and under clinical rule. Everything now—and everyone now—fell into place. They were going to make her happy by rubbing her existence out for her, along with her brother's. How ironic, too, that she had been in on the game as well, had been an active participant in razing her own soul, by hiding from the truth—hiding, in fact, by living, speaking, and breathing for the past few weeks in Robb's head and heart, rather than her own.

The despair dropped down to the very bottom of her. She was aware of the glowing fish tank out in the foyer—even the bubbles seemed in time with the security lights now. That forest of birds.

But then—and for no apparent reason—Rose House was rising before her again. Very suddenly. Its wing had not left the whole time. It was there still as a promise. It grew out of her very recollection of that lost wall of the Kaufmann's house; it grew out of the memory of her father, now beloved and not resented. Her very mind wound up the spiral staircase toward the seasons, and the Maidens formed their circle again. She realized, and for some distant but profound reason, the lights of the burglar alarm looked like owls, but that the owls never looked like burglar alarms. Owls weren't frightening at all. They weren't responsible for the things, the inhuman things, that took on their own resemblances. She could, in fact, be surrounded by a whole circle of owls, real ones at this moment, and sleep contentedly. It wasn't birds she was afraid of—not at all. All of this—obvious, obvious—but it had not been obvious until now. So that she need not be afraid of nature, only its nightmarish facsimiles.

Twenty-seven

In bed, Bart was aware that there were motions going on in the next room—as in the old days when he could sense that Robb was coming "nearer"—that was his best way of putting it, and that the man wanted him, wanted to make love. He still told himself that this was impossible, and settled, therefore, as he turned on the pillow, on the *Men Touching* film—on the visions of the two men, the Vets, making love again and again, in youth and age. He could remember the men's hands especially—strange, he should remember them when there had been so much nudity, and beautiful, too, but there had been a close-up of one hand closing over another—the very thing he had wanted so much, and not just from Robb, but from others, especially Marcus.

And now the seascape with Rose House loomed over, began to settle him for sleep—those little tide pools which Marcus had spoken over, with their minute, hurrying life, forming an eddying weave, like birds above rooftops, moving in the still air. Yes, but as he turned, in sleep, the currents in his own bedroom ushered in Robb, who stood beside the bed—Bart could see that, as he opened his eyes and stared, as though coming up for air himself; he could see that the man was there.

"How can I help you?" Bart asked, almost as though he were back at work, with his students. "Is there something I can get for you?"

Robb sat on the edge of the bed—and looked humiliated. Bart had turned on the light. "Would you hold me?" he asked. "I can't sleep. Not without my drug. So would you hold me? Just like before. But I promise this time I won't ruin everything."

Bart opened the covers. He felt the weight of the naked man against him, and Bart wrapped him tight in answer.

"Whatever happens," Robb said, "even if I get lost again, I want you to know that I love and appreciate you."

Suddenly Bart moved over him. This time—and perhaps it was the first, he covered him. And now, in folding over, he felt himself being drawn down into the tide pools he was remembering, only this time, he was diving with a companion—roving under sea—and above this rushing tide was Rose House, with Laura taking the two of them, Bart and Robb, through, landing by landing; the sun struck colors on the wall, up, up the light tendriled, branching out at the corners, forming candelabra-like shapes—up, up again, until Laura smiled at both of them, as they, Robb and himself, clung together and became one flesh.

(And Robb himself felt as though he were sidling up a wall of the house, its columns of inner light covering him and Bart, the long windows opening on to the ocean, to the garden below; the leaves, glancing from wall to wall in silhouette, formed slow climbing nets of shadow, and as his fingers clung to Bart's own naked shoulders, he felt he acknowledged the man for the first time, in himself, for himself, with the sun spreading across the circular mural at the top of the ceiling, then down as the ruby light from all the lanterns of glass shaded, protected their lovemaking, as he admitted to himself that he was capable of loving a man, and as he did so, the garden, the light, the sea, lifted him racing toward the dome of the sky, and then through—up amongst the planets and beyond, and into a special galaxy which he recognized within a second's pause, and he saw, suspended mid-air and from the canopy-like heavens, small chrysalises, one of which he entered, quite suddenly, and there found his father, as though the man were being prepared to be a spirit, angel-like. There. It was settled. His forgiveness for him, his father, and his father's forgiveness for him. It was quite finished, resolved, and with that, he was spun back down, into Rose House again—with suddenness, holding onto Bart, in one of the rooms. Under him.)

Bart awoke satisfied and happy—at just one minute, as per usual, before the alarm.

But at work he felt the whole craziness of Easter Week, and was aware, suddenly, that the show was to open in just four days. And the AIDS results were on Friday. Why hadn't he had the presence of mind to schedule it otherwise? To set himself up for tension like this. Ridiculous.

And the vulnerability of the time with Robb kept nudging inside of him, like a fledgling bird, trying to get out. But he felt that if he were to feel the full blush of tenderness, he'd be completely stymied in trying to put this rehearsal together—specifically with Laura, another Laura, a high school Laura, who was having a terrible time remembering her steps for the "Hosanna" number. She was in tears and he was trying to reassure her.

"Here it is, Dear. You turn just like this."

"But I keep bending backwards." She arced her body to show him how she was doing it wrong.

"Never mind remembering doing it wrong. Just put your left in front of your right, like this."

Beautiful as she was, she did it awkwardly, and Bart thought of a gosling and Hans Christian Andersen.

Her tears were still there.

He patted her on the shoulder, and one of the beefier students— who was to be a Soldier, of course—smiled and punched his buddy. Pointed.

"Never mind, Dear," Bart went on. "As soon as you get in costume, the steps will come on their own."

Costumes. Oh fuck, costumes. They simply must do a go-through, without stops. He hadn't even had a moment to get a grasp of the colors, of the musical's composition, he'd been so ragged, and *behind*, running late, fragmented. And even so, they'd fire the ass off him, if it got too obvious to everybody, the parents especially, that he was gay.

So he stood there, and threw an unusual tantrum, so that everybody listened up, and told them to get into costume within the next ten minutes. He'd show them he could kick ass and take names. Who's boss. And they scurried—at this unusual behavior—so fast, he felt guilty.

He got into his chair in the empty auditorium, the backstage people pulling the curtains back shut, for the complete go-through. No stops, this time. And as he sat there, he thought, If they only knew. If they could only see me backstage in my head. Fireworks going off, demons popping up through trapdoors, props falling down, and chaos rising like a tier of Esther Williams and Company (sparklers lit on water skis), they'd have me out on the street within the bat of an eye.

And so the curtains opened, and "Heaven on Their Minds" lit up the stage with one spotlight, and when Judas stepped into it, he knew it was exactly right—simple, perfect classic dress—and Kelly (Judas), who could sing like an angel, filled the whole auditorium with his torment, yielding (for this was when Bart became aware again), to the moment when Brian (Simon Zealotes) suddenly stood upon a rock, and the robed throng broke into dancing frenzy—their robes and colors forming the perfect motion (really, an undulation) that had gone on the paper—red, green, brown, and again, and again, with the shaking of the tambourines and the rioting of feet, in perfect step, Laura's among them. Clapping hands. And she did fine.

And when he surfaced once more—for he didn't want to think about King Herod just now—he saw the Arrest and the sparks flying suddenly between Brian and Mack (who was Jesus), both singing right on key (after he had worked and worked with them), right on key, and the sparks flying—flying because this theatre was becoming once again more than the sum of its parts, Brian and Mack *were* Judas and Jesus, because the sparks not only came from the composers themselves; they went back to motions and inspirations which perhaps the creators had had no awareness of—Shakespeare, for example, in his Brutus and Caesar. He had seen, one time, Johnny and June Cash singing—and in Folsom Prison, too—"Phaedra" ("Some Velvet Morning"), and all he could think was, Johnny Cash and Euripides? But that's the way it happened, in theatre and in performance, all influences were alive at once, and jumped arcs and millennia.

And so Christ was flagellated, and Judas hung himself, in the frenzy which the music stirred up and gathered. Then they all were transformed in the Resurrection which he had reverently added— even the beefy soldiers which Bart in all humor had put in leather and helmets and little pleated mini-skirts, bringing wolf whistles from the girls the moment they had come out on stage, in full dress, for the first time.

And so he went home, satisfied enough that he did not even worry when Robb told him that he had decided to see a psychiatrist, as suggested by his brother-in-law. And that he would be spending Easter with his stepdaughter, if possible. He would give driving another go again. Why not? And he would take Valerie to a church service, if she was willing, one run by the minister who'd been visiting him at the hospital.

And Bart felt perfectly cool when he heard this. "That's great. But doesn't that man have strong feelings that being gay is a sin?"

And Robb smiled. "Yes, but the trick is—I'm going to tell him about us, if he says I'm in the wrong."

"Good. I like that clarity," Bart replied. "And in return I'll be absolutely clear with you when I get my AIDS results on Friday."

"AIDS?" Robb asked. "Is there a chance you might be HIV positive?"

"No, no chance. It's just routine. But I just wanted you to know. I'm having it checked."

"Yes."

And they settled into their routine of getting dinner, and of even cleaning up the house. Robb went off with someone to one of the Meetings, and Bart even took a moment to sit in the shadow of the mimosa.

Twenty-eight

But on Saturday morning, Robb awoke feeling very crazy. Again. The sudden and wonderful intimacy he had shared with Bart had not saved him. In fact, everything had been shaken by what had happened on the day before. What he would later call Black Good Friday.

Dr. Oppenheimer had urged him to get back into the classroom, and so Friday was the day he had started back.

The students hadn't been told much—but they had known he had been sick. And so when he had stepped to the lectern, there had been uproarious applause, and immediately Robb noticed that there was a plant as a gift over on the lab table.

In an instant the wind went out of him—and he saw their beautiful faces—and the fear went straight into his heart. He babbled and stammered, he thought—behaved quite crazy, and did all he possibly could to get the notes in front of him out there. Articulated.

Afterwards, he was aware of a haze being sort of everywhere, outlining the green purgatorial hills of the neighborhood, and to settle himself, he took a walk through Woodland Park, discovering small pockets of mist, surrounded by the evergreens, which seemed very much like the mystery inside his head. Bits of lines from *Mary Stuart* and *Iphigenia of Tauris* flitted through him like lost birds above the sea, fragments from his German days in high school; he heard their wing beats, as the afternoon, the sunlight, struggled to focus itself. Easter. He wanted so desperately to get to Easter, and to show Valerie he was capable of getting back on track again—a successful teacher, a responsible father, someone safe.

But at home, Bart was not sympathetic—for starters—when Robb told him about his day. It was, in fact, a mess.

"I've had a terrible day myself," Bart said. "I'm HIV Negative, at least right now, but they told me that since my last contact is still not six months away, I'm going to have to come back."

Robb couldn't quite believe what he had heard. And he started to feel very slow again—as though the medication was in his bones once more. "But your last contact was me."

Bart glared at him. "Exactly."

"But I"—and for some reason, he had never considered that he himself might be Positive. Out of all the tests that he had been given in the hospital, HIV had not been one of them.

He sat there in a stupor.

"It's very, very unlikely," Bart said, friendly again. "But you and I haven't been as completely safe as I would have liked us to have been. And I'm just totally bummed that I'm going to have to wait. And it was strongly recommended when I was there that you get one, too."

"But the only person I've really been with is you."

"'Really' isn't good enough."

Robb tried to search along the fence of fog—which barred him from his past. "There's only been one other in the past six months—Buddy."

"Exactly. But who knows where Buddy's been?"

"But we were safe."

"Were you? Are you sure?"

Robb paused. Because he felt it was required. But only because of that. He knew, actually. "Absolutely," he said at last. "Absolutely."

Bart waited as well. "But the way I remember it was—you were drunk on your ass when you finally got here."

He thought back, trying to be humble. But he was still sure. "I'm sorry," Robb said. "About Buddy. Very, very sorry. But I came right to you right after, and I remember that I was safe, and I wasn't drunk!" And he heard himself almost shout for the first time in months.

But out of the blue, Bart was saying at last, "I don't know why I'm standing here lying. Lying like this. Getting angry at you like this. Because I was with Buddy, too."

"With Buddy?"

"Yes. He called while you were in the hospital. And so we got together, just for a hug session. It wasn't anything more than that—just hugging without our clothes, or some of them, but it was wrong. It's what I meant to tell you when I came to you in the Unit. Do you remember? When you were telling me about how sorry you were? And I wanted to answer you back with what I had done?"

Robb held his head. "I can't remember. I can't. My mind's so foggy."

And so now, as Robb had awakened on this Saturday—Holy Saturday—he had felt crazy.

Some memories were starting to come in—make themselves available now, as he dressed, and began to get ready for his short trip to Port Townsend—putting together a few overnight things, for he was to stay over. And see Valerie on both Saturday and Sunday.

There was that word he didn't want to say to himself, "Honolulu," which kept coming up, as was the other word, "AIDS." They were connected somehow, although he couldn't say why. He was actually getting into the car—what a miracle, and heading for the psychiatrist, Dr. Branton, for he had planned it this way, an unusual Saturday appointment, to gird him up before going to Port Townsend—but as he was doing so, the little wheels that were everywhere (for example, making cars run) were starting to become frightening, formidable. Within his field of vision.

He had that feeling of being debased—it was returning—once more. That he was lower than—as though, as though he contained the seeds of AIDS or something other malignant property, and he could spread them. A creeping vision of being in Church, of sitting there with Valerie and being unworthy, of being toxic and wrong and contagious settled in, ushered itself in, as he was sitting among all those people, and made the lanes once more tentative on the main road.

Honolulu. What did he have to do with Honolulu? There had just been that white building there, where he had gotten discharged. It was quite medical and on the up and up. He had been in a ward where all the men had been in white gowns. Men like himself. The doctors had looked at them, and then he had gotten discharged.

And there had been the white envelope—from his mother— saying that his father, according to report, had rowed to the center of a lake, dropped in and drowned himself. He had been staring out the window as the nurse had read the letter to him, looking at a palm tree as though it were in a water-color haze, quite beautiful against the green. He could see the Ocean tossing, avalanching upon itself, as though to remind him of the inexorable violence of water, which was so neutral and vital otherwise—for example in a glass on his bed stand. His father had drowned himself, and had been pulled up covered with seaweed. That's what he saw. And in dreams for a long time after, his father would pursue him as a green man. But he had not remembered this until now, because the drug had always wiped the recollection clean at every morning awakening.

So the windshield in front of him became just a little like a goldfish bowl, or aquarium, just a little, where things swam through. At least there were no fiery things on bicycles, but, he had to admit, lots of beings seemed to swim in front of him. Mermaids and mermen, and AIDS viruses, which no doubt were there, and a vision of him together with Buddy and Buddy together with Bart and Bart together with himself—all locked in that embrace which had at least at the time seemed to redeem everything. But not now. Who knew what contaminations he was passing on to Bart and what contaminations Buddy had passed on to him. He knew, knew, knew, it was scientifically absurd to think AIDS could be spread by casual contact, but he began to worry that just by being around, he was making the world worse—from Buddy it could have gone to him, from him it could have gone to Bart, from Bart it could have gone to his students, and around and around, until the whole world was circumnavigated and poisoned.

But that was silly. The whole thing was silly. The beings were silly—those that were swimming around. His optometrist at one time had simply called them floaters. Now he was getting out, and going into the psychiatrist's building—where he would be set straight and he could tell him about the optometrist.

But the psychiatrist said something terrible. He couldn't believe his ears again, once it happened. He had thought the man would be there to help him, set him straight. But he said things that were beyond imagination. We want to get you asleep, he said, and wrote out a prescription. You were the one driving that jeep, and until you realize it, admit it, you're going to need the means to get yourself to sleep. Here—the paper flew at him, again and again, and Robb dodged it, as though it were a hot flame; it fell to the floor, and he refused to pick it up. And all about him, the microbes seemed to invade the office; Robb wanted to cry out that they were here, but he knew he'd be hauled off again, if he said so. It wasn't just AIDS! It was the wheels, too, especially in Dr. Branton's grandfather clock, back and forth, like the sea itself, tossing back and forth, as seen from the Honolulu ward window.

A strong eddying began to fill the office. Robb knew the doctor saw that he was beside himself—for the paper still lay there. "I did not drive that jeep!" Robb shouted. "I did not!" And it was the truth; he hadn't. Because Mason had, and he loved Mason, still. Mason was his example, now; he would not die like him.

"Torturer! Pharmaceutical madman!" Robb screamed at last, and bolted from the room, bolted for his car. He must now get to Valerie. That was his only answer. He must show her that he was worthy, that he could take her to church, could bring her Easter presents—like the ones loaded in the car—and no Teddy Bears, but mature things, real presents for a young lady at Easter. He would show her he loved her, and that he wouldn't fight on her doorstep, and they would sit quietly in the pew together on Easter Sunday, and the Reverend, his Reverend, would see he was capable, gay though he was, of nurturing his daughter and steering her on to the right path.

But as the freeway opened up before him again, the landscape did go on tilt. There were no fiery phantoms—that was still a blessing. But there were the great wheels of the semis which rushed past, and it was beginning to rain an Easter rain with rainbows. All was fresh with freedom. And wheels. And now those wheels were forming a bicycle, and on the bicycle was Lily and the jeep was rounding the corner, and he, Robb, was driving, because Dr. Branton had put him there. No! he yelled again, and because the car went out of control at that moment, he slowed, and took an exit, and ended in an out-of-the-way town, not four miles from the ferry landing.

Yes, yes. He drew a breath. It was O.K. at first. For an instant, he consoled himself that he could make it to Port Townsend once again. He could. He breathed a sigh of relief. But after he'd swung back on to the highway, the lanes, even these slower ones, got impossible once more—he was expected to go up to fifty-five, and cars were buzzing around him like hornets, because he was finding thirty-five to be tops. No, twenty-five. No, fifteen. He went to a back road.

And once more he came to a standstill.

He couldn't drive, because he knew that there was that piece of paper on the floor of Dr. Branton's office for valium, or at least its cousin.

That was the drug.

The man had prescribed it for him.

His death.

And Robb knew that if he drove any further, the car would turn straight around, go back to the office, where he could pick it up.

The drugstores were after him.

The doctor's office was after him.

He had a perfectly legitimate and insane reason to take what had nearly killed him.

And the visions, the microbes had been there to make that seem O.K.

That's what he knew.

That his brain accommodated him with reasons to take what killed him. From doctors.

He had heard the word. And he had known the drug on the prescription was one of the very same nature—of the one which had almost killed him.

But he wouldn't do that. He wouldn't go back. If it took walking on water to Port Townsend where he was safe, he would get there. And be with Valerie.

And suddenly Rose House was before him. A place of childhood, hovering, at the far end of the water. And the snatches of song and loving iambic pentameter arose from memory—and someone—a queen was speaking of the freedom she felt when she had been let out for a moment's reprieve from prison (totally apocryphal) in the lovely park. Her words were like shadows across the lawn, flying toward the mist-lined hills, which now advanced upon Robb, as he wandered from the car, now parked beside the road.

Twenty-nine

On Easter morning, Bart got up with a pang, remembering that it had been weeks since he had heard from his family. A pang for the familiar days of having orange juice and frozen waffles at the Six-Ten, at five in the morning. Daniel was no doubt being served at this moment by his mother—Daniel who was lucky enough to have been born blind and nothing else.

The bitter reflection struck his heart like a bell, and with the clang came the thought that the review of last night's performance would be in the paper today. Words about him and his children would be right there, rolled up, on his doorstep, waiting.

But he had had such a moment last night. Crossing backstage, he had seen Renaissance Laura, in beige lace, standing there like a midsummer night's dream, reading a program, fairy-like, as still as a wax figurine. The light had fallen on her so beautifully. It could have just as well been the spell of Christmas, rather than Easter, striking timelessness upon every object, every performer, for he had felt these moments too when, in winter, he'd looked (particularly in Port Townsend) at views into houses, where the panes had been frosted. No need to worry. It was all the same. His gallery.

He opened the paper. There. Under news and notes. Entertainment. The neighborhood throwaway. Not recommended. He looked at the review again. Not recommended. Not Visconti's high school production. No stars. Doing King Herod as gay was old fifteen years ago. This critic found it not fair to vent such spleen on a high school production. Unless it's good. But he would do so anyway. Not good. Not recommended. News and notes. You could see the dancers counting time. High school stuff.

He sat down and tried to call back the Renaissance moment of the night before. Not there. Vanished. That review had nailed him, hung him there like a deer's head above the fireplace. And with little flowers in its antlers to boot. A doe. Marked "gay, fag, sissy." At least I could have been a moose. Now what would the parents do with him? With his very own parents not speaking to him.

The phone rang. It was Andrew. "I was just calling around," he said. "Just in case you might not know. Marcus went into the hospital yesterday. He's seriously ill."

Bart felt the hurt as one. "Which hospital?" He dare not ask why he was there. Although everyone would know by now.

"St. Stephen's. Some of us are interested in going down and visiting him, two at a time. Sometime today. I thought you might be."

"Absolutely."

"Sort of an Easter surprise," Andrew said.

"I'd be happy to," Bart told him.

"We're meeting there at four. Front lobby. Can you make that?"

"Absolutely."

Bart got up, and was about to steady himself, when the phone rang again. It was Robb. "I don't know where I am," he said. "But I'm scared. I cancelled dinner with Valerie last night. And we were supposed to go to church this morning. But all of a sudden in the motel just a few hours ago, I knew I'd never get back, if somebody didn't come up and get me right now."

"Robb, you'll do fine," Bart said. "Besides, I've got some emergencies myself—"

"You don't understand. I panicked yesterday, and I didn't get to Port Townsend. I'm over by the ferry, and I'm on the other side. And the car's gone back into nothing again. I can't drive it above ten miles an hour. Please, Bart, come and get me."

"How can I come get you when I don't know where you are?"

Robb muffled the phone a moment and seemed to be shouting.

"Near Edmonds, just two miles up from the ferry landing."

"And you're on the Seattle side?" Bart asked.

"Yes."

"And what about Valerie? She'll be waiting for you to take her to church this morning."

"But I can't. Can you come like I asked?"

"All right," Bart said. "I'll get there as soon as I can."

He dressed, feeling the pain of the review, and Marcus, and Robb all at once. He thought, in the mirror, he looked like a wreck—thought, as he passed a framed picture of Robb, that the man looked a total hunk, by comparison. And that was the man who was draining the life out of him. Just for good measure, he wrote down the name and number of Robb's psychiatrist from the phonebook, just in case things got too unwieldy. He would just have to do this, move forward, increment by increment—otherwise, he'd get too overwhelmed and sink himself.

But he was no further than the door when the phone rang again, and Andrew was telling him, "No need to visit Marcus after all. I just called the unit to get clearance, and they told me he died ten minutes ago."

"My God."

"It's true," Andrew said. "I'm sorry. Because I know how you felt about him."

"But how could he have gone so suddenly?" Bart asked.

"With AIDS, anything's possible. You know that."

"I have to sift this out," Bart heard himself saying. "And I'll need more time to talk, but right now I'm on my way to another emergency—may I call you later?"

"Of course."

Flying out the door, Bart felt everything rush straight away from him. The long line of the road stretched before him, and for a moment, he wondered how such a thing could be so frightening to a man like Robb. It was, after all, just motor and movement and gears. But then, just at the instant he feared for Robb's safety and actually saw the road the way his lover might see it, he, quite simply, went through a red light, and ended up being smashed by a car, t-boned, passenger's side.

Maybe it was the worst moment in his life when he got out and waited for the other driver to emerge. At last she did. "Are you all right?" he asked.

And she hid her face in her hands. "Yes," she said, "I think so."

But it was clear both cars were totaled.

He was just about to pull out his license and offer the particulars, when everything—review, Marcus, Robb, and now this—dropped on him at once, and he felt himself sinking to his knees. The last thing he remembered before going out, was handing the address and phone of Robb's psychiatrist to a police officer, and saying, "Please call this man. Would you? And tell him that my friend Robb is stranded just outside Edmonds?"

The breath that it took to say all this finished him off. Even fainting, he had been courteous and off in the great beyond of somebody else's life.

Thirty

Robb woke up in Chester's psychiatric ward. He knew he had been there a while.

"Robb, Buddy," Chester said, coming into his hospital room and holding out his hand. "I didn't know you'd entered into my humble abode."

Robb took his hand. Didn't say anything. Just felt terrified. Because Branton had come in, too. Come and gone. He had a vague, sleeping memory.

"Did you know this place was mine?" he went on asking.

"Yes."

"You're trembling," Chester said. "Easy, now. Just tell me what happened."

Branton came back in the room.

Robb found he had to say, "When I got to Dr. B's office, I was so beside myself trembling, Dr. B insisted on giving me valium—which I know is basically the same thing as that drug that nearly killed me—and so I said no, no—and I ran off. And then I couldn't get my car going, I called Bart, but he didn't show up, and then Dr. B does, and I think he put me here.

Chester face fell with that. "Wait, wait, you mean your Dr. Branton here prescribed valium for you?"

He looked at Dr. Branton. The doctor acknowledged "yes."

"That's what I remember."

"Well, then, I'm going to have to ask you to leave."

And the man, floored, said, "What?"

"I said get the fuck out of here!"

"I'll have your job for that," Branton said.

"And I'll have your job for prescribing addictive drugs to an addict!" And he was glowering in disbelief, because he was reading the orders on the chart. Branton stormed out. Chester went after him.

Robb just sat there in the wake of the storm.

At last a timid and totally nonplussed nurse came in and told him it was time for his orientation session here in the Depression Ward. After an hour of that, soon he was back in his room. Olivia came in.

"I came as soon as I heard," she said. "I'm so sorry you had to go through this all by yourself."

"My problem my whole life," Robb said, "is that I *haven't* gone through things myself."

She looked surprised. "Really?" She paused, awkward. "Well, but it looks like you survived Branton. And Chester."

"Something blew up between them," he said. "I don't know what's coming next."

"I don't know what it would be," she said. "I passed Chester in the hall, and he didn't say anything."

She came close and took his hand.

"How long do I have to stay here?" he asked.

"I understand there's to be a review of your case. I'm told Bart, Valerie, and Laura will all be there, too. To decide if you can leave. There's a problem with Chester being your brother-in-law. One thing—" she began. And he observed now that she was dressed in green. And looked ruddier, somehow, and healthier. "Don't expect me, Robb, to make up your mind for you. On anything. As you probably know, Chester and I are having problems, and my own life is more than enough for me to handle right now."

"Problems?" he asked. "And with him being so . . . concerned now?"

"How they will go I don't know," she answered quickly. "We may separate."

"But what about Nathan? Where will you live?"

"I may be moving back to Port Townsend. That's where I was when all this happened. Searching out housing. In fact"—she looked at him—"we must have both been there, nearly running into each other, on Easter weekend."

The pain of her situation was upon him now, as well as the pain that the one person who might have helped him best had slipped from him just minutes, perhaps, before he'd jumped ship.

"Anyway," she said, "I came to see if you are all right. Have you recovered again?"

"Yes, I think so," he answered. "Now that I know they're not going to foist addictive drugs on me. I don't blame Chester for yelling at Branton. He was horrible."

That night, he had a hard time of it getting ready for bed, as he anticipated what the "family" might say or do in a few days. Strange, but he had never even considered that he did have a family until now. It had been so fragmented and scattered, and he had spent so much time in the past avoiding the pieces, that he had always considered himself a wanderer, and this had been true even when he used to talk to Olivia on the phone. But something else was forming.

As he dallied there in his pajamas, the Night Nurse came in and asked him if he wanted a sleeping pill just to take the edge off. For sure she could give him one the night before the family conference.

"No," he told her.

The morning of the family conference, he awoke with his wits about him. He did not know exactly what he would say—and his back ached painfully—but he felt a center of force.

Bart was the first to come into the ward office, which Chester had reserved for them. "Robb," he said, sounding rehearsed, "I can't ask you home with me. I've thought about it and thought about it. I lost my car and I could have lost a lot more. I'm reduced to a bicycle state."

"I don't think it's a good idea, either," he answered. "Me coming to live with you."

Bart looked completely surprised.

They were interrupted; Valerie and Laura were in the room. The sudden collision of two different worlds—how strangely they stared at one another—dropped him back, into fear. He had not realized, until now, how entirely separate he had kept his lives, one orbiting Rose House, the other Bart, in his small home with the mimosa. No wonder he considered himself a wanderer.

Olivia and Chester came in, coincidentally together, apparently, and looking awkward.

Chester lifted some papers on a clipboard and tried to look friendly. "It looks like Robb is ready to leave. We just want to be sure he feels he is, and if he has anything he needs to say to his family, he'll say it now. We've got his medication regulated at last, and with nothing addictive."

"I don't think I have anything else to say," Robb answered.

He couldn't help but look at Valerie, who came to him, and put her arm around his shoulder.

"As far as we've been able to determine," Chester went on, "Robb has been suffering from Post-Traumatic-Stress-Disorder, on account of a brief encounter in Vietnam."

Valerie did not leave him when she heard this, but he could see she was beginning to cry.

"He's developed," Chester went on, "a plan of recovery which seems entirely feasible to me and to the staff. He will continue with the A.A. Meetings, and also start with some support sessions at the Vietnam Vet Center. He will go back to work in the summer, and he'll resume a pattern of exercise All that remains to decide is how and where Robb is to live."

"I have proposed," Robb answered, speaking for himself at last, "that I go back to Mrs. Molyson's, just like before."

"And I've wondered if that's wise." Chester said. "Your living alone. Especially with your propensity for depression."

"It seems to me perfectly clear," Laura said, "that Robb should come and live with us. At Rose House." She seemed to have been gathering all of her energy for this moment. "His adopted daughter is there. I'm there. And there's plenty of room. Port Townsend will give him a break from the trials of Seattle. And he can move back to his old place here in Seattle, if he wants it, in the summer. Rose House is his original family home anyway."

"Please come back," Valerie said. "I'll drive you wherever you want."

Olivia seemed as though she were burning to speak, but didn't.

For his part, Bart was looking at Laura. "What does your husband think of all this?"

"You mean my first husband?"

"Yes," Bart said. "It's my understanding that he's back with you. And excuse me for saying so."

"No," she said, looking at Valerie. "That was only for a brief period. It was my mistake. Now Rose is entirely free and safe for Robb."

The attention of the room was all turned on him. Now he had to say something.

"Rose is not my life anymore. I need to stay in Seattle."

Valerie had started to cry.

"I love you," Robb said, feeling tears himself. "I love all of you. But I have to go with what I think is best."

"It was a week ago," Laura said, "when you had no idea what was best. You wouldn't even take the medicine they pled with you to take."

"It was fortunate he didn't," Chester said.

Olivia now urged herself forward. "I'd love to see Robb in Port Townsend. Since I might be living there. As a matter of fact, I could offer him a place to stay, the way I did in the past."

Chester looked over at her while she spoke.

"But the fact is," she went on, "this is Robb's decision."

"I'm sorry, Olivia," Laura said, "but you don't know Robb the way I do. You've been out of his life these many years, and you haven't seen what he's capable of when he gets isolated."

"Living alone doesn't necessarily mean living isolated," Olivia answered hotly. "In any case, I don't think any of us can say we know Robb now he's clean and sober."

"Yes," Robb answered. But immediately he had to turn to Valerie. "But just because I'm living by myself doesn't mean I won't stay in touch with all of you. I promise I will." And he took Valerie's hand a second time. "I mean to show up. The way I didn't at Easter."

He waited. He wasn't quite finished. "I neglected to say something else." He looked squarely ahead. "I'm staying in Seattle also because I love Bart. If it works out, and he'll take me."

Part Three

Families of Separation

Thirty-one

It was a while before Bart got back into his rehearsal gallery mode. Of living dreams. Stripped down to his bicycle while his car was in the shop (almost totaled but saved at the wire), he rode home one afternoon and took a shovel to his garden while Robb was still in the Ward, and found that he veritably hated the son-of-a-bitch.

He was tackled full-body just as he was digging into what he'd planned as pumpkin hills. And he'd been so innocent about it, too. Just that morning he'd been in to see Robb and had taken full blame for Robb's being there in the first place. And Bart had done some real "if-onlys" on himself—if only he'd had his wits about him enough, he would have seen the red light, if only he hadn't been thinking about Marcus, too, then he could have picked Robb up right there near Edmonds, and Branton would have never been the wiser, and there would have never been any shove into any Depression Ward, and there wouldn't have been any skirmish between Branton and Robb's brother-in-law, which Olivia had told him about later.

Then the spade hit the soil. One turnover of dirt, and Bart felt himself fry with anger. What the fuck was he apologizing about? The spade went down, turned over some moss. The soil was damp, damp, damp. All of Seattle seemed to be in a bathysphere, with green and seaweed covering the window looking out. Spooky sea creatures with neon fins wormed their way past. At these depths and after these rains, what could you expect? Worms, earthworms, slugs turned up in the soil in front of Bart now. That Robb, that worm. He unearthed your life, ransacked the daylights out of it, and then walked away.

A rotten little tune along the lines of a torch song of yesteryear began to form itself again in his head, as it struggled to fix on the soil.

No matter where I go

I'm justa goner for the massive man

He knew he was a goner in just that way—take any man in the street. (Over the soil went, as he sliced it, again and again. Pulverizing it. Pounding the hell out of it.) Which he was seeing now, over the fence. It being a Sunday. The hulking chest—tanned—of the brute, any brute, coming up the avenue magnetized him every time, because it meant sooner or later an intrigue with it would unearth his life.

And then there was this little matter of his parents. Who'd shown up at the hospital. Where Bart had been treated briefly and then discharged. They had shown up with flowers and fern and a refusal to talk about anything except the weather and auto parts. There was this place called Schuck's out on Aurora where his father insisted they get all the missing pieces to Bart's poor decimated Datsun. Should he, Bart's father, go over and supervise the reassembly?

"No, that's unnecessary," Bart said. "Robb's sister's father-in-law is doing the rebuilding. He's the best auto rebuild around."

"Robb? Who's Robb?"

Good question, Bart thought, still digging.

"Robb is," Bart answered, not very graceful in his neck brace, "my partner, lover, significant other, better half. We just celebrated our second anniversary on Valentine's Day. Or I at least did."

His lack of decorum on that subject— (Spade in the soil, turning again. Maybe now he could bury Robb!). His lack of decorum on that subject, just drove them further inward. The compassion in his father's face dried up. A thick tension filled the hospital room, as it had that day, Pink Triangle Day, back at the Six-Ten. Sorry about that!

Now where was Daniel, Bart wanted to know. And still sitting there with his pain in the neck. Being one, too.

"Had to work," his father replied. "But he sends his, send his, sends his—"

Well, let's get this car started. Sends his—?

"Love," his mother replied.

Love, but he had to work. When he really doesn't work at all.

Sitting there in that hospital room, Bart thought himself a total turd. And toad, too. (Bart would be soon planting toad lilies, in honor of himself. He must give his mother some when they bloomed in the fall. He was serious.) Ungracious. Incapable of acknowledging what his parents were going through, as they had sat there and looked as if they had disgraced themselves somehow. Bart, trying to get out of his turd-like state, pushed and pushed against his own limited field of vision, to get through to how his parents saw things, how they felt things, but just couldn't budge, or at least no further than the knowledge that he was confined so.

So he thanked them for coming. Made promises he would drop by the Six-Ten again (which he had vowed he would never do; never again would he darken the door of that place which offered nothing better than stale paperbacks and saran-wrapped muffins. Well, guess what, he was taking a saran-wrapped muffin these days!). Soon as I get my car back, I'll come running (and I'm serious) bearing a bouquet of toad lilies.

And I'll do that, Bart thought again, back to his digging, as soon as I get Robb buried and in due order among the roots of my nasturtiums. And he was seized with fury again, thinking of his reduced-to-bicycle state. Because while Olivia's father-in-law seemed conscientious, he also seemed like someone who could not meet deadlines, and would keep him checking in on the progress forever.

"And," Howard (Howard the Mechanic—why did he think Howard the Duck?) said, when Bart finally did call on the phone, "how's Robb?"

That family! Always asking about Robb.

"That's right," Bart answered, avoiding the question. "You know him, don't you?"

"Know him? I was there when he almost dropped into the Christmas punchbowl," Howard answered. "Saw him carried to the couch by Olivia and Chester. Chester, my son. Poor guy."

"Well, he's doing better," Bart answered. "Much better."

Glad to hear it.

Glad to hear it. Now Bart dug a pit seemingly deep enough to inter Robb's dead body and keep it safe from grave robbers (every pun intended). Hauled in a rhododendron. One big enough to cover the body. So the plant stood there in its green strength, while Bart steamed over the way Robb's family was giving him all the attention now, and he was so fucking jealous over it—all his family did was provide florist's fern and disappear—leaving him to his bicycle, while now there was this universal rally over the Head Depressive of the year, who was nearly out of the Ward now, ready for a new life. Well, what was Robb waiting for him to do? Stand up and cheer?

Maybe it was then that he knew that never in a million years could he have Robb come back to share his house. He would have to go elsewhere. Strange, but this to-do in his head had been predicated on Robb's still coming back, sharing his bedroom, right there, north, facing the transplanted rhododendron. Maybe he had even transplanted it with the idea that Robb could look out and see it. Be comforted by it. Insane. When he had been burying the Incredible Hulk's body at the same time.

And the very moment he said that to himself—Robb, you have to go elsewhere—the anger died down and up came the fear that Laura would swoop in for the kill (Robb was vulnerable, he could see it), swoop down like a vulture, with Valerie as bait, and carry him off to her nest in her rookery of Rose House. Forever.

So be it. So be it! It was a chance he would have to take. For Robb was a big boy now, and would have to make up his own mind, anyway.

And so he went to his own Al-Anon Meetings, and then said his piece at the Family Interview. Robb, you can't come back home. And he meant it.

And so he gave up this hateful gardening. And took to his bike. To and from work, and even the grocery store. Called Howard the Mechanic almost daily at the Body Shop, to remind him not to forget his car, which, like himself, he had almost totaled.

But not quite. Because the strange thing on his bike was—he suddenly felt in command of his own business, as though these Cycle Days were just exactly what he was intended to have, to have this bridge, for example, coming up at the end of the road, with the moss and the scrolled faces—always a surprise, really, in Woodland Park. It reminded him of when, in dreams, he used to invent his own special vehicle, propelled perfectly by the light treadle of his own right foot at the end of the bed, as though on a loom, and he could go anywhere, but always it seemed, in dreams, it was through greenery, through the profound Rain Forest of the Upper Peninsula, and then back again through the Rain Shadow, where it rained less, and meadows appeared, like those in Jack and the Beanstalk and *To Think that I Saw It on Mulberry Street*, for mulberry street was a meadow, too—at least it was when he was driving in his treadle car, in his bed, at five, ten, even fifteen years old, in sleep, in dreams.

He loved, especially, the way his shadow moved ahead of him on evenings. He was supposed to watch the road carefully, very carefully, for bumps, for his bumped-up skeleton was not supposed to tolerate dips, but he just couldn't help being fascinated, riveted by the shadows of the street on evenings, twilight evenings, where everything seemed to be shadows in a florist's or a nursery, with those silhouette dramas (parrots, hanging plants, blinking rabbits) playing themselves out on the pavement and wrapped in fern.

His civilized, shadow world of biking brought him back to his Jesus Christ Superstar, which had just squeaked through despite his accident and with the even worse repercussions of the review. It seemed as though everyone was having to bear humiliation these days, and Bart had to rally himself in order to rally his friends and students. He found he could do this, though, despite his being plagued as well by the humiliating insurance settlement, which labeled him as culprit (which he was) and awarded money and a substitute car to the woman involved. Not that that wasn't right.

Nevertheless, this humiliation as well as the public shattering of his hardworking production, kept the dream world of Rehearsal from coming back sooner. Will Shakespeare and Ben Jonson were far from him for a while. So his life of biking, his dream world of treadling out into the shadows, through 1950s streets with names like "Cottage," "Dravus," "Arapahoe" (which had a brick-like color to it), meant even more.

His principal called him in. Robb thought he was going to get it.

She took one look at him and said, "I'm so sorry about your accident. It was that review which did you in, wasn't it? You've been under such a strain lately."

And Bart, suddenly feeling sorry for himself, burst into tears and said, "Yes, yes," while lying in his teeth.

"There, there," she said, patting his hand. "Bart, I just want you to know how proud of you we are, and that you have done us proud with a splendid production, no matter what your lifestyle happens to be."

Come again. Bart's tears dried up.

"Personally," the principal went on, "I liked the King Herod number."

"Thank you."

"It's about time," the principal concluded, showing her aged banner as a self-stylized protofeminist, "it's about time men did a hoochie-coochie like Yvonne de Carlo and our other imprisoned sisters of the 1950s."

"Yes, Ma'am. Thank you."

Well, be that as it may (what was that conversation, anyway?), he had some things to do, in keeping the cast's heart up, for the final two performances. The Assistant Director was a closet case who taught biology, and who pinch-hit as the girls' softball coach, and when Bart got everybody reassembled for Saturday and Sunday (sold-out, no less, just the same), he found everything in pieces, like bits of a puzzle scattered all over the children's playroom. Bart almost wanted to say, "Now I want everything picked up in the next ten minutes or no allowance for two weeks."

Instead, of course, he spoke from the heart and told them how much he admired them for getting out there and singing and dancing like angels (how many angels can dance on the head of a pin, when they've been given bad reviews?), despite the antics of some know-nothing critic. He praised certain people specifically, and then allowed the filaments to ramify outward, so that no one was excluded. He was always careful to name the easily forgotten ones, trusting that the Super-Confident knew they were good (in his opinion as well as their own) without his saying so. He told them (which was true, too, even though it had not struck him until now) that in the hospital, he had seen them as an example of picking up and carrying on.

Mary Magdalene began to cry.

Simon Zealotes smiled, showing the space between his teeth.

Peter, Simon's boyfriend in real life, gave him an elbow and smiled, too.

When he got done, Laura came up and gave him some flowers, as though for his speech. But really as welcome home. That knocked the wind out of him.

"I don't know what to say," he said at last. "But this is something I'll cherish."

He dismissed class, and told them to come back Saturday night, ready to break a leg.

On his way out, however, he saw that the costume room looked as if a tornado had hit it, and he thought—if only my assistant could have it as much together as my kids. What a total flake. These closet faggots can't even do a wardrobe right.

But when he reached the house, there was his Men's Group, sitting on his porch. "We've brought you a portable get-well party," Andrew said. "Even though you've gotten well."

"Welcome home. On wheels," Lance added.

Bart felt sufficiently humbled. He hadn't been in touch with anyone.

Immediately the group turned into a cyclone, as though it contained not only half the dirt of Kansas, but all of the Emerald City and Oz as well. There was a flurry of dust and Technicolor, as they stormed the house, changing everything over into a potluck, meant to cheer Bart's spirits against his will. Put out pink flamingo napkins. They had heard things had gone from bad to worse with Robb—and then the news of the car wreck, and so here it was, May 1, as a matter of fact, and they were determined to do an intervention on his bad luck, and have a May Day, May Day, party in his honor (so of course, the house was covered from head to foot with flowers). Someone, too, who had done a little pillaging of the past, and had learned about Bart's "screen persona," put a *Revenge of the Creature* poster on the wall. Bart's alter-ego was presently carrying off Lori Nelson, in 3-D. Interesting to say, however, the Gillman, in poster color, looked as though he were wearing lipstick. Candy apple red.

Andrew, who seemed much warmer and more approachable, came up and gave him a hug. "Forget about that bad review."

Through the cloth of the polo shirt, Bart felt the angular muscles, and thought again of his last night with Robb. How much he missed him, now that the hate had passed.

"Yeah," Bill said, seeing them hug. "Forget about all that. Bad news"—and he spoke now in a very black voice, as he put Bart's own flowers in a vase—"bad news is none of your business. That's what I do. I just don't acknowledge its *existence*."

"I'll do that," Bart said, "as soon as I get my car back."

And then it hit him.

"Oh shit! I forgot all about Marcus." And then like a fool again: "How is he?"

"Well, he's dead," Andrew said.

"No, I mean, how was he taken care of?" Bart asked, breaking out into a sweat of embarrassment.

"The hospital would not allow his body to stay in the building one second after he passed," Andrew answered. "And his family wouldn't acknowledge him, so we had to take care of the cremation."

"But you O.K.," Bill said, holding him, "you O.K., the memorial service isn't until this weekend."

"But I feel like such a self-centered idiot for forgetting."

"You be cool," Bill went on, in his tank-top. His skin shone, giving him a vulnerability which made Bart's eyes water. "You be cool. We come and pick you up personally and take you to *church*. You're not too late. You don't need to do no negative track on yourself."

"Sorry," and while Bart sat down and cried and felt himself become even more a genius for the maudlin, the room filled up with wild Sylvester and "Do You Wanna Funk," for old-time's sake. But Bart felt even sadder when he heard it, for the star diva and hero was said also to be coming down with the plague, too.

But now taffeta and ribbons were flying, and the potluck table was filling. Pink flamingo paper plates. When the news about Sylvester did finally come up, some people refused to believe, and insisted they were going to write him a fan letter instead, right then and there, before the night was out. Just to say they still believed in him. And they didn't have to mention whether he was sick or not.

A knock at the door. Bart knew it must be someone new to the group, because anybody else would have come right in.

It was Buddy.

"Just thought I would drop by—I didn't know you had guests," Buddy said.

"He's our guest," Andrew said, pointing to Bart.

Buddy just stood there.

"Please come in," Bart said, still off-center.

The man looked freshened-up and perfect, the way newly-out men usually do. He gave Bart another squeeze strong enough to take his breath away. And to tell the truth, there was a bit of Robb in him, just the way there had been a bit in Andrew as well. The disco just continued on, with men dancing in the kitchen, dancing in the hall, eating meanwhile, and breaking into Chubby Checker's the Twist, just for old times' sake, which none of them, hardly, were old enough to remember. Buddy just eddied around him— food, poster, and flowers, as though in a vortex, and Bart felt his body light up again with the sight of his strong flanks.

"That awful review of your play," Buddy said. "I saw it. You and Robb have sure been through enough tough times. And how is Robb, anyway?"

"He's all right."

Lance looked over and raised a brow, as the song came to an end.

"Are you still together?" Buddy asked.

Bart could tell that Andrew was listening intently, and he realized, in the moment, Andrew had at last put serious sights on him.

Sylvester's "Take Me to Heaven" started up.

"No, we're not still together," Bart said. "We're living apart while Robb recovers. Later, we'll check in and see where we are. After he's a year sober. I can't put it any more definitely than that."

"That's pretty definite for two that are breaking up," Andrew said.

Buddy seemed relieved, and began to move in closer, while the dancing and eating and the flying about got wilder and wilder—to the point that Bart began to wonder about the neighbors. Buddy started to fill the conversation with stories about his last experience with Men in the Woods—a gay group which got together and touched for three days in various forms of undress. And at the other end of the room, Andrew, pissed off with Buddy's advances, filled his own story corner with a queeny rendition of how Universal International might have done Revenge of the Creature, if the Creature had been in the closet.

Thirty-two

At home, Robb felt different than when he had been in the ward. He had had so many insights—so balanced, so serene—in that hospital room, and he couldn't think of one now. His mind slowed down to a snail's crawl again. And everything in this huge, ungainly house belonging to Mrs. Molyson seemed frozen, polished, and grinding. All the banisters, superhumanly polished, threw plates of burning sun—still pools—right into his eyes. As he got himself situated again, he seemed to go up and down those stairs ten thousand times, glacial step by glacial step.

However, at night, it was all right for sleep. It was extraordinary, it was a miracle, how all that had changed—that the great fear of his life had been taken care of. He'd lie there, and he'd ask himself, Where do I want to sleep tonight, and his mind would go out searching, like a faithful friend or golden lab, nosing his way through every corner of his past, until it found a safe place. Like last night. His mind decided on the Blue Mouse Theater in Seattle. And it couldn't be just any place in the Blue Mouse Theater. But in the back of the back row of the last balcony. Underneath the seat of the center aisle. In his dream-like state, he'd clear away Buttercorn tubs from the floor around him, and put them underneath his head for a pillow. Then, just when the feature was coming on—he could hear it distantly below—he'd fall asleep.

Or he'd lie in the middle of the street of 42nd Avenue West and Armour in Seattle, just about dusk. The cars wouldn't run over him exactly; they'd just rush lightly over the top, like a wind. And there would be so few at that hour anyway. Because everyone would be at home having a twilight dinner. Behind wrought iron.

Lying just over the manhole cover, he'd look to the west, and see the ships beyond Magnolia Boulevard, framed by the madronas, which had the shade of brick, at sunset. And as the sun would set he'd fall asleep.

There was this matter of his job. He still hadn't lost it. But he knew that if he was to be in any shape to teach in the fall, he must use summer school as practice. And so Dr. Oppenheimer, who'd been close to a saint in his patience with him, gave him the one section of Introduction to Science which the department had to offer. "We need to get you back in the saddle," he had said.

Alone in his office, Robb would stare at his lecture notes as if they were written by somebody else—they looked so good; for his handwriting now, so changed by the medication, looked crabbed, almost ashamed. Entirely illegible unless he made the most concerted of efforts. And the old notes of yesteryear were so clear and beautiful. And the weather of this new season was getting terribly hot; his thumbprints dampened the page, and he imagined himself trying to stand in front of the group one more time—those beloved kids who had believed in him enough to give him a plant, and now he would fail them—and try to put words together. But he didn't want to let them down.

This polished, banistered life was so distinctly his own. He saw the shadows in the street, and he thought of his paper route in Port Townsend years ago—how silent things had been all along Clay Avenue. It was a world, almost, that the sea and the cliffs and the old pioneer architects of the town had seemed to provide for him. This is my world, he thought, leaving the campus of Jutland College behind, and staring into the quiet avenue. And when, suddenly, he turned a corner, and Jutland General was upon him, attached to all the memories of what he'd been through, he turned down another street, and he would be overwhelmed, again, that two worlds, which he had kept so separate, could suddenly collide like that, in just an instant.

Nevertheless, this was his world—a world of banisters, meetings, and preparation for class. Of shadows, and a garden (a few of the hollyhocks had made it, just barely) which was still well beyond him. The simplest tasks were still that way.

So he went back to getting ready to teach. And again his old notes for class seemed very Leonardo-like, so well-organized, nicely scrolled, and bordered with clear illustrations which were to go up on the board. A child in the womb. A close-up of leaves. An arbor to indicate the way the Renaissance saw deciduous trees. Even some reference to perspective in painting. How in the world could he have sat down and gone from point A to point B so easily? And the answer was—drugs and alcohol. They had made him cool, calm, and collected. But he couldn't do that anymore. He'd just have to jitter some new notes together, and jitter himself up to the podium and do his dance for an hour and a half. And not expect to be worshipped this time, either.

The fear carried over. In finding a safe mental place to sleep one night, he discovered he was in the back row of Miss Emerson's art class, lying on the floor, underneath one of the tables, hearing a lesson in "Light and Shade," with the cadet's voice ringing up and down the room. All were to draw a bottle and teapot in charcoal, and then divide the picture into checker squares, which were to be painted alternate pink and purple. His own drawing had not been very good—John Kurosawa, the exchange student from Japan, sat right in front of him, and drew beautifully, every time, and Robb, staring over his shoulder, began to cry, thinking he'd drawn such a disaster. Miss Emerson—perfect white hair and always wearing turquoise and always pulling at her slip strap, always, always— came up and said, "Why, what's the matter, Robb?" causing everyone to turn and see that here a boy was, crying in eighth grade.

The dream was changed, however, and the next thing Robb knew he was not lying in Miss Emerson's art room at all, but was watching his father's body being lowered into some remote gravesite near the Kingston ferry. Killer, killer, killer, he thought as he saw the coffin drop down in the hole. Wrought iron light was everywhere. Killer, killer, killer; you killed him. You should have been there to pull him out of the water. You could be fishing with him now, if you hadn't had to do your manly thing and prove yourself by *enlisting* in Vietnam. Killer, killer, killer—he was drinking, because you were in that stinkhole. He pleaded with you to come back, but you didn't.

Killer, killer, killer, he thought, as he stood before Rose House and saw it, the next year, in 1970, all gone to wrack and ruin. I'll make it up to you, Father, I'll restore it, I'll marry.

But he never restored it. Never. Laura had been the one. Every time he tried to make a correction, it had been as though the house had been built upon an earthquake fault. It had shaken and crumbled at his every touch.

But the dream turned and provided him with a view inside the restored Rose, as done by Laura's hand, and he saw himself making love to her—over and over, he pushed his love into her, and over and over, he saw her naked arms fast about his neck, but suddenly he knew he couldn't breathe, and he awoke yelling, her arms pulling in.

He got up and washed his face and hands. Once more, he had slept too long. His mother would be visiting soon, and he must learn to sleep a reasonable length of time—not ten, twelve, fourteen hours, as before, in the past few months. He got up and hauled himself down to the Y. How different from that ecstatic time back in October. It was a cold, dinny place at ten o'clock in the morning, full of people in wheelchairs and braces, and of old folks, too. He got dressed again in his t-shirt and shorts, and allowed himself to look in the mirror. No ecstasy there, either. His weight still ballooned over the waistband. All flab and formlessness in just seven easy months. An erstwhile marathoner, now, with medication in his joints, he was lucky if he could get around the block. Nevertheless, Chester insisted this was what he was to do. He stared in the mirror and wished he could look like Chester.

For now there was this matter of going to see Tyler the physical therapist again, and cooperating this time with no back talk. So to speak. Sometimes when the large, t-shirted man turned him this way and that on the table, Robb felt as if he were being cradled.

But he was going to get used to the Clinic; it was less stainless steel now, and more mats and pulleys and weights, which had been assembled in the exercise room. There were other people there, pushing and pulling, too, each with an injury, and each looking better and better each time he saw them. One crippled man arrived there by bike and endlessly hauled himself up, bearded and gnome-like, on to the nautilus bench press and pushed and pushed against the bar—in fact, did a full circuit on the universal. Week by week, the man's hips seemed to free themselves up, so that his body began flickering with energy again. Robb, in fact, had felt that in himself. And although all of them rarely spoke, they still all seemed a family.

And he improved, too. Tyler showed him all the ways of strengthening his back, so that it would stay in place. And the procedures—shown to him on the floor and in diagrams—seemed impossible at first, given the terrifying slowness of his mind. In fact, he was such a glacier on the floor of Total Balance Physical Therapy (TBPT), he thought that no one save a snow god like Tyler (dressed in all white, still) could be so patient. It seemed as if Tyler could move on the same tracks of Robb's slow mind, knew where the turns where, so that he could teach him the next step.

One day, when Tyler was adjusting his sacrum, Robb found himself one more time, in memory, swinging on the swings in his childhood neighbors' yard. It was a beautiful flight at first, the recollection as smooth as before, and then, as in Miss Emerson's art class, things went dark again underneath the shadow of his father, and he was suddenly having a drink with him—in the bar on the Port Townsend waterfront, with Robb saying, "I think Vietnam would make a man of me," and his father, totally wasted, saying, "Yes, I think you're right," just before collapsing into a puddle. Snap. The bones went back into position, and Robb felt like yelling with relief and anger at the same time. If his father hadn't been plastered, there would have been no Lily, no Depression Ward, no car wreck, no break-up of marriages, his own as well as Olivia's.

His father.

But what about himself?

That was the question he asked now, as he sat up, bones all articulated and in order, on the therapy table.

What about himself? He was the one who had gotten that idea about manhood in the first place. He was the one who had gone running into Vietnam with the deficit. If he forgot everything else, if his mind became too slow to tolerate anything more than one insight, he had to remember this one undeniable thing—that he was the one who had gotten himself into this.

He dressed and went out of the clinic. Out on another stroll (for there was time, still—a very few days—before summer school). He stood on the Jutland bridge again, and looked once more at the broad expanse of city, of water. And there were these emblematic fish, rusted to blue, right above him, by the bridge's 1930s signal (for it opened to let boats through). He looked again, and had no desire to jump. There were fish in the wrought iron below, too. He wanted to stay put this time. And it occurred to him that his mind was like that tide in France, the extraordinary one he had heard about back in the 1950s, which had ebbed so far out, by some millennial turn of the moon, a Roman arch had appeared, islanded and long forgotten, a treasure house of monumental clues to the past. Who knows what it would come up with next? That was the way his mind worked.

And so it was time for his mother to come. She arrived, as was typical, with just one piece of luggage, and slept like a trooper on the fold-out bed. Her eyesight, which had nearly failed her in the past year, was corrected at last by heavy lenses. She seemed thinner somehow, but just as athletic—she still carried with her, as always, the air of sail boating.

"I wish," she said, "I could have been here to take care of you, but as I wrote, I could hardly get out of the house myself, my eyes being what they were."

Nevertheless, while she was there, in those several rooms on the third landing, she did seem to take charge, as a sort of come-lately nurse, and obviously wanted to make up for lost time. Robb, who was perfectly capable now of preparing his own food, and washing and cleaning up, would sit and be served by her, and think of the mornings when the best he could do was crawl across the floor, and day after indistinct day would fade him into nothing better than an invalid. It reminded him of a moment, also recently retrieved, when he had served the nightmare of MACV, and, returning to Port Townsend, he had found that his mother had been so worried about him, because the ferry had put him an hour late! An hour late! What about the days, weeks, months, when he could have gone up in smoke in half a second?

"I would like to see Rose again," she told him at his house, "and if we went, we could save Olivia the trip from coming down." And although classes would be starting Monday, he thought they could do it on the weekend. And so he said, "sure," and he actually was the one to drive, ferry and all, which had been such a terror before.

At Port Townsend, they went out for a sail, until Olivia was done with a job interview. And the Strait opened up before them, into a view of the Olympics which were like fresh triangles of ice in the distance. And then it seemed as if it was hardly another moment before they were back and standing before a deserted-looking Rose House, up for sale now, with the Victorian poppy garden all wild and gone to hell. Sitting on the stone in the backyard—no one was around or seemed to care, it being a Saturday afternoon—they talked, his mother saying how it was, taking care of those three floors, complete with that fresco of the maidens, and seeing to it that his father was never too drunk to scare off customers. And somewhere in the conversation (was it out on the water, when she was luffing out the sail; or was it here on the bench, with the wind lifting the ferns?), he told her he was gay, and she said, "I know."

There it is, he thought. At last. But is this all there is to it?

They had been sitting on the bench when he had said it. And then Olivia had arrived. That he remembered.

"What is it, Robb?" she asked.

"She knows about me," he said. "I just told her."

Olivia's face softened.

"The wonder is," his mother said, "you didn't say so sooner."

"Yes," Robb said.

were you afraid?" she asked. "I would have been delighted all along to have you tell me."

"Maybe I was afraid of Dad," he said.

"Your father? He loved you so much—both of you—" his mother said, "it scared me."

"And he scared us," Olivia said.

"Yes," his mother said, "although—"

"What were you about to say?" Robb asked, seeing her face.

"I was about to say that it was a shame you didn't get home in time, Robb."

"I know that," he answered.

"No, I mean, he was just in the process of getting sober," his mother answered.

"But he died out in the lake drunk," Olivia said.

"Maybe."

"What do you mean 'maybe'?" Olivia asked, her voice rising.

"The fact is," his mother said, "your father and I were separated when he died, and I don't know the exact details. The information I got was imprecise. It could have been a heart attack."

"So he could have died sober?" Robb asked.

"Yes."

He sat still. Then the "I love you, Robb" in his final letter could have been true. My dear Robb, come home. I am sober.

"Oh the amends I'll have to make to his memory," Olivia was saying. "What I've thought about him, said about him. I've never even imagined he knew about trying to stay sober."

"You and I share a lot in common," his mother answered, looking at her. "We're the very seat of judgment. Very hard sometimes."

Olivia didn't answer.

His mother went on, "I say all this now, because I want you to think twice, Olivia, think twice about staying here and leaving Chester behind. You know what a wonderful man he is. I judged your father harshly all these years, and I ultimately—infinitely regretted leaving him those last months. Chester is a good man, and loneliness, particularly late in life, is a horror, my Dear. You, too, Robb. Remember that. If there's a man in your life, don't be too hard on him."

"At first that was the problem," Robb answered. "Now it's a matter of whether or not it will work out."

"Precisely," Olivia said, with an edge.

But Robb could see that the day had decided to end their conversation for them; the wind was coming up from the water, blowing things here and there. Olivia got a speck in her eye. And besides, she was angry with the advice, especially within Robb's hearing. Close by, Rose House was registering the five o'clock hour like a sundial. Inside, the ruby filaments of the carpet would be brightening that particular way. And there would be many diamonds of light, now, on the maiden. The rocking horse planted on top of the china cabinet (why was it there?) would look more discontent, its jaw ragged with shadows, but the window seat, beneath the glass of the chandelier, would be friendlier, calling to you to come and sit—read through your memoirs until dinner. Father, I am gay.

But it was time to up and leave. They couldn't get into the house even if they'd wanted to. It would be sold soon, and Robb wondered, distantly, if Olivia would be the buyer. Having engineered something. But the thought didn't stay long, because he was too busy again thinking about his father. And himself.

Thirty-three

Olivia decided that the ferry lines being what they were, Robb and her mother best eat before going back. She invited them up to her little place above the Fine Arts Theater, but, no, her mother insisted on a restaurant on the water, for all of them.

So she went to pick Nathan up at daycare, and, pulling up to the house (Jack and Jill painted on the overhang above the porch), saw Nathan standing at the window, his eyes wide and vulnerable. Clear. And as she swooped him up, she saw a big-cheeked little girl standing by another window and wiping tears as though she were polishing a large apple on either side of her face. Down and down they slid, silently, and Olivia thought her own heart would break. The little girl always stood there, waiting for her father. For some reason, she heard, out of memory, an old 78 record, on pasteboard, painted with a fairy tale in full color, the way they did it in those days, about looking out a window and what did I see? And still the little girl stood there. We all seem to be at windows, she thought, waiting.

Then she felt herself fade. There it was—the thought—of her father sober in his last months. Could words describe how much she had hated that man! Allowed herself to! And then she had let go, years ago, with all the astonishing clemency which says, "The man was not well. I loved him." Period. It had flown from her, the hate, had turned all into magnanimity. But now?

Perhaps she should follow Nathan's instincts as a child—for he looked at her with a clear, blue gaze, that was beseeching, now—and repair all at all costs. For why, why, why, Mother, Nathan had asked her, why, why, why is Dad not here? Why don't we go back to Seattle, Mama? Was the other alternative any better—the four o'clock hour, alone in Port Townsend? She remembered getting, once, a brochure, with an explanatory sticky tab, sent out to all seeking a dissolution of marriage which involved children, entitled "Families of Separation." Inside, there were two sets of houses with cartoon faces, one set sad, one happy. The sad twins had tension between them, with talk behind each other's backs—no cooperation. The happy families had—"respect," "honesty." She had simply stood there, struck by the idea.

As though pulled by gravitation, she was rounding another corner, and finding Rose before them once more, although this time by an opposite street, so that she passed the cottage this time and saw that it was for rent, as a separate. "Office space available, 2000 square feet."

At dinner, Valerie was there, and Olivia actually asked Robb when Valerie's mother expected to move, and the answer still was—very soon to Seattle, to make it easier for him to visit, and for Valerie to stay with him. Somehow somewhere in this conversation, things changed, in this Victorian restaurant on the water, with her mother paying; Olivia could not quite define at first what it was, but she knew, even without a pat answer, that this apparently insoluble problem of what to do with her new life was going to resolve itself. Her cousin's (Quarterdeck's) song came on in from the kitchen, and the china reverberated a little. She saw her cousin Cindy take another puff on a cigarette, add another line to the score. The Tiffany window (lute and lyre) formed a scale, as the sun came through. Solution.

For now, she freed herself from the restaurant at last and kissed them all, and let them go—all except Nathan, who went back with her to the apartment above the Fine Arts. She did promise Valerie a visit, now that the wall had dropped, and that actually was a comfort to her, because she knew, with the way clear, things were going to get lonely at times in Port Townsend. She rounded that extraordinarily dim corner, with the summer sun already below the Strait, and felt that she could stare right into the Renaissance, into timelessness itself. Her own isolation was like that salt-lined apple tree on the bluff, clutching the air for dear life and yet relentlessly vital. Sometimes there would be no solace—and tomorrow was Saturday in Port Townsend, which was the loneliest and night of all.

But when she got home, there was Chester was. Standing in front of the building. The painted tragic and comic masks beside the marquee and just above him were frightening this time, as she took Nathan sleeping from his car seat, and hauled him toward the stairs like a small sack of potatoes.

"I just thought we could talk for a few minutes," Chester said.

"All right," she answered. "Help me put him to bed."

When Nathan was finally tucked in, Chester sat on the old couch, and said, "There's something I need to say."

So it wasn't going to be a marriage proposal.

"I was in Kent State," he went on. "At the time of the shooting."

"You told me that before we were married," she answered. "'So 'you know what you're getting' is the way you put it."

Yet, never had he looked more appealing than now—when he had just said that; his neck bowed and fine and vulnerable, his eyes blue and full of suffering. She felt she could see through to the very fit of his bones. Beautiful. That was always the word for him.

"But what I didn't tell you," he said at last, "is that I was one of the guardsmen."

The words were so extraordinary, she stood up.

"I didn't kill anybody," he told her hurriedly, "I just shot my gun and deliberately missed."

"But were you wearing your glasses?" she asked with her wife's hectoring voice. "How could you know for sure?" She was angry that her impression of his beauty was ruined.

"I don't know," he said, struck to the heart, as she knew he would be. "I'll never know."

"Why didn't you tell me?" she asked. "I could have helped you. It could have made us better friends."

"I was afraid," Chester said honestly. "I was afraid you would think less of me."

"So much less," she answered—again with merciless cogency—
"that I might think I knew more than you?"

"Yes."

She had been standing so much on his mental tracks, she
dared not, now, say another word. For fear of hurting him again.
It was obvious to her this was part of a larger plan. This confession.
"Please forgive me and take me back" was to come next.

"I forgive you," she said, "if that's what you're asking. But I don't
know what it has to do with anything. You'll have to work it out
for yourself. It's just like you say to all your patients. Self-reliance."

"But don't you see," he answered, "it explains why I've been so
overbearing in the past, why I got all muddled up in Robb's life,
why I wouldn't accept your way of looking at things. How could
I—when I had so much to hide."

She came up and put her hands on his shoulders. "For what it's
worth, Chet, I love you. Always have and always will. This doesn't
change that. But can't you see, even now, in this very conversation,
I'm not being myself."

"Yes, you are."

"And there you are. Just what I mean. Let me speak for who I
am, please."

Chester started cowering again.

"I feel like a complete and total bitch," she went on, finally
getting at it. "I don't care if I don't look that way, sound that way
or act that way. I feel it. And I'm not that—at all, when I'm myself.
And I feel your pain, but I've got my own life now—or at least the
start of it. There have been whole days gone by—not all of them
by a long shot, but some—where I've been able to say to myself
at night—yes, that's been me, most of the time. I couldn't say that
when we were together. I can't say it even now. Hopefully we can
grow to a time when we can support each other. But right now"—
she said, withdrawing, ever so slightly—"it's sheer poison."

"Then you don't believe," he said, "that I could begin to see
things the way you do?" He was crying.

"Do you believe that Robb and I are getting well, because we
believe in something spiritual?"

"No," he said, shaking his head through his tears. "No, not at all. But I believe that you and I could create something strong enough to help you both get well."

"My Dearest," she said, "that would only put us back to where we were. You being kingpin and once again pressing me, subtly but constantly to give up my job."

Chester seemed to experience some hideous void settling in. He wiped his eyes. "Tell me," he said at last, "tell me what it's been like for you. I still don't understand."

She tried to think of how she could explain it. It was embarrassing and trivial, what she came up with.

"Do you remember," she said finally, "one night, years ago, when we stayed up late and watched *Rebecca*?"

"Yes, sort of."

"I saw that movie again recently, and I realized that I've been just like Joan Fontaine. She was under the shadow of her artistic father until he died, then jumped into being a paid companion until Mr. de Winter came along."

Chester was still trying to recall.

"It doesn't matter, really," she said, "if you remember it or not." And she began to feel the clarity now at last. "What happens in most of the film, in fact, doesn't really apply. It's only at the beginning. Joan Fontaine is an artist herself when the movie opens, is beginning to get a life of her own, even though it's behind her paid companion's back. She'll dump that witch soon enough. After all, it's just her job. So she spends her free time sketching on the south of France, perfectly at ease with her own life. She has moxy and she has direction. Is on the very verge of herself. And it doesn't matter how good an artist is—that's not the point! It's only when the rich Mr. de Winter comes along, sweeps away her art by her own consent, harangues and marries her, that things go to hell, and she gets all tangled up in his past—so much, she never gets a past or even a name of her own."

"And so I'm Mr. de Winter," Chester said.

"Only when I make you that way," she said emphatically. "I've used you as my excuse to avoid my own life. And now I'm finally getting one. This is going to be my existence—not perfect, because I'll have to earn my keep—but mine anyway."

"But what will you do?"

"I'm going to start my own counseling practice. Right on the grounds of Rose House, once it's vacated and the new owners take over, if that's possible. Rent space."

That was final. It was over. There was nothing more that could be said. She'd lost him. For it was evident that even if she could take him back, his face told her that he could never live with that part of her—the one who could go out and rent office space, hang out a shingle, which said, "Olivia Jorgenson," and live guided by some principle or Being which even she herself could not explain. And on her own. As one who must give love and care as well as take it.

"It's what you've always wanted to do," he admitted. "I suppose in a way it makes sense."

"It really doesn't matter, in some ways, what I do," she answered. "It only matters that it's happening and happening now."

There was silence. At last, he kissed her. Frightened, cowering. "I also came here to say I was wrong for getting involved in Robb's situation," he said. "Now I'm going to have to pay the price. I'm going to have to go before the Board for what I said to Branton."

"I'm sorry," she said, stunned by his directness

""I don't even know if I have a job now," he went on. "How can I do with that without you?"

"I'm being silent and that's not me," she said. "I don't know what to say. I feel like such a dunce some times."

"Tell me we can come back together."

There was silence. At last, he kissed her and left. Frightened, head still inclined.

She sat down. Now there was only the green dot on her answering machine—but not at all like the owls' eyes back in Seattle.

And the next morning she knew she could only carry forward with her plans. By tomorrow afternoon, she would be sitting at the outdoor table in the Port Townsend square, with the sun splashing every which way and that on the grass, the pansies, and the palm-like ferns. Getting ready to see about that caretaker's cottage. A cupid in the fountain would hold up a shell as trumpet—a geyser on either side. A bouquet of lions' heads spitting continuously in, too. And as crown, "Galatea" would dance and throw off her wrap. But this time she was not going to set her suitcases down in somebody else's tragedy. And now the sights and smells of autumn (sumac, cones and all, reflected in the fountain; the rich pumpkin smell of decayed leaves) were coming at her, and Olivia was filled at last by her grief for Chester, and felt ashamed, sitting there, at her own table, crying like a child.

She took out a handkerchief. That would be her four o'clock tomorrow. But it would be with herself.

Thirty-four

October. Night. He was walking toward The Vietnam Vet Rap group.

Robb still felt as though he belonged nowhere.

All these men, in the past months, talking about their real experiences in Vietnam, and all Robb had was an as-yet-undisclosed "episode." These men had experienced the unspeakable. They talked about snakes and torture over there, talked about harassments and being spit on back home. In Robb's mind, it was all just another coming out. They had disclosed themselves to the world at large, had marched in parades, had talked with one another, and had been through it. And now were on top. And he—had hung out in Biology, stayed in a closeted marriage, and run like hell from anything even faintly sounding like "Vietnam." Or gay, for that matter.

One time, he'd passed the Gay Bull bar in Seattle in the early seventies, during afternoon hours, and a couple of men had been sitting out in front, at a cafe table, one of them in a Vietnam jacket, and looking surly. They had both eyed him up and down as he had passed, and in his heart he had despised them both, especially during the moment their glance had gone straight to his butt. But there was something else. On a deeper level, he envied them, and the residue had stayed, long after the memory had gone.

Nothing had changed since. At least as far as coming out was concerned. While he had been drinking and using, he had only been out when it had been safe and convenient or dramatic. But in any continuous way, he had never known what it might be like to be himself towards others, because the logic in his mind kept saying that he couldn't say he was gay because he couldn't say he was a Vet—and he couldn't say he was a Vet because he couldn't say he was gay.

But he had said at last he was a Vet. And tonight he must also say he was gay to the entire group—even though two of them, Jason and of course Buddy, already knew. Even if he didn't mention all the other things—Lily and his panics—at least he could say he was gay. Yes. That was something he could manage that night.

Still, he never imagined that once he was off drugs and alcohol, he'd have something like this to deal with. And constantly! He could only think of a mountain pass somewhere in Idaho where there had been perennial signs saying "Expect Delays," with neon arrows going off and on, shrinking the lanes, and the traffic coming to a crawl. And then there had been the roadmen up ahead, holding signs. Impossible beauty on either side of the road—mountain landscapes, meadows, a lake, but all at a snail-slow pace. Sometimes as he moved on this journey, he felt he would die of vulnerability without his armor. People looking in at him at keyholes, coming to windows. Gay man coming! Gay man coming! And sometimes, in his nakedness, Robb had felt like swishing down the street just to show them. But once the bravado was over, Robb had also felt like hiding under the bed.

One time, during group, Galen had urged him to march with "us Vets" in the upcoming parade, and Robb had felt—at last, I have a place where I belong. But how would it be possible, he wondered, to put one foot in front of the other, when he felt such shame like a hundred-pound weight? The spring months of therapy with Chester were easy by comparison. He was merely given, then, what was indicated. But right now it felt like he was hitting a series of walls, and only finding his way by bumping into them. Besides, he doubted if Galen would be that crazy about having him march if he truly knew what he, Robb, was.

Well. The Vet Center was upon him now, with its sign, and its windows all lit up, ready for a "rap." He could see through the window that Galen was arranging chairs. You were supposed to arrive early, so as to develop your social skills. This would be the first time that Robb would be walking in—not on the dot—but doing exactly this—allowing himself to say hello. That impossible closeness of human beings waiting for something to begin and meanwhile trying to think of something to say.

"Hello, how are you?" Robb said to Galen.

"Hello there," Galen answered.

And to his dismay, Robb saw that all the chairs were arranged, that the coffee was made, and there was nothing else to do.

Jason was nowhere to be seen. And Richard, the group therapist, who could have smoothed things over, too, never arrived until the stroke of seven, because he wanted the men to fend for themselves. Thus Galen sat, smoking, apparently at ease, but waiting for Robb—Robb was sure—to make the next move. Galen was something like a weathervane; you could tell what was going on just by looking at him. This way, that. His arms, bared to the elbows, were scrolled with tattoos and maps and weapons. A veiled girl, too, and a pierced heart. These souvenirs seemed to come from lands that he, Robb, had never even heard of, places utterly out of reach, exotic, arcane almost: where you might park your camel under a lantern. Robb, sitting there, thought, Why should I be the one to speak? This man has everything on me.

"Cat got your tongue again?" Galen asked at last.

"Guess so," Robb answered.

"You know it's hard," Galen said, under his smoke, "having someone like you around." He smiled. "I keep wondering when the lab practical is going to be."

"What do you mean?"

"I mean," Galen answered, "I feel like maybe you're just sitting back and watching instead of getting down on your hands and knees and crawling in the dirt like the rest of us."

Robb, now, only wanted to say less. He wished he were resting in that oasis where Galen seemed to be, the one at the center of his tattoos. He wanted to say something like, "Why would I want to say anything when you're the who's listening, Joe Camel?"

The rest were coming in, now. Robb was so relieved when Jason sat down next to him, and blocked out the need to give Galen an answer. Only Jason could understand—and maybe Richard—what coming here could mean, and why it was so hard for him to talk. And then there was Buddy, Bud to everybody else, who was so healthy and ruddy and full of his doctor's experience of Vietnam. News as it happened. He was the delight of everybody's eye, and yet he had not said a word, either, about being gay or bisexual, or whatever he was. Amphibious. Robb, thinking this, felt his whole soul retreat like a toad into its cave. He had informed Buddy about the group and he wondered if this had been a mistake.

They were in a circle. By then, the last man, Mick, had joined them. Richard said, "Who needs time in group tonight?"

Galen said, "Robb does."

The men laughed. Robb wanted to deck him.

Buddy, of course, chose to ignore this, and rushed right in. "I have something."

Richard said, "Wait a minute. Galen, what did you mean by that?"

"Exactly," Robb said staring at him menacingly. "What the fuck did you mean?"

"I'm feeling 'resistant,'" Galen answered, using the appropriate vocabulary, "because I'm tired of coming here week after week and having Robb sit on the outside and judge everybody."

"Look who's talking," Jason said—and Robb noticed for the first time how very tattooed Jason was, too—"you're judging someone before he's even had a fucking chance to open his mouth."

Richard, not very comfortable, was smoking, too. He looked sideways at Robb. "Well, do you want time?"

"Yes," Robb answered, nettled out of his cave. "But it's going to be hard to talk when Galen is doing this number on me."

"I'm not doing a number," Galen said. "I only meant it as a joke in the first place."

Within just a few minutes, Robb felt the whole group reach a dead space. It had happened before. Many times. And it was only now he knew why. With two group members in the closet, the whole contraption couldn't move another inch. Or at least smoothly. He came back to what he had originally set out to do this very evening when he had been admiring the Vet Center on the outside, and then later when he had been admiring Galen's tattoos from within.

"Well, I'll go first," Buddy said, "I can't stand these silences. Besides, I'm feeling compassionate tonight."

I'll bet you are.

Buddy then took off like a shot into a description of his problems with his wife. Reconciling with her. Knowing whether he ought to. Especially since she was so beautiful and sexy. And so much younger than he was. It was hard to make a rational decision. Also he had just come out to her—about his Vietnam experiences—while they had been lying in bed awake at night after doing it again and again, and he wasn't sure how she was taking them. Oh, these confessions. Robb knew them well. From other closeted men. The main point was to talk your way around your life without stepping on a landmine, which was your real sexuality. You just took pains to appear pornographic in your exploits with the ladies instead.

When he was done, and had gotten a lot of "positive feedback" from the group, Richard turned to Robb and asked him how he felt.

"Totally hostile," Robb answered. "Excuse me, resistant."

"Why?"

Suddenly Buddy looked at him and seemed to plead that he not blow his cover.

"I'm having a hard time identifying with the macho crap in this group."

"Macho crap?"

"Yeah, all these war stories. And all this constant making it with women."

Richard looked at him, too. "Everybody's got to tell what he's got to tell."

"It's just," Robb went on, "that I don't have any to offer when it finally gets around to me."

"At last it comes out," Galen said. "Well, at least you're telling us why."

"You know," Jason said, "if we're going to sit around and judge Robb all evening, I'm going to leave."

The room was heating up now. It was as though they had hit December, and a great hearth had been started. Robb noticed that everybody was starting to look pretty hot and involved. Maybe because they could see the light cracking out of the closet.

"It sounds to me," Richard said, huffing a little through his smoke and turning to Jason, "like you're rescuing."

"I am not rescuing," Jason said, "I'm speaking for my fucking self. I feel threatened in a support group when somebody else is getting the screws. And why not? I could be next. Galen is talking out both sides of his mouth about whether he's harassing Robb or not. First he accuses him and then says it's all in fun. I could be next on his list."

"You're saying I don't have a right to talk," Galen said.

"Not when it's none of your goddamn business," Jason answered. "And you're fucking contradicting yourself."

"Always standing up for him," Galen went on. "Always and forever the godfather."

"Hold on, Galen," Richard said, "we'll get to you in a minute. But I think Robb got lost in the shuffle. What were you about to say?"

"It's just," Robb answered, "that my story has to do with something else. I was," he continued, "in love with a man in Vietnam. A man named Mason."

The group snapped to attention, as though Jack Webb himself had cracked the whip.

"This man named Mason maybe killed a woman on a bicycle when we'd been driving through Saigon. I was in the jeep. Hit and run. Later he made love to me in the dorms and then killed himself afterwards. That's my story, men, the one that drove me off the edge. The one that came back after I got off drugs. That's it in three, maybe four sentences. I'm gay, a drug addict, alcoholic, and recovering crazy. I've kept myself quiet, because I'd like to have more stories like the ones you tell. It's not out of judgment, it's out of envy. I was only in Vietnam a few months before the panic attacks sent me home."

Silence. Robb remembered a long, crazy water-slide out at the old Funland in Seattle. He had gone down it and landed with a splash. Just like then, he seemed to see everything underwater but was, still, coming up for air.

"Hell," Mick said, speaking up for the first time that evening, "I had lots of gay experiences in Vietnam."

Galen was holding himself so tight, he seemed to be squeezing the anger out of himself. "Christ, Robb, why didn't you say so?"

Was there any answer to that? There didn't seem to be, although he'd asked it himself, many times.

"Galen," Richard said, shaken, "you look like you haven't finished—that is, if Robb wants feedback."

"Why not?" Robb said. "It's all out in the open anyway."

"I just don't like —," Galen began. "I just—." Robb could see he was obviously fumbling here and there again for some pre-approved word. Over and above and beyond "faggot." "I just can't stand the idea of men being together."

"Well that doesn't keep you from doing it with other men," Mick said. He was a solid wall of a man, and looked like he could clean anybody's clock. "I'm here to tell you."

"I don't like to hear that," Galen said. "That's not good news."

"It just sounds to me," Buddy said, "like a case of combat blue-balls. I mean wouldn't you have felt differently, Robb"—fixing him with a stare—"if you had stayed the whole time, and proved your mettle? I mean, I felt that, because I was patching guys up instead of mowing them down."

"I don't think that's it," Robb said.

"I don't either," Jason said, and for some reason, he had his arm along the top of Robb's chair. A show of solidarity? "I don't see what difference that would have made. At least to me. We were all in the same horrible absurd situation. What you brought home as trophies, whether it was medals, or insanity, doesn't make any difference."

"There. That's it," Robb said. "That's what I've been trying to say or believe, at least. That I belong, regardless. It doesn't matter how long I was there. Or how much I lied to myself or to other people. Eventually the whole thing caught up with me. I've paid my dues."

"As if you had any to pay in the first place," Richard said, having recovered himself. "But, Robb, can I ask something else?"

"Yes."

"To what extent do you hold yourself responsible for the death of that Saigon woman?"

"Completely."

"Oh come on," Galen said, "you may as well as take responsibility for all of Vietnam."

"Galen," Richard said, "I'll get to you later."

There was another dead space. Robb, sitting there and feeling slimmer, lighter, felt it was so good to say "completely." He realized it didn't matter whether it was rational or not. He felt it! "Yes, completely," he repeated.

"Now can I really push on you?" Richard asked.

"Yes. Go ahead."

"Then I need to point out," he said, "that you haven't paid your dues. You're still holding yourself accountable for her."

Mick bridled at that. "Now wait a minute! What the fuck are you asking him to do? For once I agree with Galen. He may as well take responsibility for the whole fucking nation."

"You're not hearing me," Richard said. "I'm not asking him to do anything. I'm merely pointing out how he himself is looking at it."

"And you're right," Robb said, still trying to make a clean breast of it. "It is an immense debt. And I don't know what to do about it yet"—Mick was wiping tears as he said this—"but I'm in a program which will show me, when the time presents itself. When I'm ready. Restitution has to be paid for my not speaking up. But it's down the road—or at the end of a long dark hall where I can't see around the corner."

"You could begin by marching in the Parade come November," Galen said.

"Maybe," Robb answered. "Maybe. I'll just have to wait and see."

Richard checked his watch. He seemed so slender and thin, too, a mere wisp of a man. "We're just about out of time. I just need to say something like 'great' to Robb for breaking the silence and ask if he has anything else he wanted to say."

He did. But he didn't know exactly how to put it. "Only this. Ever since this happened, I've felt such a strong need to touch men. Even when I was sealed down in the healing medications they gave me, I had the desire, even though I couldn't show it. I wonder if anybody else here has felt that."

"Not me," Galen said. "Not like that."

"Sometimes so bad," Mick said, "I think I'll explode."

"Ditto," Buddy said. "Touching is, now, my whole life. I'm going to retrain again, in fact, to do massage."

"Beyond anything I've ever known," Jason said. "There's something I heard when I got back to the States, and was in a group hug with other Vets—'tissue needs tissue.' I've never forgotten that."

Robb sat still. "That's what I needed to know. I just wondered if I was the only one."

"Well—" Richard began. But he obviously didn't know what else to say.

"What about you," Galen asked at last, turning to the group leader. "Do you have a burning desire to touch other men?"

Richard looked uncomfortable. "Yes . . . at times. But certainly not here." He looked at his watch a second time.

"It would be nice," Jason said, "if we could spend a little longer this time in our group hug. In light of what's been said."

"Oh, come on now," Galen said.

"I said," Richard answered, "that we'd get around to you and Jason once we were through with Robb. Looks like we'll just have to start with the two of you next time. O.K.?"

"I don't know about that," Mick said, "but I think a longer group hug is a terrific idea."

The circle, now, seemed to get up as one identity and, Richard and Galen notwithstanding, huddled together. The very resistance of muscle coming from Richard and Galen caused the rest of them to come together tighter, taking the other two with them. For the moment, Robb, feeling the arms around him, thought he might pass out from warmth and acceptance and fear.

Thirty-five

Toward noon, Bart drove up to Port Townsend, heading for the Carnegie Free Library in Old Town. He knew that his brother's unemployed and totally voluntary status at the place looked less obvious if he took him out for lunch, and besides, this way neither of them would have to deal with the Six-Ten. In fact, Bart thought it best if he saved seeing his mother and father for a ten-minute slot. No more than that—and just before he was about to go back.

The trip up had been a test-drive for his bones. Since Chester's father got him the car back, Bart had thought that it had been doing better than himself. He was always shaky, out at last on the road again. Today he'd been driving too slowly for some on that two-laner through the farmlands, and they had ridden his tail and given him honks a good part of the way. There had been one spot, where they had gone into a brief swatch of the forest, and Bart had had to turn his headlights on—where it had been just like a spook ride.

But now the Carnegie Free Library was before him, and he had been surprised into recognition by those sphinxes, which he had forgotten and which were on either side of the start of the stairs. He knew he was approaching something frightening and strange, because he knew his brother did not see him as the same—not any more. At first there had been acceptance, and then—he could sense it—a retreat, an edict which said, or at least, implied, he was less than he ought to be. A disappointment as a younger brother. Bart wanted that edict wiped away, here and now, as he passed the benign face of the sphinx. Whenever all had gone to hell with his mother and father, there had always been Daniel—a constant—standing there, blind and solid.

He began climbing the nearly perpendicular stairs. The place seemed like a stone lookout, perched on top of the hill, just like the post office. The library, like the clock face tower, had been his friend in the old days. But now he felt that tension that seems like a job interview. Absolutely, because at first, he thought he saw his brother open the door and start down to meet him. But as soon as the face became apparent, he realized it was his father. His father carrying an armload of books! Which he had never seen him do—not ever .

His father sauntered on down, not looking at first— and then instant recognition—so that he clutched his books, almost to his bosom, Bart thought.

"Well, hello," he said—and hung his head.

"Father," Bart said, rarely using that word before, "what a surprise."

"You didn't call, you didn't let us know."

"No," Bart answered. And he realized then that his father was actually trying to hide the books. "I thought I'd drop in just before leaving, the way I always do."

His father nodded, looked from side to side, and in one shift, Bart saw that he carried with him virtually every gay book in the library. They were Bart's old friends.

"Just catching up on my reading," his father said.

"Right," Bart answered, backing off a little. "How are things?"

His father looked so loaded down, Bart thought he might drop everything at any moment.

"Oh, I suppose they're fine."

But people—which is always the case in moments like these—started coming down the stairs, and being members of a small town, couldn't help but try to overhear a word or two.

"We'll talk more," Bart said, as his father tried to budge away, now protecting the titles from the onlookers. "I'll be there tonight after dinner."

"Right."

Bart felt as if he were rattling with this news—that his father was actually thinking about him. The climb seemed like Mount Everest—when the climber is virtually out of provisions, is low on oxygen, but has been rescued in the last minute.

The library was sequestered, and seemed to be one shelf of "Northwest History" after the next. Daniel was in the back vault, being read to slowly by a student reader, while he punched away at a Braille machine. "'Through light blue vapor,'" the teenager— nearly a child—read, "the Straits are seen below, and to the southward lie Admiralty Inlet, Possession Sound and Hood Canal, resembling in the distance mighty rivers like the Columbia and the Fraser winding their way to the sea; and on a clear day in June or July the reflection of the sun on the windows of Seattle flash like heliographic—'"

"What?" Daniel asked.

"Heliographic," the student answered.

"Heliographic"—and Daniel's lion's smile filled his entire face—"what the hell is that?"

"Do you want me to look it up?" the young man asked in his meekness.

"No, who the hell cares. Just tell me how you spell it."

"Hi, Daniel," Bart called out.

"Hi, Bart," Daniel said. "Let me just finish this section."

And in the still catacombs, the yawning face went on listening, striking the raises on the sheets. "—'flash like heliographic signals from a battleship,'" the student concluded. "Directly south the towering walls and spires of Constance stand, with dark green gorges of varying shades like the varying shades of ocean water according to depth.'"

The assembly broke up. "Of all things," Daniel said, "this partially sighted lady wants C.H. Handford's *Halcyon Days in Port Townsend* translated into Braille, and the library won't even let it out of the vault.

"It's quite beautiful, isn't it?" Bart said, still feeling porous and humble.

"Beautiful? I hadn't even thought about it. It certainly doesn't make *me* want to dance."

The shy student disappeared.

Daniel turned like a weathervane. "Did Greg skip out?"

"Yes."

"That kid—all you have to do is say Boo and he vanishes."

"That's just the way I feel myself sometimes," Bart said, taking his arm, and leading him out. "We're still having lunch, aren't we?"

As they went down those long stairs together (Daniel didn't even mention that he was leaving), Bart felt as if he were escorting someone out of the underworld, his brother's face brightened so with the sunshine. Bart discovered that his mother had packed them a huge lunch, which Daniel had been keeping in his backpack. They went on out to Chetzemoka Park and just sat.

"You wanted to see me?" Bart asked at last, stating the obvious. And with irritation, added, "You sent word through Mom, keeper of the National Board Exchange."

Daniel's face was in the shadow. The Park could do strange things. "Yes, I've been keeping myself scarce lately."

"Yes," Bart answered, "I noticed."

"I haven't been doing too well with your surprise information. When I got the word, I thought I might be gay too. You know in that School for the Blind I went to, we had very little boundaries on touching. Later on, women, when I would date them, would say, 'You don't have the usual defenses of a man. I mean, about protecting your body space.'"

"'Body space,'" Bart said. "What a phrase!" Nevertheless, he did notice that he was keeping his distance from his brother, and vice versa.

"There was another time," Daniel went on, "when I was at a rally in behalf of the gays and I didn't like it because it wasn't the same as a rally for the blacks."

"Why not?"

"Because people watching the gay rally could think I was one of them."

"One of us," Bart said.

"That's it. Don't get me wrong," Daniel followed up quickly. "I'm not blaming you. I'm just saying I can't handle it, because I don't know who the hell I am. My tactile relation to people is crazy, polymorphous (if that's a word), almost. I'm like an amoeba."

"Don't say that," Bart said, and nearly smiled at the coincidence of their thoughts. From the far end of the park, he could hear Quarterdeck playing. Rain, rain, rain on me. Rain on me with your love.

"Don't say that," he repeated. "I don't know how you could keep from living your life by anything except touch. In many ways, I envy you."

"Envy me?"

"Instead of having all this bullshit of words, you can just go up to someone and say, 'Let me see you,' and instantly you've got that person's face in your hands. I've spent a year trying to figure out my former partner. I wonder what would have happened if I had done that in the first place."

"Mom said you had a partner," Daniel answered. "Tell me about him."

And Bart said a few things. When he came to the part about their meeting at the Crescent, and had spent a spring roaming Port Townsend, Daniel seemed shocked by the way Bart had kept the secret so well. A whole relationship with the co-owner of Rose! The Jorgenson family. And he had never known. "If secrets work this well," Daniel said, "work this well, and this smoothly, you wonder when the next one is going to sneak up and bite you on the butt. Like the idea that maybe you're gay like you're brother."

They had eaten their lunch very, very quickly. They got up to meander back. Once again, he took Daniel's arm, and wondered if the people who had just entered the park would think just what Daniel was worried about. At this point, as was often the case, it didn't matter, because the perspective on the Strait was overpowering. He heard a flash of the beautiful, shaded prose the student had been reciting back at the Library, and somehow it combined with the rhythm of the children on the swings.

"So what next for you?" Daniel asked.

"Waiting it out," Bart said. "Seeing what happens for us."

"Strange," Daniel said. "I always thought you'd stay single, and when Mom and Dad went, you'd be around to take care of me. And we'd live together, like brothers. I'd been harboring the hope that you'd remain an old maid like me—it's given me an excuse to hide out."

The cheerleaders from the high school were running through the park. There was some kind of exercise, meant to entertain the children. "We're with you team, so fight. We're with you team, so fight. We're with you team, we're with you team, so fight, fight, fight!"

The two of them couldn't help but laugh.

But an instant of bravado later, he had to stop. He saw that one of the cheerleaders was Robb's stepdaughter, and he wanted to run from the place.

"I think I'd better get back," Daniel said conveniently.

As they did, the cheerleaders' eyes followed them, Bart was sure.

Handing Daniel back into the library—and with no parting hug or recognition, either—Bart wondered what he would do with his time, until four o'clock rolled slowly around in this town—like a liberty half dollar, dropped in a sunlit kitchen, with the flies buzzing. But the time dissolved quickly, in reflections on how far he had come since spying out on Laura at Rose House. Besides he could tell his parents good-bye now, and then leave immediately for the City—and its discos, on the ready.

But when he got to the Six-Ten, his father wasn't there, and for the first time in his life, Bart found that that was a disappointment. There was just his mother, toward the back. Save for the brief visit in the hospital, Bart had not seen her since he had gotten her letter. She was still in that mode.

Her mode was—queenly. Her blonde hair, with silver highlights, was braided perfectly, and she conveyed an air now of regality and lightness. Together.

She only said, "I wish your father was here. But he went out long ago." In their hug, she seemed to test for remaining cracks. "We haven't seen you since the accident. Are you all right?"

"I was a little shaky driving up, but I'm doing fine."

As she stood back from him, she said "Well!" in a way that meant he should leave, since there was no more to say, but something told Bart he was to stay and have it out, whatever "it" was.

He didn't have to wait long. He saw the direction of her stare, and realized "it" was his pink triangle pin.

"So you haven't changed your mind," she said at last. "You're going to stay just where you are."

"More like what I am," Bart answered. "I appreciated your letter and your concern," he lied, "but I'm completely incapable of changing, even if I wanted to."

"I saw the review of your play," she said. "You realize now, I hope, how hostile the world can be when you stage things that way."

"I was fully aware of that when I was doing the choreography," Bart replied, sounding huffy and not at all himself.

His mother was starting to stock shelves while they were talking, but she paused long enough for them to hear his father's footfalls upstairs. There was a room in the Six-Ten where the family could nap.

"Well, then," she said, sighing, "there's this other part, too, about your father. You have no idea, as I said in the letter, how hard this has hit him."

Bart suddenly began to glow hot. When he'd just seen his father not two hours ago. His father hadn't been at all that way—not at all what his mother pictured. Wasn't now and wasn't then.

"I took this problem to my sisters in our earth-goddess circle," she said, "and they said it was time I came to accept you for who you are, but I don't believe you're really being true to your inner nature by being this way. How can it be natural when men are dying by the thousands of AIDS? How can it be natural when your father drinks every day over this?"

"You caring about me," Bart said. "I find that hard to believe."

His mother turned from lifting the cans from her cart; he had never spoken to her like that before. "I don't believe I heard you," she said.

"I said I find it hard to believe," Bart answered loudly. And in his mind, he went on. You foul hypocrite. Sisters and an earth circle. Don't you think I remember the way you brutalized Daniel when he was growing up, hounded him to behave like the crowd so he wouldn't be noticed. Don't you think I remember how you used to harangue him so much, he'd hide under the bed, just because you were furious with the drunk you married? He was your ideal stooge, wasn't he? And still is.

He came over and stood by her. "Don't talk to me about how I should live my life, Mother," he actually said, "you hide behind Dad's behavior for everything. I'm not to be treated this way. Not anymore. If you don't like him, divorce him, if you want to stay, stay, but stop foisting the family in between the two of us."

She dropped one of the cans. "Don't say that! If you say one more word, I don't think I can bear it." She pointed to herself at last. "I can't."

His father had heard the noise and had come down. He was still carrying one of his gay books. "What's going on?" he asked.

"Mother," Bart said, ready for this, "she didn't want to talk about something."

His mother was rubbing her forehead and saying nothing.

"I was just asking Mom that I be treated as an equal in the family."

"Oh," his father answered, "I think I read that was the way to do it somewhere."

But his mother clearly wanted none of this. "It would be best if you left," she said.

"Why?" his father asked.

"It just would be best."

"I'm not leaving," Bart said, "until I get an answer. Am I going to be treated as an equal or not?"

His father was frightened by his tone.

His mother had started to cry, and Bart turned out of the grocery, and went straight down to the fountain square. He could sit for a moment. It was nearly four o'clock anyway, and nearly time to take the ferry back.

Thirty-six

So October passed into November, December. Robb marched in the parade and felt more like he belonged. Both he and Bart came out negative on their HIV tests. Galen pressed him less in group, and an almost physical connection formed between them. He and Jason continued with their own A.A. Meetings, and as the months went by, they felt bound together even further.

Valerie and Laura moved down to Seattle, and having Valerie visit and stay over at Mrs. Molyson's was the highlight of his life. He saw Tara again, but did not try to take her back. He was incapable as yet of taking care of a dog. Just buying groceries for their dinners together sometimes seemed more than he could do. The holidays were spectacularly lit for him, like a shower of meteors falling on evergreens—the severe presence of all the ghosts at once, among them his father, who seemed to take his shape behind the reddened Christmas tree. Had Valerie been aware of this while she had been opening presents? His dreams then had had a hearth fire cast to them, and the storage vaults at the back of his mind, started letting loose with Christmases and New Years long since past and apparently bundled away, and sometimes when he got up in the morning he wasn't sure where he was—Idaho or Seattle or Port Townsend or even Vietnam. He had even thought at one moment that he was back at Olivia's party where he had almost collapsed into the Christmas tree.

But while the days pressed toward spring again, and he was led to remember all the days of horror of the previous year, the longing for Bart came up again, and tackled him hard. It seemed unfair and then finally unspeakable that just as he was nearing his first year of sobriety and the "first date" they had set, that the grapevine divulged and finally confirmed that Bart was seeing someone else. And that it was serious. It was so horrible and inexplicable that Robb almost drank over it. He sat down one night and seriously considered going out dancing and getting drunk—then taking someone home. Fortunately he called Jason, and they went to a Meeting. Telling it there, he felt like a fool, but he had not known, up until then, how much he cared about Bart.

He was able to recognize—and he thought of this often now, when days when he wasn't teaching put him out in the spring beds again, trying those hollyhocks a second time—that Bart, his seeing someone else aside, was just the right man for him. He was loving and caring and humorous—just the right balance to his own wintry seriousness and hulkiness. He knew there were times—although he was foggy on this—times well before he had hit bottom, when he had come in all furious about something, and Bart had simply smiled and gone about his business. That was it—Bart did not reflect his weather—the way all his other partners had, male and female alike, consequently making things worse for everybody; Bart had simply gone about his business. Bart loved him too much to take him seriously. And for that, among many other things, Robb loved him. In fact, even now, he had also heard it rumored that he was doing a new musical, and was directing a whole series of one-acts for the high school. The man truly had his own life. And loved it. And now Robb had to suffer over this—and feel cheated out of the gift of a lifetime, too. He deserved, after all, to have this man. For hadn't, after all, he been his husband? And for several years.

But it wasn't just Bart himself—or even his lost suitability— that pained and grieved him. It was also this whole matter of marriage itself. He missed it; it had been good for him, even with Laura. It was his natural condition, and being single was too odd for words.

Which was his natural state now, as March approached and left, with the celebration of his first A.A. birthday, and April began burning him with its heat, as he worked in the yard. His bared muscles, now active again at the gym, longed to return to Bart, and their intimacy. He stood in the garden plot, bared to the waist, and arched his back in the beneficent sun. Tissue needs tissue. He could, in fact, stand here forever, if he had had his arms around Bart, around all the years they had shared, and which now were so out of reach. And yet—this sun, these roses he was about to plant, these bulbs—seemed enough, too. He felt like he was one of them, as he did with all the people in the Meetings and in the Vet circle, the ones who were in pain. Yes, he felt like he was a plant, embedded in their plot of light, growing.

But now the time for their date was coming up—they had agreed to stay separate for a year. And he must call. Face the music—even endure having Andrew answer the telephone—for Andrew was the one people said Bart had taken up with. He'd do it, and if Bart answered, and he lost it over the phone, O.K.

Because he was filled with gratitude to Bart—strange, even when he was at this painful point of loss—he couldn't help but think of all the times Bart had put up with his outrages, his drunkenness, his impossibility—and not just those times he'd apologized for, but also moments he only now remembered. How could he, in fact, blame Bart for choosing someone else, given everything he had put him through? It was only a sign that Bart was at last getting healthy himself. Finding someone he deserved.

But oh, the self-pity when Robb at last lifted up the phone a week before they were to have the date. If Andrew answers, I'll go over and deck him. But he dialed nevertheless.

Bart answered laughing. "You'll never guess," he said, "what I just saw now. There was a man going past who I thought was schizophrenic. Turns out he was just using a cellular phone!"

Robb, despite himself—and as usual with Bart—couldn't help but laugh. "I'm sure glad you're around," he said. "Nobody sees things like you."

"Yes," Bart answered, "but it's a good thing there's just one of us. Anyway, I'm so glad you called. I've been thinking about you."

A dead space.

"Have you?" Robb asked. And for some reason, he felt as though he were back at the Rap Group, about to come out all over again. "I've been thinking about you, and missing you. But tell me," he said, still feeling guarded, "what it's been like these past six months?" And with Andrew, he wanted to add.

"I've started working on a new show. You may have heard about it. It got a little write-up in the local *Times*. It was nice," he said, "to have it described rather than panned. And you—have you—"

"Stayed sober? Yes. Miraculously. Of course," he added, "that's what it takes in the Program."

Another dead space. Well, Robb decided, we can't sit here all day. "Bart," he went on—and it was coming as though from a Victorian letter, scented even—"I heard about you and Andrew, and I just want you to know that I wish you all the happiness in the world. And I want to thank you for everything you've given me, which, unfortunately, I'm just beginning to appreciate. I love you very much—and I've only realized that now—but I know," he said (still self-pity), "I can learn to let go."

Bart was silent, still. "What in the world are you talking about?" he asked at last. "There's never been anyone but you. Count on it. Even when I got off on Buddy, it was still you. I told you that. I just plain don't know what you're talking about. Me and Andrew?"

"I heard that the two of you were a couple."

"What? No. I see a lot of him, because he's my friend, and he needs my help right now. The Men's Group has been looking after him, because he has AIDS. You knew that, of course?"

"No."

"Well, he does." Obviously it was taking Bart time to digest this all. "Oh Robb," he laughed at last, "that was the sweetest farewell letter I've ever received, but you don't get off that easy! We have a date for Mozart, don't forget."

Robb was so relieved, he felt like crying. He didn't even refer to it. He just wiped his eyes and went on talking, asking about Andrew, and then going on about the date—tickets, who would drive, and whether or not they were to have dinner. It felt like the first date of his entire life, because, to be honest, he had never dated sober before, and, apart from those few weeks out of Treatment, had never known Bart except when he himself had been loaded, politely or otherwise. And now that he actually was going to see the great love of his life again—and without tragedy looming on the horizon—the prospect terrorized him. He could, in fact, blow it completely.

The week of waiting for Bart was filled with sun. He taught his classes at Jutland with the windows open, and the frights did not visit him quite as much. He prepared, in fact, to tell Bart everything when the right moment came—just as he and Chester had discussed in the session—even about the Minotaur. If he and Bart were to have their life again, it must begin on an honest footing. He'd see to that. He wanted to get this done, especially now that the sessions with Chester were over.

In his garden, the sunlight was like an ecstasy; it seemed to run like veins through the new leaves. The plum had popped open overnight, and the apple trees were dropping their snow all over Mrs. Molyson's lawn. It wouldn't be long before her Rose of Sharon would be out with all its peacock eyes. And the unveiling of his own body these past weeks—untouched by sun for so long—seemed like a part of the strategy of the season, and he worked, planting the last of the roses, until his skin went red.

He noticed it when Tyler worked on him the next day, and when he finally put on his dress shirt the night of Mozart. He felt like fire fitted into starched cloth. Felt like that, as he drove through the clarity of the evening, toward Bart's—for he had insisted that he, for once, do the driving, since Bart had seemed the constant chauffeur in their other life together.

He felt terribly awkward as he pulled up to the house with the pale mimosa, which was also getting ready to spread its feathers again. He couldn't help but think of that night, only a year ago October, when he had barged in and torn Bart's life apart. He hoped—no, he believed—he could do better this time.

"Won't you come in?" Bart said formally at the door, and showed him into a living room, neat as usual, and asked him to sit on the sofa where, many of a night, Robb had yanked off his clothes and hauled him off to bed. Now he timidly took the place indicated to him, and sat with his hands folded across his chest.

He had to admit how good Bart looked. He was slender still, but looked more tightly made, not from exercise, but from a clearer sense of direction. "Can I get you something?" he asked, and as he drew out the soda water, and poured it into a crystal, the crystal seemed to match him, along with the rowed garden and its tiers through the window.

"I see," Robb said at last, still not much beyond a stammer, "that you've been working in your yard. It's beautiful."

"Yes," Bart answered, laughing, "at last I've got those rhododendrons right. But many died in the transplanting, and many had to be replaced."

Bart was sitting in the easy chair while he was saying this. "Well," he said, putting down his glass, "and I see that you've been out in the sun, like me. May I hug you and all that sunburn at once?"

"I don't know why not," Robb answered, getting up before he finished.

Robb felt enfolded as they joined, and then there was the long kiss. He was sure for a moment he would suffocate from the intense sunshine smell which must have come from them both— and his skin hurt with all the comfort of contact.

Then tightness came in upon him. It was a mist coming further and further in, until he felt he did not have another breath in him. And once again, he felt himself climb up the walls of Rose House.

In his mind, he came to a window, and looked out. He saw Bart, still there in front of him. "Please," Bart said, "that's enough for now."

They went to their restaurant, and in a back booth, Robb found himself at last telling Bart everything that had happened to him, Minotaur and all. The occasion, in fact, was so dramatic, Robb found he could hardly eat a bite. He was sure, again, this time Bart would head for the exits.

Bart was indeed quiet when Robb finished, but he had, in fact, cleaned his whole plate as Robb had talked. "You know," he said at last with his mouth still full, "that Minotaur reminds me of the story I was reading in Apuleius' *Golden Ass*. That myth about half-man, half-beast does seem to go a long way back, doesn't it?"

"That's all you've got to say?" Robb asked, finding himself both relieved and angry.

"Well," Bart went on, making things worse, "I was going to add that eventually the Golden Ass is cured by Isis, and I've wondered for years if there was any connection between the Roman goddess Iris and the Eastern one Isis."

Robb found himself sitting there, resisting another move. "I'm glad you're taking this in your stride. But this is my ordeal we're talking about."

"I know," Bart said, "I was in on it. And I'm not quite finished. I want to say that I know from all this that you're being taken care of—and it's not me who's been doing this. It must be someone like Isis or Iris." He took his hand.

"You know," Robb said, "that this is still hard to hear. I was hoping for more drama after this great confession."

Bart drew his mouth down as though to say, "What were you expecting? Puccini?"

So it was time for Mozart on this very, very, checkered evening. Still, somewhere in the middle of the *Laudamus Te* of the soprano solo (the Mass in C Minor was one of the few classical works he remembered by name), he felt his skin hot again beneath his sport jacket, beneath his dress shirt, complete with tie. And he saw Bart's skin match his own as his partner sat in complete concentration with the choral voices rising. He thought of candle flames. Somewhere, lustfully, he wondered if the two of them would ever make love again, because while he sensed the heat between them he could also sense a great wall.

At intermission, the two of them milled shyly about (they had gotten there late and had not had time to feel the crowd), as though they were two hicks fresh from Port Townsend, walking between Seattle skyscrapers and looking scared. Nevertheless, Bart, brash in his pink triangle, had taken Robb's hand, just as the lobby lights were flashing for the first time, and they ran into Jacques, a former member of their Men's Group.

"I haven't seen you guys in ages," he said. "Has it been two years?"

"Two years," Robb said.

"Anything new and exciting?" Jacques asked. "Or just the same two perfect love birds—Robb and Bart, Bart and Robb."

They could only look at each other.

"It's great, though," Jacques concluded, waving himself past, on the second flash, "to see you stick together for so long. By golly," he said, mock-heroically, "it's refreshing, given the mortality rate of most gay relationships. The other day a couple told me they were celebrating their second anniversary. I inquired a little further and found out it was two months!"

By then Robb could see that Jacques was actually cruising and that his target was, in fact, Buddy.

"Hello Buddy!" Robb heard himself call out. "Long time no see."

Buddy—and to his surprise—saw the humor of it, too, and just waved goodbye.

Thirty-seven

Toward June, Bart knew he had to make a decision about seeing his family again. He and Robb were talking about an August commitment ceremony, and the whole idea was not to sweep things under the rug. Not anymore. His mother had not spoken to him for over half a year, and her coldness had run an icicle through his contact with Daniel. For some reason, Daniel was just a little bit stonier every time Bart called him—especially when Bart asked how she was doing. His father, on the other hand, had turned almost cordial.

Go figure. Nevertheless, he found that the recovery of his life with Robb was just the start of all kinds of dilemmas, which he had never even considered in their world of storms over the past many years. What about Valerie? Robb was out to her, but how was he to explain this odd new man in his life? And how was he, a sort of stepfather, to take to her? Apart from his own beloved students, he never really liked kids much, if that made any sense, and now there was a new ripple—which was entirely his business—of introducing Robb to his family.

As school ended, he decided to make another trip up to Port Townsend, and, if not to heal the breach completely, at least to try to clear a few things up. He simply couldn't stand this silence from his mother—silence which not only defied his many apologies for his hard words but in fact seemed to draw strength from them.

With school out, he started arranging, he started bustling. He and Robb were looking for a house to buy in Seattle—they'd already tried having Robb take the second bedroom in his own home, and that hadn't worked—and he now found himself becoming extremely officious about narrowing down the possibilities. He was also becoming fussy about this planned weekend to Port Townsend—it was only a weekend for God's sake—and he found at last that this was drawing its source from the fear both of them had about sex.

He wasn't sure they were ever going to have it, and, in fact, both of them had seemed to become reconciled to living like good friends for the rest of their lives. Perhaps the tenderness of their hugs was a huge gift by itself, since they had both abused sex so badly in the earlier days—especially between themselves. They slept tender and naked, reveling in the contact, but Robb had confessed one night that he had never known full sex with anyone which could be called honest. Unfortunately, Bart felt exactly the same way. As he saw Robb's mind drifting toward his summer work at the College again—and the amends he was going to make by returning to Vietnam some time in the future—Bart found himself thinking up a new musical, not just one to direct in the autumn, but another one which he would write himself—and one much better, even, than his own *Houdini*. But this drift on both of their parts was also an attempt to avoid each other.

He knew that he should go on with his creative life, that he should not put things on hold just because he now he had a man. And he was thrilled with the whole prospect of writing *The Night Elvis Went to the Movies*, giving Elvis a whole new gay slant—and especially in the Sun Record Sessions. Yes. It was wonderful, but there was this other matter of what Robb called the "i-word," Intimacy.

He worked on the musical, and made ready to go to Port Townsend over the weekend. The plan was somewhat complicated, because now both of them had a life. First, he couldn't stay at his parents', so he'd reserved a room at Rose House (now under new management), just to treat himself. Robb, who had Valerie that weekend and had no objections against the place, was to come up on Saturday and stay with him the second night, leaving her with one of her past school friends, who was having a slumber party. Somewhere in there he and Valerie were to meet—maybe over lunch—and somewhere in there he, Bart, was to try to reconcile with his mother. Somewhere in there. Olivia, also part of the plan, was to have them over for dinner Saturday night, and then join him for lunch Sunday, after Robb took Valerie back to Seattle. For Bart had decided he needed an entire Port Townsend day just to himself, especially after seeing his family.

The next morning he packed and went up to Rose, and at least felt all the relief that came from being above board this time. Today, he and Robb would not have to steal into the basement and make love on the sly. He almost broke out into an embarrassed sweat, thinking about it now. How could he have done such a thing?

Bart dropped the pen back down on the sign-in roster, and smiled at the new proprietress, wondering what she would say, of course, if she had known his outrageous thoughts. Rather, she smiled back, handing him the key and pointed up the spiral staircase, where he had spied on Laura over a year ago.

The day passed with a visit from Olivia, who was conducting her practice at last in the adjacent cottage, and was very busy with a full clientele. It was obvious she was much loved in Port Townsend. Obvious, too, she missed Chester unspeakably, and was anguished, because she still knew there was no going back. The divorce had become final. Strange, she had said, how she had noticed the steady stream of couples into Rose on the adjacent grounds—the overnighters, during all this intervening time. And then after the passage of a mere few months, she had seen some of the people reappearing, only this time not linked with their original partners but in new combinations, new families—as if, as if she were finally being shown (by Rose) that no one had a corner on partnership.

Friday night, he drove over to the Six-Ten, but found, still, he was not welcome. His father, ironically, had just left for a purchase in Seattle, and wouldn't be back until Sunday night, and Daniel just didn't seem to be able to cope with an icy mother in one room, and a brother-in-exile in the other.

"She can't see you just now," Daniel said.

"Well," Bart answered, angrily, bitterly, and with a force that he was to regret later, "just tell her then that Robb and I expect to have a commitment ceremony come August, and if she would like to talk to her newly engaged son, I'll be at Rose until Monday morning. Just in case she changes her mind."

But, damn, Bart thought, trying to sleep that night and thinking about how dramatic he had been, now he'd driven the final wedge at last. Talk about triangulation! Why hadn't I had the guts to speak to her myself?

While there was time the next morning, he sent her a rose and a card, explaining everything directly. That he still needed to be who he was but that he loved her and wanted to hear from her. That he was sorry for how he had sounded the last time he'd seen her. Then the hours before noon passed in angst about the note and also meeting Valerie.

But at last when Robb and Valerie did pull up to Rose, the whole moment was quite spectacular, really. Valerie merely got out of the car, shook Bart's hand, and handed him a flower. Bart instantly misted up, and felt his whole facade crash like a sheet of ice on the sidewalk, so that he stood there like a fool in front of everyone. And Robb just remained in his tracks and let Bart have his cry. At last he said, "Well, now that you've met, we need to get Valerie to her friends. Take my suitcase up, will you? I'll be right back."

Bart, carrying the luggage slowly up the steps toward the "rose" window in the front door, wondered how he could be so uncharitable as to think there ought to be more in his life.

But when Robb finally joined him in the room, he knew what it was.

Robb, kissing him, put his hands on his shoulders. "I love you," he said.

"Yes," he answered, "I love you, too."

Robb nodded, and simply unbuttoned his shirt.

Bart followed.

Midway in the room, he felt caught up in the current, as their skin met, and the hurt came over him again.

"Tyler just got through working me over this morning," Robb said, "so every part of me will be along for the ride."

"And Marian worked me over just the other day," Bart answered.

Without answering, Bart removed his pants, his shorts, and with himself full and strong, went up against Robb's haunches, and found he could enter him this time, and thought of a furrow, which was being hoed back, again and again, as Robb responded, and Bart was aware, only now, that this was just the second time that he had ever taken him, and that that was the wrong way of putting it—Robb was being not taken, anymore than he was.

And he, Bart, moved down and across, and he was spent, but even after he was spent, he found himself opening again, becoming vital, so he discovered he was ready for Robb's penis and breastplate of chest against him. Then Robb was penetrating him as a rain is penetrating.

And when they were done, Bart found that it was not over. They lay together, and he felt himself spill. "I want to be married here," he said. "How does that sound?"

"Yes," Robb said, but with reluctance. He smiled. "Married here, yes. But live here, no. This house and I need to be apart."

"I know that."

"In fact," Robb said. "I'm finding I need to cut lose from the past more and more."

But later that night, after dinner with Olivia, Bart had awakened, fully aware that Robb was awake, too. "What is it?" he asked.

"Tell me," Robb said, out of the dark, "tell me what it was like in those years we were together. Bart, my mind is so foggy still, sometimes I don't remember."

"We started," Bart said, "by hoping we could be everything to each other. When you saved me from that bakery fight, you were more than my Mr. Right, you were my hero. I can remember us going out in tuxedos or swim wear and being everybody's beautiful couple, but only ending with me running a stoplight on your behalf and you nearly going under with drugs."

"But now that we're no longer that to each other," Robb said, "either of us could leave at any time."

"Absolutely," Bart said.

"But I want that assurance that you won't," Robb said, moving over and holding him naked again. "More than anything."

"So do I," Bart heard himself answering, "but I don't feel I can demand it."

"But we haven't lost everything?" Robb asked.

"No, I don't think so at all."

So the next morning, Bart watched Robb leave at eleven a.m., as planned. He could have the whole day to himself before they met up again. But turning to the window at noon, he was surprised. For instead of seeing Olivia, who was expected again for lunch, he saw his brother and his mother down below, making their way toward the stairs, and coming up.

About the Author

Henry Alley is a Professor Emeritus of Literature in the Honors College at the University of Oregon. He has four novels, *Through Glass* (Iris Press, 1979), *The Lattice* (Ariadne Press, 1986), *Umbrella of Glass* (Breitenbush Books, 1988), *Precincts of Light* (Inkwater Press, 2010), as well as a collection of stories, *The Dahlia Field* (Chelsea Station Editions, 2017). For nearly half a century, such journals as *Seattle Review, Outerbridge, Virginia Quarterly Review, Chelsea Station* and *Virginia Woolf Quarterly* have published his short fiction. His stories have been the recipient of awards from Gertrude Press as well as Ooligan Press. More recently, in 2017 he was included in Best Gay Stories and was awarded a Mill House Residency by Writing by Writers.

His essays have appeared in *The Journal of Narrative Technique, Studies in the Novel, Twentieth Century Literature, Kenyon Review*, and *Papers on Language and Literature*. In 1997, The University of Delaware Press published his book-length study, *The Quest for Anonymity: The Novels of George Eliot*.

He lives in Eugene, Oregon, with the writer and teacher Austin Gray.

Of his new collection, *The Dahlia Field*, *Kirkus Review* wrote, "With sensitivity and deadpan humor, Alley's luminous stories explore a wealth of characters and social types thrown into fertile combinations. His prose is limpid and straightforward, laced with droll psychology . . . and sometimes opening into an evocative, elegiac poetry . . . . The results are funny, poignant, and engrossing. . . . A fine collection that explores and celebrates the ebb and flow of gay life."— (starred review)